ODDSFISH!

ODDSFISH!

ROBERT HUGH BENSON

WILDSIDE PRESS

ODDSFISH!

Published 2005 by Wildside Press, LLC.
www.wildsidepress.com

AUTHOR'S NOTE.

I wish to express my gratitude for great help received in the writing of this book to Miss MacDermot, Miss Stearne and others, as well as to three friends who submitted to hearing it read aloud in manuscript, and who assisted me by their criticisms and suggestions.

Further, I think it worth saying that in all historical episodes in this book I have taken pains to be as accurate as possible. The various plots, the political movements, and the closing scenes of Charles II's life are here described with as much fidelity to truth as is compatible with historical romance. In particular, I do not think that the King himself is represented as doing or saying anything — except of course to my fictitious personages — to which sound history does not testify. I have also taken considerable pains in the topographical descriptions of Whitehall.

PROLOGUE

The day from which I reckon the beginning of all those adventures which occupied me in the Courts of England and France and elsewhere, was the first day of May in the year sixteen hundred and seventy-eight — the day, that is, on which my Lord Abbot carried me from St. Paul's-without-the- Walls to the Vatican Palace, to see our Most Holy Lord Innocent the Eleventh.

It had been a very hot day in Rome, as was to be expected at that season; and I had stayed in the cloister in the cool, as my Lord Abbot had bidden me, not knowing whether it would be on that day or another, or, indeed, on any at all, that His Holiness would send for me. I knew that my Lord Abbot had been to the Vatican again and again on the business; and had spoken of me, as he said he would, not to the Holy Father only, but to the Cardinal Secretary of State and to others; but I did not know, and he did not tell me, as to whether that business had been prosperous; though I think he must have known long before how it would end. An hour before *Ave Maria*, then, he sent to me, as I walked in the cloisters, and when I came to him, told me, all short, to dress myself in my old secular clothes, as fine as I could, and to be ready to ride with him in half an hour, because our Most Holy Lord had consented to receive me one hour after Ave Maria. He said nothing more to me than that; he did not tell me how I was to bear myself, nor what I was to say, neither as I stood in his cell, nor as we rode as fast as we could, with the servants before and behind, into Rome and through the streets of it. I knew nothing more than this — that since neither I nor my novice-master were in the least satisfied as to my vocation, and since I had considerable estates of my own in France (though I was an Englishman altogether on my father's side), and could speak both French and English with equal ease, and Italian and Spanish tolerably — that since, in short, I was a very well-educated young gentleman, and looked more than my years, and bore myself — (so I was told) — with ease and discretion in any company, and could act a part if it were required of me — I might perhaps be of better service to the Church in some secular employment than in sacred. This was all that I knew. The rest my Lord Abbot left to my own wits to understand, and to our Holy Father, if he would, to discover to me: and that, indeed, was presently what he did.

* * *

I had been within the Vatican before three or four times, both when I had first come to Rome four years ago, and once as attendant upon my Lord Abbot; but never before had I felt of such importance within those walls; for this time it was myself to whom the Holy Father was to give audience, and not merely to one in whose company I was. I was in secular clothes too — the peruke, buckles, sword, and all the rest, which I had laid aside two years ago, though these were a little old and tarnished — and I bore myself as young men will (for I was only twenty-one years old at that time), with an air and a swing; though my heart beat a little faster as we passed through the great rooms, after leaving our cloaks in an antechamber and arranging our dress after the ride; and at last were bidden to sit down while the young Monsignore who had received us in the last saloon went in to know if the Holy Father were ready to see us.

It was a smaller room — this in which we sat — than the others through which we had passed, and in which the crimson liveried servants were; and its walls were all covered with hangings from cornice to floor. That which was opposite to me presented, I remember, Jacob receiving the blessing which his brother Esau should have had; and I wondered, as I sat there, whether I myself were come, as Jacob, to get a blessing to which I had no right. Idly Lord Abbot said nothing at all; for he was a stout man and a little out of breath; and almost before he had got it again, and before I was sure as to whether I were more like to the liar Jacob, who won a blessing when he should not, or to unspiritual Esau, who lost a blessing which he should have had, the young Monsignore in his purple came back again, and, bowing so low that we saw the little tonsure on the top of his head, beckoned to us to enter.

*   *   *

By the time that, behind my Lord Abbot, I had performed the three genuflections and, at the third, was kissing the ring of our Most Holy Lord, I had already taken into my mind something of the room I was in and of him who sat there, wheeled round in his chair to greet us. The room was far more plain than I had thought to find it, though pretty rich too. The walls had sacred hangings upon them; but it was so dark with the shuttered windows that I could not make out very well what their subjects were. A dozen damask and gilt chairs stood round the walls, and three or four tables; and, in the centre of all, where I was now arrived, stood the greatest table of all, carved of some black wood, and at the middle of one side the chair in which sat the Holy Father himself.

He had very kind but very piercing eyes: this was the first thing that I thought; his hair beneath his cap, as well as his beard, was all iron-grey; his complexion was a little sallow, and seemed all the more sallow because of his red velvet cap and white soutane; (for he wore no cloak because of the heat). As soon as I had kissed his ring he bade me stand up — (speaking in Italian, as he did all through the audience) — and then beckoned me to a chair opposite to his, and my Lord Abbot to another on one side. And then at once he went on to speak of the business on which we were come — as if he knew all about it, and had no time to spend on compliments.

Now our Holy Father Innocent the Eleventh was, I suppose, one of the greatest men that ever sat in Peter's Seat. I would not speak evil, if I could help it, of any of Christ's Vicars; but this at least I may say — that Pope Innocent reformed a number of things that sorely needed it. He would have no nepotism at the Papal Court; men stood or fell by their own merits: so I knew very well that my estates in France, even if they had been ten times as great, would serve me nothing at all. He was very humble too — (he asked pardon, it was said, even of his own servants if he troubled them) — so I knew that no swashbuckling air on my part would do me anything but harm — (and, indeed, that was all laid aside, willy nilly, so soon as I came in) — since, like all humble men he esteemed the pride, even of kings, at exactly its proper worth, which is nothing at all. He was, too, a man of great spirituality, so I knew that my having come to St. Paul's as a novice and now wishing to leave it again, would scarcely exalt me in his eyes. I felt then a very poor creature indeed as I sat there and listened to him.

"This, then, is Master Roger Mallock," he said to my Lord Abbot, "of whom your Lordship spoke to me."

"This is he, Holy Father," said my Lord.

"He has been a novice for two years then; and his superiors are not sure of his vocation?"

"Yes, Holy Father."

The Pope looked again at me then, and I dropped my eyes.

"And you yourself, my son?" he asked.

"Holy Father," I said, "I am sure that at present I have no vocation. What God may give me in the future I do not know. I only know what He has not given me in the present."

Innocent tightened his lips at that; but I think it was to prevent himself smiling.

"And he is an English gentleman," he went on presently, "and he has estates in France that bring him in above twenty thousand francs yearly; and he is twenty-one years of age; and he is accustomed to all kinds of society, and he is a devoted son of Holy Church, and he speaks French and English and Italian and Spanish and German —"

"No, Holy Father, not German — except a few words," I said.

"And he is discreet and courageous and virtuous —"

"Holy Father —" I began in distress, for I thought he was mocking me.

"And he desires nothing; better than to serve his spiritual superiors in any employment to which they may put him — Eh, my son?"

I looked into the Pope's face and down again; but I said nothing.

"Eh, my son?" he said again with a certain sharpness.

"Holy Father, I have been taught never to contradict my superiors; but indeed in this —"

"Bravo!" said Innocent.

Then he turned to my Lord Abbot, as if I were no longer in the room.

"The question," he said, "is not only whether this young gentleman is capable of hearing everything and saying nothing, of preserving his virtue, of handling locked caskets without even desiring to look inside unless it is his business, of living in the world yet not being of it — but whether he is willing to do all this without being paid for it — except perhaps his bare expenses."

My Lord Abbot said nothing.

"I can have a thousand paid servants," said Innocent, "who are worth exactly their wages; but, since money cannot buy virtue or discretion or courage, in such servants I cannot demand those things. And I can have a thousand foolish servants who could earn no wages anywhere because of their foolishness, and these never have discretion and not often either virtue or courage. But what I wish is to have servants who are as wise sons to me — who have all these things, and will use them for love's sake — for the love of Holy Church and of Christ and His Mother, and who will be content with the wages that These give."

He stopped suddenly and looked at me quickly again; and my heart burned in my breast; for this that he was saying was all that I most desired; and I saw by that that my talk must have been reported to him. I loved Holy Church then, and the cause of Jesus and Mary, as young men do love, and as I hope to love till I die. I asked nothing better than to serve such causes as these even to death. It was not for lack of ardour that I wished to leave the monastery; it was because, truthfully, I had a fever on me of greater activity; because, truthfully, I was not sure of my vocation; because, truthfully, I doubted whether such gifts and such wealth and such education as were mine could not be used better in the world than in the cloister. I knew that I could take a place tomorrow in either the French or the English Court, without disgracing myself or others; and it was precisely of this that I had spoken to my Lord Abbot; and here was our Holy Father himself putting into words those very ambitions that I had. I met his eyes, and knew that I was beginning to flush.

"Well, my son?" he said.

"Holy Father," I said, "my virtues and capacities, such as they are, I must leave to my superiors. But my desires are those of which your Holiness has spoken. I ask no wages: I ask only to be allowed to serve whatever cause my superiors may assign to me."

He continued to look at me, and for very shame I presently dropped my eyes again.

"Well, my Lord Abbot?" he said again. "Let us hear what you have to say."

Then my lord began to speak; and before he was half-done I wished myself anywhere else in the world. For, as great men alone are capable, he could be as lavish of praise as of blame. He said that I was all that of which His Holiness had spoken; that I had been obedient and exact as a novice; and he said other things too of which even under obedience I could not speak. Then too he added what he had never said to me before, that he was not sure that I had no vocation; but that since God spoke through exterior circumstances as well as through interior drawings, His Holy Will seemed to point, at least at present, to a life in the world for me; that he was sure I would be as obedient there as here; that I had learned not only to use my tongue but, what is much harder, to hold it. And he ended by begging the Holy Father to take me into his service and to use me in the ways in which perhaps I might be useful. All this, of course, I now understand to have been rehearsed before; but just at that time I had no more than a suspicion that this was so.

When he had finished, His Holiness once more turned and looked at me; and I upon the ground: and then at last he spoke.

"My son," he said, "you have heard what his Reverence has said of you; and I too have heard it, and not today for the first time. It seems that you are right in thinking that for the present at any rate you have no vocation to Holy Religion. Well, then, the question is as to what is your Vocation, for Our Lord never leaves any man without a Vocation of some kind. You are very young for such service as that on which we think to send you; for we shall send you to the Court of England first, and then perhaps now and again to France; but you look five years at least older than your age, and, I am told, have ten times its discretion. I need not tell you that you will have no very heavy mission given to you at first; you must mix freely with the world and use your wits and see what is best to be done, sending back reports to the Cardinal Secretary. You will live at your own charges, as you yourself have said that you wished to do; but you may draw upon us here for any journeys that you may undertake upon our business up to a certain amount. In a word you will be in the diplomatic service of the Holy See, though without direct office or commission beyond that which I now give you myself. You will have full liberty to make a career for yourself in the English or French Courts, so long as this comes always second to your service to ourselves. If you acquit yourself well — in the way which will be explained to you later — you may make a career with us too, and will have rewards if you want them: but for the present there must be no talk of that. As you must be in the world yet not of it; so you must be of the Court of Rome yet not in it. It is a delicate position that you will hold; and, to compensate for the informality of it, you will have the more liberty on your side, to make a career, as I have said, or to marry, if God calls you to that, or in any other way.... Does that content you, my son?"

I do not know what I said; for all that the Holy Father had told me was what I myself had said to my Lord Abbot. I knew that affairs in England were in a very strange condition, that the Duke of York who was next heir to the throne was a Catholic, and that Charles himself was favourably disposed to us; and I knew a number of other things too which will appear in the course of this tale; and I had said to my Lord that sometimes even a hair's weight will make a balance tip; and had asked again and again if I might not, with my advantages, such as they were, be of more service to Holy Church in a more worldly place than the cloister; and now here was our Most Holy Lord himself granting and confirming all that I had wished.

"There! there!" he said to me presently, when I had tried to say what was in my heart. "Go and serve God in this way as well as you can; and remember that you can be as well sanctified in the Court of a King as in a cloister — and better, if it is the Court that is your Vocation. Go and do your best, my son; and we shall see what you can make of it."

*   *   *

When we were outside again I saw that my Lord Abbot's face was all suffused, as was my own, for there was something strangely fiery and keen and holy about Innocent; but he said nothing, except that we must now go and see His Eminence the Cardinal Secretary of State, for I was to receive my more particular instructions from him.

PART ONE

CHAPTER I

I came to London on the fifteenth of June, having left it seven years before in company with my father, to go to Paris, two years before he died.

It was drawing on to sunset as we rode up through the Southwark fields and, at the top of a little eminence in the ground saw for the first time plainly all the City displayed before us.

We came along the Kent road, having caught sight again and again of such spires as had risen after the Great Fire, and of the smoke that rose from the chimneys; but I may say that I was astonished at the progress the builders had made from what I could remember of seven years before. Then there had still been left great open spaces where there should have been none; now it was a city once more; and even the Cathedral shewed its walls and a few roofs above the houses. The steeples too of Sir Christopher Wren's new churches pricked everywhere; though I saw later that there was yet much building to be done, both in these and in many of the greater houses. My man James rode with me; (for I had been careful not to form too great intimacies with the party with whom I had ridden from Dover); and I remarked to him upon the matter.

"And there, sir," he said to me, pointing to it, "is the monument no doubt that they have raised to it."

And so we found it to be a day or two later — a tall pillar, with an inscription upon it saying that the Fire had been caused by the Papists — a black lie, as every honest man knows.

By the time that we came to London Bridge the sun was yet lower, setting in a glory of crimson, so that it was hard to see against it much of Westminster, across the Southwark marshes and the river; but yet I could make out the roofs of the Abbey and of some of the great buildings of Whitehall, where my adventures, I thought, were to lie. But between that and the other end of London Bridge, just before we set foot on it, the rest of the City was plain enough; and, indeed, it was a splendid sight to see the river, all, as it seemed, of molten gold with the barges and the wherries plying upon it, and the great houses on the banks and their gardens coming down to the water-gates, and the forest of chimneys and roofs and steeples behind, and all of a translucent blue colour. The sounds of the City, too, came to us plainly across the water — the chiming of bells and the firing of some sunset gun, and even the noise of wheels and the barking of dogs and the crowing of cocks — all in a soft medley of human music that made my heart rejoice; for in spite of my long exile abroad and my French and Italianate manners, I counted myself always an Englishman.

Now the first design that I had in mind, and for which I had made my dispositions, was to go straight to my lodging that had been secured for me by my cousin Tom Jermyn, where he was to meet me, and where he too would lie that night. It was with him that I was to present my letters at Whitehall in a day or two, after I had bought my clothes and other necessaries; in short he was to be my *cicerone* for a while — for he was a Catholic too, like myself — but he was not to be told that I had come on any mission at all, until at anyrate I had well tested his discretion.

*　　*　　*

Now the mission on which I had been instructed by the Cardinal Secretary was in one sense a very light one, and in another a very difficult one; for its express duties were of the smallest.

Affairs in England at this time were in a very strange condition. First, the Duke of York, who was heir to the throne, was a declared Catholic; and then the King himself was next door to one, in heart at anyrate. Certainly he had never been reconciled to the Church, though the report among some was that he had been, during his life in Paris: but in heart, as I have said, he was one, and waited only for a favourable occasion to declare himself. For he had been so bold seventeen years before, as to send to Rome a scheme by which the Church of England was to be reunited to Rome under certain conditions, as that the mass, or parts of it, should be read in English, that the Protestant clergy who would submit to ordination should be allowed to keep their wives, and other matters of that kind. His answer from Rome, sent by word of mouth only, was that no scheme could be nearer to the heart of His Holiness; but that he must not be too precipitate. Let him first show that his subjects were with him in his laudable desires; and then perhaps the terms of the matter might be spoken of again. For the King himself, and indeed even the Duke too at this time (though later he amended his life), Catholic in spirit, were scarce Christian in life. The ladies of the Court then must not be overlooked, for they as much as any statesman, and some think, more, controlled the king and his brother very greatly at this time.

But this was not all. Next, the King was embroiled in a great number of ways. The more extreme of his Protestant subjects feared and hated the Catholic Church as much as good Catholics hate and fear the Devil; and although for the present our people had great liberty both at Court and elsewhere, no man could tell when that liberty might be curtailed. And, indeed, it had been to a great part already curtailed five years before by the Test Act, forbidding the Catholics to hold any high place at the Court or elsewhere, though this was largely evaded. There was even a movement among some of them, and among the most important of them too, in the House of Lords and elsewhere, to exclude the Duke of York from the succession; and they advanced amongst themselves in support of this the fear that a French army might be brought in to subdue England to the Church. And, worst of all, as I had learned privately in Rome, there was some substance in their fear, though few else knew it; since the King was in private treaty with Louis for this very purpose. Again, a further embroilment lay in the propositions that had been made privately to the King that he should rid himself of his Queen — Catherine — on the pretext that she had borne no child to him, and could not, and marry instead some Protestant princess. Lastly, and most important of all, so greatly was Charles turned towards the Church, that he had begged more than once, and again lately, that a priest might be sent to him to be always at hand, in the event of his sudden sickness, whom none else knew to be a priest; and it was this last matter, I think, that had determined the Holy Father to let me go, as I had wished, though I was no priest, to see how the King would bear himself to me; and then, perhaps afterwards, a priest might be sent as he desired.

This then was the mission on which I was come to London.

I was to present myself at Court and place myself at His Majesty's disposal. The letters that I carried were no more than such as any gentleman might bring with him; but the King had been told beforehand who I was, and that I was come to be a messenger or a go-between if he so wished, with him and Rome. So much the King was told, and the Duke. But on my side I was told a little more — that I was to do my utmost, if the King were pleased with me, to further his conversion and his declaration of himself as a Catholic; that I was to mix with all kinds of folks, and observe what men really thought of all such matters as these, and send my reports regularly to Rome; that I was to place myself at the King's service in any way that I could — in short that I was to follow my discretion and do, as a layman may sometimes even more than a priest, all that was in my power for the furtherance of the Catholic cause.

Now it may be wondered perhaps how it was that I, who was so young, should be entrusted with such matters as these. Here then, I am bound to say, however immodest it may appear, that I have had always the art of making friends easily and of commending myself quickly. I had lived too in the societies of both Paris and Rome; and I had the accomplishments of a gentleman as well as his blood. I was thought a pleasant fellow, that is to say, who could make himself agreeable; and I certainly had too — and I am not ashamed to say this — but one single ambition in the world, and that was to serve God's cause: and these things do not always go together in this world. Last of all, it must be observed, that no very weighty secrets were entrusted to me: I bore no letters; and I had been told no more of affairs in general than such as any quick and intelligent man might pick up for himself. Even should I prove untrustworthy or indiscreet, or even turn traitor, no very great harm would be done. If, upon the other hand, I proved ready and capable, all that I could learn in England and, later perhaps, in France, would serve me well in the carrying out of weightier designs that might then be given into my charge.

Such then I was; and such was my mission, on this fifteenth day of June, as I rode up with James my man — a servant found for me in Rome, who had once been in the service of my Lord Stafford — to the door of the lodgings engaged for me in Covent Garden Piazza above a jeweller's shop.

*   *   *

It was after sunset that we came there; and all the way along the Strand, until we nearly reached the York Stairs, I had said nothing to my man, but had used my eyes instead, striving to remember what I could of seven years before. The houses of great folk were for the most part on my left — Italianate in design, with the river seen between them, and lesser houses, of the architecture that is called "magpie," on the right. The way was very foul, for there had been rain that morning, and there seemed nothing to carry the filth away: in places faggots had been thrown down to enable carts to pass over. The Strand was very full of folk of all kinds going back to their houses for supper.

Covent Garden Piazza was a fairer place altogether. It was enclosed in railings, and a sun-dial stood in the centre; and on the south was the space for the market, with a cobbled pavement. To the east of St. Paul's Church stood the greater houses, built on arcades, where many fashionable people of the Court lived or had their lodgings, and it was in one of these that I too was to lodge: for I had bidden my Cousin Jermyn to do the best he could for me, and his letter had reached me at Dover, telling me to what place I was to come.

As I sat on my horse, waiting while my man went in to one of the doorways to inquire, a gentleman ran suddenly out of another, with no hat on his head.

"Why, you are my Cousin Roger, are you not?" he cried from the steps.

"Then you are my Cousin Tom Jermyn," I said.

"The very man!" he cried back; and ran down to hold my stirrup.

All the way up the stairs he was talking and I was observing him. He seemed a hearty kind of fellow enough, with a sunburnt face from living in the country; and he wore his own hair. He was still in riding-dress; and he told me, before we had reached the first landing, that he was come but an hour ago from his house at Hare Street, in Hertfordshire.

"And I have brought little Dorothy with me," he cried. "You remember little Dorothy? She is a lady of quality now, aged no less than sixteen; and is come up to renew her fal-lals for her cousin's arrival; for you must come down with us to Hare Street when your business is done."

I cannot say that even after all this heartiness, I thought very much of my Cousin Tom. He spoke too loud, I thought, on the common stair: but I forgot all that when I came into the room that was already lighted with a pair of wax candles and set eyes on my Cousin Dorothy, who stood up as we came in, still in her riding-dress, with her whip and gloves on the table. Now let me once and for all describe my Cousin Dorothy; and then I need say no more. She was sixteen years old at this time — as her father had just told me. She was of a pale skin, with blue eyes and black lashes and black hair; but she too was greatly sunburnt, with the haymaking (as her father presently told me again; for she spoke very little after we had saluted one another). She was in a green skirt and a skirted doublet of the same colour, and wore a green hat with a white feather; but those things I did not remember till I was gone to bed and was thinking of her. It is a hard business for a lover to speak as he should of the maid who first taught him his lessons in that art; but I think it was her silence, and the look in her eyes, that embodied for me at first what I found so dear afterwards. She was neither tall nor short; she was very slender; and she moved without noise. All these things I write down now from my remembrance of the observations that I made afterwards. It would be foolish to say that I loved her so soon as I saw her; for no man does that in reality, whatever he may say of it later; I was aware only that here was a maid whose presence made the little room very pleasant to me, and with whom taking supper would be something more than the swallowing of food and drink.

The rooms of my lodging were good enough, as I saw when my Cousin Tom flung open the doors to show me them all. They were three in number: this room into which we had first come from the stairs was hung in green damask, with candles in sconces between the panels of the stuff; the door on the left opened into the room where my Cousin Dorothy would lie, with her maid; and that on the right my Cousin Tom and I would share between us. The windows of all three looked out upon the piazza.

He said a great number of times that he was sorry that he had brought up his daughter without giving me warning; but that the maid had set her heart on it and would take no denial. (This I presently discovered to be wholly false.) For a week, he said, and no more, I should be discommoded; and after that, when I had come back from Hare Street, I should be able to entertain my friends in peace.

I answered him, of course, with the proper compliments; but I liked his manner less than ever. He was too boisterous, I thought, on a first meeting; and too hearty in his expressions of goodwill. When we were set down to supper, he began again, with what I thought a good deal of indiscretion.

"So you are come from Rome!" he said loudly, "and from a monastery too, as I hear. Well, no man loves a monk more than I do — in their monasteries; but I am glad you are not to be one. We will teach him better here — eh, Dolly, my dear?"

It was only my man James who was in the room when he spoke; yet as soon as he was gone out to fetch another dish I thought I had best say a word.

"Cousin," I said, "with your leave; I think it best not to speak of monasteries —"

He interrupted me.

"Why, you need fear nothing," he cried. "We Catholics are all in the fashion these days. Why, there is Mr. Huddleston that goes about in his priest's habit: and the Capuchins at St. James', and the very Jesuits too —"

"I think it would be better not —" I began.

"Oho!" cried Cousin Tom. "That is in the wind, is it? Why, I'll be as mum as a mouse!"

I did not know what he meant; and I supposed that he did not know himself, unless indeed by sheer blundering he had pitched upon the truth that I was come on a mission. But so soon as James was in the room again, he began upon the other tack, and talked of Prince this and the Duke of that, with whom I might be supposed to be on terms of intimacy, winking on me all the while, so that my man saw it. However, I answered him civilly. I could do no less; for he was my cousin, and in a manner my host; and, most of all, I must depend upon him for a few days at least, to tell me how I must set about my audiences and my personal affairs.

My Cousin Dorothy said little or nothing all this time; but sat with downcast eyes, giving a look now and again at the table to see if we had all that we needed; for she was housekeeper at Hare Street, her mother having died ten years before, and she herself being the only child. She did not look at me at all, or shew any displeasure; and yet it seemed to me that she was not best pleased with her father's manners. Once, towards the end of supper, when James came behind him with the wine-jug, I saw her shake her head at him; and, indeed, Cousin Tom was already pretty red in the face with all that he had drunk.

When the meal was finished at last, and the table cleared, and the servants gone downstairs to their own supper, he began again with his talk, stretching his legs in the window-seat where he sat; while I sat still in my chair wheeled away from the table, and my Cousin Dorothy went in and out of the rooms, bestowing the luggage that she and her maid had unpacked. I watched her as she went to and fro, telling myself (as some lads will, who pride themselves on being come to manhood) that she was only a little maid.

"As to your affairs, Cousin Roger," he said, "they will soon be determined. I take it that when you have kissed His Majesty's hand and paid your duty to the Duke, you will have done all that you should for the present."

I did not contradict him; but he was not to be restrained.

"You are come to seek your fortune, no doubt:" (he winked on me again as he said this, to draw attention to his discretion); "and there is nothing else in the world but that, no doubt, that brings you to England." (He said this with an evident irony that even a child would have understood.) "Not that you have not a very pretty fortune already: I understand that it is near upon a thousand pounds a year; and great estates in Normandy too, when you shall be twenty-eight years old. I am right, am I not?"

Now he was right; but I wondered that he should take such pains to know it all.

"There or thereabouts," I said.

"That condition of twenty-eight years is a strange one," he went on. "Now what made your poor father fix upon that, I wonder?"

I told him that my father held that a man's life went by sevens, and that every man was a boy till he was twenty-one, a fool till he was twenty-eight, and a man, by God's grace, after that.

"Ah, that was it, was it?" he said, stretching his legs yet further. "I have often wondered as to how that was."

And that shewed me that his mind must have run a good deal upon my fortunes; but as yet I did not understand the reason.

When, presently, my Cousin Dorothy had shut the door of her room, and my man was gone down again to the horses, he began again on his old tack.

"You and I, Cousin Roger," he said, "will soon understand one another. I knew that as soon as I clapped eyes on you. Come, tell me what your business is here. I'm as close as the grave over a friend's secrets."

"My dear cousin," I said, "I do not know what business you mean. Was not my letter explicit enough? I am come to live here as an English gentleman. What other business should I have?"

He winked again at me.

"Yes, yes," he said. "And now having done your duty to your discretion, do it to your friendship for me too. I know very well that a man who comes from a Roman monastery, with letters from the French ambassador, does not come for nothing. Is there some new scheme on hand? — for the honour of Holy Church, no doubt?"

I thanked God then that I had said not one word in my letter that Shaftesbury himself might not have read. I had been in two minds about it; but had determined to wait until I saw my cousin and learned for myself what kind of man he was.

"My dear cousin," I said again, "even if I had come on some such mission, I should assure you, as I do now, that it was nothing of the kind. How else could such missions be kept secret at all? It would be a *secretum commissum* in any case; as the theologians would say. I can but repeat what I said in my letter to you; and, if you will think of it, you will see that it is not likely that any matter of importance would be entrusted to a young man of my age."

That seemed to quiet him. I have often noticed that to appeal to the experience and wisdom of a fool is the surest way to content him.

He began then to talk of the Court; and it would not be decent of me to record even a tenth part of the gossip he told me regarding the corruption that prevailed in Whitehall. Much of it was no doubt true; and a great deal more than he told me in some matters; but it came pouring out from him, and with such evident pleasure to himself, that it was all I could do to preserve a pleasant face towards him. He told me of the little orange-girl, Nell Gwyn, who was now just twenty-eight years old; and how she lived here and there as the King gave her houses — in Pall Mall, and in Sandford House in Chelsea, and at first at the "Cock and Pie" in Drury Lane; and how her hair was of a reddish brown, and how, when she laughed her eyes disappeared in her head; and of the Duchess of Cleveland, that was once Mrs. Palmer and then my Lady Castlemaine, now in France; and of the Duchess of Portsmouth, and her son created Duke of Richmond three years ago; and of the mock marriage that was celebrated, in my Lord Arlington's house at Euston, seven years ago between her and the King. And these things were only the more decent matters of which he spoke; and of all he spoke with that kind of chuckling pleasure that a heavy country squire usually shews in such things, so that I nearly hated him as he sat there. For to myself such things seem infinitely sorrowful; and all the more so in such a man as the King was; and they seemed the more sorrowful the more that I knew of him later; for he had so much of the supernatural in him after all, and knew what he did.

Then presently my Cousin Jermyn began upon the Duke; and at that I nearly loosed my tongue at him altogether. For I knew very well that the guilt of the Duke was heavier even than the guilt of the King, since James had the grace of the Sacraments to help him and the light of the Faith to guide him. But I judged it better not to shew my anger, since I was, as the Holy Father had told me, to be "in the world," though interiorly not of it: and so I feigned sleep instead, and presently had to snore aloud before my cousin could see it: and, as he stopped speaking, my Cousin Dorothy came in to bid us good-night.

"Why, I have been half asleep," I said. "I am tired with my journey. What were you saying, cousin?"

He leered again at that, as if to draw attention to his daughter's presence.

"Why, we were talking of high matters of state," he said, "when you fell asleep — matters too high for little maids to hear of. Give me a kiss, my dear."

When she came to me, I kissed her on the forehead, and not upon the cheek which she offered me.

"Is that the Italian custom?" cried my Cousin Tom. "Why, we can teach you better than that — eh, Dolly?"

She said nothing to that; but looked at me a little anxiously and then at the table where the wine stood; and I thought that I understood her.

"Well, cousin," I said, "I, too, had best be off to bed. We had best both go. I do not want to lie awake half the night; and if you wake me when you come to bed, I shall not sleep again."

He tried to persuade me to stay and drink a little more; but I would not: and for very courtesy he had to come with me.

In spite of my drowsiness, however, when I was once in bed and the light was out I could not at once sleep. I heard the watchman go by and cry that it was a fine night; and I heard the carriages go by, and the chairs; and saw the light of the links on the ceiling at the end of my bed; and I heard a brawl once and the clash of swords and the scream of a woman; as well as the snoring of my Cousin Tom, who fell asleep at once, so full he was of French wine. But it was not these things that kept me awake, except so far as they were signs to me of where I was.

For here I was in London at last, which, whatever men may say, is the heart of the world, as Rome is the heart of the Church; and there, within a gunshot, was the gate of Whitehall where the King lived, and where my fortunes lay. Neither was I here as a mere Englishman come home again after seven years, but as a messenger from the Holy See, with work both to find and to do. Tomorrow I must set out, to buy, as I may say, the munitions of war — my clothes and my new periwigs and my swords and my horses; and then after that my holy war was to begin. I had my letters not only to the Court, but to the Jesuits as well — though of these I had been careful to say nothing to my cousin; for I could present these very well without his assistance. And this holy war I was to carry on by my own wits, though a soldier in that great army of Christ that fights continually with spiritual weapons against the deceits of Satan.

I wondered, then, as I lay there in the dark, as to whether this war would be as bloodless as seemed likely; whether indeed it were true (and if true, whether it were good or bad) that Catholics should again almost be in the fashion, as my cousin had said.

There were still those old bloody laws against us; was it so sure that they would never be revived again? And if they were revived, how should I bear myself; and how would my Cousin Jermyn, and all those other Catholics of whom London was so full?

Of all these things, then, I thought; but my last thoughts, before I commended myself finally to God and Our Lady, were of my Cousin Dorothy — that little maid, as I feigned to myself to think of her. Yes; I would go down to Hare Street in Hertfordshire so soon as I conveniently could, without neglecting my business. It would be pleasant to see what place it was that my Cousin Dorothy called her home.

CHAPTER II

It was again a fair evening, five days later, when, in one of my new suits, with my new silver-handled sword, I set out on foot to Whitehall to see the King first and the Duke afterwards, as word had been brought me from the Chamberlain's office; for I had presented my letters on the morning after I had come to London.

Those four days had passed busily and merrily enough in company with my cousins. The first two days I had spent in the shops, and had expended above forty pounds, with both my cousins to advise me. It would not be to the purpose to describe all that I bought; but there was a blue suit I had, that was made very quickly, and that was the one I wore when I went to see the King, that was very fine. All was of blue; the coat was square-cut, with deep skirts, and had great laced cuffs that turned up as high as the elbow, showing the ruffled wristbands of the shirt beneath; the waistcoat below — in the new fashion — was so hung as to come down to my knees; and both coat and waistcoat had buttons all the way down the front, with silver trimming. My stockings — for the brodequins were out of fashion again now — were of a darker blue, and my shoes of strong leather, with a great rosette upon each, for buckles were not usual at this time. Then my cravat was of Flanders lace; and my Cousin Dorothy showed me how to fasten it so that the ends lay down square in front; and my hat was round with a blue favour in it upon the left side; and I wore it with what was called the "Monmouth cock." I carried a long cane in my hand, with a silver head, and a pair of soft leather gloves, without cuffs to them. Then, as my own hair was still short, I bought a couple of dark periwigs of my own colour, and put on, the better to go to Whitehall in. Besides these things I had three other suits, one very plain, of grey, and two less plain; a case of pistols, and a second sword, very plain and strong, in a leather scabbard, with its belt; two pair of riding-boots, besides other shoes; and two dozen of shirts and cravats, of which half were plain, without lace.

While we went to and fro on all those businesses, we saw something both of the town and of the folks. On our way back from Cheapside one day, we turned aside to see the Monument, with the lying inscription upon it; and then to see the Cathedral, which was already of a considerable height. Of the persons of importance we saw one day the Duke of Buckingham in his coach, drawn by two white horses, with riders before and behind, pass along towards Whitehall; and a chair went by us one evening in which, it was said, was the Duchess of Portsmouth (once Madame de la Querouaille, or Mrs. Carwell); but it was so closely guarded that I could not see within. Also, we saw my Lord Shaftesbury, a sly yet proud looking fellow, I thought him, walking with Mr. Pepys, who fell later under suspicion of being a Catholic, because his servant was one.

On the Saturday evening we went to take the air in St. James' Park, and walked by Rosamund's pond; and here we but just missed seeing the King and Queen; for as we came into it from Charing Cross (where I had seen for the first time in the public street the Punch-show, which I think must take its origin from Pontius Pilate) their Majesties rode out — hand in hand, I heard later — through the Park Gate into the Horse-Guards, and so to Whitehall, with guards in buff and steel following. There was a great company of gentlemen and ladies who rode behind, of whom we caught a sight; but they were too far away for us to recognize any of them. (I saw, too, the cress-carts come in from Tothill fields.)

On the Sunday morning we went all three together to hear mass sung in St. James'; and here for the first time I saw Mr. Huddleston, who was of the congregation, who was in his priest's habit — as my cousin had told me — for this was allowed to him by Act of Parliament, because he had saved the King's life after the battle of Worcester. He was a man that looked like a scholar, but was very brown with the sun, too. We could not see the Duke, for he was in his closet, with the curtains half drawn — a tribune, as we should call it in Rome. It was very sweet to me to hear mass again after my journey; and it was not less sweet to me that my Cousin Dorothy was beside me; but the crush was so great, of Protestants who had come to see the ceremonies, as well as of Catholics, that there was scarcely room even to kneel down at the elevation. On our way back we saw Prince Rupert, a fat pasty-faced man, driving out in his coach. He spent all his time in chymical experiments, I was told. As Sedley said, he had exchanged Naseby for Noseby.

I had been bidden, on the Monday, to present myself first at Mr. Chiffinch's lodgings that were near the chapel, between the Privy Stairs and the Palace Stairs; and, as I was before my time, when I came into the Court, behind the Banqueting Hall, I turned aside to see the Privy Garden. A fellow in livery, of whom there were half a dozen in sight, asked me my business very civilly; and when I told him, let me go through by the Treasury and the King's laboratory, so that I might see the garden: and indeed it was very well worth seeing. There were sixteen great beds, set in the rectangle, with paved walks between; there was a stone vase on a pedestal, or a statue, in the centre of each bed, and a great sundial in the midst of them all. There were some ladies walking at the further end, beneath the two rows of trees; and the sight was a very pretty one, for the sunlight was still on part of the garden and on the Bowling-Green beyond the trees; and the flowers and the ladies' dresses, and the high windows that flashed back the light, all conspired to make what I looked upon very beautiful. The lodgings that looked on to the Privy Garden and the Bowling-Green were much coveted, I heard later; and only such personages as Prince Rupert, my Lord Peterborough, Sir Philip Killigrew, and such like, could get them there.

Mr. Chiffinch's lodgings, when I came to them, were not so fine; for they looked out upon little courts on both sides, and my Lady Arlington's lodgings blocked his view to the river. I went up the stairs, and beat upon the door with my cane: and a voice cried to me to enter.

Now I had heard enough of Mr. Chiffinch to make me prejudge him; for his main business, it seemed, was to pander to the King's pleasures; and he had his rooms so near the river, it was said, that he might more easily meet those who came by water and take them up to His Majesty's rooms unobserved: yet when I saw him, I understood that any prejudgement was unnecessary. For if ever man bore his character in his face it was Mr. Chiffinch.

He had risen at my knock, and was standing in the light of the window. He was dressed in a dark suit, very plain, yet of very rich stuff, and had laid his periwig aside, so that I could see his features. He was a dark secret-looking man with his eyes set near together, and with a lip so short that it seemed as if he sneered; he stooped a little too. Yet I am bound to say that his manner was perfection itself.

"Mr. Chiffinch," I said. And at that he bowed.

"I am Mr. Roger Mallock," I said; "and I was bidden to come here at this hour."

"I am honoured to meet you, Mr. Mallock," he said. "I have had His Majesty's instructions very particular in your regard. I am ashamed that you should find me so unready; but I will not keep you above five minutes, if you will sit down for a little."

He made haste to set me a chair near the window; and with another apology or two he went out of a second door. The room in which he left me was like the suit that he wore — in that it was both plain and rich. There were three or four chairs with arms; a table, with twisted legs, on which lay a great heap of papers and a pair of candlesticks: and there was a tall lightly-carved press, with locks, between the windows. The walls were plain, with a few good engravings hung upon them. I went up to examine one, and found it to be a new one, by Faithorne.

Now that I was drawing so near to the King, I found my apprehensions returning upon me, for half my success, I knew, if not all, turned upon the manner I first shewed to him. I knew very well that I could bear myself with sufficient address; but sufficient address was not all that was needed: I must so act that His Majesty would remember me afterwards, and with pleasure. Yet how was I to ensure this?

As I was so thinking to myself, Mr. Chiffinch came in again, having, with marvellous speed, changed his suit into one of brown velvet, with a great black periwig, from which his sharp face looked out like a ferret from a hole.

"I must ask your pardon, Mr. Mallock," he said, as I stood up to meet him, "again and again; but I have scarcely an hour to myself day or night. Duty treads on the heels of duty all day long. But we have still time: His Majesty does not expect us till half-past five."

I made the usual compliments and answers, to which he bowed again; and then, as I thought he would, he began upon what was not his business — at least I thought not then.

"You are come from Rome, I hear. I trust that His Holiness was in good health?"

"The reports were excellent," I said, determined not to be taken in this way.

"You have seen His Holiness lately, no doubt?"

"It was the French and Spanish ambassadors," I said, "who gave me my letters. A poor gentleman like myself does not see the Holy Father once in a twelvemonth."

He seemed contented with that; and I think he put me down as something of a well-bred simpleton, which was precisely what I wished him to think; for his manner changed a little.

"You have seen His Majesty before, no doubt?"

"I have not been in England for seven years," I said, smiling. "I saw His Majesty once when I was a lad, as he went to dinner; and I have seen him once, on Saturday last; at least, I saw the top of his hat from a hundred yards off."

"And the Duke of York?" he asked.

"I have never seen the Duke of York in my life, to my knowledge," I said.

Now I saw well enough what he was after. Without a doubt he had a suspicion that I was an emissary in some way from the Holy Father, or at least that I was more than I appeared to be; and being one of those men who desire to know everything, that they may understand, as the saying is, which way the cat will jump, and how to jump with her, he was determined to find out all that he could. On my side, therefore, I assumed the air of a rather stupid gentleman, to bear out better the character that I had — that I was a mere gentleman from Rome, recommended by the Catholic ambassadors; and I think that, for the time at anyrate, he took me so to be; for his manner became less inquisitive.

"We must be going to His Majesty, sir," he said presently, rising; and then he added as if by chance: "You are a Catholic, Mr. Mallock?"

"Why, yes," I said: for there was no need of any concealment on the point of my religion.

*　　*　　*

As we went downstairs and along the passage that led by Sir Francis Clinton's lodgings, he began to speak of how I was to behave myself to the King, and how kiss his hand and the rest. I knew very well all these things, but I listened to him as if I did not, and even put a question or two; and he answered me very graciously.

"You should be very modest with His Majesty," he said, "if you would please him. He likes not originals over-much; or, rather, I would say — (but it must not be repeated) — that he likes to be the only original of the company."

And when Mr. Chiffinch said that I knew that he was lying to me; for the very opposite was the truth; and I understood that he still had his suspicions of me and wished me to fail with the King. But I nodded wisely, and thanked him.

A couple of Yeomen of the Guard — of which body no man was less than six feet tall — stood at the foot of the little stairs that led up to the King's lodgings: and these made no motion to hinder the King's page and his companion. So English were they that they did not even turn their eyes as we went through, Mr. Chiffinch preceding me with an apology.

At the door on the landing of the first floor he turned to me again before he knocked.

"His Majesty will be within the second room," he said. "Will you wait, Mr. Mallock, please, in this first anteroom, and I will go through. This is a private reception by His Majesty. There will be no formalities."

He tapped upon both the doors that were one inside the other; and then led me through. The first chamber was very richly furnished, though barely. There was a long table with chairs about it; and he led me to one of these. Then with a nod or two he passed on to a second door, tapped upon it softly and went through, closing it behind him. I heard a woman's laugh as he went through, suddenly broken off.

There was, I supposed (and as I learned afterwards to be the case) one other way at least out of the King's lodgings, through his private library, where he kept all his clocks and wheels and such-like; for when, after a minute or two, the door opened again and Mr. Chiffinch beckoned me in, there was no woman with the King.

It was a great room — His Majesty's closet as it was called — which he used for such solitary life as he led; and while I was with him, and afterwards upon other occasions, I saw little by little how it was furnished. The table in the midst, at which His Majesty wrote, was all in disorder; it was piled high with papers and books, for he would do what writing or reading he cared to do by fits and starts. The walls were hung with panels of tapestry, and tall curtains of brocade hung at the windows. Between the panels were pictures hung upon the walls — three or four flower-pictures by Varelst; three pictures of horses and dogs by Hondius, and a couple of Dutch pictures by Hoogstraaten. Over the fireplace was a chimney-breast by Gibbons; and the ceiling was all a-sprawl with gods and goddesses, I suppose by Verrio. In the windows, which looked out on two sides, over the river and into a little court, were little tables covered with curious things, for His Majesty delighted in such ingenuities — Dutch figures in silver, clockwork, and the like, and a basket of spaniels lay beneath one of the tables. A second great table stood against the wall on the further side from that on which I entered, covered with retorts and instruments, and behind it a press, and near it sat the King. The floor was carpeted with rush matting, loosely woven, with rugs upon it. But of all these things I saw little or nothing at the first, for Mr. Chiffinch was gone out behind me, and I was alone with His Majesty. One of the spaniels had given a little yelp as I came in; but disposed himself to sleep again.

Now I am not one of those who think that those who are noble by birth must always be noble by character, though I know that it should be so. I knew, too, very well that Charles was less than noble in a great number of ways. His women did what they liked with him; he would spend fortunes on those who pleased him and did him nothing but injury, and would let his faithful lovers and servants go starve. He lived always, you would say, only for the flesh and the pride of the eyes; he was careless and selfish and ungrateful; in short, he was as dissolute as a man could be, or, rather, as dissolute as a king could be, and that is much more. Yet for all this, he was a man of an extraordinary power, if he had cared to use it. It was said of him that "he could, if he would, but that he would not"; and of his brother that "he would if he could, but that he could not"; and I know no better epigram on the two than that. James was all intention without success; and Charles all success without intention. And so James at the end lived and died as a saint, though he was far from being one at this time; and Charles lived and died a sinner, though, thank God, a penitent one.

Now although I knew all this well enough, and how Charles' private life stank in the nostrils of God and man, I cannot describe how he affected me with loyalty and compassion and even a kind of love, in this little while that I had with him in private, nor how these emotions grew upon me the more that I knew him.

He was sitting in his great chair, not yet dressed for supper, for his wristbands were tumbled and turned back, and his huge dark brown periwig was ever so little awry. He was in a dark suit, with a lace cravat; and his rosetted shoes were crossed one over the other as he sat. The light of the window fell full upon him from one side, shewing his swarthy face, his thin close moustaches, and his heavy eyes under his arched brows — shewing above all that air of strange and lovable melancholy that was so marked a trait in those of the Stuart blood. He smiled a little at me, but did not move, except to put out his hand. I came across the floor, kneeled and kissed his hand, then, at a motion from him, stood up again.

"So you are Mr. Roger Mallock," he said. "Welcome to England, Mr. Roger Mallock. You bring good news of His Holiness, I hope."

"His Holiness does very well, Sir," I said.

"We should all do as well if we were as holy," said the King. "And you come to look after my soul, I am informed."

(He said this with a kind of gravity that can scarcely be believed.)

"I am no priest, Sir," I said, "if you mean that. I am only a forerunner, at the best."

"*Vox clamantis in deserto,*" said the King. "I hope I shall be no Herod to cut off your head. But it is very kind of you to come to this wilderness. And have you seen my brother yet?"

"I am to see his Royal Highness immediately," I said. "I waited upon Your Majesty first."

"Poor James!" said the King. "He wants looking after, I think. And what have you come to do in England, Mr. Mallock?"

Now I felt that I was cutting a poor figure at present; and that I must say something presently, if I could, to make the King remember me afterwards. It appeared to me that he was trying me, as he tried all newcomers, to see whether they would be witty or amusing; but, for the life of me, I could think of nothing to say.

"I am come to put myself wholly at Your Majesty's disposal," I said.

"Come! come! That's better," said Charles. "It is usually the other way about. *Servus servorum Dei*, you know. And in what manner do you propose that I should use you?"

"I will clean Your Majesty's shoes, if you will. Or I will run errands in my own. Or I will sing psalms, or ditties; or I will row in a boat; or I will play tennis, or fence. I am what is called an accomplished young gentleman, Sir."

Now I think I put in a shade too many clauses, for I was a little agitated. But the King's face lightened up very pleasantly.

"But I have plenty of folks who can do all that," he said. "In what are you distinguished from the rest?"

Then I determined on a bold stroke; for I knew that the King liked such things, if they were not too bold.

"I am a Jesuit at heart, Sir;" I said. "I desire to do these things, if Your Majesty wills it so, simply that I may serve His Holiness in serving Your Majesty."

"Oho!" said Charles; and he gathered his feet under him and looked at me more closely. I met his eyes fairly and then dropped my own.

"Oho! That is frank enough, Mr. Mallock. You know all about me, I suppose. You seem very young for such work. How old are you? Twenty-five?"

"I pass as twenty-five, Sir. But I am only twenty-one!"

"I would that I were!" said Charles earnestly. "And so you are a Jesuit in disguise — a wolf in sheep's clothing."

"No, Sir. I am a Jesuit at heart only, in that I would do anything in God's cause. But I am rather a sheep in wolf's clothing. I was a Benedictine novice till lately."

He seemed not to hear me. He had dropped his chin on his hand, and was looking at me as if he were thinking of something else.

"So you are come to serve me," he said presently, "in any way that I will; and you will serve me only that you may serve your master better. And what wages do you want?"

"None that Your Majesty can give," I said.

"Better and better," said Charles. "Nor place, nor position?"

"Only at Your Majesty's feet."

"And what if I kick you?"

"I will look for the halfpence elsewhere, Sir."

Then the King laughed outright, in the short harsh way he had; and I knew that I had pleased him. Then he stood up, and I saw that he was taller than I had thought. He was close upon six feet high.

"Well, Mr. Mallock," he said, "this seems all very pleasant and satisfactory. You said you would run errands. I suppose you mean to Rome?"

"To Rome and back, Sir," I said. "Or to anywhere else, except Hell."

"Oh! you draw the line there, do you?"

"No, Sir. It is God Almighty who has drawn it. I am not responsible."

"But you observe God His line?"

"Yes, Sir. At least, I try to."

"We all do that, I suppose. The pity is that we do not succeed more consistently ... Well, Mr. Mallock, I have nothing for you at present. I am a great deal too busy. These ladies, you know, demand so much. I suppose you heard one of them laugh just now?"

"I hear nothing but Your Majesty's commands," I said very meekly.

Charles laughed again and began to walk up and down.

"Well — and there are all these clockwork businesses, and chymical and the like. And there is so much to eat and drink and see: and there are the affairs of the kingdom — I had forgot that. Well; I have no time at present, Mr. Mallock, as you can see for yourself. But I will not forget you, if I want you. Where do you lodge?"

I named my lodgings in Covent Garden.

"And I have a cousin, Sir," I said, "who has bidden me to his house in Hare Street. I shall be here or there."

"His name?"

"Thomas Jermyn, Sir."

The King nodded.

"I will remember that," he said. "Well, it may be a long time before I have anything more to say to His Holiness. 'He that will not when he may —' You know all about that, I suppose, Mr. Mallock?"

"I know that Your Majesty has the reunion of Christendom at heart," I said discreetly.

"Yes, yes; I understand," said Charles. "I have received very favourable accounts of you, sir. And your letters, which are for the public eye, are perfectly in order. Well; I will remember, Mr. Mallock. Meanwhile you had best not shew yourself at Court in public too much." (And this he said very earnestly.)

He put out his hand to be kissed.

"And you will give my compliments to my brother James," he said.

*   *   *

One of the spaniels snored in his sleep as I went out again.

CHAPTER III

My interview with the Duke was a very different matter. I was informed at his lodgings that he was not yet come from tennis; and upon asking how long he would be, or if I might go to the tennis-court, was told that he might be half an hour yet, and that I might go there if I wished; so I went up from the river again, with a fellow they sent to guide me, down through the Stone Gallery, across the Privy Garden, and so across the street, midway between the gates, and so by the Duke of Monmouth's lodgings to the tennis-court. Here, as I went across the street, I caught sight of the sentries changing guard. These were the Coldstream Guards, in their red coats; for it was these foot-guards who did duty for the most part in the Palace and round about at the gates. The other troops about His Majesty were, first the King's Guards proper, who attended him when he rode out: these were in buff coats and cuirasses, very well mounted, and very gay with ribbons and velvet and gold lace and what not: and to each troop of these were attached a company of grenadiers with their grenades. Besides these were the Blues, also cavalry; and the dragoons, who were infantry on horseback, and carried bayonets. Of the foot-soldiers, such as the Buffs, most were mousquetaires; but some trailed pikes, and every one of them had a sword. These troops I saw constantly in town; besides the Yeomen who were closely attached to the person of his Sacred Majesty.

It was by the Duke of Monmouth's lodgings that I had my first sight of the Duke of Monmouth himself; for as I came towards the archway, by which were the lodgings of my Lady Suffolk, he himself came out from his own. I did not know who he was, until the fellow by me saluted him and doffed his cap, whereupon I did the same. I think I have never seen a more handsome lad in all my life (for he looked no more, though he was near thirty years old). His face was as smooth as a girl's, though not at all effeminate; he had a high and merry look with him, and bore himself, with his two friends, like a prince; he had violet eyes and arched brows over them. It is piteous to me now to think of his end, and that it was against his uncle by blood (whom I was to see presently) that he rebelled later, and by his uncle that he was condemned; and it is yet more piteous to think how he met that end, crying and cringing for fear of his life, both in the ditch in which he was discovered, and afterward in prison. He looked very kindly on me as he passed, lifting his hand to his hat; but I think he would not have so looked if he had known all about me; for he was as venomous against the Catholics as a man could be, or at least feigned himself so, for I think he had not a great deal of religion at any time. But he was to know me better afterwards.

When I came up into the gallery of the tennis-court I found it pretty full; yet not so full but that I could get a sight of the players. The Duke was in the court of the *dédans* when I first came in, so I could see no more of him than his back and his cropped head; but when, after two chaces he crossed over, I had a good view of him.

He was more heavily built than Charles; but his features were not unlike the King's, though he was fairer in complexion, I suppose; and his lip was shorter, and he wore no hair on his face. He had somewhat of a heavier look too in his face, without the fire that burned like embers in his brother's eyes. All this I noticed somewhat of, even from the gallery, though he was all a-sweat with his exercise.

I had left word with one of the men below as to my name and my business; and when the game was ended and the Duke went out, I remained still upstairs for a little, thinking that perhaps another would be played, and then perhaps he would send for me. But a servant came up presently and told me I was to follow to the Stone Gallery, where the Duke would walk for a while before changing his clothes, as his custom was. This Stone Gallery, as I had seen, was roofed, with skylights in it, and had presses of books all along the walls, together with collections of all kinds.

When I came to the Gallery he was at the further end, walking with Sir Robert Murray, as I learned afterwards, who was a very earnest Protestant, but always at Court; but when he saw me he sent Sir Robert away and beckoned to me to come. So I went up to him and kissed his hand, and he bade me walk with him for a little. (He had put on a cloak and hat to prevent his taking cold.)

Now his manner was wholly different from His Majesty's. There was a courtesy always in Charles that was not in James; for the Duke said nothing as to his receiving me here in his *déshabille*, but began immediately to talk in a low voice.

"I am pleased that you are come to England, Mr. Mallock. I have had news of you from Rome."

Then he asked very properly of the Holy Father, and of a Cardinal or two that he knew; and I answered him as well as I could. But I very soon saw that His Royal Highness wanted nothing like wit from me: he was somewhat of a solemn man, and had great ideas of his rights, and that all men who were below his own station should keep their own. He desired deference and attention above all things.

He spoke presently of Catholics in England.

"God hath blest us very highly," he said, "both in numbers and influence. But we can well do with more of both; for I never heard of any cause that could not. There is a feeling against us in many quarters, but it is less considerable every year. You are to attach yourself to His Majesty, I understand?"

"But I am to have no place or office, sir," I said. "I am rather to be at His Majesty's disposal — to fetch and carry, I may say, if he should need my services."

His Highness looked at me sidelong and swiftly; and I understood that he did not wish any originality even in speech.

"We must all be discreet, however," he said — (though I suppose there was never any man less discreet than himself, especially when he most needed to be so). "It is useless to say that we are altogether loved; for we are not. But you will soon acquaint yourself with all our politics."

I did not say that I had already done so; but assured him that I would do my best.

"As a general guide, I may say," he went on; "where there is Whiggery, there is disloyalty, however much the Whigs may protest. They say they desire a king as much as any; but it is not a king that they want, but his shadow only."

He talked on in this manner for a little, for we had the Gallery to ourselves, telling me, what I knew very well already, that the Catholics and the High Churchmen were, as a whole, staunch Royalists; but that the rest, especially those of the old Covenanting blood, still were capable of mischief. He did not tell me outright that it was largely against his own succession that the disaffection was directed; nor that the Duke of Monmouth was his rival; but he told me enough to show that my own information was correct enough, and that in the political matters my weight, such as it was, must be thrown on to the side of the Tories — as the other party was nicknamed. I understood, even in that first conversation with him, why he was so little loved; and I remembered, with inward mirth, how His Majesty once, upon being remonstrated with by his brother for walking out so freely without a guard, answered that he need have no fears; for "they will never kill me," said he, "to set you upon the throne."

"You have seen Father Whitbread, no doubt," said the Duke suddenly.

"No, sir. I waited to pay my homage first to His Majesty and to yourself."

He nodded once or twice at that.

"Yes, yes; but you will see him presently, I take it. You could not have a better guide. Why —"

He broke off on a sudden.

"Why here is the man himself," he said.

A man in a sober suit was indeed approaching, as His Highness spoke. He was of about the middle-size, clean-shaven, of grave and kindly face, and resembled such a man as a lawyer or physician might be. He was dressed in all points like a layman, though I suppose it was tolerably well known what he was, if not his name.

He saluted as he came near, and made as if he would have passed us.

"Mr. Whitbread! Mr. Whitbread!" cried the Duke.

The priest turned and bowed again, uncovering as he did so. Then he came up to the Duke and kissed his hand.

"I was on my way to see your Royal Highness," he said, "but when I saw you were in company —"

"Why, this is Mr. Mallock, come from Rome, who has letters to you. This will save you a journey, Mallock."

The priest and I saluted one another; and I found his face and manner very pleasant.

"I have heard of you, Mr. Mallock," he said, "but I hope His Highness is misinformed, and that this will not save you a journey, after all."

"I was just telling this gentleman," broke in the Duke, as we continued our walking, "that he must take you for his mentor, Dr. Whitbread, in these difficult times. Mr. Mallock seems very young for his business, but I suppose that the Holy Father knows what he is about."

"The Holy Father, sir," I said, "has committed himself in no sort of way to me. I am scarcely more than a free-lance who has had his blessing."

"Well, well; it is all the same thing," said James a little impatiently. "Free-lance or drilled soldier — they fight for the same cause."

He continued to talk in the same manner for a little, as if for my instruction; and I listened with all the meekness I had. He did not tell me one word which I did not already know; but I had perceived by now what kind of man he was — well intentioned, no doubt, as courageous as a lion, and as impatient of opposition, and not a little stupid: at least he had not a tenth of his brother's wits, as all the world knew. He solemnly informed me therefore of what all the world knew, and I listened to him.

When he dismissed me at last, however, he remembered to ask where I lodged, and I told him.

"A very good place too," he said. "I am glad your cousin had the sense to put you there. Then I will remember you, if I need you for anything."

"I will go with Mr. Mallock," said the priest, "if Your Royal Highness will permit. I came but to pay my respects; and it is a little late."

The Duke nodded; and gave us his hand to kiss.

As we went out through the Courtyard, Father Whitbread pointed out a few things to me which he thought might be of interest; and I liked the man more at every step. He was a complete man of the world, with a certain gentle irony, yet none the less kindly for it. He did not say one disparaging word of anyone, nor any hint of criticism at His Royal Highness; yet he knew, and I knew that he knew, and he knew that again, that our Catholic champion was a shade disappointing; and that, not in his vices only — of which my Lady Southesk could have given an account — but in that which I am forced to call his stupidity. But, after all, our Saviour uttered a judgment generally as to the children of light and the children of this world, that must always be our consolation when our friends are dull or perverse. Father Whitbread only observed emphatically that the Duke was a man of excellent heart.

He showed me the windows of a number of lodgings on the way, and the direction of a great many more: for indeed this Palace of Whitehall was liker a little town than a house. Father Patricks, he said, had a lodging near the Pantry, which he shewed me.

"There be some of us priests who have an affinity, do you not think, Mr. Mallock? with pantries and butteries and such like — good sound men too, many of them. I have not a word to say against Mr. Patricks."

He shewed me too how the Palace was in four quarters, of which two were divided from two by Whitehall itself and the street between the gatehouses. That half of it that was nearer to the Park held the tennis-court and the cock-pit and the lodgings of the Duke of Monmouth and others nearer Westminster, and the other half the Horse Guards and the barracks: and that nearer the river held, to the south the Stone Gallery, the Privy Garden, the Bowling Green and a great number of lodgings amongst which were those of the King and of his brother and Prince Rupert, and of the Queen too, as well as of their more immediate attendants — and this part contained what was left of the old York House; to the north was another court surrounded by lodgings, the Wood-Yard, the two courts called Scotland Yard, and the clock-house at the extremity, nearest Charing Cross. In the very midst of the whole Palace, looking upon Whitehall itself, was the Banqueting House where His Majesty dined in state, and from a window of which King Charles the First, of blessed memory, went out to lose his head. Indeed as we went by the end of the Banqueting House the trumpets blew for supper; and we saw a great number of cooks and scullions run past with dishes on their heads.

*   *   *

As we went up Whitehall, Mr. Whitbread began to speak of more intimate things.

"You are a stranger in England, Mr. Mallock, I think."

I told him I had not been in the country for seven years.

"You will find a great many changes," he said; "and I think we are on the eve of some more. Certainly His Majesty has wonderfully established his position; and yet, if you understand me, there is a great and growing disaffection. It is the Catholic Faith that they fear; and I cannot help thinking that some victims may be required again presently, though I do not know what they can allege against us. There is a deal of feeling, too, against the Queen; she has borne no children — that is true; but the main part of it arises from her religion: and so with the Duke of York also. Certainly we are in the fashion in one way: but those who are on the top of the wave must always look to come down suddenly."

Here again, Father Whitbread did not tell me anything that I did not know; yet he put matters together as I had not heard them put before; and he seemed to me altogether a shrewd kind of man whose judgment I might very well rely upon; and as we went up the Strand he spoke again of the Queen.

"His Majesty hath been urged again and again to divorce her; but he will not. He said to the Duke himself in my hearing one day that an innocent woman should never suffer through him — which is good hearing. But Her Majesty is not very happy, I am afraid."

When we came to the Maypole, which I had already seen, in the midst of the Strand, he spoke to me of how it had been carried there and set up with great rejoicing, after the Restoration. It was a great structure, hung about by a crown and a vane; and he said that it stood as a kind of symbol against Puritanism.

"There are many," he told me, "who would pull it down tomorrow if they could, as if it were some kind of idol."

He saw me as far as the door of my lodgings; but he would not come in. He said that he had no great desire to be known more widely than be was at present known.

"But if you have time to come in tomorrow morning about ten o'clock to Mr. Fenwick's lodgings in Drury Lane — over the baker's shop — I shall be there, and Mr. Ireland also — all Fathers of our Society; and I will very gladly make you known to them. My own lodgings are in Weld Street — at the Ambassador's."

I thanked him for his kindness, and said I would be there; and so I bade him good-night.

*　　*　　*

Although I had learned very few things that day which I had not known already, I felt that evening as I sat at supper, and afterwards, in the coffee house at 17, Fleet Street (which he recommended to me) that I knew them in a different manner. For I had spoken with some of the principal actors, and, above all, with the King himself. My cousin questioned me delightedly upon my experiences when we were alone with our pipes at one end of the great room that had been a council-chamber; and related to me all his own experiences with the King at great length; and how Charles had made to him some witty remarks which I think must have lost in the telling, for they were not witty at all when I heard them. It appeared that my cousin had spoken with the King three or four times, at City-banquets and such like; and he would know all that His Majesty had said to me. But much I would not tell him, and some I could not: I could not that is, even if I would, have conveyed to him the strange compassion that I felt, and the yet more strange affection, for this King who might have done so much, and who did so little — except what he should not; and I would not on any account tell him of what the King had said as to Rome and his desires and procrastinations. But I told him how I had met Father Whitbread, and how I was to go and see him on the morrow.

"Why, I will come with you myself," he said. "I know Mr. Fenwick's lodgings very well: and we will ride afterwards as far as Waltham Cross, and lie there; and so to Hare Street for dinner next day."

All the way home again, and when my Cousin Dorothy was gone to bed, and we sat over a couple of tankards of College Ale, he would talk of nothing but the Jesuits.

"They are too zealous," he said. "I am as good a Catholic as any man in England or Rome; but I like not this over-zeal. They are everywhere, these good fathers; and it will bring trouble on them. They hold their consults even in London, which I think over-rash; and no man knows what passes at them. Now I myself —" and so his tongue wagged on, telling of his own excellence and prudence, and even his own spirituality, while his eyes watered with the ale that he drank, and his face grew ever more red. And yet there was no true simplicity in the man; he had that kind of cunning that is eked out with winks and becks and nods that all the world could see. He talked of my Cousin Dorothy, too, and her virtues, and what a great lady she would be some day when these virtues were known; and he, declared that in spite of this he would never let her go to Court; and then once more he went back again to his earlier talk of the corruptions there, and of what my Lady this and Her Grace of that had said and done and thought.

*   *   *

Mr. Fenwick's lodgings in Drury Lane were such as any man might have. The Jesuit Fathers lived apart in London — Father Whitbread in the City, Father Ireland in Russell Street, and Father Harcourt, who was called the "Rector of London," I heard, in Duke Street, near the arch — lest too much attention should be drawn to them if they were all together. They were pleasant quiet men, and received me very kindly — for my cousin who had forgot some matter he had to do before he went into the country, was gone down into the City to see to it. Mr. Grove, whom I learned later to be a lay brother of the Society, opened the door to me; and shewed me to the room where they were all three together.

They were all three of them just such men as you might meet anywhere, in coffee-houses or taverns, none of them under forty or over sixty years old. Father Harcourt was seventy — but he was not there. They were in sober suits, such as a lawyer might wear, and carried swords. These were not all the Jesuits thereabouts; for I heard them speak of Father John Gavan and Father Anthony Turner (who were in the country on that day), and others.

As I talked with them, and gave my news and listened to theirs, again and again I thought of the marvellous misjudgments that were always passed upon the Society; of how men such as these were always thought to be plotting and conspiring, and how any charge against a Jesuit was always taken as proven scarcely before it was stated; and that not by common men only, but by educated gentlemen too, who should know better. For their talk was of nothing but of the most harmless and Christian matters, and of such simplicity that no man who heard them could doubt their sincerity. It is true that they spoke of such things as the conversion of England, and of the progress that the Faith was making; and they told many wonderful stories of the religion of the common people in country places, and how a priest was received by them as an angel of God, and of their marvellous goodness and constancy under the bitterest trials; but so, I take it, would the Apostles themselves have spoken in Rome and Asia and Jerusalem. But as to the disloyalty that was afterwards charged against them, still less of any hatred or murderous designs, there was not one such thought that passed through any of their minds.

It was a plain but well-furnished chamber in which we sat. Beneath the windows folks came and went continually. There were hangings on the wall; and a press full of books and papers, and two or three tables; but there was no concealment of anything, nor thought of it. Through the door I saw Mr. Grove laying for dinner.

"But you will surely stay for dinner," said Father Fenwick, when I said that I must be gone presently.

I told him that I was to ride to Waltham Cross with my cousins, and that I was to meet them for dinner first at the coffee-house beside the Maypole in the Strand.

"And to Hare Street tomorrow, then," said Father Whitbread — or Mr. White as he was called sometimes.

I told him, Yes; and that I did not know how long I should be there.

"The King will be at Windsor next month, I think," he said; "but he will be back again for August. You had best be within call then, if he should send for you." (For I had told them all freely what had passed between myself and His Majesty, and what His Holiness had said to me too.)

"You can command any of us at any time," he added, "if we can be of service to you. There are so many folks of all kinds, here, there and everywhere, that it is near impossible for a stranger to take stock of them all; and it may be that our experience may be of use to you, to know whom to trust and of whom to beware. But the most safe rule in these days is, Trust no man till you know him, and not entirely even then. There are men in this City who would sell their souls gladly if any could be found to give them anything for it; how much more then, if they could turn a penny or two by selling you or me or another in their stead!"

I thanked him for his warning; and told him that I would indeed be on my guard.

"Least of all," he said, "would I trust those of my own household. I know your cousin for a Catholic, Mr. Mallock, but you will forgive me for saying that it is from Catholics that we have to fear the most. I do not mean by that that Mr. Jermyn is not excellent and sincere; for I know nothing of him except what you have told me yourself. But zeal without discretion is a very firebrand; and prudence without zeal may become something very like cowardice; and either of these two things may injure the Catholic cause irreparably in the days that are coming. St. Peter's was the one, and Judas', I take it, was the other; for I hold Judas to have been by far the greater coward of the two."

*   *   *

When I came out into the passage with him, I kneeled down and asked his blessing; for I knew that this was of a truth a man of God.

CHAPTER IV

It was a little after noon next day that first we saw the Norman church upon the hill, and then the roofs of Hare Street.

I had been astonished at the badness of the roads from London, coming as I had from Rome, where paved ways go out in every direction. We came out by Bishopsgate, by the Ware road, and arrived at Waltham Cross a little before sunset, riding through heavy dust that had hardly been laid at all by the recent rains. We rode armed, with four servants, besides my Cousin Dorothy's maid, for fear of the highwaymen who had robbed a coach only last week between Ware and London. My Cousin Dorothy rode a white mare named Jenny which mightily became her. We lay at the *Four Swans* at Waltham Cross, and went out before supper to see the Cross which was erected where Queen Eleanor's body had lain — of which the last was at Charing Cross — and I was astonished that the Puritans had not more mutilated it. The beds were pretty comfortable, and the ale excellent, so that once more my Cousin Tom drank too much of it. And so, early in the morning we took horse again, and rode through Puckeridge, where we left for the first time the road by which the King went to Newmarket, when he went through Royston; and we found the track very bad thenceforward. My Cousin Tom carried with him, though for no purpose except for show, a map by John Ogilby which shows all the way from London to King's Lynn, very ingeniously, and which was made after the Restoration to encourage road traffic again; but it was pleasant for me to look at it from time to time and see what progress we made towards Hormead Magna which is the parish in which Hare Street lies.

Now it was very pleasant for me to ride, as I did a good deal, with my Cousin Dorothy; for her father, for a great part, rode with the men and cracked stories with them. For journeying with a person sets up a great deal of intimacy; and acquaintance progresses at least as swiftly as the journey itself. She spoke to me very freely of her father, though never as a daughter should not; and told me how distressed she was sometimes at the quantity of ale and strong waters that he drank. She told me also how seldom it was that a Catholic could hear mass at Hare Street: sometimes, she said, a priest would lie there, and say mass in the attic; but not very often; and sometimes if a priest were in the neighbourhood they would ride over and hear mass wherever he happened to be. The house, she said, lay near upon the road, so that they would hear a good deal of news in this way. But she told me nothing of another matter — for indeed she could not — which distressed her; though I presently guessed it for myself, as will appear in the course of this tale.

My horse, Peter (as I had named him after the Apostle when I bought him at Dover), was pretty weary as we came in sight of the church of Hormead Parva; for I had given him plenty to do while I was in London; and he stumbled three or four times.

"We are nearly home," said my Cousin Dorothy; and pointed with her whip.

"It is pleasant to hear such a word," I said: "for, as for me, I have none."

She said nothing to that; and I was a little ashamed to have said it; for nothing is easier than to touch a maid's heart by playing Othello to her Desdemona.

"I have no business to have said that, cousin," I went on presently: "for England is all home to me just now."

"I hope you will find it so, cousin," she said.

The country was pretty enough through which we rode; though in no ways wonderful. It was pasture-land for the most part, with woods here and there; and plenty of hollow ways (all of which were marked upon the map with great accuracy), by which drovers brought their sheep to the highway. I saw also a good many fields of corn. The hills were lowish, and ran in lines, with long valleys between; and there was one such on the right as we came to Hare Street, through which flowed a little stream, nearly dry in the summer.

The house itself was the greatest house in the village, and lay at the further end of it upon the right; sheltered from the road by limes, in the midst of which was the gateway, and the house twenty yards within. My Cousin Tom came up with us as we entered the village, and shewed me with a great deal of pride his new iron gate just set up, with a twisted top.

"It is the finest little gate for ten miles round," he said, "and cost me near twenty pound."

We rode past the gate, however, into the yard just beyond; and here there was a great barking of dogs set up; and two or three men ran out. I helped my Cousin Dorothy from her horse; and then all three of us went through a side-door to the front of the house.

The house without was of timber and plaster, very solidly built, but in no way pretentious; and the plaster was stamped, in panels, with a kind of comb-pattern in half circles, peculiar, my cousin told me, to that part of the country. Within, it was very pleasant. There was a little passage as we came in, and to right and left lay the Great Chamber (as it was called), and the dining-room. Beyond the little passage was the staircase, panelled all the way up, with the instruments of the Passion and other emblems carved on a row of the panels; and at the foot of the staircase on the right lay a little parlour, very pretty, with hangings presenting the knights of the Holy Grail riding upon their Quest. Upon the left of the staircase, lay a paved hall, with a little pantry under the stairs, to the left, and the kitchens running out to the back; and opposite to them, enclosing a little grassed court, the brewhouse and the bakehouse. Behind all lay the kitchen gardens; and behind the brewhouse a row of old yews and a part of the lawn, that also ran before the house. The house was of three stories high, and contained about twenty rooms with the attics.

It is strange how some houses, upon a first acquaintance with them, seem like old friends; and how others, though one may have lived in them fifty years are never familiar to those who live in them. Now Hare Street House was one of the first kind. This very day that I first set eyes on it, it was as if I had lived there as a child. The sunlight streamed into the Great Chamber, and past the yews into the parlour; and upon the lawns outside; and the noise of the bees in the limes was as if an organ played softly; and it was all to me as if I had known it a hundred years.

My Cousin Tom carried me upstairs presently to the Guest-chamber — a great panelled room, with a wide fire-place, above the dining-room — that I might wash my hands and face before dinner; and my heart smote me a little for all my thoughts of him, for, when all was said, he had received me very hospitably, and was now bidding me welcome again, and that I must live there as long as I would, and think of it as my home.

"And here," he said, opening a door at the foot of the bed, "is a little closet where your man can hang your clothes; it looks out upon the yard; and my room is beyond it, over the kitchen."

I thanked him again and again for his kindness; and so he left me.

*　　*　　*

We dined below presently, very excellently. The room was hung with green, with panels of another pattern upon it; and the dishes were put in through a little hatch from the kitchen passage. My man James waited with the rest, and acquitted himself very well. Then after dinner, when the servants were gone away, my Cousin Tom carried me out, with a mysterious air, to the foot of the stairs.

"Now look well round you, Cousin Roger," he said, when he had me standing there; "and see if there be anything that would draw your attention."

I looked this way and that but saw nothing; and said so.

"Have you ever heard of Master Owen," he said, "of glorious memory?"

"Why, yes," I said, "he was a Jesuit lay-brother, martyred under Elizabeth: and he made hiding-holes, did he not?"

"Well; he hath been at work here. Look again, Cousin Roger."

I turned and saw my Cousin Dorothy smiling — (and it was a very pretty sight too!) — but there was nothing else to be seen. I beat with my foot; and it rang a little hollow.

"No, no; those are the cellars," said my Cousin Tom.

I beat then upon the walls, here and there; but to no purpose; and then upon the stairs.

"That is the sloping roof of the pantry, only," said my Cousin Tom.

I confessed myself outwitted; and then with great mirth he shewed me how, over the door into the paved hall, there was a space large enough to hold three or four men; and how the panels opened on this side, as well as into the kitchen passage on the other.

"A priest or suchlike might very well lie here a week or two, might he not?" asked my Cousin Tom delightedly; "and if the sentry was at the one side, he might be fed from the other. It is cunningly contrived, is it not? A man has but to leap up here from a chair; and he is safe."

I praised it very highly, to please him; and indeed it was very curious and ingenious.

"But those days are done," I said.

"Who can tell that?" he cried — (though a week ago he had told me the same himself). "Some priest might very well be flying for his life along this road, and turn in here. Who knows whether it may not be so again?"

I said no more then on that point; though I did not believe him.

"And there is one more matter I must shew you in your own chamber; if you have any private papers and suchlike."

Then he shewed me in my own room, by the head of the bed that stood along the wall, how one of the panels slid back from its place, discovering a little space behind where a man might very well keep his papers or his money.

"Not a living soul," he said, "knows of that, besides Dolly and myself. You are at liberty to use that, Cousin Roger, if you like."

I thanked him; and said I would do so.

The rest of that day I spent in going about the house, and acquainting myself with it all. My Cousin Dorothy shewed me the rooms. Her own was a little one at the head of the stairs; and she told me, smiling, that a ghost was said to walk there.

"But I have never been troubled with it," she said. "It is a tall old, woman, they say, who comes up the stairs and into the room; but she does no harm to anyone."

Next her room, along the front of the house, lay two other greater rooms, one with a fire-place and one without: then was my chamber, and then her father's: and upstairs were the attics where the men lay. The maids lay in two little rooms above the kitchen.

It was mighty pleasant to me to be with my Cousin Dorothy. She had changed her riding clothes into others more suitable for a country maid — with a white starched neckerchief that came down upon her shoulders, and a grey dress and petticoat below that. Her sleeves were short, as the custom is in the country, with great linen cuffs folded back upon them, so as to leave her hands and arms to the elbow free for her occupations. But most of all I loved her simplicity and her quietness and her discretion. Her father bade her expressly to shew me all the house; or she would not have done it, for she was very maidenly and modest; but as soon as he said that, she did it without affectation. She shewed me the parlour too, with the hangings upon the walls, and the chapel of the Grail, with the Grail itself upon an altar within, flanked by two candlesticks, that was represented over the fire-place. She came out with me too to shew me the bakehouse where the baking was already begun, and the brewhouse — both of which too were all built of timber and plaster; and there my Cousin Tom came upon us, and carried me off to see his garden and his pasture; for he farmed a few acres about here, and made a good profit out of it: and it was while I walked with him that for the first time I understood what his intention was towards me.

He was speaking, as he very often did, of his daughter Dorothy — which I had taken to be a father's affection only. (We were walking at the time up and down in the pasture below the garden; and the house lay visible among the gardens, very fair and peaceful with the sunlight upon it.)

"She will be something of an heiress," he said; "and when I say that, I do not mean that she will have as many acres as yourself. But she will have near a thousand pound a year so soon as poor Tom Jermyn dies: and I may die any day, for I am short in the neck, and might very well be taken with an apoplexy. I wish above all things then, to see her safely married before I go — to some solid man who will care for her. There is a plenty of Protestants about here that would have her; for she is a wonderful housewife, and as pure as Diana too."

He paused at that; and looked at me in that cunning way of his that I misliked so much. Yet even now I did not see what he would be at; for gentlemen do not usually fling their daughters at the head of any man; and he knew nothing of me but that I was pretty rich and would be more so one day. But I suppose that that was enough for him.

"I had thought at one time," he went on, "of sending her to Court. I could get her in, under the protection of my Lady Arlington. But the Court is no place for a maiden who knows nothing of the world. What would you advise, Cousin Roger? I would not have her marry a Protestant, if I could help it."

And with that he looked at me again.

Then, all of a sudden I saw his meaning; and my heart stood still; for not only did his words reveal him to me, but myself also; and I understood why he had questioned me so closely in town, as to my fortune. I cannot say at this time that I loved my Cousin Dolly — for I had not known that I loved her — but his words were very effective. Indeed I had not thought to marry, though I was free to do so; for a novice does not quickly shake off his monkishness. I had thought far more of the mission I was come to England upon, and what I could accomplish, with God's blessing, for Christ and His Church. But, as I say, my heart stood still when my cousin said that to me; for, as in a vision, I saw myself here as her husband, and her as my wife, in this house among its gardens. Here we might live a life which even the angels might envy — harmless, innocent, separate from sinners, as the Apostle says — not accomplishing, maybe, any great things, but at least refraining from the hindering of God's Kingdom. The summers would come and go, and we still be here, with our children growing about us, to inherit the place and the name, such as it was. And no harm done, no vows broken, no offence to any. Such thoughts as these did not as yet shew any very great ardour of love in me; and indeed I had not got this yet; but she was the first maid I had ever had any acquaintance with, at least for some while; and this no doubt, had its effect upon me. All this came upon me of a sudden; and as I lifted my eyes I saw my Cousin Dolly's sunbonnet going among the herbs of the garden; and saw her in my mind's eye too as I had seen her just now, cool and innocent and good, with that touch of hidden fire in her eyes that draws a man's heart. Neither had she looked unkindly on me: our intimacy had made wonderful progress, though I had known her scarcely more than a week: she had spoken to me of her father, too, as one would speak only to a friend. Yet I could not say one word of this to him; for he had not said anything explicit to me: and I knew, too, that I must give myself time; for a man does not, if he is wise, change the course of his life on an instant's thought. Yet I must not say No outright, and thereby, maybe, bang the door on my new hopes.

"I could not advise you at present," I said. "I do not know my cousin well enough to advise anything. I am one with you so far as concerns the Court: I cannot think that any Catholic father should send his daughter into such a den of lions — and worse. And I am one with you as concerns marrying her to a Protestant. Yet I can say no more at present."

And at that my Cousin Tom looked at me in such a manner as near to ruin his own scheme; for his eyes said, if his mouth did not, that now we understood one another; and were upon the same side, or at least not opposed; and to think that I was leagued with him against her made my heart hot with anger.

"Very well," he said; "we will say no more at present." And he bade me observe an old ram that was regarding us, with a face not unlike Cousin Tom's own: but I suppose that he did not know this.

*   *   *

In this manner, then, began our life at Hare Street; for I was there six weeks before I went back again to London in the way I shall relate presently. The days were passed for the most time, from rising until dinner, upon the farm, or in hunting; for we rode out now and again with the neighbours after a stag who had come from the woods. But we did not, because of the Papistry of the house, see a great deal of the neighbours, or they of us. The parson of Hormead came to see us now and again, and behaved very civilly: but during those six weeks we had no sight of a priest, except once when we rode to Standon to hear mass. After dinner, I gave myself up to writing; for I thought that I could best serve His Holiness in this way, making my diary each day in shorthand (as I had learned from an Italian); and it is from that very diary that this narrative is composed; and I wrote too a report or two, apologizing for the poverty of it, which I determined to send to the Cardinal Secretary as soon as I had an opportunity. I read too a little Italian or Spanish or French every day; and thus, for the most part kept to my chamber. But all my papers I put away each afternoon in the little hiding-place in my chamber; and made excuse for keeping my room on the score of my practice in languages.

We supped at five o'clock — which was the country hour; and after that, to me, came the best part of the day.

For my Cousin Dorothy, I had learned, was an extraordinary fine musician. We had, of course, no music such as was possible in town; but she had taught a maid to play upon a fiddle, and herself played upon the bass-viol; and the two together would play in the Great Chamber after supper for an hour or two, when the dishes were washed. In this manner we had many a corrant and saraband; and I was able to prick down for them too some Italian music I remembered, which she set for the two instruments. Sometimes, too, when Cousin Tom was not too drowsy after his day and his ale, the three would sing and I would listen; for my Cousin Tom sang a plump bass very well when he was in the mood for it. As for me, I had but a monk's voice, that is very well when all the choir is a-cry together, but not of much use under other circumstances. In this way then I made acquaintance with a number of songs — such as Mr. Wise's "It is not that I love you less" and his duet "Go, perjured man!" of which the words are taken from Herrick's "Hesperides," and of which the music was made by Mr. Wise (who was a gentleman of the Chapel Royal) at His Majesty's express wish.

*   *   *

I have many very pleasant memories of Hare Street, but I think none more pleasant than of the music in the Great Chamber. I would sit near the window, and see them in the evening light, with their faces turned to me; or, when it grew late with the candlelight upon them and their dresses or sometimes when the evening was fair and warm I would sit out upon the lawn, and they at the window, and listen to the singing coming out of the candlelight, and see them move against it. My Cousin Dorothy would make herself fine in the evening — not, I mean, like a Court lady, for these dresses of hers were put away in lavender — but with a lace neckerchief on her throat and shoulders, and lace ruffles at her wrists.

Yet all this while I made no progress with her or even with myself; for every time that I was alone with her, or when her father was asleep in his chair, a remembrance of what he had said came over me with a kind of sickness, and I could not say one word that might seem to set me on his side against her; and so I was torn two ways, and the very thing by which he had hoped to encourage me, (or rather to help himself) had the contrary effect, and silenced me when I might have spoken.

For I understood very well by now what was in his mind. He saw no prospect of marrying Dolly to a Protestant — or I take it, if I know the man, he would have leapt at it; neither was there any hope of marrying her to a Catholic; and as for his talk about my Lady Arlington I did not believe one word of it. Therefore, since I was at hand, and would be a wealthy man some day, and indeed even now did very well on my French *rentes*, he had set his heart on this. It was not wholly evil; yet the cold-bloodedness of it affected me like a stink....

*   *   *

The matter ended, for the time, on the evening of the thirteenth of August, in the following manner, when my adventures, of which my life, ever since my audience with our Most Holy Lord the Pope, had been but a prelude, properly began — those adventures for whose sake I have begun this transcript from my diary, and this adventure was pre-shadowed, as I think now, by one or two curious happenings.

On the morning of the thirteenth of August, two days before the Feast of the Assumption (on which we had intended to hear mass again at Standon) my Cousin Dorothy came down a little late, and found us already over our oatbread and small beer which we were accustomed to take upon rising — and which was called our "morning."

"I slept very ill," she said; and no more then.

Afterwards, however, as I was lighting my pipe in the little court at the back of the house, she came out and beckoned me in; and I saw that something was amiss. I went after her into the little hung parlour and we sat down.

"I slept very ill, cousin," she said again; and I observed again that her eyes looked hollow. "And I dare not tell my father my fancies," she said, "for he is terrified at such things; and has forbade the servants to speak of such things."

"The tall old woman, then?" I said; for I had not forgotten what she had told me before.

"Yes," she said, smiling a little painfully — "and yet I was not at all afraid when she came; or when I thought that she did."

"Tell me the whole tale," I said.

"I awakened about one o'clock this morning," she said, "and knew that my sleep was gone from me altogether. Yet I did not feel afraid or restless; but lay there content enough, expecting something, but what it would be I did not know. The cocks were crowing as I awakened; and then were silent; and it appeared to me as if all the world were listening. After a while — I should say it was ten minutes or thereabouts — I turned over with my face to the wall; and as I did so, I heard a soft step coming up the stairs. One of the maids, thought I, late abed or early rising, for sickness. When the steps came to my door they ceased; and a hand was laid upon the latch; and at that I made to move; but could not. Yet it was not fear that held me there, though it was like a gentle pricking all over me. Then the latch was lifted, and still I could not move, not even my eyes; and a person came in, and across the floor to my bed. And even then I could not move nor cry out. Presently the person spoke; but I do not know what she said, though it was only a word or two: but the voice came from high up, as almost from the canopy of the bed, and it was the voice of an old woman, speaking in a kind of whisper. I said nothing; for I could not: and then again the steps moved across the floor, and out of the door; and I heard the latch shut again; and then they passed away down the stairs."

My Cousin Dorothy was pale as death by this time; and her blue eyes were set wide open. I made to take her by the hand; but I did not.

"You were dreaming," I said; "it was the memory of the tale you have heard."

She shook her head; but she said nothing.

"You have never had it before?" I asked.

"Never," she said.

"You must lie in another chamber for a week or two, and forget it."

"I cannot do that," she said. "My father would know of it." And she spoke so courageously that I was reassured.

"Well; you must cry out if it comes again. You can have your maid to sleep with you."

"I might do that," she said; and then —

"Cousin Roger; doth God permit these things to provide us against some danger?"

"It may be so," I said, to quiet her; "but be sure that no harm can come of it."

At that we heard her father calling her; and she stood up.

"I have told you as a secret, Cousin Roger; there must be no word to my father."

I pledged myself to that; for I could see what a spirit she had; and we said no more about it then.

As the day passed on, the sky grew heavy — or rather the air; for the sky was still blue overhead; only on the horizon to the south the clouds that are called *cumuli* began to gather. The air was so hot too that I could scarcely bear to work, for I had set myself to take some plant-cuttings in a little glass-house that was in the garden against the south wall; and by noon the sky was overcast.

After dinner I went up to my chamber; and a great heaviness fell upon me, till I looked out of the window and saw that beyond the limes the clouds spewed a reddish tint that marked the approach of thunder; and at that grew reassured again; and not only for myself but for my Cousin Dorothy, whose tale had lain close on my heart through the morning: for this thought I, is the explanation of it all: the maid was oppressed by the heat and the approaching storm, and fancied all the rest.

I fell asleep in my chair, over my Italian; and when I awakened it was near supper-time, and the heaviness was upon me again, like lead; and my diary not written.

After supper and some talk, I made excuse to do my writing; and as it was growing dark, and I was finishing, I heard music from the Great Chamber beneath. They were singing together a song I had not heard before; and I listened, well pleased, promising myself the pleasure too of going downstairs presently and hearing it.

Between two of the verses, I heard on a sudden, over the hill-top beyond the village, the beat of a horse's hoofs, galloping; but I thought no more of it. At the end of the next verse, even before it was finished, I heard the hoofs again, through the music; I ran to the window to see who rode so fast; and was barely in time to see a courier, in a blue coat, dash past the new iron gate, pulling at his horse as he did so; an instant later, I heard the horse turn in at the yard gate, and immediately the singing ceased.

As I came down the stairs, I saw my Cousin Dolly run out into the inner lobby, and her face, in the dusk, was as white as paper; and the same instant there came a hammering at the hall door.

"What is it? What is it?" cried she; and clung to me as I came down.

I saw, through the inner door, my Cousin Tom unbolting the outer one; he had taken down a pistol that hung upon the wall, for the highwaymen waxed very bold sometimes; then when he opened the door, I heard my name.

I went forward, and received from the courier, a sealed letter; and there, in the twilight I opened and read it. It was from Mr. Chiffinch, bidding me come to town at once on King's business.

"I must ride to town," I said. "Cousin Tom, will you order my horse for me; and another for this man? I do not know when I shall be back again."

And, as I said these words, I saw my Cousin Dorothy's face looking at me from the dusk of the inner hall, and knew what was in her mind; and that it was the matter of the tall old woman in her room.

CHAPTER V

The storm was broken before we could set out, and the ride so far as Hoddesdon was such as I shall never forget; for the wind was violent against us; and it was pitchy dark before we came even to Puckeridge; the thunder was as if great guns were shot off, or bags of marbles dashed on an oak floor overhead; and the countryside was as light as day under the flashes, so that we could see the trees and their shadows, and, I think, sometimes the green colour of them too. We wore, all three of us — the courier, I and my man James — horse-men's cloaks, but these were saturated within half an hour. We had no fear of highwaymen, even had we not been armed, for the artillery of heaven had long ago driven all other within doors.

The hardest part of the journey was that I knew, no more than the dead — indeed not so much — why it was that Mr. Chiffinch had sent for me. He had said nothing in his letter, save that His Majesty wished my presence at once; and on the outside of the letter was written the word "Haste," three times over. I thought of a hundred matters that it might be, but none of them satisfied me.

It is near forty miles from Hare Street to Whitehall; but so bad was the way that, though we changed horses at Waltham Cross — at the *Four Swans* — we did not come to London until eight o'clock in the morning; and it was half-past eight before we rode up to Whitehall. The last part of the journey was pretty pleasant, for the rain held off; and it was strange to see the white hard light of the clouded dawn upon the fields and the trees. But by the time we came to London it was long ago broad day — by three or four hours at the least; and all the folks were abroad in the streets.

I went straight to Mr. Chiffinch's lodgings, sending my man to the lodging in Covent Garden, to bestow the horses and to come again to the guard-house to await my orders. Mr. Chiffinch was not within, for he had not expected me so early, a servant told me; but he had looked for my coming about eleven or twelve o'clock, and had given orders that I was to be taken to a closet to change my clothes if I needed it. This I did; and then was set down to break my fast; and while I was at it, Mr. Chiffinch himself came in.

He told me that I had done very well to come so swiftly; but he smiled a little as he said it.

"His Majesty is closeted with one or two more until ten o'clock. I will send to let him know you are come."

I did not ask him for what business I had been sent for; since he did not choose to tell me himself; and he went out again. But he was presently back once more; and told me that His Majesty would see me at once.

My mind was all perturbed as I went with him in the rain across the passages: I felt as if some great evil threatened, but I could make no conjecture as to what it was about; or how it could be anything that was at once so sudden and that demanded my presence. We went straight up the stairs, and across the same ante-room; and Mr. Chiffinch flung open the door of the same little closet where I had spoken with the King, speaking my name as he did so.

His Majesty was sitting in the very same place where he sat before, with his chair wheeled about, so that he faced three men. One of them I knew at once, for my cousin had pointed him out to me in the park — my Lord Danby, who was Lord Treasurer at this time — and he was sitting at the end of the great table, nearest to the King: on the other side of the table, nearer to me as I entered, were two men, upon whom I had never set eyes before — one of them, a little man in the dress of an apothecary or attorney; and the other a foolish-looking minister in his cassock and bands. All four turned their eyes upon me as I came in, and then the two who were standing, turned them back again towards His Majesty. There was a heap of papers on the table below my Lord Danby's hand.

His Majesty made a little inclination of his head to me, but said nothing, putting out his hand; and when I had kissed it, and stood back with the other two, he continued speaking as if I were not there. His face had a look, as if he were a little *ennuyé*, and yet a little merry too.

"Continue, my Lord," he said.

"Now, doctor," said my Lord, in a patient kind of voice as if he encouraged the other, "you tell us that all these papers were thrust under your door. By whom were they thrust, do you think?"

"My Lord, I have my suspicions," said the minister; "but I do not know."

"Can you verify these suspicions of yours, do you think?"

"My Lord, I can try."

"And under how many heads are they ranged?" asked the King, drawling a little in his speech.

"Sir; they are under forty-three heads."

The King rolled his eyes, as if in a droll kind of despair; but he said nothing.

"And you tell me —" began my Lord; but His Majesty broke in:

"*Mon Dieu!*" he said; "and here is good Mr. Mallock, come here hot-foot, and knows not a word of the proceedings. Mr. Mallock, these good gentlemen — Doctor Tonge, a very worthy divine and a physician of the soul, and Mr. Kirby, a very worthy chymist, and a physician of the body — are come to tell me of a plot against my life on the part of some of my faithful lieges, whereby they would thrust me swiftly down to hell — body and soul together. So that, I take it is why God Almighty hath raised up these physicians to save me. I wish you to hear their evidence. That is why I sent for you. Continue, my Lord."

My Lord looked a little displeased, pursing up his mouth, at the manner in which the King told the tale; but he said nothing on that point.

"Grove and Pickering, then, it appears, were to shoot His Majesty; and Wakeman to poison him —"

("They will take no risks you see, Mr. Mallock," put in the King.)

"Yes, my Lord," said Tonge. "They were to have screwed pistols, with silver bullets, champed, that the wounds may not heal."

("Prudent! prudent!" cried the King.)

Then my Lord Danby lost his patience; and pushed the papers together with a sweep of his arm.

"Sir," he said, "I think we may let these worthy gentlemen go for the present, until the papers are examined."

"With all my heart," said the King. "But not Mr. Mallock. I wish to speak privately with Mr. Mallock."

So the two were dismissed; but I noticed that the King did not give them his hand to kiss. They appeared to me a pair of silly folks, rather than wicked as others thought them afterwards, who themselves partly believed, at any rate, the foolish tale that they told. Mr. Kirby was a little man, as I have said, with a sparrow-like kind of air; and Doctor Tonge had no great distinction of any kind, except his look of foolishness.

When they were gone, my Lord Danby turned to the King, with a kind of indignation.

"Your Majesty may be pleased to make a mock of it all; but your loving subjects cannot. I have permission then to examine these papers, and report to Your Majesty?"

"Why, yes," said the King, "so you do not inflict the forty-three heads upon me. I have one of my own which I must care for."

My Lord said no more; he gathered his papers without a word, saluted the King at a distance, still without speaking, and went out, giving me a sharp glance as he went.

"Now, Mr. Mallock," said His Majesty, "sit you down and listen to me."

I sat down; but I was all bewildered as to why I had been sent for. What had I to do with such affairs as these?

"Do you know of a man called Grove?" the King asked me suddenly.

Now the name had meant nothing to me when I had heard it just now; but when it was put to me in this way I remembered. I was about to speak, when he spoke again.

"Or Pickering?" he said.

"Sir; a man called Grove is known to me; but no Pickering."

"Ha! then there is a man called Grove — if it be the same. He is a Papist?"

"Sir, he is a lay-brother of the Society of Jesus, and dwells —"

The King held up his hand.

"I wish to know nothing more than I am obliged. Pickering is some sort of Religious, too, they tell me. And what kind of a man is Grove?"

"He is a modest kind of man, Sir. He opened the door to me, and I saw him a-laying of the table for dinner. I know no more of him than that."

Then the King drew himself up in his chair suddenly, as I had seen him do before, and his mocking manner left him. It was as if another man sat there.

"Mr. Mallock," he said, shaking his finger at me with great solemnity, "listen to me. I had thought for a long time that an attempt would be made against the Catholics. There is a great deal of feeling in the country, now that my brother is one of them, and I myself am known not to be disinclined towards them. And I make no doubt at all that this is such an attempt. They have begun with the Jesuits; for that will be the most popular cry; and they have added in Sir George Wakeman's name, Her Majesty's physician, to give colour to it all. By and by they will add other names; (you will see if it be not so), until not a Jesuit, and scarce a Catholic is left who is not embroiled in it. I do not know who is behind this matter; it may be my Lord Danby himself, or Shaftesbury, or a score of others. Or it may be some discontented fellow who will make his fortune over it; for all know that such a cry as this will be a popular one. But this I know for a verity — that there is not one word of truth in the tale from beginning to end; and it will appear so presently, no doubt. Yet meanwhile a great deal of mischief may be done; and my brother, may be, and even Her Majesty, may suffer for it, if we are not very prudent. Now, Mr. Mallock, I sent for you, for I did not know who else to send for. You are not known in England, or scarcely: you come commended to me by the Holy Father himself; you are neither priest nor Jesuit. What, then, you must do for me is this. First, you must speak not one word of the matter to any living soul — not even your confessor; for if we can quash the whole matter privately, so much the better. I had you in just now, that Danby and the others might see that you had my confidence; but I said nothing of who you were nor where you came from; and, if they inquire, they will know nothing but that you come commended by the ambassadors. Very well then; you must go about freely amongst the Jesuits, and rake together any evidence that you can that may be of use to them if the affair should ever be made public; and yet they must know nothing of the reason — I lay that upon you. And you must mix freely in taverns and coffee-houses, especially among the smaller gentry, and hear what you can — as to whether the plot hath yet leaked out — (for it is no less) — and what they think of it; and if not, what it is that they say of the Catholics. You understand me, Mr. Mallock?"

I said, Yes: but my heart had grown sick during the King's speech to me; for all that I had ever thought in Rome, of England, seemed on the point of fulfilment. His Majesty too had spoken with an extraordinary vehemence, that was like a fire for heat. But I must have commanded my countenance well; for he commended me on my behaviour.

"Your manner is excellent, Mr. Mallock," he said, "both just now and a few minutes ago. You take it very well. And I have your word upon it that you will observe secrecy?"

"My word on it, Sir," I said.

Then His Majesty leaned back again and relaxed a little.

"That is very well," he said; "and I think I have chosen my man well. You need not fear, Mr. Mallock, that any harm will come to the good Fathers, or to Grove or Pickering either. They cannot lay a finger upon them without my consent; and that they shall never have. It is to prevent rather the scandal of the whole matter that I am anxious; and to save the Queen and my brother from any trouble. You do not know yet, I think, all the feeling that there is upon the Catholics."

I said nothing: it was my business to listen rather, and indeed what His Majesty said next was worth hearing.

"There be three kinds of religion in my realm," he said. "The Presbyterian and Independent and that kind — for I count those all one; and that is no religion for a gentleman. And there is the Church of England, of which I am the head, which numbers many gentlemen, but is no religion for a Christian; and there is the Catholic, which is the only religion (so far as I am acquainted with any), suited for both gentlemen and Christians. That is my view of the matter, Mr. Mallock."

The merry look was back in his eyes, melancholy though they always were, as he said this. For myself, it was on the tip of my tongue to ask His Majesty why, if he thought so, he did not act upon it. But I did not, thinking it too bold on so short an acquaintance; and I think I was right in that; for he put it immediately into words himself.

"I know what you are thinking, Mr. Mallock. Well; I am not yet a good enough Christian for that."

I knew very well what His Majesty meant when he said that: he was thinking of his women to whom as yet he could not say good-bye; and the compassion surged up in me again at the thought that a man so noble as this, and who knew so much (as his speeches had shewed me), could be so ignoble too — so tied and bound by his sins; and it affected me so much — here in his presence that had so strange a fascination in it — that it was as if a hand had squeezed my throat, so that I could not speak, even if I would.

"Well, sir," he said, "I must thank you for coming so quickly when I sent for you. Mr. Chiffinch knows why you are come; but no one else; and even to him you must not say one word. You will do well and discreetly; of that I am sure. I will send for you again presently; and you may come to me when you will."

He gave me his hand to kiss; and I went out, promising that no pains should be spared.

*   *   *

It was indeed a difficult task that His Majesty had laid upon me. I was to speak freely to the priests, yet not freely; and how to collect the evidence that was required I knew not; since I knew nothing at all of when the conspiring was said to be done, nor what would be of avail to protect them; and all the way to my lodgings with my man James, I was thinking of what was best to do.

My man had ordered that all things should be ready for my enter-tainment, and I found the rooms prepared, and the beds laid; and the first thing I did after dinner was to go to bed, after I had written to my Cousin Tom at Hare Street, and sleep until the evening.

*　　*　　*

When I was dressed and had had supper in the coffee-house, listening as well as I could to the talk, but hearing nothing perti-nent, I went back again to Drury Lane, to Mr. Fenwick's lodging, to lay the foundation of my plan. For I had determined, between sleeping and waking, that the best thing to be done, was to shew myself as forward and friendly as I could, so that I might mix with the Fathers freely, in the hope that I might light on something; and it so fell out, that although my small adventures that evening had no use in them in the event, yet they were strangely relevant to what took place afterwards.

The first small adventure was as follows:

I was walking swiftly up Drury Lane, scanning the houses, for it was falling dark, and the oil-lights that burned, one before every tenth house, cast but a poor illumination, when just beyond one of the lights I knocked against a fellow who was coming out suddenly from a little passage at the side, just, as it chanced, opposite to Mr. Fenwick's house. I turned, to beg his pardon, for it was more my fault than his, that we had come together; and I set my eyes upon the most strange and villainous face that I have ever seen. The fellow was dressed in a dark suit, and wore a crowned hat, and carried a club in his hand, and he appeared to be one of the vagrom-men as they are called, who are at the bottom of all riots and such like things. He was a smallish man in his height, but his face was the strangest thing about him; and in the light from the lamp I thought at first that he had some kind of deformity in it. For his mouth was, as it were in the very midst of his face; there was a little forehead above, with eyes set close beneath it, and a little nose, and then his mouth, turned up at the corners as if he smiled, and beneath that a vast chin, as large as the rest of his face.

He cried out "Lard!" as I ran against him; by which I under-stood him to say "Lord!"

I asked his pardon.

"O Lard!" he said again, "'tis nothing, sir. My apologies to you, sir."

I bowed to him civilly again, and passed on; but as I knocked upon Mr. Fenwick's door, I saw that he was staring after me, from the entrance to that same passage from which he had come.

*   *   *

My second adventure was that, upon coming upstairs, I found that in the chamber with Mr. Fenwick were the mother and sister of Mr. Ireland, waiting for him to come and take them back to their lodging. They were quiet folks enough — a little shy, it appeared to me, of strange company. But I did my best to be civil, and they grew more talkative. Mrs. Ireland would be near sixty years old, I would take it, dressed in a brown sac, such as had been fashionable ten years back, and her daughter, I should think about thirty years old. They told me that they had been to supper, and to the play in the Duke's Playhouse, where Mr. Shirley's tragi-comedy *The Young Admiral* had been done; and that Mr. Ireland was to come for them here, as presently he did, for it was scarce safe for ladies to be abroad at such an hour in the streets without an escort, so wild were the pranks played (and worse than pranks), by even the King's gentlemen themselves, as well as by the riff-raff.

We sat and talked a good while; and Mr. Grove brought chocolate up for the ladies. But for myself, I had such a variety of thoughts, as I talked with them all, knowing what I did, and they knowing nothing, that I could scarce command my voice and manner sometimes. For here were these innocent folk — with Mr. Grove smiling upon them with the chocolate — talking of the play and what-not, and of which of the actors pleased them and which did not — and I noticed that the ladies, as always, were very severe upon the women — and the good fathers, too, pleased that they were pleased, and rallying them upon their gaiety — (for it appeared that these ladies did not go often into company); and here sat I, with my secret upon my heart, knowing — or guessing at least — that a plot was afoot to ruin them all and turn their merriment into mourning.

But I think that I acquitted myself pretty well; and that none guessed that anything was amiss with me; for I spoke of the plays I had seen in Rome, before that I was a novice, and of the singers that I heard there; and I listened, too, to their own speeches, gathering this and that, of what they did and where they went, if by chance I might gather something to their own advantage thereafter.

It was pretty to see, too, how courteous and gallant Mr. Ireland was with his mother and sister; and how he put their cloaks about them at the door, and feigned that he was a constable to carry them off to prison — (at which my heart failed me again) — for frequenting the company of suspected persons; and how he gave an arm to each of them, as they set off into the dark.

*   *   *

That night too, as I lay abed, I thought much of all this again. I had established a great friendliness with the Fathers by now, telling them I was come up again to London, as Mr. Whitbread had recommended me, until the Court should go again to Windsor, and that perhaps I should go with it thither. They had told me at that, that one of their Fathers was there, named Mr. Bedingfeld (who was of the Oxburgh family, I think), and that he was confessor to the Duke of York, and that they would recommend me to him if I should go. But all through my anxiety I comforted myself with the assurance the King had given to me, that, whatever else might ensue, not a hair of their heads should be touched, for I had great confidence in His Majesty's word, given so solemnly.

CHAPTER VI

Now begins in earnest that chapter of horrors that will be with me till I die; and the learning of that lesson that I might have learned long before from one that was himself a Prince, and knew what he was talking of — I mean King David, who bids us in his psalm to "put no trust in princes nor in any child of man."

For several days all passed peacefully enough. I waited upon Mr. Chiffinch, and asked whether the King had spoken of me again, and was told he had not; so I went about my business, which was to haunt the taverns and to frequent the company of the Jesuits.

I made an acquaintance or two in the taverns at this time, which served me later, though not in the particular manner that I had wished; but for the most part matters seemed quiet enough. Men did not speak a great deal of the Catholics; and I always fenced off questions by beginning, in every company that I found myself in, by speaking of some Church of England divine with a great deal of admiration, soon earning for myself, I fear, the name of a pious and grave fellow, but at the same time, of a safe man in matters of Church and State.

One of these acquaintances was a Mr. Rumbald, a maltster (which was all I thought him then), who frequented the Mitre tavern, without Aldgate, where I went one day, dressed in one of my sober country suits, wearing my hat at a somewhat rakish cock, that I might seem to be a simple fellow that aped town-ways.

The tavern was full when I came to it, and called for dinner; but I made such a to-do that the maid went to an inner room, and presently returning, told me I might have my dinner there. It was a little parlour she spewed me to, with old steel caps upon the wall, and strewed rushes under foot; and there were three or four men there who had just done dinner, all but one. This one was a ruddy man, with red hair going grey, dressed very plain, but well, with a hard kind of look about him; and he had had as much to drink as a man should have, and was in the merry stage of his drink. Here, thought I, is the very man for me. He is of both country and town; here is a chamber of which he seems lord — for he ordered the maid about royally, and cursed her once or twice — and it is a chamber apart from the rest. So I thought this a very proper place to hear some talk in, and a very proper fellow to hear it from. For a while I thought he had something of the look of an old soldier about him; but then I thought no more of it.

When the others were gone out, and there was a little delay, I too — (God forgive me!) — cursed the poor maid for a slut once or twice, and bade her make haste with my dinner; and my manner had its effect, for the fellow warmed to me presently and told me that he was Mr. Rumbald, and I said on my part that my name was Mallock; and we shook hands upon it, for that was the mood of the ale that was in him. (But he had other moods, too, I learned later, when he was very repentant for his drink.)

I began then, to speak of Hare Street, and said that I lodged there sometimes; and then began to speak of the parson there, and of what a Churchman he was.

"Of Hare Street, eh?" said he. "Why I am not far from there myself. I am of Hoddesdon, or near to it. Where have you lodged in Hare Street, and what is your business?"

I was in a quandary at that, for it seemed to me then (though it was not in reality), a piece of bad fortune that he should come from thereabouts.

"I am Jack-of-all-trades," I said. "I did some garden work there for Mr. Jermyn, the Papist."

"The Papist, eh?" cried Mr. Rumbald.

"I would work for the Devil," said I, "if he would pay me enough."

The words appeared to Mr. Rumbald very witty, though God knows why: I suppose it was the ale in him: for he laughed aloud and beat on his leg.

"I'll be bound you would," he said.

And it was these words of mine which (under God's Providence, as I think now) established my reputation with Mr. Rumbald as a dare-devil kind of fellow that would do anything for money. He began, too, at that (which pleased me better at the time), to speak of precisely those matters of which I wished to hear. It was not treasonable talk, for the ale had not driven all the sense out of him; but it was as near treasonable as might be; and it was above all against the Catholics that he raged. I would not defile this page by writing down all that he said; but neither Her Majesty nor the Duke of York escaped his venom; there appeared nothing too bad to be said of them; and he spoke of other names, too, of the Duchess of Portsmouth whom he called by vile names (yet not viler than she had rightfully earned) and the Duchess of Cleveland; and he began upon the King, but stopped himself.

"But you are a Church of England man?" he said. "Well, so am

I now, at least I call myself so, though I should be a Presbyterian; but —" And he stopped again.

Now all this was mighty interesting to me; for it was worse than anything I had heard before; and yet he said it all as if it was common talk among his kind, where he came from; and it was very consonant with what the King had set me to do, which was to hear what the common people had to say. My gorge rose at the man again and again; but I was a tolerable actor in those days, and restrained myself very well. When he went at last he clapped me on the back, as if it were I who had done all the bragging.

"You are the right kind of fellow," he said, "and, by God, I wish there were more of us. You will remember my name — Mr. Rumbald the maltster — I am to be heard of here at any time, for I come up on my business every week — though I was not always a maltster."

I promised I would remember him: and indeed after a while all England has remembered him ever since.

*　　*　　*

It was that same evening, I think (for my diary is confused at this time, and no wonder), that when I came back to my lodgings about supper-time, I found that a man had been from Mr. Chiffinch to bid me come to Whitehall as soon as I returned; but the messenger had not seemed greatly perturbed, James told me; so I changed my clothes and had my supper and set out.

It would be about half-past seven o'clock when I came to Mr. Chiffinch's; and when I tapped I had no answer. I tapped again; and then a servant of Mr. Chiffinch's came running up the stairs (who had left his post, I suspect) and asked me what I wanted there. When I told him he seemed surprised, and he said that Mr. Chiffinch had company in his inner closet; but that he would speak with him. So he left me standing there; and went through, and I heard a door shut within. Presently he came out again in something of a hurry, and bade me come in; and, to my astonishment we went through the first room that was empty, and out again beyond and down a dark passage. I heard voices as I went, talking rapidly somewhere, but there was no one to be seen. Then he knocked softly upon a door at the end of the passage; a voice cried to us to come in; and I entered; and, to my astonishment, not only was the little closet half full of persons, but these persons were somewhat exceptional.

At the end of the table that was opposite me, sat His Majesty, tilting his chair back a little as if he were weary of the talk; but his face was flushed as if with anger. Upon his right sat the Duke, with his periwig pushed a little back, and his face more flushed even than the King's. Opposite to the Duke sat two men, whom I took to be priests by their faces — one fair, the other dark — (and I presently proved to be right) — and beside him Mr. Chiffinch, very eager-looking, and lean, talking at a great speed, with his hands clasped upon the table. Finally, my Lord Danby sat next to the Duke, opposite to Mr. Chiffinch, with a sullen look upon his face. There was a great heap of papers, again, upon the table, between the five men. All these persons turned their eyes upon me as I came in and bowed low to the company; and then Mr. Chiffinch jerked back a chair that was beside him, and beckoned to me to sit down in it. The room appeared to me a secret kind of place, with curtains pulled across the windows, where a man might be very private if he wished. Mr. Chiffinch ended speaking as I came in, and all sat silent.

His Majesty broke the silence.

"You are very late, Mr. Mallock," he said — no more than that; but I felt the reproof very keenly. "Tell him, Chiffinch."

Then Mr. Chiffinch related to me an extraordinary story; and he told it very well, balancing the two sides of it, so that I could not tell what he thought.

It appeared that a day or two ago, Doctor Tonge had come to my Lord Danby, in pursuance of the tale he had told before, saying that he had received further information, from the very man whom he had suspected, and now had certified, to be the writer of the first information under forty-three heads, to the effect that a packet of letters was on its way to Windsor, to that very Mr. Bedingfeld (of whom Mr. Whitbread had spoken to me), on the matter of the plot to murder the King, and the Duke too unless he would consent to the affair. My Lord Danby posted immediately to Windsor that he might intercept these letters and examine them for himself; but found that not only had Mr. Bedingfeld received them, but had taken them to the Duke, saying that he did not understand one word that was written in them. Those letters purported to have been written from a number of Jesuits, and others — amongst whom were a Mr. Coleman, an agent of the Duke's, and Mr. Langhorn, a lawyer; and related to a supposed plot, not only to murder the King, and his brother, too, perhaps, but to re-establish the Popish domination, to burn Westminster, as they had already burned the City; and that the new positions in the State had already been designed to certain persons, whose names were all mentioned in the letters, by the Holy Father himself. The matter that was now being discussed in this little chamber was, What was best to be done?

Mr. Chiffinch told me this, as shortly almost as I have written it down, glancing at His Majesty once or twice, and at the Duke, as if he wished to know whether he were telling it properly; and as soon as he ended His Majesty began:

"That is where we stand now, Mr. Mallock. As for me, I do not believe one word of the tale, as I have said before: and I say that it is best to destroy the letters, to tell Doctor Tonge that he is a damned fool, if not worse, so to be cozened, and to say no more of it. I would not have this made public for a thousand pounds. It is as I said before: I knew that the matter would grow."

"And I say, Sir," put in the Duke savagely, "that Your Majesty forgets who it is who are implicated — that it is these good Jesuit Fathers, and my own confessor, too" — (he bowed slightly to the fair man, who returned it) — "and that if the matter be not probed to the bottom, the names of all will suffer, in the long run."

"Brother, brother," said Charles, "I entreat you not to speak so violently. We all know how good the Fathers are, and do not suspect any one of them. It is to save their name —"

"And I tell you," burst in James again, "that mine is the only way to do it! Do you think, Sir, that these folks who are behind it all will let the matter rest? It will grow and grow, as Your Majesty said; and we shall have half the kingdom involved."

Here was a very pretty dispute, with sense on both sides, and yet there appeared to me that there was more on His Majesty's than on the other. If even then Dr. Tonge had been sent for and soundly rated, and made to produce his informant, and the matter sifted, I believe we should have heard no more of it. But it was not ordained so. They all spoke a good deal, appealing to the two priests — Mr. Bedingfeld and Mr. Young — and they both gave their opinions.

Presently Charles was silent; letting his chair come forward again on to its four legs, and putting his head in his hands over the table. I had never seen him so perturbed before. Then I ventured on a question.

"Sir, may I ask who is Doctor Tonge's informant?"

His Majesty glanced up at me as if he saw me for the first time.

"Tell him, Chiffinch," he said.

"His name is Doctor Oates," said the page. "He was a Papist once, and is turned informer, he says. He still feigns secretly to be friends with one or two of the Jesuits, he says."

"But every word you hear here is *sub sigillo*, Mr. Mallock," added the King. I knew no such name; and said no more. I had never heard of the man.

"Have you anything to say, Mr. Mallock?" asked the King presently.

"I have some reports to hand in, Sir," I said, "but they do not bear directly upon this matter."

The King lifted his heavy eyes and let them fall again. He appeared weary and dispirited.

*   *   *

When we broke up at last, nothing was decided. On the one hand the letters were not destroyed, and the Duke was still unforbidden to pursue his researches; and, on the other there was no permission for a public inquiry to be held. The counsels, in short, were divided; and that is the worst state of all. The Duke said nothing to me, either at the table or before he went out with Mr. Bedingfeld — or Mr. Mumford as he was usually called: he appeared to consider me too young to be of any importance, and to tolerate me only because the King wished it. I handed to Mr. Chiffinch the reports of what folks had said to me in taverns and elsewhere: and went away.

The days went by; and nothing of any importance appeared further. I still frequented the company of the Jesuit Fathers, and the taverns as before; but no more was heard, until a few days before the end of September. On that day I was passing through the Court of Whitehall to see if there were anything for me at Mr. Chiffinch's — for the King was at Windsor again — when I saw Father Whitbread and Father Ireland, coming swiftly out from the way that led to the Duke's lodgings — for he stayed here a good deal during these days. They were talking together, and did not see me till I was close upon them. When I greeted them, they stopped all of a sudden.

"The very man!" said Mr. Whitbread.

Then he asked me whether I would come with them to the lodgings of Mr. Fenwick, for they had something to say to me; and I went with them very willingly, for it appeared to me that perhaps they had heard of the matter which I had found so hard to keep from them. We said nothing at all on the way; and when we got within, Mr. Whitbread told Mr. Grove to stand at the foot of the stairs that no one might come up without his knowledge. They bolted the door also, when we were within the chamber. Then we all sat down.

"Now, Mr. Mallock," said Father Whitbread, "we know all that you know; and why you have been with us so much; and we thank you for your trouble."

I said nothing; but I bowed to them a little. But I knew that I had been of little service as yet.

"It is all out," said the priest, "or will be in a day or two. Mr. Oates hath been to Sir Edmund Berry Godfrey, the Westminster magistrate, with the whole of his pretended information — his forty-three heads to which he hath added now thirty-eight more, and he will be had before the Council tomorrow. Sir Edmund hath told Mr. Coleman his friend, and the Duke's agent, all that hath been sworn to before him; Mr. Coleman hath told the Duke and hath fled from town tonight; and the Duke has prevailed with the King to have the whole affair before the Council. I think that His Majesty's way with it would have been the better; but it is too late for that now. Now the matter must all come out; and Sir Edmund hath said sufficient to shew us that it will largely turn upon a consult that our Fathers held here in London, last April, at the White Horse Tavern; for Oates hath mingled truth and falsehood in a very ingenious fashion. He was at St. Omer's, you know, as a student; and was expelled for an unspeakable crime, as he was expelled from our other college at Valladolid also, for the same cause: so he knows a good deal of our ways. He feigns, too, to be a Doctor of Divinity in Salamanca University; but that is another of his lies, as I know for a truth. What we wish to know, however, is how he knows so much of our movements during these last months; for not one of us has seen him. You have been to and fro to our lodgings a great deal, Mr. Mallock. Have you ever seen, hanging about the streets outside any of them, a fellow with a deformed kind of face — so that his mouth —"

And at that I broke in: for I had never forgotten the man's face, against whom I had knocked one night in Drury Lane.

"I have seen the very man," I cried. "He is of middle stature; with a little forehead and nose and a great chin."

"That is the man," said Mr. Whitbread. "When did you see him?"

I told them that it was on the night that I found Mrs. Ireland and her daughter come from the play.

"He was standing in the mouth of the passage opposite," I said, "and watched me as I went in."

"He will have been watching many nights, I think," said Mr. Whitbread, "here, and in Duke Street, and at my own lodgings too."

I asked what he would do that for, if he had his tale already.

"That he may have more truth to stir up with his lies," said Mr. Whitbread. "He will say who he has seen go in and out; and we shall not be able to deny it."

He said this very quietly, without any sign of perturbation; and Mr. Ireland was the same. They seemed a little thoughtful only.

"But no harm can come to you," I cried. "His Majesty hath promised it."

"Yes: His Majesty hath promised it," said Mr. Whitbread in such a manner that my heart turned cold; but I said no more on the point.

"Now, Mr. Mallock," said the priest, "we must consider what is best to be done. When the case comes on, as it surely will, the question for us is what you must do. I doubt not that you could give evidence that you have found us harmless folk" — (he smiled as he said this) — "but I do not know that you will be able to add much to what other of our witnesses will be able to say. I am not at all sure but that it may not be best for you to keep away from the case at first at any rate. You have the King's ear, which is worth more to us than any testimony you could give."

"Why do you not fly the country?" I cried.

He smiled again.

"Because that," he said, "would be as much as to say that we were guilty; and so the whole Society would be thought guilty, and the Church too. No, Mr. Mallock, we must see the matter out, and trust to what justice we can get. But I do not think we shall get a great deal."

So it was decided then, that I would not give testimony unless there was some call for it; and I took my leave, marvelling at the constancy of these men, who preferred to imperil life itself, sooner than reputation.

*   *   *

Well; all went forward as Mr. Whitbread had said it would. On the twenty-eighth day of September Dr. Oates appeared before the Council to give his testimony; and it was to the same effect as was that which I had heard Mr. Chiffinch relate before, as to the Jesuit plot to murder the King, and if need be, the Duke too, and to establish Catholic domination in England.

I went into a gallery in the Council room for a little, to confirm with my own eyes whether it were Dr. Titus Oates himself against whom I had knocked in Drury Lane; and it was the man without doubt, though he looked very different in his minister's dress. It was not a very great room, and only those were admitted who had permission. His Majesty himself was there upon the second day; and sat in the midst of the table, at the upper end, with the Duke beside him, and the great officers round about; amongst whom I marked my Lord Shaftesbury, who I was beginning to think knew more of the plot than had appeared; Dr. Oates stood in a little pew at one side, so that when he turned to speak I could see his face. Dr. Tonge and Mr. Kirby and others sat on a seat behind him.

He was dressed as a minister — for he had been one, before his pretended reconciliation to the Catholic Church — in gown and bands and wore a great periwig; and not his face only — which no man could forget who had once set eyes on it — but the strange accent with which he spoke, confirmed me that it was the man I had seen.

My Lord Danby, I think it was, questioned him a good deal, as well as others: and he repeated the same tale with great fluency, with many gibes and aphorisms such as that the Jesuits had laid a wager that if Carolus Rex would not become R.C. — which is Roman Catholic — he should not much longer remain C.R. He said too that he had been reconciled to the Church on Ash Wednesday of last year; but that "he took God and His holy angels to witness that he had never changed the religion in his heart," but that it was all a pretence to spy out Papistical plots.

His Royal Highness broke out, when he had done, declaring the whole matter a bundle of lies; and when one or two asked Oates for any writings or letters that he had — since he had been so long amongst the Jesuits, and was so much trusted by them — he said that he had none; but could get them easily enough if warrants and officers were given him. I suppose the truth was that he had not wit enough to write them as yet, but had thought the Windsor letters (as I may call them) would be enough. (These questions had also been put to him on the day before, but were repeated now for the King's benefit.)

His Majesty himself, I think, proved the shrewdest examiner of them all.

"You said that you met Don Juan, the Spaniard, in your travels, Doctor Oates. Pray, what is he like in face and figure?"

"My Lard — Your Majesty," said Oates, "he is a tall black thin faylow, with swatthy features" — (for so he pronounced his words.)

"Eh?" asked the King.

Dr. Oates repeated his words; and the King turned, nodding and smiling, to His Royal Highness; for the Spanish bastard is far more Austrian than Spanish, and is fair and fat and of small stature.

"Excellent, Doctor Oates," said the King. "And now there is another small matter. You told these gentlemen yesterday that you saw — with your own eyes — the bribe of ten thousand pound paid down by the French King's confessor. Pray, where was this money paid?"

"In the Jesuits' house in Paris, your Majesty," said the man.

"And where is that?"

"That — Your Majesty — that house is — is near the King's own house." (But he spoke hesitatingly.)

Then the King broke out in indignation; and beat his hand on the table.

"Man!" he cried. "The Jesuits have no house within one mile of the Louvre!"

It pleased me to hear the King say that; for I was a little uneasy at Father Whitbread's manner when he had spoken of the King's promise; but I was less pleased a day or two afterwards to hear that His Majesty was gone to Newmarket, to the races, and had left the Council to do as best it could; and that the Jesuits had been taken that same night — Michaelmas eve — after Oates had been had before the Council. There had been a great to-do at the taking of Father Whitbread, for the Spanish soldiers had been called out to save the Ambassador's house, so great was the mob that went to see him taken.

*   *   *

The next public event in the whole affair was the last and worst of all the links that were being forged so swiftly: and the news of it came to me as follows.

I had gone to sup in Aldgate, where I had listened to a good deal of talk from some small gentry, as to the Papist plot; and had been happy to hear three or four of them declare that they believed there was nothing in it, and even the rest of them were far from positive on the matter; and I had stayed late over my pipe with them, so that it was long after my usual time when I returned towards my lodgings, walking alone, for I said good-bye to the last of my companions in the City.

As I came up into the Strand, I saw before me what appeared to be the tail of a great concourse of people, and heard the murmur of their voices; and, mending my pace a little, I soon came up with them. I went along for a little, trying to hear what they were saying upon the affair, and to learn what the matter was; for by now the street was one pack of folk all moving together. Little by little, then, I began to hear that someone had been strangled, and that "he was found with his neck broken," and then that "his own sword was run through his heart," and words of that kind.

Now I had heard talk before that Sir Edmund Berry Godfrey was run away with a woman, and to avoid the payment of his debts, which, if it were true, were certainly a very strange happening at such a time, since he was the magistrate before whom Oates had laid his information; but six days were gone by, and I had not thought very much of it, for his running away could not now in any way affect the information that had been laid. He was a very gentle man, though melancholy; and, though a good Protestant, troubled no man that was of another religion than himself — neither Papist nor Independent.

But when I heard the people about me speaking in this manner, the name of Sir Edmund came to my mind; and I asked a fellow that was tramping near me, who it was that was strangled and where the body was. But he turned on me with such a burst of oaths, that I thought it best to draw no more attention to myself, and presently slipped away. Then I thought myself of a little rising ground, a good bit in advance, whence, perhaps I might be able to see something of what was passing; and I made my way across the street, to a lane that led round on the north. As I came across, in the fringes of the crowd, I saw a minister walking, in his cassock; so I saluted him courteously, and asked what the matter was.

He looked at me with an agitated face, and said nothing: his lips worked, and he was very pale, yet it seemed to me with anger: so I asked him again; and this time he answered.

"Sir, I do not know who you are," he said. "But it is Sir Edmund Berry Godfrey who has been foully murdered by the Papists. He hath been found on Primrose Hill, and we are taking him to his house. I do not know, sir —"

But I was gone; and up the lane as fast as I could run. All that I had heard, all that I had feared, all even that I had dreamed, was being fulfilled. The links were forging swiftly. I do not know, even now as I write, how it was that Sir Edmund met his end, whether he had killed himself, as I think — for he was of a melancholiac disposition, as was his father and his grandfather before him — or whether, as indeed I think possible, he was murdered by the very man who swore so many Catholic lives away, by way of giving colour to his own designs — for if a man will swear away twenty lives, what should hinder him from taking one? One thing only I know, that no Catholic, whether old or young, Jesuit or not, saint or sinner, had any act or part in it; and on that I would lay down my own life.

By the time that I arrived at the rising mound — for a force mightier than prudence drove me to see the end — the head of the great concourse was beginning to arrive. Across the street from side to side stretched the company, all tramping together and murmuring like the sound of the sea. It was as if all London town was gone mad: for I do not believe there were above twenty men in that great mob, who were not persuaded that here was the corroboration of all that had been said upon the matter of the plot; and that the guilt of the Papists was made plain. Some roared, as they came, threats and curses upon the Pope, the Jesuits, and every Catholic that drew breath; but the most part marched silently, and more terribly, as it appeared to me. The street was becoming as light as day, for torches were being kindled as they came; and, at the last, came the great coach, swaying upon its swings, in which the body was borne.

I craned my head this way and that to see; and, as the coach passed beneath me, I saw into its interior, and how there lay there, supported by two men, the figure of another man whose face was covered with a white cloth.

CHAPTER VII

It would occupy too much space, were I to set down in detail all that passed between the finding of Sir Edmund Berry Godfrey's body, and the being brought to trial of the Jesuit Fathers. But a brief summary must be given.

The funeral of Sir Edmund was held three or four days later in St. Martin's, and the sermon was preached by Dr. Lloyd, his friend, who spoke from a pulpit guarded by two other thumping divines, lest he should be murdered by the Papists as he did it. There was a concourse of people that cannot be imagined; and seventy-two ministers walked in canonicals at the head of the procession. Dr. Lloyd spoke of the dead man as a martyr to the Protestant religion.

By the strangest stroke of ill-fortune Parliament met ten days before the funeral, which happened on the thirty-first of October; so that the excitement of the people — greatly increased by the exhibition of the dead body of Sir Godfrey — was ratified by their rulers — I say their rulers, since His Majesty, it appeared, could do nothing to stem the tide. It was my Lord Danby who opened the matter in the House of Peers that he might get what popularity he could to protect him against the disgrace that he foresaw would come upon him presently for the French business; and every violent word that he spoke was applauded to the echo. The House of Commons took up the cry; a solemn fast was appointed for the appeasing of God Almighty's wrath; guards were set in all the streets, and chains drawn across them, to prevent any sudden rising of the Papists; and all Catholic householders were bidden to withdraw ten miles from London. (This I did not comply with; for I was no householder.) Besides all this, both men and women went armed continually — the men with the "Protestants' flails," and ladies with little pistols hidden in their muffs. Workmen, too, were set to search and dig everywhere for "Tewkesbury mustard-balls," as they were called — or fire-balls, with which it was thought that the Catholics would set London a-fire, as Oates had said they would — or vast treasures which the Jesuits were thought to have buried in the Savoy and other places. Folks took alarm at the leastest matters; once my Lord Treasurer himself rode into London crying that the French army was already landed, when all that he had seen were some horses in the mist; once it was thought, from the noise of digging that some fat-head heard, that the Papists were mining to blow up Westminster. The King, whom I dared not go to see in all this uproar, and who did not send for me, went to and fro even in Whitehall, guarded everywhere — in private, as I heard, pouring scorn upon the plot, yet in public concealing his opinion; and upon the ninth of November he made a speech in the House of Lords, confirming all my fears, thanking his subjects for their devotion, and urging them to deal effectually with the Popish recusants that were such a danger to the kingdom! In October, too, five Catholic Lords — the Earl of Powis, Viscount Stafford, my Lord Petre, my Lord Arundell of Wardour, and my Lord Bellasis were committed to the Tower on a charge of treason.

I saw Dr. Oates more than once during these days, coming out of Whitehall with the guards that were given to protect him, carrying himself very high, in his minister's dress; and no wonder, for the man was the darling of the nation and was called its "Saviour," and had had a great pension voted to him of twelve hundred pounds a year. He did not think then, I warrant, of the day when he would be whipped from Newgate to Tyburn at a cart's tail; and again, laid upon a sled and whipped again through the City, for that he could not stand by reason of his first punishment. Another fellow too had come forward, named Bedloe, once a stable-boy to my Lord Bellasis, who had given himself up at Bristol, with "information," as he called it, as to Sir Edmund's murder, which he said had been done in Somerset House itself, by the priests and others, saying that the wax that was found upon the dead man's breeches came from the candles of the altar that the priests had held over him while they did it! Presently too, at the trial and even before it, Bedloe made his evidence to concur with Oates', though at the first there was no sign of it. Even before the trial, however, the audacity of the two villains waxed so great, as even to seek to embroil Her Majesty herself in the matter, and to make her privy to the whole plot; and this Oates did, at the bar of the House of Commons. But the King was so wrath at this, that little more was heard of it.

The Duke of York, during these proceedings, saved himself very well. When the Bill for the disabling of Papists from the holding of office or of sitting in either House of Parliament, had passed through the Commons, he made a speech upon it in the House of Lords, speaking so well that others as well as he were moved to tears by it. He said that his religion should be a matter between his soul and God only; and should never affect his public conduct; and this with so much weight that the decision was given in his favour, since he was the King's brother. I should never have thought that he could have done so well.

Mr. Coleman was the first to be brought to trial, at the beginning of December, for he came back and gave himself up the day after he had at first fled. He was already pre-judged; for so violent was the feeling against the Papists that my Lord Lucas said in the House of Lords that if he could have his way, he "would not have even a Popish cat to mew and purr about the King." Coleman, I say, was the first of those who had before been accused; but a Mr. Stayley, a Catholic banker (who had his house not far from me in Covent Garden), was even before him judged and executed, on account of some words that a lying Scotsman had said he had heard him use in the tavern in the same place.

I did not go to the trial of Mr. Coleman; for that I had nothing to say for him; and indeed Mr. Coleman's own letters — written three or four years ago — were the severest witnesses against him, in which he had written to Father La Chaise — (whom Oates at first called Father Le Shee) — the French King's confessor, and others, that if he could lay hands on a good sum of money, he could accomplish a great project he had for the restoration of the Catholic religion in England. (These letters were found in a drawer he had forgotten, when he had burned all the rest; and proved very unfortunate for him.) He meant by this, I have no doubt, the bribing of many Parliament-men to win toleration, and to get His Royal Highness restored as Lord High Admiral. He said this was his meaning; and I see no reason to doubt it, for he was a pragmatical kind of man, full of great affairs; but Chief Justice Scroggs waved it all away; and it was made to appear exactly consonant with all that Oates and Bedloe had said as to the project of killing the King. So great was the excitement, not of the common people only, but of those who should have known better, and so shrewd were these who took advantage of it, that my Lord Shaftesbury, who was waxing very hot upon the supposed Plot, for his own ends, was heard to say that any man that threw doubt on the plot must be treated as an enemy. Mr. Coleman was executed at Tyburn on the third day of December.

*   *   *

The trial of Father Ireland, Mr. Grove and Mr. Pickering — who was a Benedictine lay-brother — was opened on the seventeenth day of December, in the Sessions House at Justice Hall in the Old Bailey.

I was in the Court early, before the trial began, carrying a letter with me which Mr. Chiffinch got for me from my Lord Peterborough, that I might have a good place; and I had a very good one; for it was in a little gallery that looked down into the well of the court, so that I could see all that I wished, and the faces of all the prisoners, judges and witnesses, and yet by leaning back could avoid observation — for I had no wish, for others' sake, if not for my own, to be recognized by any of the witnesses. The seats for my Lords were on the left, under a state, with their desks before them; the place for the prisoners on the right, facing the judges; and for the witnesses opposite to me. The jury was beneath; and the counsels in front of them with their backs to me.

When the Court was full to bursting, my Lords came in, with the Chief Justice — that is Sir William Scroggs — in the midst. I had never seen him before, though I knew how hot he was against Catholics, and I looked to see what he was like. It was a dark morning, and the candles were lighted on my Lords' desks; and I could see his face pretty well in their light. He was in scarlet, and wore his great wig; and he talked behind his hand, with what seemed a great deal of merriment to Mr. Justice Bertue, who sat on one side of him, and the Recorder Jeffreys who sat upon the other. He had very heavy brows; his face was clean-shaven, and his mouth was like a trap when he shut it, and looked grave, as he did so soon as the clerk had done his formalities. He was a strong man, I thought, who would brook no opposition, and would have his way — as indeed he did; and the rest of my Lords had little or no say in the proceedings; and least of all had the jury, except to do what the Lord Chief Justice bid them.

The three prisoners — for Mr. Whitbread and Mr. Fenwick were presently withdrawn to be tried later, since they could not get two false witnesses against them at that time — were Mr. Ireland, Mr. Grove and Mr. Pickering, and I looked upon them with infinite compassion, to see how they would bear themselves. Mr. Pickering I had never seen before; so I could not tell whether or no he bore himself as usual. But the two others I had seen again and again; yet, with respect to them both I remembered principally that occasion when Mr. Ireland had entertained his mother and sister in Mr. Fenwick's lodging on that one night he was in town, and gone off with them into the dark so merrily; and Mr. Grove had brought up the chocolate in white cups, and we had all been merry together. Now they stood here in the dock together, and answered to their names cheerfully and courageously; and I could see that neither anguish of heart nor the fear of death had availed to change their countenances in the leastest degree. They stood there, scarcely moving, except once or twice to whisper to one another, while Dr. Oates told his lying tale.

It was now for the first time that I understood how shrewdly, and yet how clumsily now and then, the man had weaved together his information. He spoke with an abundance of detail that astonished me; he spoke of names and places with the greatest precision; he related how himself had been sent from St. Omer's with fifty pounds promised him, to kill Dr. Tonge who had lately translated a book from the French named "The Jesuits' Morals"; he spoke of a chapel in Mrs. Sanders' house, at Wild-House, where he had been present, he said, at a piece of conspiring; and so forth continually, interlarding his tale with bursts of adjuration and piety and indignation, so evidently feigned — though with something of the Puritan manner in it — that I marvelled that any man could be deceived who did not wish to be; and all with his vile accent. He spoke much also, as Mr. Whitbread had told me that he would, of the consult of the Fathers — of all that is, who had the *jus suffragii* in England — that had been held at the White Horse Tavern in the Strand, in April; pretending that at this the murder of the King was again decided upon, and designed too, in all particulars; how Mr. Pickering and Mr. Grove had been deputed to do the killing in St. James' Park with screwed pistols, as His Majesty walked there, or if not there, at Newmarket or Windsor; and how commissions had been given to various persons (whom he named), which they were to hold in the army that was to be raised, when His Majesty had been murdered, and the French King Louis let in with his troops. Worst of all, however, was the assertion which he made again and again that no Catholic's oath, even in Court, could be taken to be worth anything, since the Pope gave them all dispensations to swear falsely; for such an assertion as this deprives an accused man of all favour with the jury and destroys the testimonies of all Catholic witnesses. And, what amazed me most of all was that Chief Justice Scroggs supported him in this, and repeated it to the jury again and again. He said so first to Mr. Whitbread, before he was withdrawn.

"If you have a religion," he said, "that can give a dispensation for oaths, sacraments, protestations and falsehoods, how can you expect that we should believe you?"

"I know no such thing," said Mr. Whitbread very tranquilly.

Bedloe, too, told the same tale as he had told before, but with many embellishments; and was treated by my Lords with as much respect, very nearly, as Oates himself; and they were both given refreshment by the Chief Justice's order.

*   *   *

I could have found it in my heart to kill that man — Oates, I mean — as he stood there in his gown and bands and periwig, with his guards behind him, swearing away those good men's lives; now standing upright, now leaning on the rail before him, and now reposing himself on a stool that was brought for him. His monstrous countenance was as the face of a devil; he feigned now to weep, now to be merry. But most of all I hated the man, when the piteous sight was seen of the entrance of Mrs. Ireland and her daughter, who came to testify that Mr. Ireland was not in London at all on those days in August when Oates had sworn that he had spoken with him there. They stood there, as gallant women as might be, turning their eyes now and again upon the priest who was all the world to them by ties both of nature and grace; but all their testimony went for nothing, since, first my Lord had told the jury that a Catholic's oath was worth nothing, and next the prisoners had had no opportunity to know what charges precisely they were that were to be brought against them, and had had therefore no time to get their witnesses together. They complained very sharply of this; but my Lord puffed it all away, and would scarcely allow them to finish one sentence without interruption.

Mr. Ireland said upon one occasion that though he had no witnesses, for he had had no time to get them, yet he could get witnesses that there were witnesses.

"I know," said the Chief Justice, "what your way of arguing is; that is very pretty. You have witnesses that can prove you have witnesses, and those witnesses can prove that you have more witnesses, and so *in infinitum*. And thus you argue in everything you do."

It was growing dark when the evidence (for so it was called) was done; and the end was drawing near; and the candles which had been put out long ago were lighted again by an usher, who came in with a taper when the Lord Chief Justice called for lights. But the candles burned very badly, by reason of the closeness of the Court in which so many persons had been gathered for so long; and shed but a poor illumination. My eyes were weary too with staring upon the people — now upon the monstrous face of Oates, that was like a nightmare for terror, now upon the prisoners so patient in the dock, and now upon my Lords on their high seats beneath the state, and especially upon that hard and bitter face of Chief Justice Scroggs who, if ever a man murdered innocent folk, was murdering today the three men before him, by the direction which he gave to the jury, and the manner he conducted the case. I could, by now, see the faces only one by one, as each leant into the light of the candles; and it appeared to me, again and again, that these were mocking demons and not men, and Oates the lord of them all and of hell itself from which they all came, and to which they must return. I closed my eyes sometimes, both to rest them, and that I might pray for bare justice to be done; but my prayers were to me like the lifting of weights too great for my strength. One hope only remained to me, and that lay in His Majesty; for, although he had permitted the deaths of Coleman and of Stayley, these might indeed have appeared guilty to one who knew nothing of them; but I could not find it in my heart to believe that he would suffer these Jesuits to die, of whom he had sworn to me that not a hair of their heads should be injured. I had determined, too, to go to His Majesty, so soon as the trial was done, and the verdict given as I knew it would be, and hear from his own lips that he would keep his word, at whatever cost to himself.

It was dark then, by the time that all the evidence had been given, and the Chief Justice had done his directing of the jury. The Court, crowded though it was with the people, was as still as death, so soon as the jury came back after a very short recess. I could hear only the breathing of the folks on all hands. A woman sat beside me, who had been as early as myself that morning; but she had roared and clapped with the rest, at the earlier stages, when the Chief Justice had silenced the prisoners or thrown doubt upon what they said. She was quiet now, however, and I wondered how the evidence had affected her.

When the jury were ready to give their verdict, the talking that had broken out a little, grew silent again; but when the verdict of Guilty was given, it broke out once more into a storm of shouting; so that the rafters rang with it. The woman beside me — for I sat at the end of a bench and had nothing but the wall beyond me — appeared to awaken at the tumult and join her voice to it, beating with her hand at the edge of the gallery in front of her. As for me I looked at the prisoners. They were all upright in their places, Mr. Ireland in the midst of the three; and were as still as if nothing were the matter. They were looking at the Lord Chief Justice, at whom I too turned my eyes, and saw he was grinning and talking behind his hand to the Recorder. It was a very travesty of justice that I was looking at, and no true trial at all. There were a thousand points of dissonance that I had remarked myself — as to how it was, for instance, that one fellow had been promised twenty guineas for killing the King and another fifteen hundred pounds; as to how it was that Oates, who professed himself so loyal, had permitted four ruffians to go to Windsor (as he said), with intent to murder the King, and that he had said nothing of it at the time. But all was passed over in this lust for the Jesuits' blood.

I knew that my Lord would make a great speech on the affair, before he would make an end and give sentence; for this was a great opportunity for him to curry favour not only with the people, but with men like my Lord Shaftesbury who was behind him in all the matter; and as I had no wish to hear what he would have to say (for I knew it all by heart already) and, still less to hear the terrible words of the sentence for High Treason passed upon these three good men in the dock, I rose up quietly from my place, and slipped out of the door by which I had come in. As I was about to close the door behind me I heard silence made, and my Lord Justice Scroggs beginning his speech — and these were the words which first he addressed to the jury.

"Gentlemen," he said, "you have done like very good subjects and very good Christians; that is to say like very good Protestants; and now much good may their thirty thousand masses do them!" When he said this, he was referring to a piece of Dr. Oates' lying evidence as to a part of the reward that they should get for killing the King. But I closed the door; for I could bear to hear no more. But afterwards I heard that they then adjourned for an hour or two, and that it was the Recorder — Sir George Jeffreys — that gave sentence.

When I presented myself, half an hour later, at Mr. Chiffinch's lodgings, I had very nearly persuaded myself that all would yet be well. For I thought it impossible that any man to whom the report of the trial should be brought, could ever think that justice had been done; least of all the King who is the fount of it, under God. I knew very well that His Majesty would have to bear the brunt of some unpopularity if he refused to sign the warrants for their death; but he appeared to me to care not very much for popularity — since he outraged it often enough in worse ways than in maintaining the right. He had said to me, too, so expressly that no harm should come to the Fathers or to Mr. Grove and Mr. Pickering either; and he had said so, I was informed, even more forcibly to the Duke and those that were with him — saying that his right hand should rot off if ever he took the pen into his hand for such a purpose. I remembered these things, even while the plaudits of the crowd still rang in my ears, and the bitter cruelty of my Lord Chief Justice's words to the jury. His Majesty, I said to myself, is above all these lesser folk, and will see that no wrong is done. And, besides all this, he is half a Catholic himself and he knows against what kind of men these charges have been made.

I was pretty reassured then, when I knocked upon the door of Mr. Chiffinch's lodgings, and told the man who opened to me that I must see his master.

He took me through immediately into the little passage I had been in before, and himself tapped upon the door of the inner parlour; then he opened it, and let me through: for Mr. Chiffinch was accustomed by now to receive me at any hour.

He rose civilly enough, and asked me what I wished with him, so soon as the door was shut.

"The verdict is given," I said. "I must see His Majesty."

He screwed up his lips in a way he had.

"It is Guilty, I suppose," he said.

I told him Yes;

"And I have never seen," I said, "such a travesty of justice."

He looked down upon the table, considering, drumming his fingers upon it.

"That is as may be," he said. "But as for His Majesty —"

I broke out on him at that: for I was fiercely excited.

"Man," I cried, "there is no question about that. I must see His Majesty instantly."

He looked at me again, as if considering.

"Well," he said. "What must be, must. I will see His Majesty. He is not yet gone to supper."

At the door he turned again.

"The verdict was Guilty?" he said. "You were there and heard it?"

I told him Yes; for I was all impatient.

"And how was that verdict received in court?"

"It was applauded," I said shortly.

He still waited an instant. Then he went out.

*　　*　　*

I was all in a fever till he came back; for his manner and his hesitation had renewed my terrors. Yet still I would not let myself doubt. I went up and down the room, and looked at the pictures in it. There was a little one by Lely, not finished, of my Lady

Castlemaine, done before she was made Duchess, which I suppose the King had given to him; but I remembered afterwards nothing else that I saw at that time.

In about half an hour he came back again; but he shut the door behind him before he spoke.

"His Majesty will see you in a few minutes," he said, "but he goes to supper presently; and must not be detained. And there is something else that I must ask you first."

I was all impatient to be gone; but impatience would not help me at all.

"Mr. Mallock," he said, sitting down, "did you see any man following you from the Court? Or at the doors of the Palace?"

My heart stood still when he said that; for though I had done my best at all times for the last month or two to pass unnoticed so far as I could, I had known well enough that having been so much with the Jesuits as I had, it was not impossible that I had been marked by some spy or other, or even by Oates himself, since he had seen me go into Mr. Fenwick's lodgings. But I had fancied of late that I must have escaped notice, and had been more bold lately, as in going to the Court today.

"Followed?" I said. "What do you mean, Mr. Chiffinch?"

"You saw no fellow after you, or loitering near, at the gates, as you came in?"

"I saw no one," I said.

"The gates were barred, as usual?"

"Yes," I said. "And the guard fetched a lieutenant before he would let me in."

(For ever since the late alarms extraordinary precautions had been taken in keeping the great gates of the Palace always guarded.)

"And you saw no one after you?"

"No one," I said.

"Well," said Mr. Chiffinch, "a fellow was after you. For when you were gone in he came up to the guard and asked who you were, and by what right you had entered. The lieutenant sent a mail to tell me so, and I met him in the passage as I went out."

"Who was the fellow?"

"Oh! a man called Dangerfield. The lieutenant very prudently detained him; and I went across and questioned him before I went to His Majesty. I know nothing of the man, except that he hath been convicted, for I saw the branding in his hand when we examined him. We let him go again immediately."

"He knows my name?"

Mr. Chiffinch smiled.

"We are not so foolish as that, Mr. Mallock. He thinks you have some place at Court; but we did not satisfy him as to your name."

I said nothing; for there was nothing to say.

"You had best be very careful, Mr. Mallock," went on the page, standing up again. "You have been mixing a great deal with unpopular folks. You will be of no service to His Majesty at all if you fall under suspicion. You had best go back by water to the Temple Stairs."

He spoke a little coldly; and I perceived that he thought I had been indiscreet.

"Well," he said, "we had best be going to His Majesty's lodgings."

I had flattered myself, up to the present, that I knew His Majesty's capacities tolerably well. I thought him to be an easily read man, with both virtues and vices uppermost, wearing his heart on his sleeve, as the saying is — indolent, witty, lacking all self-control — yet not, as I might say, a deep man. I was to learn the truth, or rather begin to learn it, on this very night.

*   *   *

When I entered his private closet he was sitting not where I had seen him before, but at the great table in the midst of the floor, with his papers about him, and an appearance of great industry. He did not do more than look up for an instant, and then down again; and I stood there before him, after I had bowed and been taken no notice of, as it were a scholar waiting to be whipped.

He was all ready for supper, in his lace, with his hat on his head; and he was writing a letter, with a pair of candles burning before him in silver candlesticks. His face wore a very heavy and preoccupied look; and I was astonished that he paid me no attention.

He finished at last, threw sand on the paper from the pounce-box, and pushed it aside. Then he leaned his cheeks in his hands, and his elbows on the table, and looked at me. But he did not speak unkindly.

"Here you are then," he said. "And I hear you bring news from the Old Bailey?"

"I came from there half an hour ago, Sir."

"Ah! And the verdict was Guilty, Mr. Chiffinch tells me?"

"Yes, Sir."

"How did the people take it?"

"They applauded a great deal, Sir."

"They applauded, you say. At the end only, or all the while?"

"They applauded, Sir, whenever any of my Lords made a hit against the Catholics."

"Were there any who did otherwise?"

"Not one, Sir, that I could hear."

"The Chief Justice. What did he say?"

"He made many protestations of devotion to your Majesty, Sir, and to the Protestant Religion. He beat down the Catholics at every point. He permitted none of their witnesses to speak freely."

The King was silent a moment. Then he went on again.

"And the prisoners. How did they bear themselves?"

"They bore themselves like gallant gentlemen, Sir. They fought every point, so far as the Chief Justice would permit them."

"Did they shew any fear when the verdict was brought in?"

"None, Sir. They relied upon your Majesty's protection, no doubt."

Again His Majesty was silent. I still stood on the other side of the table from him, waiting to say what I had to say. The King shewed no sign of having heard what I had last said.

Then, to my astonishment he turned on me again very sharply.

"Mr. Mallock," he said, "I have a fault to find with you. Mr. Chiffinch tells me that you were followed from the Court, and that a fellow was asking after you at the gate. You say that you wish to serve me. Well, those who serve me must be very discreet and very shrewd. Plainly, you have not been so in this instance. You are a very young man; and I do not wish to be severe. But you must remember, Mr. Mallock, that such a thing as this must not happen any more."

My mouth was gone suddenly dry at this attack of His Majesty upon me. I licked my lips with my tongue in readiness to answer; but before I could speak, the King went on again.

"Now I had a little business to entrust to you; but I am not sure if it be not best to give it to another hand."

He took up from the table before him a newly sealed little packet that I had not noticed before; and sat weighing it in his hand, as if considering, while his eyes searched my face.

"Sir —" I began.

"Yes, Mr. Mallock, I know what you would say. That is all very well; but my servants must not make mistakes such as you have made. It was the height of madness for you to go to the Court at all to-day. I have no doubt that you were seen there, and followed; and you could have been of no service to your friends there, in any case. Mr. Chiffinch tells me he will provide a wherry for you immediately, that you may go back without observation. You must do this. The question before my mind is as to whether you shall take this packet with you, or not. What do you say, Mr. Mallock?"

All the while he had been speaking, I had been in a torment of misery. As yet I had done little or nothing for His Majesty, after all my commissioning from Rome; and now that the first piece of work was on hand, it was doubtful whether I had not forfeited it by my clumsiness. For the moment I forgot what I had come for. I was all set on acquitting myself well. I was but twenty-one years old!

"Sir," I cried, "if your Majesty will entrust that to me, you shall never repent it."

He smiled; but his face went back again to its heaviness. "It is a very difficult commission," he said. "And, what is of more importance than all else is that the packet should fall into no hand other than the one that should have it. For this reason, there is no name written upon it. But I have sealed it with a private signet of my own, both within and without; and you must bear the packet with you until you can deliver it."

"I understand, Sir."

"I can send no courier with it, for the reasons of which I have spoken. No man, Mr. Mallock, but you and I must know of its very existence. Neither can I tell you now to whom the packet must be given. You must bear it with you, sir, until you have a message from me, signed with the same seal as that which it bears, telling you where you must take it, and to whom. You understand?"

"I understand, Sir."

"You must leave London immediately until your face is forgotten, and until this storm is over. You have a cousin in the country?"

"Yes, Sir; Mr. Jermyn at Hare Street."

"You had best lie there for the present; and I can send to you there, so soon as I have an opportunity. Meanwhile you must have this always at hand, and be ready to set out with it, so soon as you hear where you must go with it. That is all plain, Mr. Mallock?"

"I understand, Sir."

The King rose abruptly, pushing back his chair; and as he rose I heard the trumpets for supper, in the Court outside.

"Then you had best be gone. Take it, Mr. Mallock."

I came round and received the packet; and I kissed the King's hand which he had not given to me as I had come in. My heart was overjoyed at the confidence which he shewed me; and I slipped the packet immediately within my waistcoat. It was square and flat and lay there easily in a little pocket which the tailor had contrived there. Then, as I stood up again, the memory of what I had come for flashed back on me again.

"Sir," I said, "there is one other matter."

His Majesty was already turning away; but he stopped and looked over his shoulder.

"Eh?" he said.

"Sir, it is with regard to the Jesuits who were condemned today."

He jerked his hand impatiently in a way he had.

"I have no time for that," he said, "no time."

Then he was gone out at the other door, and I heard him going downstairs.

Now as I came downstairs again the further way, and heard the trumpets go, to shew that the King was come out, I had no suspicion of anything but my own foolishness in not speaking of what I had come about. But, by the time that I was at the Temple Stairs, I wondered whether or no the King had not had that very design, to put me off from which I wished to say. And at the present time I am certain of it — that His Majesty wished to hear from me at once of the proceedings at the trial, and then spoke immediately of that other matter of the packet, and of my being followed to the Palace Gates, with the express purpose of hindering me from saying anything; for I am sure that at this time he had not yet made up his mind as to what he would do when the warrants were brought to him, and did not wish to speak of it.

CHAPTER VIII

The first thing that I did when I got home was to call for my man James, and bid him shut the door. (My man was about forty years old, and he had been got for me in Rome, having fallen ill there in the service of my Lord Stafford — being himself a Catholic, and a very good one, for he went to the sacraments three or four times in the year, wherever he was. He was a clean-shaven fellow, and very sturdy and quick, and a good hand at cut and thrust and the quarter-staff, as I had seen for myself at Hare Street on the summer evenings. I had found him always discreet and silent, though I had not as yet given him any great confidence.)

"James," I said to him with great solemnity, "I have something to say to you which must go no further."

He stood waiting on my word.

"A fellow hath been after me today — named Dangerfield — a very brown man, with no hair on his face" (for so Mr. Chiffinch had told me). "He hath been branded on the hand for some conviction. I tell you this that you may know him if you see him again. I take him to be a Protestant spy: but I do not know for certain."

He still stood waiting. He knew very well, I think, that I was on some business, and that therefore I was in some danger too at such a time; though I had never spoken to him of it.

"And another thing that I have to say to you is that we must ride for Hare Street tomorrow, and arrive there by tomorrow night — without lying anywhere on the road. You must have the horses here, and all ready, by seven o'clock in the morning. And you must tell no one where we are going to, to hinder any from following us, if we can help it. We must lie at Hare Street a good while.

"And the third thing I have to say is this; that you must watch out very shrewdly for any signs that we are known or suspected of anything. I tell you plainly that both you and I may be in some danger for a while; so if you have no taste for that, you had best begone. You will keep quiet, I know very well."

"Sir, I will stay with you, if you please," said James, as the last word was out of my mouth.

I gave him a look of pleasure; but no more; and he understood me very well.

"Then that is all that I have to say. You may bring supper in as soon as you like."

Before I lay down that night I had transferred His Majesty's packet to a belt that I put next to my skin; and so I went to bed.

*   *   *

It was still pretty dark when we came out upon the Ware road upon the next morning. I did not call James up to ride with me; for I had a great number of things to think about; and first amongst them was the commission which His Majesty had given me. What then could such a business be? — a packet that I must carry with me, and deliver to a man whose name should be given me afterwards! Why, then, was it entrusted to me so soon? And why could not the name be given to me immediately? But to such riddles there was no answer; and I left it presently alone.

The second thing that I had to think of was the matter of the men whom I had seen condemned yesterday; and even of that I did not know much more than of the packet. His Majesty had not spoken of them, except to ask questions at the beginning; and this seemed as a bad omen to me. Yet I had the King's word on it that they should not suffer; and, when I considered, there was no obligation or even any reason at all that he should talk out the matter with myself. Yet, though I presently put this affair too from my mind, since I had no certain knowledge of what would happen, it came back to me again and again — that memory of Mr. Ireland and Mr. Grove in the lodgings in Drury Lane, so harmless and so merry, and again as I had seen them yesterday in the dock, with Mr. Pickering, so helpless and yet so courageous in face of the injustice that was being done on them.

The third thing that I had to think upon was Hare Street to which I was going as fast as I could, and of those who would greet me there, and most of all, I need not say, of my Cousin Dolly. Her father had written to me two or three times during the four months that I had been away; and his last had been the letter of a very much frightened man, what with the news that had come to him of the proceedings in London and the feeling against the Catholics. But I had written back to him that nothing was to be feared if he would but stay still and hold his tongue; and that I myself would be with him presently, I hoped, and would reassure him; for in spite of the hot feeling in London the country Catholics suffered from it little or not at all, so long as they minded their own business. But it was principally of my Cousin Dolly that I thought; for the memory of her had been with me a great deal during the four months I had lived in London; but I was deter-mined to do nothing in a hurry, since the remembrance of her father's words to me, and, even more, of his manner and look in speaking, stuck in my throat and hindered me from seeing clearly. I knew very well, however, that my principal reason why I urged Peter on over the bad roads, was that I might see her the more quickly.

Nothing of any importance happened to us on the way. At Hoddesdon the memory of Mr. Rumbald came back to my mind, and I wondered where it was in Hoddesdon or near it that he had his malt-houses; and before that we stayed again for dinner at the *Four Swans* in Waltham Cross, where the host knew me again and asked how matters were in London; and we came at last in sight of the old church at Hormead Parva, just as the sun was going down upon our left. Peter, my horse, knew where he was then, and needed no more urging, for he knew that his stable was not far away.

They knew of course nothing of my coming; and when I dis-mounted in the yard there was not a man to be seen. I left my horse with James; and went along the flagged path that led to the door, and beat upon the door. The house seemed all dark and deserted; and it was not till I had beaten once more at the door that I saw a light shewing beneath it. Presently a very unsteady voice cried out to know who was there; and I knew it for my Cousin Tom's; so I roared at him that it was myself. There fol-lowed a great to-do of unlocking and unbarring — for they had the house — as I found presently — fortified as it were a castle; and when the door was undone there was my Cousin Tom with a great blunderbuss and two men with swords behind him.

"Why, whatever is forward?" I said sharply; for I was impa-tient with the long waiting and the cold, for a frost was beginning as the sun set.

"Why, Cousin Roger, we knew nothing of your coming," said my Cousin Tom, looking a little foolish, I thought. "We did not know who was at the door."

"I only knew myself of my coming yesterday," I said. "And whatever is the house fortified for?"

My cousin was putting up the bolts again as I spoke; (the two men were gone away into the back of the house); — and, as soon as he had done, he said:

"Why, there are dangerous folks about, Cousin Roger. And it is a Catholic house, you see."

I smiled at that; but said no more; for at that moment my Cousin Dolly came through from the back of the house where she had been sent by her father for safety; and at that sight I thought no more of the door.

I saluted her as a cousin should; and she me. She looked mighty pretty to me, in her dark dress, with her lace on, for supper was just on the table; and I cannot but think she was pleased to see me, for she was all smiling and flushed.

"So it is you, Cousin Roger," she said. "I thought it might very well be. We looked for you before Christmas."

* * *

At supper, and afterwards, I learned in what a panic poor Cousin Tom had lived since the news of the plot, and, above all, of Sir Edmund Berry Godfrey's death; and what he said to me made me determine to speak to him of my own small peril, for he had the right to know, and to forbid me his house, if he wished. But I hoped that he would not. It appeared that when the news of Sir Edmund's death had come, there had been something of a to-do in the village, of no great signification; for it was no more than a few young men who marched up and down shouting together — as such yokels will, upon the smallest excuse; and one of them had cried out at the gate of Hare Street House. At Barkway there had been more of a business; for there they had burnt an effigy of the Pope in the churchyard; and the parson — who was a stout Churchman — had made a speech upon it. However, this had played upon Cousin Tom's fears, and he had fortified the house with bolts, and slept with a pistol by his bed.

I told him that same night — not indeed all that happened to me; but enough of it to satisfy him. I said that I had been a good deal at the Jesuits' lodgings; and at the trial of the three; and that a fellow had attempted to follow me home; but that I had thrown him off.

Cousin Tom had the pipe from his mouth and was holding it in his hand, by the time I had done.

"Now, Cousin," I said, "if you think I am anything of a danger to the house, you have but to say the word, and I will be off. On the other hand, I and my man might be of some small service to you if it came to a brawl."

"You threw him off?" asked Cousin Tom.

"It was at Whitehall —" I began; and then I stopped: for I had not intended to speak of the King.

"Oho!" said Cousin Tom. "Then you have been at Whitehall

again?"

"Why, yes," I said, trying to pass it off. "I have been there and everywhere."

Cousin Tom put the pipe back again into his mouth.

"And there is another matter," I said (for Hare Street suited me very well as a lodging, and I had named it as such to His Majesty). "It is not right, Cousin Tom, that you should keep me here for nothing. Let me pay something each month —" (And I named a suitable sum.)

That determined Cousin Tom altogether. My speaking of Whitehall had greatly reassured him; and now this offer of mine made up his mind; for he was something of a skinflint in some respects. (For all that I did for him when I was here, in the fields and at the farm, more than repaid him for the expense of my living there.) He protested a little, and said that between kinsfolk no such question should enter in; but he protested with a very poor grace; and so the matter was settled, and we both satisfied.

*   *   *

So, once more, the time began to pass very agreeably for me. Here was I, safe from all the embroilments of town, in the same house with my Cousin Dorothy, and with plenty of leisure for my languages again. Yet my satisfaction was greatly broken up when I heard, on the last day of January that all that I had feared was come about, and that of the three men whom I had seen condemned at the Old Bailey, two — Mr. Ireland and Mr. Grove — had been executed seven days before: (Mr. Pickering was kept back on some excuse, and not put to death until May). The way I heard of it was in this manner.

I was in Puckeridge one day, on a matter which I do not now remember, and was going to the stable of the *White Hart* inn to get my horse to ride back again, when I ran into Mr. Rumbald who was there on the same errand. I was in my country suit, and very much splashed; and it was going on for evening, so he noticed nothing of me but my face.

"Why, Mallock," he cried — "It is Mr. Mallock, is it not?"

I told him yes.

He exchanged a few words with me, for he was one of those fellows who when they have once made up their minds to a thing, do not easily change it, and he was persuaded that I was of his kind and something of a daredevil too, which was what he liked. Then at the end he said something which made me question him as to what he meant.

"Have you not heard?" he cried. "Why the Popish dogs were hanged a week ago — Ireland and Grove, I mean. And there be three or four more men — accused by Bedloe of Godfrey's murder, and will be tried presently."

I need not say what a horror it was to me to hear that; for I had had more hope in my heart than I had thought. But I was collected enough to say something that satisfied him; and, as again he had been drinking, he was not very quick.

"And those three or four?" I asked. "Are they Jesuits too?"

"No," said Rumbald, "but there will be another batch presently, I make no doubt."

I got rid of him at last; and rode homewards; but it was with a very heavy heart. Not once yet had the King exercised his prerogative of mercy; and if he yielded at the first, and that against the Jesuits whom he had sworn to protect, was there anything in which he would resist?

My Cousin Dorothy saw in my face as I came in that something was the matter; so I told her the truth.

"May they rest in peace," she said; and blessed herself.

*   *   *

From time to time news reached us in this kind of manner. Though we were not a great distance from London we were in a very solitary place, away from the high-road that ran to Cambridge; and few came our way. Even in Puckeridge it was not known, I think, who I was, nor that I was cousin to Mr. Jermyn; so I had no fear of Mr. Rumbald suspecting me. Green, Berry, and Hill were all convicted of Sir Edmund's murder, through the testimony of Bedloe, who said that he had himself seen the body at Somerset House, and that Sir Edmund had been strangled there by priests and others and conveyed later to the ditch in Primrose Hill where he was found. Another fellow, too, named Miles Prance, a silversmith in Princes Street (out of Drury Lane), who was said by Bedloe to have been privy to the murder, in the fear of his life, and after inhuman treatment in prison, did corroborate the story and add to it, under promise of pardon, which he got. Green, Berry, and Hill, then, were hanged on the tenth day of February, on the testimonies of these two; and were as innocent as unborn babes. It was remarked how strangely their names went with the name of the murdered man and of the place he was found in.

For a while after that, matters were more quiet. A man named Samuel Atkins was tried presently, but was acquitted; and then a Nathaniel Reading was tried for suppressing evidence, and was punished for it. But our minds, rather, were fixed upon the approaching trial of the "Five Jesuits" as they were called, who still awaited it in prison — Whitbread, Fenwick, Harcourt, Gavan and Turner — all priests. But I had not a great deal of hope for these, when I thought of what had happened to the rest; and, indeed, at the end of May, Mr. Pickering himself was executed. At the beginning of May too, we heard of the bloody murder of Dr. Sharpe, the Protestant Archbishop in Scotland, by the old Covenanters, driven mad by the persecution this man had put them to; but this did not greatly affect our fortunes either way. One of the most bitter thoughts of all was that a secular priest named Serjeant, who, with another named Morris, was of Gallican views, had given evidence in public court against the Jesuits' casuistry.

Meanwhile, in other matters, we were quiet enough. Still I hesitated in pushing my suit with my Cousin Dolly, until I could see whether she was being forced to it or not. But my Cousin Tom had more wits than I had thought; for he said no more to me on the point, nor I to him; and I think I should have spoken to her that summer, had not an interruption come to my plans that set all aside for the present. During those months of spring and early summer we had no religious consolation at all; for we were too near London, and at the same time too solitary for any priest to come to us.

The interruption came in this manner.

I had sent my man over to Waltham Cross on an affair of a horse that was to be sold there on the nineteenth day of June (as I very well remember, from what happened afterwards); and when he came back he asked if he might speak with me privately. When I had him alone in my room he told me he had news from a Catholic ostler at the *Four Swans*, with whom he had spoken, that a party had been asking after me there that very morning.

"I said to him, sir, What kind of a party was it? And he told me that there were four men; and that they went in to drink first and to dine, for they came there about noon. I asked him then if any of them had any mark by which he could be known; and he laughed at that; and said that one of them was branded in the hand, for he was pulling his glove on when he came into the yard afterwards, so that it was seen."

I said nothing for a moment, when James said that, for I was considering whether so small a business of so many months ago was worth thinking of.

"And what then?" I said.

"Well, sir; as I was riding back I kept my eyes about me; and especially in the villages where it might be easy to miss them; and in Puckeridge, as I came by the inn I looked into the yard, and saw there four horses all tied up together."

"Did you ask after them?" I said.

"No, sir; I thought it best not. But I pushed on as quickly as I could."

"Did the ostler at Waltham Cross tell you what answer was given to the inquiries?"

"No, sir — he heard your name only from the parlour window as he went through the yard."

Now here was I in a quandary. On the one hand this was a very small affair, and not much evidence either way, and I did not wish to alarm my Cousin Tom if I need not; and, on the other if they were after me I had best be gone as soon as I could. It was six months since the fellow Dangerfield had asked after me at White-hall, and no harm had followed. Yet here was the tale of the branded hand — and, although there were many branded hands in England, the consonance of this with what had happened, misliked me a little.

"And was there any more news?" I asked.

"Why, yes, sir; I had forgot. The man told me too that the five Jesuits were cast six days ago, and Mr. Langhorn a day later, and that they were all sentenced together." (Mr. Langhorn was a lawyer, a very hot and devout Catholic; but his wife was as hot a Protestant.)

Now on hearing that I was a little more perturbed. Here were Mr. Whitbread and Mr. Fenwick, in whose company I had often been seen in public before the late troubles, condemned and awaiting sentence; and here was a fellow with a branded hand asking after me in Waltham Cross. Oates and Bedloe and Tonge and Kirby and a score of others were evidence that any man who sought his fortune might very well do so in Popish plots and accusations; and it was quite believable that Dangerfield was one more of them, and that after these new events he was after me. Yet, still, I did not wish to alarm my Cousin Tom; for he was a man who could not hide his feelings, I thought.

It was growing dark now; for it was after nine o'clock, and cloudy, with no moon to rise; and all would soon be gone to bed; so what I did I must do at once. I sat still in my chair, thinking that if I were hunted out of Hare Street I had nowhere to go; and then on a sudden I remembered the King's packet which he had given me, and which I still carried, as always, wrapped in oil-cloth next to my skin, since no word had come from him as to what I was to do with it. And at that remembrance I determined that I must undergo no risks.

"James," I said, "I think that we must be ready to go away if we are threatened in any way. Go down to the stables and saddle a fresh horse for you, and my own. Then come up here again and pack a pair of valises. I do not know as yet whether we must go or not; but we must be ready for it. Then take the valises and the horses down to the meadow, through the garden, and tie all up there, under the shadow of the trees from where you can see the house. And you must remain there yourself till twelve o'clock tonight. At twelve o'clock, as near as I can tell it, if all is quiet I will show a light three times from the garret window; and when you see that you can come back again and go to bed. If they are after us at all they will come when they think we are all asleep; and it will be before twelve o'clock. Do you understand it all?"

(I was very glib in all this; for I had thought it out all beforehand, if ever there should be an alarm of this kind.)

My man said that he understood very well, and went away, and I down to the Great Chamber where I had left my cousins.

As I came in at the door, my Cousin Tom woke up with a great snuffle; and stared at me as if amazed, as folks do when suddenly awakened.

"Well; to bed," he said. "I am half there already."

My Cousin Dorothy looked up from her sewing; and I think she knew that something was forward; for she continued to look at me.

"Not to bed yet, Cousin Tom," I said. "There is a matter I must speak of first."

Well; I sat down and told him as gently as I could — all the affair, except of the King's packet; and by the time I was done he was no longer at all drowsy. I told him too of the design I had formed, and that James was gone to carry it out.

"Had you not best be gone at once?" he said; and I saw the terror in his eyes, lest he too should be embroiled. But my Cousin Dorothy looked at me, unafraid; only there was a spot of colour on either cheek.

"Well," I said, "I can ride out into the fields and wait there, if you wish it, until morning: if you will send for me then if all be quiet."

But I explained to him again that I was in two minds as to whether I should go at all, so very small was the evidence of danger.

He looked foolish at that; but I could see that he wanted me gone: so I stood up.

"Well, Cousin," I said, "I see that you will be easier if I go. I will begone first and see whether James has the horses out; and you had best meanwhile go to my chamber and put away all that can incriminate you — in one of your hiding-holes."

I was half-way to the kitchen when I heard my Cousin Dorothy come after me; and I could see that she was in a great way.

"Cousin," she said, "I am ashamed that my father should speak like that. If I were mistress —"

"My dear Cousin," I said lightly, "if you were mistress, I should not be here at all."

"It is a shame," she said again, paying no attention, as her way was when she liked. "It is a shame that you should spend all night in the fields for nothing."

As she was speaking I heard James come downstairs with the valises. As he went past he told me he already had the horses tied under the trees. I nodded to him, and bade him go on, and he went out into the yard and so through the stables.

"I had best go help your father put the things away," I said. "They will not be here, at any rate, until the lights of the house are all out."

We went upstairs together and found my Cousin Tom already busy: he had my clothes all in a great heap, ready to carry down to the hiding-hole above the door; my papers he already had put away into the little recess behind the bed, and the books, most of which had not my name in them, he designed to carry to his own chamber.

We worked hard at all this — my Cousin Tom in a kind of fever, rolling his eyes at every sound; and, at the last, we had all put away, and were about to close the door of the hiding-hole. Then my Cousin Dorothy held up her hand.

"Hush!" she said; and then, "There was a step on the paved walk."

CHAPTER IX

When my Cousin Dorothy said that, we all became upon the instant as still as mice; and I saw my Cousin Tom's mouth suddenly hang open and his eyes to become fixed. For myself, I cannot say precisely what I felt; but it would be foolish to say that I was not at all frightened. For to be crept upon in the dark, when all is quiet, in a solitary country place; and to know, as I did, that behind all the silence there is the roar of a mob — (as it is called) — for blood, and the Lord Chief Justice's face of iron and his bitter murderous tongue, and the scaffold and the knife — this is daunting to any man. I made no mistake upon the matter. If this were Dangerfield himself, my life was ended; he would not have come here, so far, and with such caution; he would not have been at the pains to smell me out at all, unless he were sure of his end; and, indeed, my companying so much with the Jesuits and my encounter with Oates, and my seeking service with the King, and for no pay too — all this, in such days, was evidence enough to hang an angel from heaven.

This passed through my mind like a picture; and then I remembered that it was no more than a step on a paved path.

"If it is they," I whispered, "they will be round the house by now. We had best look from a dark window."

But my Cousin Tom seized me suddenly by the arm in so fierce a grip that I winced and all but cried out; and so we stood.

"If you have brought ruin on me —" he began presently in a horrid kind of whisper; and then he gripped me again; for again, so that no man could mistake it, came a single step on the paved path; and in my mind I saw how two men had crossed from lawn to lawn, to get all round the house, each stepping once upon the stones. They must have entered from the yard.

In those moments there came to me too a knowledge, of the truth of which I neither had nor have any doubt at all, that my Cousin Tom was considering whether he might save himself or no by handing me forthwith to the searchers. But I suppose he thought not; for presently his hand relaxed.

"In with you," he whispered; and made a back for me to climb up into the hiding-hole. I looked at my Cousin Dolly, and she nodded at me ever so gently; so I set my foot on my Cousin Tom's broad back, and my hands to the ledge, and raised myself up. It was a pretty wide space within, sufficient to hold three or four men, though my clothes and a few books covered most of the floor; but the only light I had was from the candle that my Cousin Dolly carried in her hand. As I turned to the door again, I caught a sight of her face, very pretty and very pale, looking up at me: I remember even now the shadow on her eyes and beneath her hair; and then the door was put to quickly, and I was all in the dark.

*   *   *

It was a very strange experience to lie there and to hear all that went on in the house, scarcely a hand's-breadth away.

I lay there, I should think, ten minutes or a quarter of an hour before the assault was made; and during that time too I could tell pretty well all that went on. There remained for a minute or thereabouts, a line of light upon the roof of my little chamber from the candle that my Cousin Dolly carried; (and that line of light was as a star to me); then I heard a little whispering; the light went out; and I heard soft steps going upstairs. Then I heard first the door of my Cousin Dolly's chamber close, and then another door which was my Cousin Tom's. Then followed complete silence; and I knew that the two would go to bed, and be found there, as if ignorant of everything.

The assault was made on two doors at once, at front and back. They had another man or two, I have no doubt, in the stable-yard; and more beneath the windows everywhere, so that I could not escape any way. There came on a sudden loud hammerings and voices shouting altogether; but I could not tell what it was that they cried; but I suppose it must have been, "Open in the King's name!"

Then the house awakened, all, that is, that were asleep; and the rest feigned to do so. I heard steps run down the stairs, and voices everywhere; as the maids over the kitchen awakened and screamed as maids will, and the men awakened and ran down from the garret. Then, overhead, across the lobby I heard my Cousin Tom's footsteps, and I nearly laughed to myself at the thought of the part that he must play, and of how ill he would play it. And all the while the beating on the doors went on; and I heard voices through the lath and plaster from the back-hall; and then the sound of unbolting, and the knocking ceased on that side, though it still went on upon the, other.

My hiding-hole, as I have said, was in the very centre of the house; one side faced upon the back-hall; and the opposite down the front passage; and, of the other two, one upon the stairs and one upon the kitchen passage, and these two had the doors in them. Above me was the lobby; and beneath me, first the little way into the back-hall, and beneath that the cellars. It was strange how prominent the place was, and yet how well concealed. One might live ten years in the house without suspecting its presence.

Presently the whole house was full of talking; and the front door was opened; and I heard a gentleman's voice speaking. He was Mr. Harris, I learned afterwards, a Justice of the Peace from Puckeridge, whom Dangerfield had brought with him.

Much of what was said I could not hear; but I heard enough to understand why I was being looked for, and what would be the charges against me. Now the voices came muffled; and now clear; so that I would hear half a sentence and no more, as the speaker moved on.

"I tell you he left for Rome tonight," I heard my Cousin Tom say (which was an adroit lie indeed, as no one could tell whether I had or no), "and he hath taken his man with him."

"That is very well —" began the gentleman's voice; and then no more.

Presently I heard one of the men of the house, named Dick — a good friend of mine, ask what they were after me for; and some fellow, as he went by, answered:

" — Consorting with the Jesuits, and conspiring —" and no more.

So, then, I lay and listened. Much that I heard had no relevance at all, for it was the protesting of maids and such-like. The footsteps went continually up and down; sometimes voices rose in anger; sometimes it was only a whisper that went by. I heard presses open and shut; and once or twice the noise of hammering overhead; and then silence again; but no silence was for long.

Here again I find it very hard to say all that I felt during that search. My thoughts came and went like pictures upon the dark. Now my heart would so beat that it sickened me, of sheer terror that I should be found; and this especially when a man would stay for a while talking on the stairs within an arm's length of where I lay: now it was as I might say, more of the intellect; and I pondered on what I heard my Cousin Tom say, and marvelled at his shrewdness; for fear, if it does not drive away wits, sharpens them wonderfully. He had, of course, put me in greater peril, by saying that I was gone to Rome; but he had saved himself very adroitly, for no witness in the house could tell that I had not done so; for here was my chamber empty, and I and my man and my clothes and my books and my horses all vanished away. At one time, then, I was all eyes and ears in the muffled dark, hearing my heart thump as it had been another's; at another time I would be looking within and contemplating my own fear.

Again and again, however, I thought of my Cousin Dorothy and wondered where she was and what she was at. I had not heard her voice all that time; and, on a sudden, after the men had been in the house near an hour I should say, I heard her sob suddenly, close to me, in a terrified kind of voice.

"Keep them, Nancy, keep them here as long as you can. It will give him —"

"Eh?" said a man's voice suddenly beneath. "What was that?"

"I said nothing," stammered my Cousin Dolly's voice.

Well; there was a to-do. The fellow beneath called out to Mr. Harris, who was upstairs; and I heard him come down. My Cousin Dolly was sobbing and crying out, and so was the maid Nancy to whom she had spoken. At first I could make nothing of it, nor why she had said what she had; and then, as I heard them all go into the parlour together, I understood that if my Cousin Tom had been shrewd, his daughter had been shrewder; and had said what she had, knowing that a man was within earshot.

But there was nothing for me to do but to lie there still; for I could hear nothing from the parlour but a confused sound of voices, now three or four speaking at once, now a man's voice (which I took to be the magistrate's), and now, I thought my Cousin Dolly's. I heard, too, above me, my Cousin Tom speaking very angrily, and understood that he was kept from his daughter — which was the best thing in the world for me, since he might very well have spoiled the whole design. At last I heard Dolly cry out very loud; then I heard the parlour-door open and three or four men came tumbling out, who ran beneath my hiding-hole and out through the kitchen passage to the stable. I was all a-tremble now, especially at my cousin's cry; but I gave her credit for being as shrewd still as I had heard her to be on the stairs; and I proved right in the event; for almost immediately after that my Cousin Tom was let come downstairs, and I heard every word, of the colloquy.

"Well, Mr. Jermyn," said the gentleman's voice, immediately without my little door, "I am sorry indeed to have troubled you in this way; but I am the King's justice of the peace and I must do my duty. Which way did you say Mr. Mallock was gone?"

"By...by Puckeridge," stammered poor Tom.

"Ah! indeed," said the other voice, with something of a sneer in it. "Why Mistress Dorothy here says it was by Barkway and so to Harwich; and of the two versions I prefer the lady's. For, first, we should have seen him if he had come by Puckeridge, since we have been lying there since three o'clock this afternoon; and second, no such man in his senses would go to Rome by London. I am sorry I cannot commend your truthfulness, Mr. Jermyn, as much as your professions of loyalty."

"I tell you —" began my Cousin Tom, angrily enough.

"I need no telling, Mr. Jermyn. Your cousin is gone by Barkway; and my men are gone to get the horses out to follow him. We shall catch him before Newmarket, I make no doubt."

Then I heard Dolly's sobbing as she clung to her father.

"Oh! father! father!" she mourned. "The gentleman forced it out of me. I could not help it. I could not help it!"

(As for me, I smiled near from ear to ear in the dark, to hear how well she feigned grief; and I think I loved my Cousin Dolly then as never before. It would have made a cat laugh, too, to hear the gentleman's chivalry in return.)

"Mistress Dorothy," he said, "I grieve to have troubled you like this. But you have done your duty as an English maid should; and set your loyalty to His Majesty before all else."

Mistress Dorothy sobbed so admirably in return that my own eyes filled with tears to hear her; and I was a little sorry for the poor gentleman too. He was so stupid, and yet so well mannered too now that he had got all that he wanted, or thought he had.

"Well, mistress, and Mr. Jermyn, I must not delay any longer. The horses will be ready."

They moved away still talking, all except my Cousin Dolly who sank upon the stairs still sobbing. She cried out after Mr. Harris to have mercy; and then fell a-crying again. When the door of the kitchen passage shut — for they were all gone out by now — her crying ceased mighty soon; and then I heard her laugh very softly to herself, and break off again, as if she had put her hand over her mouth. But I dared not speak to her yet.

I listened very carefully — for all the house was still now — for the sound of the horses' feet; and presently I heard them, and reckoned that a dozen at least must have come after me; and I heard the voices of the men too as they rode away, grow faint and cease. Then I heard my Cousin Dolly slip through the door beneath me, and she gave me one little rap to the floor of my hiding-hole as she went beneath it.

I did not hear her come back; for Cousin Tom's footsteps were loud in the kitchen passage; and the men too were tramping in and upstairs, while the maids went back to bed through the kitchen; and then, when all was quiet again I heard her voice speak suddenly in a whisper.

"You can open now, Cousin Roger, they be all gone away." I unbolted and pushed open the little door quickly enough then; and though I was dazed with the candlelight the first thing that I saw was Dolly's face, her eyes as bright as stars with merriment and laughter, and her cheeks flushed to rose, looking up at me.

CHAPTER X

That ride of mine all night to London was such as I shall never forget, not from any outward incident that happened, but for the thoughts that went continually through my heart and brain; and I do not suppose that I spoke twenty words to James all night, until we saw about seven o'clock the smoke and spires of London against the morning sky.

*   *   *

So soon as the coast was clear, and the last sound of the horses was died away on the hill beyond the Castle Inn — for the men rode fast and hard to catch me — I was out and away in the opposite direction, to Puckeridge; but first we brought the horses back as softly as we could, with James (who, like a good servant had not stirred an inch from his orders through all the tumult which he had heard plainly enough from the meadow), round to the head of the little lane that leads from Hormead Magna into Hare Street. There we waited, I say, all four of us in silence, until we heard the hoofs no more; and then James and I mounted on our horses.

I had said scarcely a word to Dorothy, nor she to me; for we both felt, I think, that there was no great need of words after such an adventure, and that it had knit us closer together than any words could do; and, besides, that was no place to talk. Yet it was not all pure joy; for here was the knowledge which we both had, that I must go away, and that God only knew when I should get back again; and, whatever that knowledge was to Dorothy, it was as a sword for pain to me. As for my Cousin Tom, he was no better than a dummy; for he was still terrified at all that had happened, and at the magistrate's words to him. I told them both, while we were still in the house, that I must go to London, partly for that that was the last place in the world that any would look for me in, and partly — (but this I told neither of them) — for that I must return the packet to His Majesty: and I said that from London I would go to France for a little, until it seemed safe for me to get back again. But there, waiting in the dark, I said nothing at all; but before I mounted I kissed Dorothy on the cheek; and her cheek was wet, but whether with the feigned tears she had shed in the house, or with tears even dearer to me than those, I do not know. But I dared not delay any longer, for fear that when Mr. Harris came to Barkway, which was five miles away, he might learn that no one that could be James and I had passed that way, and so return to search again.

*   *   *

The clouds had rolled away by now; and it was a clear night of stars until they began to pale about two o'clock in the morning; and I think that for a lover who desires to be alone with his thoughts, there is no light of sun or moon or candle so sweet as the light of stars; and by that time we were beyond Ware and coming out of the valley.

It was solemn to me to watch that dawn coming up, for it was, I thought, the last dawn that I should see in England for a while, since I was determined but to see the King in London, and push straight on to Dover and take the packet there: and it was a solemn dawn too, in another way, for it was the first I had seen since I had been certain not only that I loved my Cousin Dolly as I had my own heart, but that she loved me also; and that is a great day for a lover.

To see the King then, and to push on to Dover, was all that I had rehearsed to myself; but Providence had one more adventure for me first, that was one of the saddest I have ever had in all my life, and yet not all sad.

*   *   *

My road took me in through the City and down Gracechurch Street; but here I took a fancy to turn to the right up Leadenhall and Cornhill, which were all crowded with folks, though at first I did not think why, that I might go by Newgate where the Jesuits lay, and see at least the walls that enclosed those saints of God; for I was pretty bold here, knowing that Mr. Dangerfield who was my chief peril, was off to Harwich to find me; and even if they found that I was not gone through Barkway, I did not think that they could catch me, for their horses were tired and ours fresh; and you do not easily get a change of a dozen horses, or anywhere near it, in Hertfordshire villages. So I went very boldly, and made no pretence not to look folks in the face.

After we had passed up Cheapside it appeared to me that the streets were strangely full, and that all the folk were going the same way; and so astonished was I at this — for no suspicion of the truth came to me — that I bid my man ask someone what the matter was. When he came up with me again I could see that something was the matter indeed; and so it was.

"Sir," he said in a low voice, so that none else could hear, "they are taking the prisoners to execution this morning."

Then there came upon me a kind of madness — for, although by God's blessing it brought no harm to me — yet it was nothing else; and I determined to go to Newgate as I had intended, and at least see them brought out. For here was to be a martyrdom indeed — five men, all priests, all Religious — suffering, in God's eyes at least, for nothing in the world but the Catholic religion; yes, and in men's too, if they had known all, for I remembered how Mr. Whitbread had refused to escape, while he had yet a whole day for it, for fear of seeming to confess his guilt and so bringing scandal upon the Church and his order. From such a martyrdom, then, so near to me, how could I turn away? and I determined, if I could, to speak with Father Whitbread, and get his blessing.

When I got near Newgate the press grew greater every instant; but as we were on horseback and the greater number of the folks on foot, we got through them at last, and so came to the foot of the stairs by the chapel, where the sleds were laid ready with a pair of horses to each. I had never before seen an execution done in England, so I observed very carefully everything that was to be seen. The sleds were three in number, and were each made flat of strong wood with runners about an inch high; and there was a pair of horses harnessed to each, with a man to guide them. I got close to these, next behind the line of yellow trainbandmen who kept the way open, as well as the stairs. We were in the shadow here, in a little court of which the gates were set open, but the people were all crowded in behind the trainbandmen as well as in the street outside, and from them rose a great murmuring of talk, of which I did not hear a word spoken in sympathy, for I suppose that the Catholics there held their tongues.

We had not very long to wait; for, by the appointment of God, I was come just to time; and very soon the door at the head of the stairs was opened and men began to come out. I saw Mr. Sheriff How among them, who was to see execution done; but I did not observe these very closely, since I was looking for the Jesuits.

Mr. Harcourt came first into the sunlight that was at the head of the steps; and at the sight of him I was moved very deeply; for he was an old man with short white hair, very thick, and walked with a stick with his other hand in some fellow's arm. A great rustle of talk began when he appeared, and swelled into a roar, but he paid no attention to it, and came down, smiling and looking to his steps. Next came Mr. Whitbread; and at the sight of him I was as much affected as by the old man; for I had spoken with him so often. He too walked cheerfully, first looking about him resolutely as he came out at all the faces turned up to his; and at him too was even a greater roaring, for the people thought him to be at the head of all the conspiracy. He was pinioned loosely with cords, but not so that he could not lift his hands (and so were the other three that followed), and a fellow held the other end of the cord in his hand. Mr. Turner and Mr. Gavan, who came next, I had never seen before — (Mr. Gavan was he that was taken in the stables of the Imperial Ambassador — Count Wallinstein) — they came one behind the other, and paid no more attention than the others to the noise that greeted them; and last of all came Mr. Fenwick who had entertained me so often in Drury Lane, looking pinched, I thought, with his imprisonment, yet as courageous as any. Behind him came a minister and then the tail of the guard.

As I saw Mr. Fenwick come out I put into execution a design I had formed just now; and slipping from my horse I got out a guinea and begged in a low voice the fellow before me — for I was just by the sled on which Mr. Harcourt and Mr. Whitbread would be bound — to let me through enough to speak a word with him; and at the same time I pressed the guinea into his hand: so he stood aside a little and let me through, on my knees, enough to speak to Mr. Whitbread. Mr. Harcourt was already laid down on the sled, on the further side from me, and Mr. Whitbread was getting to his knees for the same end. As he turned and sat himself on the sled he saw me, and frowned ever so little. Then he smiled as I made the sign of the cross on myself and he made it too at me, and I saw his lips move as he blessed me. He was not an arm's length from me. That was enough for me; and I stepped back again and mounted my horse once more. The fellow who had let me through looked at me over his shoulder once or twice, but said nothing; for he had my guinea; and, as for myself I sat content, though my eyes pricked with tears, for I had had the last blessing (or very nearly) which that martyr of God would ever give in this world.

*   *   *

When they were all ready, and the five were bound on the sleds, with their beads to the horses' heels, I looked to see how I could best follow; and it appeared to me that it was best for me to keep close at the tail, rather than to attempt to go before. When the word was given, the whips cracked, and the sled nearest me, with Mr. Whitbread and Mr. Harcourt upon it, began to move. Then came Mr. Turner and Mr. Gavan, and last Mr. Fenwick all by himself. The minister whose name was Samuel Smith, as I learned later, and who was the Ordinary of Newgate, followed on foot, and behind him came the guards to close them all in.

My fellow in front, whom I had bribed, seemed to understand what I wanted; for in the confusion he let me through, and my man James forced his way after me; so that we found ourselves with three or four other gentlemen, riding immediately behind the guards, as we came out of the court into the street outside; and so we followed, all the way to Tyburn.

That adventure of mine was I think the most observable I have ever had, and, too, the greatest privilege to my soul: for here was I, if ever any man did, following the Cross of Christ in the passion of His servants — such a *Via Crucis* as I have never made in any church — for here was the very road along which so many hundreds of the Catholic martyrs had passed before; and at the end was waiting the very death by which they had died. I know that the martyrdom of these five was not so evident an one as that of others before them, since those died for the Faith directly, and these for an alleged conspiracy; yet before God, I think, they died no less for Religion, since it was in virtue of their Religion that they were accused. So, then, I followed them.

All the way along Holborn we went, and High Holborn and St. Giles, and at last out into the Oxford Road that ran then between fields and gardens; and all the way we went the crowds went with us, booing and roaring from time to time, and others, too, from the windows of the houses, joined in the din that was made. At first the way was nasty enough, with the pails that folks had emptied out of doors into the gutter; but by the time we reached the Oxford Road the way was dusty only; so that the five on the sleds were first nastied, and then the dust fell on them from the horses' heels. I could see only Mr. Fenwick's face from time to time; he kept his eyes closed the most of the way, and was praying, I think. Of the rest I could see nothing.

It was a terrible sight to me when we came out at last and saw the gallows — the "Deadly Nevergreen" as it was called — the three posts with the beams connecting them — against the western sky. The ropes were in place all in one line; and a cart was there beneath them. A cauldron, too, sent up its smoke a little distance away beside the brook. All this space was kept clear again by guards; and there were some of the new grenadiers among them, in their piebald livery, with furred caps; and without the guards there was a great crowd of people. Here, then, was the place of the Passion.

The confusion was so great as the sleds went within the line of guards, and the people surged this way and that, that I was forced, somewhat, out of the place I had hoped to get, and found myself at last a good way off, with a press of people between me and the gallows; so that I could see nothing of the unbinding; and, when they spoke later could not hear all that they said.

It was not long before they were all in the cart together, with the ropes about their necks, and the hangman down again upon the ground; and as soon as that was done, a great silence fell everywhere. I had seen Mr. Gavan say something to the hangman, and he answered again; but I could not hear what it was.

Then, when the silence fell, I heard Mr. Whitbread begin; and the first sentence was clear enough, though his voice sounded thin at that distance.

"I suppose," he said, "it is expected I should speak something to the matter I am condemned for, and brought hither to suffer."

Then he went on to say how he was wholly guiltless of any plot against His Majesty, and that in saying so he renounced and repudiated any pretended pardons or dispensations that were thought to have been given him to swear falsely. He prayed God to bless His Majesty, and denied that it was any part of Catholic teaching that a king might be killed as it was said had been designed by the alleged plot; and he ended by recommending his soul into the hands of his blessed Redeemer by whose only merits and passion he hoped for salvation. He spoke very clearly, with a kind of coldness.

Father Harcourt's voice was not so clear, as he was an old man; but I heard Mr. Sheriff How presently interrupt him. (He was upon horseback close beside the gallows.)

"Or of Sir Edmund Berry Godfrey's death?" he asked.

"Did you not write that letter concerning the dispatch of Sir Edmund Berry Godfrey?"

"No, sir," cried the old man very loud. "These are the words of a dying man. I would not do it for a thousand worlds."

He went on to affirm his innocence of all laid to his charge; and he ended by begging the prayers of all in the communion of the Roman Church in which he himself died.

When Mr. Anthony Turner had spoke a while, again Sheriff How interrupted him.

"You do only justify yourselves here," he said. "We will not believe a word that you say. Spend your time in prayer, and we will not think your time too long."

But Mr. Turner went on as before, affirming his entire innocence; and, at the end he prayed aloud, and I heard every word of it.

"O my dear Saviour and Redeemer," he cried, lifting up his eyes, and his hands too as well as he could for the cords, "I return Thee immortal thanks for all Thou hast pleased to do for me in the whole course of my life, and now in the hour of my death, with a firm belief of all things Thou hast revealed, and a stedfast hope of obtaining everlasting bliss. I cheerfully cast myself into the arms of Thy mercy, whose arms were stretched on the Cross for my redemption. Sweet Jesus, receive my spirit."

Then Mr. Gavan spoke to the same effect as the rest, but he argued a little more, and theologically too, being a young man; and spoke of Mariana the Jesuit who had seemed to teach a king-killing doctrine; but this sense on his words he repudiated altogether. He too, at the end, commended his soul into the hands of God, and said that he was ready to die for Jesus as Jesus had died for him.

Mr. Fenwick had scarcely begun before Mr. Sheriff How broke in on him, and argued with him concerning the murder of Sir Edmund.

"As for Sir Edmund Berry Godfrey," cried Mr. Fenwick, "I protest before God that I never saw the man in my life."

"For my part," said the Sheriff, "I am of opinion that you had a hand in it."

"Now that I am a dying man," said the priest, "do you think that I would go and damn my soul?"

"I wish you all the good that I can," said Mr. How, "but I assure you I believe never a word you say."

Well; he let him alone after that; and Mr. Fenwick finished, once more denying and renouncing the part that had been assigned to him, and maintaining his innocence.

There followed after that a very long silence, of half an hour, I should think. The five men stood in the cart together, with their eyes cast down; and each, I think, absolved his neighbour. The crowd about kept pretty quiet, only murmuring together; and cried no more insults at them. I, too, did my best to pray with them and for them; but my horse was restless, and I had some ado to keep him quiet. After a good while, Mr. Sheriff How spoke to them again.

"Pray aloud, gentlemen, that we may join with you. We shall do you no hurt if we do you no good."

They said nothing to that; and he spoke again, with some sharpness.

"Are you ashamed of your prayers?"

Still they did not speak; and he turned on Father Gavan.

"Why, Mr. Gavan," he said, "it is reported that you did preach in the Quakers' meeting-house."

The priest opened his eyes.

"No, sir," he said, "I never did preach there in all my life."

It was very solemn and dreadful to wait there while they prayed; for they were at it again for twenty minutes, I should judge, and no more interruptions from Mr. How, who, I think, was a shade uneasy. It was a clear June day, beginning to be hot; and the birds were chirping in the trees about the place — for at times the silence was so great that one could hear a pin fall, as they say. Now I felt on the brink of hell — at the thought of the pains that were waiting for my friends, at the memory of that great effusion of blood that had been poured out and of the more that was to follow. There was something shocking in the quietness and the glory of the day — such a day as many that I had spent in the meadows of Hare Street, or in the high woods — faced as it was with this dreadful thing against the blue sky, and the five figures beneath it, like figures in a frieze, and the smoke of the cauldron that drifted up continually or brought a reek of tar to my nostrils. And, again, all this would pass; and I would feel that it was not hell but heaven that waited; and that all was but as a thin veil, a little shadow of death, that hung between me and the unimaginable glories; and that at a word all would dissolve away and Christ come and this world be ended. So, then, the minutes passed for me: I said my *Paternoster* and *Ave* and *Credo* and *De Profundis*, over and over again; praying that the passage of those men might be easy, and that their deaths might be as sacrifices both for themselves and for the country. I was beyond fearing for myself now; I was in a kind of madness of pity and longing. And, at the last I saw Mr. Whitbread raise his head and look at the Sheriff.

There rose then, as he made a sign, a great murmur from all the crowd. I had thought that they would have been impatient, but they were not; and had kept silence very well; and I think that this spectacle of the five men praying had touched many hearts there. Now, however, when the end approached, they seemed to awaken again, and to look for it; and they began to move their heads about to see what was done, so that the crowd was like a field of wheat when the wind goes over it.

Then fell a horrible thing.

There broke out suddenly a cry, that was like a trumpet suddenly sounding after drums — of a different kind altogether from the murmuring that was before. I turned my head whence it came, and saw a great confusion break out in the outskirts of the crowd. Then I saw a horse's head, and a man's bare head behind it, whisk out from the trees in the direction of the park, and come like a streak across the open ground. As the galloper came nearer, I could see that he was spurring as if for life. Then once more a great roar broke out everywhere —

"A pardon! a pardon!" And so it was.

The crowd opened out to let the man through; and immediately he was at the gallows, and handing the paper to the sheriff. A roar was going up now on all sides; but as in dumb play I could see that Mr. How was speaking to the priests who still stood as before. Mr. Whitbread shook his head in answer and so did the others. Then I saw Mr. How make a sign; the hangman came forward again (for he had stepped back just now); and the roar died suddenly to silence.

Then I understood that the pardon was offered only on conditions which these men could not accept — and indeed they turned out afterwards to be that they should confess their guilt — and my anger at that bitter mockery swelled up so that I could scarcely hold myself in. But I did so.

Then the hangman climbed once more into the cart, and, one by one with each, he adjusted the rope, and then pulled down the caps over their faces, beginning with Father Whitbread and ending with Father Fenwick. Then he got down from the cart again; and the murmur rose once more to a roar.

I kept my eyes fixed upon the five, caring for nothing else; and even in that horrible instant my lips moved in the *De Profundis* for their souls' easy passage. Then I saw old Father Harcourt suddenly stagger, and then the rest staggered; and I saw that the cart was being pulled away. And then all five of them were in the air together, beginning to twist to and fro; and I shut my eyes, for I could bear no more.

CHAPTER XI

It was not till we were coming down St. Martin's Lane on the way to Whitehall, that my thoughts ran clear again, and I could think upon the designs I had formed. Until then, it seemed to me that I rode as in a dream, seeing my thoughts before me, but having no power to look within or consider myself. One thing too moved before me whenever I closed my eyes; and that was the slow twisting frieze of the five figures against the blue sky.

* * *

I spoke suddenly to James as we went.

"You will leave me," I said, "at the Whitehall gate; and go back to my lodgings. Procure a pair of good horses at the Covent Garden inn; and say we will leave them at any place they name on the Dover Road."

He answered that he would do so, and it was the first word he had spoken since we had left Tyburn. At the palace-doors I found no difficulty in admittance, for it was the hour for changing guard, and a lieutenant that was known to me let me in at once; so I went straight in and across the court, just as I was, in my dusty clothes and boots, carrying nothing but my riding-whip. My mind now seethed with bitter thoughts and words, now fell into a stupor, and I rehearsed nothing of what I should say to His Majesty, except that I was done with his service and was then going to France for a little, unless it pleased him to have me arrested and hanged too for nothing. Then I would give him back his papers and begone.

* * *

I came up the stairs to Mr. Chiffinch's lodgings, just as himself came out; and he fell back a step when he saw me.

"Why, where do you come from?" he asked.

"They are after me," I said briefly. "But that is not all."

"Why, what else?" said he, staring at me.

"I am come from seeing the martyrdoms," I said.

"For God's sake! —" he cried; and caught me by the arm and drew me in.

"Now have you dined?" he said, when he had me in a chair.

"Not yet."

He looked at me, fingering his lip.

"I suppose you have come to see His Majesty?" he said.

I told him, Yes: no more.

"And what if His Majesty will not see you?" he asked, trying me.

"His Majesty will see me," I said. "I have something for him."

Again he hesitated. I think for a minute or two he thought it might be a pistol or a knife that I had for the King.

"If I bring you to him," he said, "will you give me your word to remain here till I come for you?"

"Yes; I will do that," I said. "But I must see him immediately."

"Well —" said Mr. Chiffinch. And then without a word he wheeled and went out of the room.

I do not know how long I sat there; but it may have been half an hour. I sat like a dazed man; for I had had no sleep, and what I had seen drove away all desire for it. I sat there, staring, and pondering round and round in circles, like a wheel turning. Now it was of Dorothy; now of the Jesuits; now of His Majesty and Mr. Chiffinch; now again, of the road to Dover, and of what I should do in France.

There came at last a step on the stairs, and Mr. Chiffinch came in. At the door he turned, and took from a man in the passage, as I suppose, a covered dish, with a spoon in it. Then he shut the door with his heel, and came forward and set the dish down.

"Dinner first —" he said.

"I must see His Majesty," I repeated.

"Why you are an obstinate fellow, Mr. Mallock," he said, smiling. "Have I not given you my word you shall see him?"

"Directly?"

He leaned his hands on the table and looked at me.

"Mr. Mallock; His Majesty will be here in ten minutes' time. I told him you must eat something first; and he said he would wait till then."

*   *   *

The stew he had brought me was very savoury: and I ate it all up; for I had had nothing to eat since supper last night; and, by the time I had done, and had told him very briefly what had passed at Hare Street, I felt some of my bewilderment was gone. It is marvellous how food can change the moods of the immortal soul herself; but I was none the less determined, I thought, to leave the King's service; for I could not serve any man, I thought, whose hands were as red as his in the blood of innocents.

I had hardly done, and was blessing myself, when Mr. Chiffinch went out suddenly, and had returned before I had stood up, to hold the door open for the King.

He came in, that great Prince, — (for in spite of all I still count him to be that, *in posse* if not *in esse*) — as airy and as easy as if nothing in the world was the matter. He was but just come from dinner, and his face was flushed a little under its brown, with wine; and his melancholy eyes were alight. He was in one of his fine suits too, for today was Saturday; and as it was hot weather his suit was all of thin silk, puce-coloured, with yellow lace; and he carried a long cane in his ringed hand. He might not have had a care in the world, to all appearances; and he smiled at me, as if I were but just come back from a day in the country.

"Well, Mr. Mallock" — he said; and put out his hand to be kissed.

Now I had determined not to kiss his hand — whatever the consequences might be; but when I saw him like that I could do no otherwise; for my love and my pity for him — (if I may use such a word of a subject towards his Sovereign) — surged up again, which I thought were dead for ever; so I was on my knees in an instant, and I kissed his brown hand and smelled the faint violet essence which he used. Then, before I could say anything, he had me down in a chair, and himself in another, and was beginning to talk. (Mr. Chiffinch was gone out; but I had not seen him go.)

"It is a bloody business," he said sorrowfully — "a very bloody business. But what else could be done? If I had not consented, I would be no longer King; but off on my travels again; and all England in confusion. However; that is as it may be. What do you want to see me for, Mr. Mallock?"

He spoke so kindly to me, and with such feeling too, and his condescension seemed to me so infinite in his coming here to wait upon me — (though this was very often his custom, I think, when he wished to see a man or a woman in private) — that I determined to put off my announcement to him that I could no longer be in his service. So first I drew out from my waistcoat the packet I had taken from under my shirt, and put there, while Mr. Chiffinch was away.

"Sir;" I said, "I have brought your packet back again. I have had no word from you as to its delivery; and as I must go abroad today I dare keep it no longer. Your Majesty, I fear, must find another messenger."

His face darkened for an instant as if he could not remember something; but it lightened again as he took the packet from me, and turned it over.

"Why; I remember," he said. "It was sealed within and without, was it not?"

That seemed to me a strangely irrelevant thing to say but I told him, Yes it was.

"And you were to deliver to — eh? what was his name?"

"Your Majesty told me that the name would be sent to me."

"Why, so I did," said the King, smiling. "Well; let us open the packet and see what is within."

He took up a little ivory knife that was on the table by his elbow, and slipped it beneath the folds of the paper, so as to burst open the seals; and when he had done that, there was another wrapper, also sealed. This seal he also scrutinized, still smiling a little; and then he burst that; and when he had taken off that covering, a folded piece of paper fell out. This he unfolded, and spread flat with his fingers; and there was nothing written on that side; then he turned it over, and shewed me how there was nothing written on that either. So the message I had borne about me, was nothing in the world but a piece of blank paper.

I drew a long breath when I saw that; for my anger surged up at the way I had been fooled; but before I could think of anything to say, the King spoke.

"Mr. Mallock," he said, "you have done very well. You understand it now, eh?"

"No, Sir; I do not," I said.

"Why; it is a very old trick;" went on His Majesty, "to see if a messenger will be faithful. Your folks did it first, I think, in Queen Bess her reign; so as to risk nothing. And you have kept it all this while!"

"I obeyed Your Majesty's commands," I said.

"Well; and you have delivered it to the right person." (He tossed the papers altogether upon the table and turned to me again.) "Now, sir; I had no real doubt of you; but others were not so sure; and I consented to this to please them; so now that all has been done, I can use you more freely, if you will: I have more than one mission which must be done for me; and if you like it, Mr. Mallock, you may have the first."

"Sir; I must go to France immediately. The hunt is up, after me, too."

"What do you mean by that?" he said sharply. "The hunt! What is that?"

"I would not weary Your Majesty with it all; but the truth is that the fellow Dangerfield, who came after me here, came yesterday with a magistrate and near a dozen men, to Hare Street to take me. I eluded them, and came to London."

"You eluded them! How was that?"

Well; I told him as shortly as I could; and he laughed outright when I came to my Cousin Dolly's part in it.

"Why: that was very wittily done!" he said. "The minx!"

I did not much like that; but I could not find fault with the King.

"And I was at Tyburn this morning, Sir."

"What! At Tyburn!"

"At Tyburn, Sir; and I was so sick at heart at what I saw there — five of Your Majesty's most faithful servants murdered in the name of justice, that I would not have cared greatly if I had been hanged with them."

His face darkened a little; but not with anger at me.

"It is a bloody business, as I have said," he said gently. "But come! — it is to France that you go."

"There is as good as any other place," I said, "so I be out of the kingdom. I have estates there, too."

"But to France will suit very well," said the King. "For it is to France that I designed to send you. I have plenty of couriers who can take written messages, and I have plenty of men who can talk — some think, too much; but I have no one at hand at this moment whom I can send to Court, and who will acquit himself well there, and that can take a message too — none, that is, that is not occupied. What do you say, Mr. Mallock? Would a couple of months there please you?"

Here then was the time for my announcement; for I knew that if I did not make it then I should make it never.

I stood up; and my heart beat thickly.

"Sir," I said. "Six months ago I would have run anywhere to serve you. But in six months many things have happened; and I cannot serve a Prince any more who cannot keep his word even to save the innocent. I had best be gone again to Rome, I think, and see what they can give me there. I am sick of England, which I once loved so much."

It was those very words — or others very like them that I said. I do not know where I got the courage to say them, for my life lay altogether in the King's hand: a word from him, or even silence, and I should have kicked my heels that night in Newgate, and a week or two later in the air, on a charge of being in with the Jesuits in their plot. Yet I said them; for I could say nothing else.

His Majesty's face turned black as thunder as I began; and

when I was done it was all stiff with pride.

"That is your mind, Mr. Mallock, then?" he said.

"That is my mind, Sir," I answered him.

And then a change went over his face once more. God knows why he relented; I think it may have been that he had somewhat of a fancy for me, and remembered how I had pleased him and tried to serve him. And when he spoke, it was very gently indeed.

"Mr. Mallock," he said, "those are very brave words. But I think they are not worthy of a man of your parts. For consider; were you not sent here by the Holy Father to help a poor sinner who had need of it? And is it Catholic charity to leave the sinner because of his sins?"

I said nothing to that; for I was all confounded at his mildness. I suppose I had braced myself for something very different.

"It is true I am not a Catholic; but were you not sent here, in answer to my entreaty, that you might help to make it easy for me to become one? Is it apostolic, then, to run away so soon —"

"If Your Majesty," I burst out, "would but shew some signs —"

He lifted his eyebrows at that.

"Signs! In these days?" he said. "Why, I should hang, myself, in a week's time! Are these the days, think you, to shew Catholicism? Why; do you not think that my own heart is not near broken with all I have had to do?"

He spoke with extraordinary passion; for that was his way when he was very deeply moved (which, to tell the truth, however, was not very often). But I have never known a man so careless and indolent on the surface, who had a softer heart than His Sacred Majesty, if it could but be touched.

"The blood of God's priests," he cried, holding the arms of his chair so that it shook — "their blood cries from the ground against me! Do you think I do not know that? Yet what can I do? I am tied and bound by circumstance. I could not save them; and in the attempt I could only lose my own life or throne as well. The people are mad for their blood! Why Scroggs himself said in public at one of the trials, that even the King's Mercy could not come between them and death. And it is at this moment, then, that the servants to whom I had looked to help me, leave me! Go if you will, Mr. Mallock, and save your own soul. You shall have a safe passage to France; but never again speak to me of Catholic charity."

Every word that he said rang true in my heart. It was true indeed, as he said, that no effort of his could have saved the men, and he could only have perished himself. There were scores of men, even among his own guards, I have no doubt, who would have killed him if he had shewn at this time the least mercy, or the least inclination towards Catholicism. His back was to the wall; he fought not for himself only, but for Monarchy itself in England. There would have been an end of all, and we back again under the tyranny of the Commonwealth if he had acted otherwise; or as I had thought that he would.

He had scarcely finished when I was on my knees before him.

"Sir," I cried, "I am heartily ashamed of myself. I ask pardon for all that I have said. I will go to France or to anywhere else; and will think myself honoured by it, and by the forgiveness of Your Majesty. Sir; let me be your servant once more."

The passion was gone from his face as he looked down on me there; and he was, as before, the great Prince, with his easy manner and his unimaginable charm.

"Why that is very well said," he answered me. "And I shall be glad to have your services, Mr. Mallock. Mr. Chiffinch will give you all instructions."

*   *   *

"That was a very bold speech," said Mr. Chiffinch presently, when the King was gone away again — "which you made to His Majesty."

"Why, did you hear it?" I cried.

He smiled at me.

"Why, yes," he said. "I was behind the open door just within the further chamber. I was not sure of you, Mr. Mallock, neither was the King for that matter."

"Sure of me?"

"I thought perhaps we might have a real threatener of the King's life, at last," he said. "You had a very wild look when you came in, Mr. Mallock."

"Yet His Majesty came; and unarmed!" I cried: "and as happy as — as a King!"

"Why, what else?" asked Mr. Chiffinch.

Our eyes met; and for the first time I understood how even a man like this, with his pandering to the King's pleasures, and his own evil life, could have as much love and admiration for such a man, as I myself had.

PART II

CHAPTER I

I do not mean to set down in this volume all that befell me during the years that I was in the King's service, partly because that would make too large a book, but chiefly because there were committed to me affairs of which this French one was the first, of which I took my oath never to speak without leave. Up to the present in England nothing had been said to me which would be private twenty years afterwards; I take no shame at all at revealing what little I was able to do for the King personally in England — (except perhaps in one or two points which must not be spoken of) — nor of my adventures and my endeavours to be of service to those who were one with me in religion; but of the rest, the least said the soonest mended. So the best plan which I can think of is to leave out on every occasion all that passed, or very nearly all, when I was out of my country, both in France and Rome, for I went away — on what I may call secret service — three times altogether between my first coming and the King's death. It is enough to say that this time I was in Paris about three months, and in Normandy one; and that I had acquitted myself, so far, to His Majesty's satisfaction.[1]

I returned to London then on the night of the sixteenth of November, of the same year; and I brought with me a letter to the King from a certain personage in France.

Now to one living in a Catholic country the rumours that come from others not so happy, are either greatly swollen and exaggerated in his mind, or thought nothing of. It was the latter case with me. I was in high favour on both sides of the Channel; and this, I suppose made me think little of the troubles in my own country: so when I and James reached London late in the evening, after riding up from Kent, I went straight to Whitehall, as bold as brass to demand to see Mr. Chiffinch. We had ridden fast, and had talked with but very few folks, and these ignorant; so that I knew

---

1   Plainly this business of Mr. Mallock had some connection with Charles' perpetual intrigues with France, for Louis' support of him. At this time Charles' intrigues were a little unsuccessful; so it may be supposed that without Mr. Mallock they would have been even worse.

nothing of what impended, and was astonished that the sentinels at the gate eyed me so suspiciously.

"Yes, sir," said the younger, to whom I had addressed myself, "and what might your business with Mr. Chiffinch be?"

I had learned by now not to quack gossip or to parley with underlings; so I answered him very shortly.

"Then fetch the lieutenant," I said; and sat back on my horse like a great person.

When the lieutenant came he was one I had never seen before, nor he me; and he too asked me what I wanted with Mr. Chiffinch.

"Lord, man!" I cried, for I was weary with my journey, and a little impatient. "Do you think I shall blurt out private business for all the world to hear? Send me under guard if you will — a man on each side — so you send me."

He did not do that (for I think he thought that I might be some important personage from my way with him), but he would not let James come in too; and he said a man must go with me to show me the way.

"Or I, him," I said. "However; let it be so;" and I told James to ride on to the lodgings, and make all ready for me there.

Now I had heard in France of the events in the kingdom; but as they had not greatly affected Catholics, and, if anything, had even helped them, I was in no great state of mind. Within a week of my getting to Paris the news came of how the Duke of Monmouth had been sent with an army to Scotland and had trounced the Highlanders (who prayed and preached when they should have fought) at Bothwell Bridge on the river Clyde; and of the punishment he inflicted on them afterwards; though this was nothing to what Dr. Sharpe (who had been killed by them in May) or Lauderdale would have done to them. Of Catholic fortunes there was not a great deal of bad news, and some good: Sir George Wakeman, with three Benedictines, was acquitted of any design to murder the King; and Mr. Kerne, a priest, had been acquitted at Hereford of the charge under 27 Elizabeth — that famous statute, still in force, that forbade any priest that had received Orders beyond the seas, to reside in England. On the other hand, in the provinces, a few had suffered; of whom I remember, on the Feast of the Assumption a Franciscan named Johnson, a man of family, had been condemned at Worcester; and Mr. Will Plessington at Chester: and these were executed. Since then, no deaths that I had heard of, had taken place in England for such causes: and affairs seemed pretty quiet.

I was all unprepared then for the news I had from Mr. Chiffinch, as soon as he had greeted me, and paid me compliments on the way I had done my French business.

"You are come just in time," he said ruefully. "We are to have a great to-do tomorrow, I hear."

I asked him what that might be, lolling in my chair, for I was stiff with riding.

"Why it is your old friend Dangerfield, I hear, who is the thorn in our pillow now. He hath first feigned to discover a Covenanting plot against His Majesty; and then turned it into a Popish one. There has been much foolish talk about a meal-tub, and papers hidden in it, and such-like: and now there is to be a great procession of malcontents tomorrow, to burn the Pope and the Devil and Sir George Jeffreys, and God knows who, at Temple Bar. But that is not all."

"Why, what else?" I asked. "And why is not the procession forbidden?"

"Who do you think is behind it all?" he said. "Why; no one less than my Lord Shaftesbury himself. Dangerfield is but one of his tools. And that is not all."

"Lord!" said I. "What a troublous country!" (I spoke lightly, for I did not understand the weight of all these events.) "What else is the matter?"

"It is the Duke of Monmouth," he said, "who is the pawn in Shaftesbury's game. My Lord would give the world to have the Duke declared legitimate, and so oust James. His Grace of Monmouth is something of a popular hero now, after his doings in Scotland, and most of all since he stands for the Protestant Religion. He hath dared to strike out the bar sinister from his arms too; and goeth about the country as if he were truly royal. So His Royal Highness is gone back to Scotland again in a great fury; and His Majesty is once again in a strait betwixt two, as the Scriptures say. There is his Catholic brother on the one side; and there is this young spark of a Protestant bastard on the other. We shall know better tomorrow how the feeling runs. His Majesty was taken very ill in August; and I am not surprised at it."

*   *   *

This was all very heavy news for me. I had hoped in France that most at least of the Catholic troubles were over, and now, here again they were, in a new form. I sighed aloud.

"Heigho!" I said. "But this is all beyond me, Mr. Chiffinch. I had best be gone into the country."

"I think you had," he said very seriously. "You can do nothing in this place."

I was very glad when I heard him say that; for I had thought a great deal of Hare Street, and of my Cousin Dolly there; and it was good news to me to hear that I might soon see her again.

"But I must see the sight tomorrow," I said; and soon after that I took my leave.

*   *   *

It was a marvellous sight indeed, the next evening. I went to see a Mr. Martin in the morning, that lived in the Strand, a Catholic bookseller, and got leave from him to sit in his window from dinner onwards, that I might see the show.

It was about five o'clock that the affair began; and the day was pretty dark by then. A great number of people began to assemble little by little, up Fleet Street on the one side, the Strand on the other, and down Chancery Lane in the midst; for it was announced everywhere, and even by criers in some parts, that the procession would take place and would end at Temple Bar. My Lord Shaftesbury, who had lately lost the presidency of the Council, had rendered himself irreconcilable with the Duke of York, and his only hope (as well as of others with him) lay in ruining His Highness. All this, therefore, was designed to rouse popular feeling against the Duke and the Catholic cause. So this was my welcome home again!

It was strange to watch the folks assembling, and the gradual kindling of the flambeaux. In the windows on either side of the street were set candles; and a line of coaches was drawn up against the gutter on the further side. But still more strange and disconcerting were the preparations already made to receive the procession. An open space was kept by fellows with torches to the east of the City Gate; and here, looking towards the City, with her back to the Gate, close beside the Pillory, stood Queen Bess in effigy, upon a pedestal, as it were a Protestant saint in her shrine; for the day had been chosen on account of its being the day of her accession and of Queen Mary's death. She was set about with gilded laurel-wreaths, and bore a gilded sceptre; and beneath her, like some sacrificial fire, blazed a great bonfire, roaring up to heaven with its sparks and smoke. Half a dozen masked fellows, in fantastic dresses, tended the bonfire and replenished the flambeaux that burned about the effigy. Indeed it was strangely like some pagan religious spectacle — the goddess at the entrance of her temple (for the gate looked like that); and the resemblance became more marked as the ceremonies were performed which ended the show. A Catholic might well be pardoned for retorting "Idolatry," and saying that he preferred Mary Queen of Heaven to Bess Queen of England.

It was from Moorfields that the procession came, and it took a good while to come. But I was entertained enough by the sight of all the people, to pass the time away. A number of gentlefolks opposite to my window sat on platforms, all wrapped up in furs, and some of them masked, with a few ministers among them; and I make no doubt that Dr. Tonge was there, though I did not see him. But I did see a merry face which I thought was Mistress Nell Gwyn's; and whether it was she or not that I saw, I heard afterwards that she had been there, to His Majesty's great displeasure.

And in the same group I saw Mr. Killigrew's face — that had been page to Charles the First, and came back to be page to his son — for his grotesque and yet fine face was unmistakable; the profligate fop Sir George Etheredge, gambler and lampooner, with drink and the devil all over him; solemn Thomas Thynne, murdered two years afterwards, for a woman's sake, by Count Conigsmark, who was hanged for it and lay in great state in a satin coffin; and last, my Lord Dover, with his great head and little legs, looking at the people through a tortoiseshell glass. The Court, or at least, some of it, enjoyed itself here, in spite of the character of the demonstration. Meanwhile out of sight a great voice shouted jests and catchwords resonantly from time to time, to amuse the people; and the crowd, that was by now packed everywhere against the houses, upon the roofs and even up Chancery Lane, answered his hits with roaring cheers. I heard the name of the Duke of Monmouth several times; and each time it was received with acclamation. Once the Duke of York's was called out; and the booing and murring at it were great enough to have daunted even him. (But he was in Scotland now — too far away to hear it — and seemed like to remain there.) And once Mrs. Gwyn's name was shouted, and something else after it; and there was a stir on the platform where I thought I had seen her; and then a great burst of cheering; for she was popular enough, in spite of her life, for her Protestantism. (It was not works, they hated, thought I to myself, but Faith!)

The first that I knew of the coming of the procession was the sound of fifes up Fleet Street; and a great jostling and roaring that followed it by those who strove to see better. I was distracted for an instant by a dog that ran out suddenly, tail down, into the open space and disappeared again yelping. When I turned again the head of the procession was in sight, coming into view round the house that was next to Mr. Martin's.

First, between the torches that lined the procession through all its length, came a band of fifers, very fine, in scarlet tunics and stiff beaver-hats; shrilling a dirge as they walked; and immediately behind them a funeral herald in black, walking very upright and stiff, with a bell in one hand which he rang, while he cried out in a great mournful bellowing voice:

"Remember Justice Godfrey! Remember Justice Godfrey;" and then pealed upon his bell again. (It was pretty plain from that that we Catholics were to bear the brunt of all, as usual!)

Behind him came a terrible set of three. In the midst, led by a groom, was a great white horse, with bells on his bridle sounding as he came; and on his back an effigy, dressed in riding costume, with boots, and with white riding gloves and cravat all spattered over with blood. His head lolled on his shoulders, as if the neck were broken, turning a pale bloody face from side to side, with fallen jaw and great rolling melancholy eyes; for this was of Justice Godfrey. Beside him walked a man in black, that held him fast with one hand, and had a dripping dagger in the other — to represent a Jesuit. This was perhaps the worst of all; but there was plenty more to come.

There followed, after Justice Godfrey, a pardoner, dressed as a priest, in a black cope sown all over with death's heads, waving papers in his hands, and proclaiming indulgences to all Protestant-killers, so loud that he might be heard at Charing Cross; and next behind him a fellow carrying a silver cross, that shone very fine in the red light of the bonfire and the flambeaux, and drew attention to what came after. For behind him came eight Religious, Carmelites and Franciscans, in the habits of their Orders, going two by two with clasped hands and bowed heads as if they prayed; and after them that which was, in intention, the centre of all — for this was a set of six Jesuits in black, with lean painted faces, each bearing a dagger which he waved, gnashing his teeth and grinning on the folks.

There had been enough roaring and cheering before; but at this sight the people went near mad; and I had thought for an instant that the very actors would be torn in pieces for the sake of the parts they played.

Mr. Martin and his wife were close beside me in the window; and I turned to them.

"We are fortunate not to be Jesuits," I said, "and known to be such. Our lives would not be worth a pin."

He nodded at me very gravely: and I saw how white was his wife's face.

When I looked again a very brilliant group was come into view — four bishops in rochets and violet, with large pectoral crosses. These walked very proud and prelatical, looking disdainfully at the people who roared at the burlesque; and behind them, again, four more in gilded mitres. (I do not know what this generation knew of Catholic bishops; for not one in a thousand of them had ever set eyes on one.)

After a little space followed six cardinals in scarlet, very gorgeous, with caps and trains of the same colour. These swept along, looking to neither right nor left, followed by a lean man in a black silk suit and gown, skulking and bending, bearing a glass retort in one hand, and a phial, with a label flying from it, in the other. On this was written, I heard afterwards, the words "Jesuit-Powder"; but I could not read it from where I was.

Then at last the tail of the procession began to come into view.

Two priests, in great white copes, bore aloft each a tall cross; and behind them I could see through the flare and reek of the torches, a vast scarlet chair advancing above the heads of the people. It was borne on a platform, and was embroidered all over with gold and silver bullion. Upon the platform itself were four boys, two and two, on either side of the throne, in red skull-caps and cassocks and short white surplices, each with a tall red cross held in the inner hand, and a bloodstained dagger in the other, which they waved now and again. Upon the throne itself sat a huge effigy. It was dressed in a scarlet robe, embroidered like the throne; its feet in gold embroidered slippers were thrust forward on a cushion; its hands in rich gloves were clasped to the arms of the chair; and its grinning waxen face, very pale, was surmounted by a vast tiara on which were three crowns, one above the other. Round the neck hung a gold cross and chain; and a pair of great keys hung down on one side. A devil in tight fitting black, with a masked face, and long sprouting nails, with a tail hung behind him, and two tall horns on his head, rolled his eyes from side to side, and whispered continually into the ear of the effigy from behind the throne. A great mob of people and torches and guards came shouting on behind. And when I saw that, a kind of despair came upon me. If that, thought I, is what my countrymen think of Catholics and the Holy Father, what use to strive any more for their conversion?

By the time that the tail had come up, the rest of the procession was disposed round the bonfire, leaving a broad space in the midst where the throne and effigy might be set down.

And now there appeared on the Pillory beside the Queen's image, one of the six cardinals that had come up a little while before, and began a sort of rhyming dialogue with a choir that was set on another platform over against him. I could not hear all that was said, although the people kept pretty quiet to hear it too; but I heard enough. The cardinal was proclaiming the Catholic Religion as the only means of salvation and threatened both temporal and eternal punishment to all that would not have it; and the choir answered, roaring out the glories of England and Protestantism. The fifes screamed for the cardinal's words, as if accompanying them; and trumpets answered him for England; and at the end, shaking his fist at the Queen and with another gesture as of despair he came down from the Pillory.

Then came the end.

The devil, behind the throne, slipped altogether behind it and stood tossing his hands with delight; while meantime the effigy, contrived in some way I could not understand, rose stiffly from the seat and stood upright. First he lifted his hands as if in entreaty towards the Queen's image; then he shook them as if threatening, meanwhile rolling his head with its tiara from side to side as if seeking supporters. Two men then sprang upon the platform, as if in answer, dressed like English apprentices, bare-armed and with leather aprons; and these seized each an arm of the effigy; and at that the devil, after one more fit of laughter, holding his sides, and shouting aloud as if in glee, leapt down behind the platform, dragging the chair after him. The four boys stood an instant as if in terror, and then followed him, with clumsy gestures of horror.

The three figures that remained now began to wrestle together, stamping to and fro, up to the very edge, then reeling back again, and so on — the two apprentices against the great red dummy. At that the shouting of the crowd grew louder and louder, and the torches tossed up and down: it was like hell itself, for noise and terror, there in the red flare of the bonfire: and, at the last, all roaring together, with the trumpets and drums sounding, and the fifes too, the effigy was got to the edge of the platform, where it yet swayed for an instant or two, and then toppled down into the fire beneath.

It was a great spectacle, I cannot but confess it, and admirably designed; and I took my leave of Mr. Martin and his lady, and went home to supper through the crowded streets, more in tune, perhaps, with my country's state than I had been when I lolled last night in Mr. Chiffinch's closet.

CHAPTER II

With Dangerfield's demonstration in my mind I was not greatly inclined to embroil myself in other matters; and I kept my intention to ride down to Hare Street three days after, when I had done my business in London and kissed the King's hand; and this I had done by the evening of the second day. I saw His Majesty on that second day; but he was much pressed for time, and he did no more than thank me for what I had done: and so was gone. On that evening, however, a new little adventure befell me.

The taverns in town were rare places for making new acquaintances; and since I, for the most part, dined and supped in them, I met a good number of gentlemen. From these I would conceal, usually, most of my circumstances, and sometimes even my name, though that would not have told them much. Above all I was very careful to conceal my dealings with His Majesty, and as, following the directions he had first given me, I presented myself seldom or never at Court, and did my business through Mr. Chiffinch, and in his lodgings, usually, I do not suppose that there were five men in town, if so many, who knew that I had any private knowledge of him at all. In this manner then, I heard a deal of treasonable talk of which I did not think much, and only reported generally to Mr. Chiffinch when he asked me what was the feeling in town with regard to Court affairs. It was through this, and helped, I daresay, by what I have been told was the easy pleasantness which I affected in company, that I stumbled over my next adventure; and one that was like, before the end of it, to have cost me dear.

I went to supper, by chance, on the second day after my coming to London, to an inn I had never been to before — the *Red Bull* in Cheapside — a very large inn, in those days, with a great garden at the back, where gentlemen would dine in summer, and a great parlour running out into it from the back of the house, of but one story high. The rooms beneath seemed pretty full, for it was a cold night; and as there appeared no one to attend to me I went upstairs, and knocked on the door of one of the rooms. The talking within ceased as I knocked, and none answered; so I opened the door and put my head in. There was a number of persons seated round the table who all looked at me.

"This is a private room, sir," said one of them at the head.

"I beg your pardon, gentlemen," I said. "I was but looking for someone to serve me." And I was about to withdraw when a voice hailed me aloud.

"Why it is Mr. Mallock!" the voice cried; and turning again to see who it was I beheld my old friend Mr. Rumbald, seated next the one that presided.

I greeted him.

"But I had best be gone," I said. "It is a private room, the gentleman told me."

"No, no," cried the maltster. "Come in, Mr. Mallock." And he said something to the gentleman he sat by, who was dressed very finely.

I could see that something was in the wind; and as I was out for adventure, it seemed to me that here was one ready-made, however harmless it might turn out in the end. So I closed the door behind me; there was a shifting along the benches, and I stepped over into a place next my friend.

"How goes the world with you, sir?" demanded Mr. Rumbald of me, looking at my suit, which indeed was pretty fine.

"Very hungrily at present," I said. "Where the devil are the maids got to?"

He called out to the man that sat nearest the door, and he got up and bawled something down the passage.

"But it has treated me better lately," I said. "I have been in France on my affairs." (I said this with an important air, for there is no disguise so great as the truth, if it is put on a little awry.)

"Oho!" said Rumbald, who again, in spite of his old Presbyterianism, had had a cup too many. And he winked on the company. I had not an idea of what he meant by that; but I think he was but shewing off his friend as a travelled gentleman.

"And we have been speaking of England," he went on, "and of them that govern it, and of the Ten Commandments, in special the sixth."

I observed signs of consternation among one or two of the company when he said this, and remembering of what political complexion Mr. Rumbald had been on our previous meeting, I saw in general, at least, what they had been after. But what he meant of the Sixth Commandment which is that of killing, according to the Protestant arrangement of it, I understood nothing.

"And of who shall govern England hereafter," I said in a low voice, but very deliberate.

There fell a silence when I said that; and I was wondering what in God's name I should say next, when the maid came in, and I fell to abusing of her with an oath or two. When she was gone away again to get me my supper, the gentleman in the fine dress at the head of the table leaned forward a little.

"That, Mr. Mallock," he said, "is of what we were speaking. How did you know that?" "I know my friend Mr. Rumbald," I said.

This appeared to give the greatest pleasure to the maltster. He laughed aloud, and beat me on the back; but his eyes were fierce for all his merriment. I felt that this would be no easy enemy to have.

"Mr. Mallock knows me," he said, "and I know Mr. Mallock. I assure you, gentlemen, you can speak freely before Mr. Mallock." And he poured a quantity of his college-ale into a tankard that stood before me.

It appeared, however, that several of the company had sudden affairs elsewhere; and, before we even smelled of treason, three or four of them made their excuses and went away. This confirmed me in my thought that I was stumbled upon one of those little gatherings of malcontents, of whom the town was full, who talked largely over their cups of the Protestant succession and the like, but did very little. But I was not quite right in my surmise, as will appear presently.

By the time that my supper came up — (I cursed the maid again for her delay, though, poor wench, she was near run off her legs) — there were left but four of us in the room; the gentleman at the head of the table, a lean quiet man with a cast in his eye who sat opposite me, Mr. Rumbald and myself.

There was, however, a shade of caution yet left in my friend that the ale had not yet driven out; and before proceeding any further, he observed again that my fortunes had improved.

"Why, they have improved a great deal," I said — for he had caught me with my silver-hilted sword and my lace, and I saw him looking at them — "I live in Covent Garden now, where you must come and see me, Mr. Rumbald."

"And your politics with them?" he asked.

"My politics are what they ever were," I said; and that was true enough.

"You were at Temple Bar?" he asked.

"Why I only came from France the day before; but you may depend upon it I was there. It warmed my heart."

"You know who was behind it all?" asked the gentleman at the head of the table, suddenly.

I knew well enough that such men as these despise ignorance above all things, and that a shrewd fellow — or a man that they think to be one is worth a thousand simpletons in their eyes; so I made no pretence of not knowing what he meant.

"Why of course I do!" I said contemptuously. "It was my Lord Shaftesbury."

Now the truth of this was not known to everyone in London at this time, though it was known a little while later: and I should not have known it myself if Mr. Chiffinch had not told me. But these men knew it, it seemed, well enough; and my knowledge of it blew me sky-high in their view.

"My Lord Shaftesbury, God bless him!" said the lean squinting man, suddenly; and drained his mug.

"God bless him!" I said too, and put my lips to mine. My hand was immediately grasped by Mr. Rumbald; and so cordial relations were confirmed.

*   *   *

Well; we settled down then to talk treason. I must not deny that these persons skewed still some glimmerings of sense; they did not, that is to say, as yet commit themselves irrevocably to my mercy: they appeared to me to talk generally, with a view to trying me: but I acquitted myself to their satisfaction.

We deposed Charles, we excluded James, we legitimized Monmouth; we armed the loyal citizens and took away the arms of all others. We appointed even days of humiliation and thanksgiving; and we grew more enthusiastic and reckless with every mug. The lean man confided to me with infinite pride, that he had been one of the cardinals in the procession to Temple Bar; and I grasped his hand in tearful congratulation. We were near weeping with loyalty at the end, not to Charles but to Monmouth. The only man who preserved his self-control completely was the gentleman at the head of the table, though he too adventured a good deal, throwing it before me as a bait before a trout; and each time I gulped it down and asked for more. He was a finely featured man, with a nose set well out in his face, and had altogether the look and bearing of a gentleman.

It must have been full half-past nine before we broke up; and that was at the going of our president. We too rose and saw him to the door; and the lean man said he would see him downstairs, so Mr. Rumbald and I were left, he swaying a little and smiling, holding on to the door-post, and I endeavouring to preserve my dignity.

I was about to say good-night too and begone, when he plucked me suddenly by the sleeve.

"Come back again, Mr. Mallock," he said. "I have something to say to you."

We went back again, shutting the door behind us, and sat down. It was a pleasant little parlour this, decently furnished, and I feigned to be looking at the hanging that was over the press where they kept the tankards, as if I had no curiosity in the world.

"Here, Mr. Mallock," said my friend's voice behind me. "Look at this."

He had drawn out a little black pocket-book, leather-bound, and with it three or four loose papers. I sat down by him, and took it from him.

"It is some kind of an account-book," I said.

"You are right, sir," said Mr. Rumbald.

He sat with an air of vast importance, while I examined the book. It had a great number of entries, concerning such things as accounts for beer and other refreshments, with others which I could not understand. There were also the names of inns in London, with marks opposite to them, and times of day written down besides. I could make nothing of all this; so I turned to the papers. Here, to my astonishment, on one of them was written a list of names, some very well known, beginning with my Lord Shaftesbury's, and on the two others a number of notes in short-hand, with three or four of the same names as before written long-hand. One of these slipped to the floor as I held them, and I stooped to pick it up; when I raised my head again, the pocket-book and the other two papers had disappeared again into Mr. Rumbald's possession. He did not seem to have seen the one that fell, so I held it on my knee beneath the table, thinking to examine it later.

"Well?" I asked. "What is the matter?"

The maltster had an air of great mystery upon his face. He regarded me sternly, though his eyes watered a little.

"Enough to hang us all," he said; and I saw the fierce light in his eyes again, through the veil of drink.

"Why; how is that?" asked I, slipping the paper I held, behind me, and into the skirt pocket of my coat.

"Those accounts," he said, "they are all for the procession; for I provided myself a good deal of the refreshment; and was paid for it by a man of my Lord's, who has signed the book."

"And the two papers?" I asked.

"Ah!" said Mr. Rumbald. "That is another matter altogether."

I feigned that I was incurious.

"Well," I said, "every man to his own trade. I would not

meddle with another's, for the world."

"That is best," said my friend.

I tried a sentence or two more; but caution seemed to have returned to him, though a little late; and I presently saw I should get no more out of him. I congratulated him again on the pleasant evening we had spent; and five minutes later we went downstairs together, very friendly; and he winked upon me as I went out, after paying my account, as if there were some secret understanding between us.

*   *   *

I had a cold walk back to Covent Garden, remembering with satisfaction, as I went, that I had not told Mr. Rumbald more particularly where I lodged; and thinking over what I had heard. It was not a great deal after all, I thought. When all was said, I had only heard over again what was known well enough at Court, that my Lord Shaftesbury was behind this demonstration, and had his finger in the whole affair of Monmouth; I had but stumbled upon one of those companies, who were known, well enough, to be everywhere, who were for Monmouth against His Royal Highness: and I had but seen, what surely might be guessed to exist — the accounts of the refreshments supplied to the actors in the demonstration — and had been told that my Lord's man had paid the score. There might, indeed, be more behind; but of that I had no evidence at all; I had received no confidence that could be of any value: and as for the paper in my skirt-pocket, I valued it no more than a rush; and wondered I had taken the trouble to secure it.

When I reached my lodgings, I took it out and looked at it again. I had not even the means of reading it. The name of my Lord Shaftesbury, as I have said, was written in long-hand three or four times; and the Duke of Monmouth's twice. There also appeared other names of which I did not know a great deal, and one at least of which I knew nothing, which was "College"; though this for all I knew was for a college in an University. Other names were that of my Lord Essex and John Hampden, and Algernon Sidney. The paper was about a foot in length and six inches across; and I thought so little of it — thinking that a paper of importance would scarcely be entrusted to a man like Rumbald, who threw them about a tavern — that I was very near throwing it into the fire. But I kept it — though God knows that afterwards I wished I had not done so — and slipped it into my pocket-book where I kept three or four others, intending, when I had an opportunity, to give it to some clerk, learned in short-hand, to read for me.

And so I went to bed.

CHAPTER III

It was with a very happy heart that the next night, about seven o'clock, I rode down Hare Street village, and saw the lights of the house shining through the limes.

It was a very different coming back from my going. Then we four had stood together in the dark at the corner of the lane, fearing lest a window should be thrown up. Now I rode back with James, secure and content, fearing nothing: for Mr. Chiffinch had told me that all peril had passed from Dangerfield, even had he met me and known me, which was not likely. They were after other game now than the old conspirators.

I had sent a message to Hare Street on the day after I was come to London, that I would be with them on this day: and so soon as I rode into the yard the men ran out, and I heard a window open in the house; so that by the time I came to the door it was open, and my cousins there to meet me.

*   *   *

It was very strange, that evening there, to be so with my Cousin Dolly; for each of us knew, and that the other knew that too, that matters were advanced with us, since we had been through peril together. It was strange how diffident we both were, and how we could not meet one another's eyes; and yet I was aware that she would have it otherwise if she could, and strove to be natural. We had music again that night, and Dolly and her maid sang the setting of "Go, perjured man" which she had made from Mr. Wise's. For myself, I sat in a corner by the fire and watched her. She was in grey that night, with lace, and a string of little fresh-water pearls.

When she was gone to bed, my Cousin Tom and I had a crack together; and he seemed to me more sensible than I had thought him at first. We talked of a great number of things; and he asked me about France and my life there; and I had a great ado from being indiscreet and telling him too much. I represented to him that I was gone over to be out of the way of Dangerfield, as indeed I had; but I said nothing at all to him as to my business there: and he seemed content.

He told me also of what he had written to me as to the return of Mr. Harris, very tired and angry, the next afternoon after his search of the house. He had ridden near all the way to

Newmarket, inquiring for me everywhere: and had come to the conclusion at last that I had not gone that way after all.

"He was very high with me," said my Cousin Tom, "but I was higher yet. I told him that it was not my business both to make conspirators and to arrest them; and since he had done me the honour of thinking I had done the first, I had done him the honour of thinking that he could do the second: but that it seemed I was wrong in that."

This seemed a considerable effort of wit for my Cousin Tom; but scarcely one calculated to soothe Mr. Harris.

Finally, when I was thinking of bed my Cousin Tom opened out once again on an old matter that was before my mind continually now: and he spoke, I think, very sensibly.

"Cousin Roger," he said: "there is one other affair I must speak to you of, now that you are come again to Hare Street and seem likely to remain here for a while; and that is of my daughter. I know you would not have me say too much; and I will not. But have you considered the advice you said you would give me a great while ago?"

I did not answer him for a moment; for I was not sure if he were very wise or very foolish in opening upon it again. Then I determined to be open with the man.

"Cousin Tom," I said, "I am both glad and sorry that you have spoken of this; and I will tell you the whole truth, which I think perhaps you may have guessed. The reason why I could not give you advice before was that I was not sure of my own mind. Well; I am sure of it now; and I wish to ask my Cousin Dolly, so soon as I see an opportunity to do so, if she will marry me. But I must say this — that I am going to take no risks. I shall not ask her so long as I think she will refuse me; and I think, to tell the truth, that she would not have me if I asked her now."

My Cousin Tom began to speak: but I prevented him.

"One moment," I said, "and you shall say what you will. There is one reason that comes to my mind which perhaps may explain her unwillingness; and that is that she may think that she is being thrown at my head. You have been very kind, Cousin, in allowing me to make this my home in the country; and I know" — (here I lied vehemently) — "I know that nothing was further from your thoughts than this. Yet it may seem so, to a foolish maid who knows nothing of the world. I do not know if you have ever said anything to her —"

"Why, Cousin —" cried Tom, in such a manner that I knew he was lying too — "what do you think —"

"Just so," I said; for I did not wish him to lie more than he need; "I was sure —"

"I may have said a word or two, once or twice," pursued Cousin Tom, intent on his own exposure — "that she must think soon about getting married, and so forth. But to say that I have thrown her at your head, Cousin, is not, I think, a kindly thing —"

"My dear man!" cried I. "I have been saying expressly that I knew you had done nothing of the sort; but that perhaps Dolly thought so." (This quieted him a little, for I watched his face.) "So the best way, I think, is for us all to be quiet for a little and say nothing. You know now what my own wishes are; and that is enough for you and me. As to estates, I will make a settlement, if ever the marriage is arranged, that will satisfy you; but I think we need not trouble about that at present. I will do my utmost to push my suit; but it must be in my own way; and that way will be to say nothing at all for a while, but to establish easy relations with her. She is a little perturbed at present: I saw that, for I watched her tonight; and unless she can grow quiet again, all will come to nothing."

So I spoke, in the folly of my own wisdom that seemed to me so great at that time. I had dealt with men, but not at all with women, and knew nothing of them. If I had but followed my heart and spoken to her at once, while the warmth of my welcome, and the memory of the peril we had undergone together were still in heart, matters might have been very different. But I thought otherwise, and that I would be very prudent and circumspect, knowing nothing at all of a maid's heart and her ways. As for Cousin Tom, he had to yield to me; for what else could he do? The prospect that I opened before him was a better one than he could get anywhere else: he had no opening at Court, in spite of his bragging; and the Protestants round about were too wise, in their rustic way, to engage themselves with a Papist at such a time. So there the matter remained.

*　　*　　*

When I came to my chamber, it had a very pleasant aspect to me. The curtains were across the windows; a great fire blazed on the hearth — (I had heard my Cousin Dolly's footsteps pass across the landing, before she went to bed, — no doubt to put more wood on) — my bed was ready, and on the round table in the middle was a jug of horn-beam branches with some winter flowers. It was six months since I had been here; and matters were considerably better with me now than they had been then. Then I was being hunted; now I was free from all anxiety on that score: then I had been going up to London to resign what little position I had; now I was re-established, owing to what I had done in France, on a better footing than ever. More than all, I knew now, without any doubt at all, what my heart told me of my Cousin Dolly; and I was here, with every liberty to commend my suit to her.

Before I went to bed I opened the little secret cupboard by my bed, and put into it three or four private papers I had, and amongst them that written in cipher that I had had from Mr. Rumbald. Then I went to bed; and dreamed of Dolly.

Then began for me a time of great peace and serenity.

First came Christmas, with its homely joys, and Twelfth night on which we cut and ate a great cake that Dolly had made; then there was the winter's work to be done in preparation for the spring; and then spring itself, with the crocuses sprouting between the joints of the paved walk round the house; and the daffodils in the long box-bed beneath the limes. I write these little things down, for it was principally by these things that I remember those months; and the noise of the world outside seemed as sounds heard in a dream. I went up to London, now and again — but not very often; and saw His Majesty in private twice, and he honoured me by asking my advice again on certain French affairs; but, for the time, all these things were secondary in my mind to the cows of Hare Street and to how the pigs did. It is marvellous how men's minds can come down to such matters, and become absorbed in them, and let the rest of the world go hang. I thought now and again of my mission from Rome; yet I do not think I was faithless to it; for there was nothing at that time which I could do for the King; and he expressly had desired me not to mix much with the Court and so become known. The truth of the matter was that at this time he was largely occupied with a certain woman, whose name had best not be spoken; and when His Majesty ran upon those lines, he could think of little else. I sent my reports regularly to Rome; and the Cardinal Secretary seemed satisfied; and so therefore was I.

It was, with my Cousin Dolly, precisely as I had thought. She was at first very shy indeed, going up to her chamber early in the evening, so that we had little or no music; but relaxing a little as I shewed myself friendly without being forward. I caught her eyes on me sometimes; and she seemed to be appraising me, I thought in my stupidity, as to whether she could trust me not to make love to her; but now, as I think, for a very different reason; and I would see her sometimes as I went out of doors, peeping at me for an instant out of a window. It was not, however, all hide and seek. We would talk frankly and easily enough at times, and spend an hour or two together, or when her father was asleep, with the greatest friendliness; and meanwhile I, poor fool, was thinking how wise and prudent I was; and what mighty progress I was making by these crooked ways.

In Easter week we had a great happiness — so great that it near broke me down in my resolution — and I would to God it had — (at least in certain moods I wish so).

I was returning along the Barkway road from a meadow where I had been to look to the new lambs, in my working dress, when I heard a horse coming behind me. I stepped aside to let him go by, when I heard myself called.

"My man," said the voice. "Can you tell me where is Mr. Jermyn's house?"

"Yes, sir," I said. "I am going there myself."

He was a grave-looking gentleman, very dark; and as I looked at him I remembered him; but I could see he did not remember me, and no wonder, for he had only seen me once, on a very agitating occasion, for a short while. He was riding a very good horse, which was going lame, but without any servant, and he had his valise strapped on the crupper. In appearance he was a country-squire on his way to town. I determined to give him a surprise as we went along.

"I hope you are well, Mr. Hamerton," I said.

He gave a great start at that, and looked at me closely.

"I do not remember you," he said. "And why do you call me Mr. Hamerton?"

"I knew that is not the name you were usually known by, father. Would you be easier if I called you Mr. Young?"

"I give it up," he said. "Who are you, sir?"

"Do you remember a young man," I said, "a year and a half ago, who came into Mr. Chiffinch's inner parlour on a certain occasion? You were sitting near His Royal Highness; His Majesty was at the end of the table; and by you was Father Bedingfeld who died in prison in December."

He smiled at me.

"I remember everything except the young man," he said. "So you are he. And what is your name, sir?"

I told him.

"I am Mr. Jermyn's cousin," I said. "And I have been looking after his lambs for him. I would there was some spiritual shepherd who would look after us. We have not heard mass since Christmas." (For we had ridden over to Standon on that day.)

He seemed altogether easier at that.

"Why, that can be remedied tomorrow," he said. "If you have an altar stone and linen and vestments. I have all else with me."

We had these, and I told him so.

"Then you mean to lie at Hare Street tonight, sir?" I said.

"I had hoped to do so," he said. "I am come from Lincolnshire; and I was recommended to Mr. Jermyn's if I could not get so far as Standon; and I cannot, for my horse is lame."

*   *   *

My Cousin Tom received the priest in a surprising medley of emotions which he exhibited one by one to me who knew him so well. He was at first plainly terrified at receiving a priest and a Jesuit; but, presently recovered himself a little and strove to remember that here was one of God's priests who would bring a blessing on the house — (and said so); finally all else was swallowed up in pleasure, or very nearly, when I took occasion on Mr. Hamerton's going upstairs to pull off his boots, to tell him that I had seen this priest very intimate with His Royal Highness the Duke of York; and that he had been a near friend of Mr. Bedingfeld, the Duke's confessor.

My Cousin Dorothy received him with the reverence that pious maids can shew so easily towards a priest. She had his chamber ready for him in ten minutes; with fresh water in the basin and flowers upon the table: she even set out for his entertainment three or four books of devotion by his bedside. And all the time at supper she never ceased to give him attention, drawing the men's eyes to his plate and cup continually.

Mr. Hamerton was a very quiet gentleman, wonderfully at his ease at once, and never losing his discretion; he talked generally and pleasantly at supper, of his road to Hare Street, and told us an edifying story or two of Catholics at whose houses he had lain on his way from Lincolnshire. These Jesuits are wonderful folk: he seemed to know the country all over, and where were the safer districts and where the dangerous. I have no doubt he could have given me an excellent road-map with instructions that would take me safe from London to Edinburgh, if I had wished it.

"And have you never been troubled with highwaymen?" asked my Cousin Tom.

"No, Mr. Jermyn," said the priest, "except once, and that was a Catholic robber. I thought he was by the start he gave when he saw my crucifix as he was searching me; and taxed him with it. So the end was, he returned me my valuables, and took a little sermon from my lips instead."

*   *   *

When supper was over, and Dorothy had gone upstairs to make all ready for mass on the next morning, Mr. Hamerton, at our questioning, began to tell us a little of the state of politics and what he thought would happen; and every word that he said came true.

"His Grace of Monmouth will be our trouble," he said. "The King adores him; and he hath so far prevailed with His Majesty as to get the Duke of York sent twice to Scotland. I think few folk understand what feeling there is in the country for the Protestant Duke. It was through my Lord Shaftesbury, who is behind him, that His Royal Highness was actually sent away, for Monmouth could do nothing without him; and I have no kind of doubt that he has further schemes in his mind too."

(This was all fulfilled a couple of months later, as I remembered when the time came, by my Lord Shaftesbury's actually presenting James' name as that of a recusant, before the grand jury of Middlesex; but the judges dismissed the jury immediately.)

"And you think, father," asked my Cousin Tom very solemnly, "that these seditions will lead to trouble?"

"I have no doubt of it at all," said he. "The country — especially London — is full of disaffection. Their demonstration last year did a deal to stir it up. The Duke of York is back now, against my advice; but I have no doubt he will have to go on his travels again. Were His majesty to die now — *(quod Deus avertat!)* — I do not know how we should stand."

*   *   *

Mr. Hamerton took occasion to ask me that night, when we were alone for a minute or two, what I was doing in the country.

"I remember you perfectly now," said he. "Father Whitbread spoke to me of you, besides."

I told him that I had nothing to do in town; and with His Majesty's consent was lying hid for a little, in order that what little was known of me might be forgotten again.

"Well; I suppose you are wise," he said, "and that you will be able to do more hereafter. But the time will come presently when we shall all be needed."

It was on the tip of my tongue to ask him if he could read cipher, and to shew him my paper — reminded of it, by his talk of disaffection; but my Cousin Tom came back at that moment; and I put it off; and I presently forgot it again.

*   *   *

The memory of the mass that we heard next morning will never leave me; for it was the first time that I had heard it in the house.

We used the long attic, for fear of disturbance, and had a man posted beneath — for it was still death for a priest to say mass in England. All the servants that were Catholics were there; and all, I think, went to the sacraments. Mr. Hamerton heard confessions before the mass began.

The north end of the attic had been prepared by Dolly and her maid; and looked very pretty and fine. A couple of men had carried up a great low press, that had the instruments of the Passion painted upon its panels; and this served for an altar. Behind it Dolly had put up a hanging from downstairs, that was of Abraham offering Isaac, and had set upon the altar a pair of silver candlesticks from the parlour, and a little standing crucifix, with jugs of country flowers between the candlesticks and the cross. She had laid too, as a foot-pace, a Turkey rug that came too from the parlour; and had put a little table to serve as a credence. Mr. Hamerton had with him little altar-vessels made for travelling, with a cup that unscrewed from the stem, and every other necessary except what he asked us to provide.

*   *   *

It is the experience of everyone, I think, that mass differs from mass, as a star (in the apostle's words) differs from another star in glory — I do not mean in its essential effects, for that is the same always, but in the devotion which it arouses in those that hear it. This mass then seemed to me like scarcely any other that I had ever heard, except perhaps that at which I received my first communion in the country church in France. Mr. Hamerton said it with great deliberation and recollection; and, as my Cousin Tom served him, as a host should, I was not distracted by anything. My Cousin Dolly and I kneeled side by side in front, and again, side by side, to receive Holy Communion.

I was in a kind of ecstasy of delight, and not, I think unworthily; for, though much of my delight came from being there with my cousin, and receiving our Lord's Body with her, I do not think that is any dishonour to God whom we must love first of all, to find a great joy in loving Him in the company of those we love purely and uprightly. So at least it seems to me.

*   *   *

Mr. Hamerton told us he must be riding very early; and not much after seven o'clock we stood at the gate to bid him farewell. I made my man James go with him so far as Ware to set him on his road, though the priest begged me not to trouble myself.

When I came back to the house I was in a torment of indecision as to whether this would not be the best occasion I could ever find of telling my Cousin Dorothy all that was in my heart in her regard; and I even went into the Great Chamber after her, still undecided. But her manner prevented me; for I thought I saw in her something of a return of that same shyness which she had shewed to me when I had come last time back to Hare Street; and I went out again without saying one word except of the priest's visit and of what a good man he seemed.

Even then, I think, if I had spoken, matters might have taken a very different course; but, whether through God's appointment or my own diffidence, this was not to be; and again I said nothing to her.

CHAPTER IV

Our next adventure, not unlike the last exteriorly, was very different from it interiorly; and led to very strange results in the event. It came about in this way.

It was in May that Mr. Hamerton had come to us, for Easter that year fell in that month; and the weather after that, which had been very bitter in the winter, with so much snow as I never saw before, but clearer about Eastertime, fell very wet and stormy again in June.

It was on a Thursday evening, in the first week in June, that the bad weather set in with a violent storm of rain and a high wind. We sat in the Great Chamber after supper, and had some music as usual: and between the music we listened to the gusts of wind and the rattle of the rain, which made so great a noise that Dolly said that it was no use for her to go to bed yet, for that she would not sleep if she went. Her maid went to bed; and we three sat talking till nearly half-past ten o'clock, which is very late for the country where men rise at four o'clock.

The wind made such a noise that we heard nothing of the approach to the house; and the first that we knew of anyone's coming was a hammering at the door.

"Why, who is that;" said I, "that comes so late?"

I could see that my Cousin Tom did not like it, for his face shewed it — (I suppose it was the memory of that other time when the hammering came) — so I said nothing, but went myself to the outer door and unbolted it.

A fellow stood there in a great riding-cloak; but I could see he wore some kind of a livery beneath.

"Well," I said, "what do you want?"

He saw that I was a gentleman by my dress; and he answered me very civilly.

"My master is benighted, sir," said he; "and he bid me come and ask whether he might lie here tonight. There is no inn in the place."

"Why, who is your master?" I asked.

He did not seem to hear my question, for he went on immediately.

"There are only five of the party, sir," he said. "Two gentlemen and three servants."

I saw that my Cousin Tom was behind me now; and that

Dolly was looking from the door of the Great Chamber.

"You have not yet told us," I said, "what your master's name is."

"I think, sir, he had best answer that," said the fellow.

Now this might very well be a Catholic, and perhaps an important person who had heard of Mr. Jermyn, but did not wish to advertise who himself was. I looked at my Cousin Tom; and thought from his look that the same thought had come to him.

"Well, Cousin?" I said.

"They had best come in —" he said shortly. "Dolly, rouse some of the servants. They will want supper, I suppose."

He nodded to the man, who went back immediately; and a minute later two gentlemen came up the flagged path, also in great cloaks that appeared soaked with the rain.

"By God, sir!" said the first of them, "we are grateful to you. This is a wild night."

My Cousin, Tom said something civil, and when the door was shut, helped this man off with his cloak, while I helped the other. The former was explaining all the while how they were on their way to town from Newmarket; and how they had become bogged a little after Barkway, losing their road in the darkness. They had intended to push on to Waltham Cross, he said, or Ware at the least, and lie there. He spoke with a merry easy air that shewed him for a well-bred and pleasant fellow. My own man said nothing, but left it all to the other.

When I turned to see the one who spoke, I was more surprised than ever in all my life before; for it was no other than the Duke of Monmouth himself. He looked a shade older than when I had last seen him in the park above a year ago; but he was the very same and I could not mistake him. As for me, he would not know me from Adam, for he had never spoken with me in all his life. I did not know what to do, as to whether I should make to recognize him or not; but he saved me the trouble; for as I followed the others into the Great Chamber, he was already speaking.

"It is very good of you, Mr. Jermyn," he said, "to receive us like this. My name is Morton, and my friend's here Mr. Atkins. You can put us where you will — on the floor if you have no other place."

"We can do better than that, sir," said Tom. "There is only my daughter here and Mr. Mallock my cousin. My daughter is gone to call the servants."

The Duke looked very handsome and princely as he stood on the hearth, although there was no fire, and surveyed the room. He was in a dark blue riding-suit, darker than it should be upon the shoulders with the rain that had soaked through his cloak; but it was of the colour of his eyes that were very fine and attractive; and he wore his own hair. The other man looked pretty mean beside him; and yet he was not ill-looking. He was a fair man, too, with a rosy face; in a buff suit.

"We can manage two changes of clothes, Mr. Morton," went on my Cousin Tom, "if you fear to take a cold; or you can sup immediately; as you will."

"Why, Mr. Jermyn; I think we will sup first and go to bed afterwards. The clothes can be dried, no doubt, before morning."

In spite of all his efforts, he spoke as one born to command and with a kind of easy condescension too; and certainly this had its effect upon poor Tom; for he was all eagerness and welcome, who just now had been a shade surly. He was beginning to say that it was for his guests to choose, when my Cousin Dolly came in suddenly through the open door.

"Why here is my little maid, gentlemen —" he said; and Dolly did her reverence.

Now I had in my mind no thought of jealousy at all; and yet when I saw how the Duke bowed to my cousin, I am bound to say that a touch of it pierced me like a dart — there and gone again, I thought. But it had been there. I thought how few gentlemen poor Dolly saw down here in Hare Street: beyond the parson — and he was a man who would go out before the pudding in a great house, and marry the lady's maid — there was scarce one who might write Esquire after his name; and the breeding of most of the squires was mostly rustical. As for her, she did her reverence very prettily, without a trace of the country in it; and, strange to say, her manner seemed to change. I mean by that, that she seemed wholly at her ease in this new kind of company, fully as much as with her maids.

"You have had a very wet ride, sir," she said, without any sign of confusion or shyness; "the maids are kindling a fire in the kitchen, to dry your clothes before morning: and your men shall have beds in the attic."

The Duke made a pretty answer, which she took as prettily.

"And a cold supper shall be in immediately," she said.

Then my Cousin Tom must needs begin upon the maid, as if she were a child, or idiotic; and say what a good housekeeper his little maid was to him, and how she could do so many things; and the Duke took it all with courtesy, yet did not encourage it, as if he understood her ways better than her father did — which was, very likely, true enough.

"And you come up to London, mistress," he said, "no doubt," with a look at her dress that was not at all insolent, and yet very plain. And it was indeed a pretty good one; and I remember it very well. It was cut like a French sac — a fashion that had first come in about ten years before, and still lasted; and was a little lower at the throat than many that she wore. It was of a brownish kind of yellow, of which I do not know the name, and had white lace to it, and silver lace on the bodice. She was sunburnt again, but not too much, as I had first seen her; and her blue eyes looked very bright in her face; and she wore a ring on either hand, as she usually did in the evening, and had her little pearls round her neck. It was strange to me how I observed all this, so soon as the Duke had drawn attention to it; whereas I had not observed it particularly before.

Wen we went into supper it was the same with the Duke and her. He behaved to her with the greatest deference, yet not at all exaggerated so as to be in the least insolent. He treated her, it appeared to me, as he would have treated one of his own ladies, though there had been every excuse, especially with Cousin Tom's way of speaking to her, and the deep country we were in, if he had not noticed her at all. Mr. Atkins, as he called himself, followed suit; but said very little. Once, when the dishes had to be taken away, and Dolly rose to do it — before I could move — (my Cousin Tom, of course, sat there like a dummy) — I observed the Duke make a little movement with his eyes towards Mr. Atkins, who immediately rose up and did it for her.

The effect of all this upon me was to make me do my best in talk; but it was not very easy without betraying that I knew more of the Court than might be supposed; but the Duke outdid me every time. He listened with the greatest courtesy; and then said something a little better. I think I have never seen a man do better; but it was always so with him. Five years later he won the hearts of all the drapers in Taunton, in that terrible enterprise of his, besides ranging on his side some of the noblest blood in England. Twenty-six young maids in that town gave him a Bible and a pair of colours worked by their hands; and twenty-six young maids, it was said, went away after it in love with him. He did not prove himself very much of a hero in the field; but from his manner in company one could never have guessed at that. He had all the bearing of a prince, and all the charm of a boy with it.

My Cousin Tom said something when supper was ending about Dolly's skill in music; and how she and her maid sang together.

"May we not hear it for ourselves?" asked the Duke.

"But you are wet, sir," said my Cousin Tom.

The Duke smiled.

"I shall not think of that, sir," he said, "if Mistress Dorothy will sing to us."

Well; so it was settled. The maid was in the kitchen, and was presently fetched; and she and Dolly sang together once or twice, though it was now after eleven o'clock. They sang Mr. Wise's "Go, perjured man," I remember, again; and then M. Grabu's "Song upon Peace." The Duke sat still in the great chair, shading his eyes from the candlelight, and watching my Cousin Dolly: and once, when my Cousin Tom broke in upon the second song with something he had just thought of to say, he put him aside with a gesture, very royal and commanding, and yet void of offence, until the song was done.

"I beg your pardon, Mr. Jermyn," he said a moment afterwards, "but I have never been so entranced. What was it that you wished to say?"

As Dolly came towards him he stood up. "Mistress Dorothy," he said, "you have given us a great deal of pleasure." And he said this with so much gravity and feeling that she flushed. It was the first evident sign she had given that he had pleased her.

"And I mean it," he went on, "when I say it is a pity you do not come to town more often. Such singing as that should have a larger audience than the two or three you have had tonight."

Dolly smiled at him.

"Thank you, sir," she said. "But I know my place better than that."

This was all a little bitter to me; for by this time a wild kind of jealousy had risen again in me which I knew to be unreasonable, and yet could not check. It was true that I myself took the greatest pains never to forget my manners; but I knew very well that novelty has a pleasantness all of its own; and the novelty of such company as this, charged with the peculiar charm of the Duke's manner, must surely, I thought, have its effect upon her.

"Well," said he, "I could spend all night in this chamber with such music; but I must not keep Mistress Dorothy from her sleep another moment."

He kissed her fingers with the greatest grace, and then bowed by the door as she went out.

When we had taken them to the great guest-room that was as large, very nearly, as the Great Chamber, and over it, and bidden them good-night, my Cousin Tom remembered that we had forgotten to ask Mr. Morton at what time he must ride in the morning; so I went back again to ask.

I stayed at the door for one instant after knocking, for it seemed they had not heard me; and in that little interval I heard the Duke's voice within, very distinct.

"A damned pretty wench," he cried. "We must —"

And at that I opened the door and went in, my jealousy suddenly flaming up again, so that I lost my wits.

They stared at me in astonishment. The Duke already was stripped to his shirt by one of the beds.

"I beg your pardon, Sir," I said. "But at what hour will Your Grace have the horses?"

Mr. Atkins wheeled round full upon me; and the Duke's mouth opened a little. Then the Duke burst into a fit of laughter.

"By God, sir!" he said. "You have detected us. How long have you known it?"

"From the moment Your Grace took off your hat," I said.

He laughed again, highly and merrily.

"Well; no harm is done," he said. "We took other names to make matters easier for all. You have told Mr. Jermyn?"

"No, sir," I said.

"I beg of you not to do so," he said. "It will spoil all. Nor Mistress Dorothy. It is far easier to do without ceremony now and again."

I bowed again; but I said nothing.

"Then you may as well know," said the Duke, "that Mr. Atkins is none other than my Lord of Essex. We have been at Newmarket together."

I bowed to my lord, and he to me.

"Well — the horses," said Monmouth. "At eight o'clock, if you please."

I said nothing to Tom, for I was very uncertain what to do; and though I was mad with anger at what I had heard the Duke say as I waited at the door — (though now I cannot say that there was any great harm in the words themselves) — I still kept my wits enough to know that I was too angry to judge fairly. I lay awake a long time that night, turning from side to side after that I had heard the wet clothes of our guests carried downstairs to be dried by morning before the fire. It was all a mighty innocent matter, so far as it had gone; but I would not see that. I told myself that a man of the Duke's quality should not come to a little country-house under an *alias*, even if he had been bogged ten times over; that he should not make pretty speeches to a country maid and kiss her fingers, and hold open the door for her, even though all these things or some of them were just what I had done myself. Frankly, I understand now that no harm was meant; that every word the Duke had said was true, and that it was but natural for him to try to please all across whom he came; but I would not see it at the time.

On the next morning when I came downstairs early it seemed to me that my Cousin Dorothy was herself downstairs too early for mere good manners. The guests were not yet stirring; yet the maids were up, and the ale set out in the dining-room, and the smell of hot oat-cake came from the kitchen. There were flowers also upon the table; and my cousin was in a pretty brown dress of hers that she did not wear very often.

I looked upon her rather harshly; and I think she observed it; for she said nothing to me as she went about her business.

I went out into the stable-yard to see the horses; and found my Cousin Tom there already, admiring them; and indeed they were fine, especially a great dappled grey that was stamping under the brush of the fellow who had first knocked at our door last night.

"That is Mr. Morton's horse, I suppose?" said Tom.

The man who was grooming him did not speak; and Tom repeated his question.

"Yes, sir," said the man, with a queer look which I understood, though Tom did not, "this is Mr. Morton's."

"And the chestnut is Mr. Atkins'?" asked my cousin.

"Just so, sir; Mr. Atkins'," said the man, with the corners of his mouth twitching.

The grinning ape — as I thought him — very nearly set me off into saying that I knew all about it; and that the yellow saddle-cloth was the colour the Duke of Monmouth used always; but I did not. It appeared to me then the worst of manners that these personages should come and make a mock of country-folk, so that even the servants laughed at us.

*   *   *

Our guests were downstairs when I came in again, and talking very merrily to my Cousin Dorothy, who was as much at her ease as last night. The Duke sneezed once or twice.

"You have taken a cold, sir," said Dolly.

"It was in a good cause," he said; and sneezed again.

"*Salute,*" said I.

He gave me a quick look, astonished, I suppose, that a rustic should know the Italian ways.

"*Grazie,*" said he, smiling. "You have been in Italy, Mr. Mallock?"

"Oh! I have been everywhere," I said, with a foolish idea of making him respect me.

*   *   *

When they rode away at last, we all stood at the gate to watch them go. The storm had cleared away wonderfully; and the air was fresh and summerlike, and ten thousand jewels sparkled on the limes. They made a very gallant cavalcade. The horses had recovered from their weariness, for they were finely bred, all five of them; and the Duke's horse especially was full of spirit, and curvetted a little, with pleasure and the strength of our corn, as he went along. The servants' liveries too were gay and pleasant to the eye: — (they were not the Duke's own liveries; for when he went about outside town he used a plainer sort) — and the Duke's dark blue, with his fair curls and his great hat which he waved as he went, and my Lord Essex's spruce figure in his buff, all made a very pretty picture as they went up the village street.

It was this, I think, and my Cousin Dolly's silence as she looked after them, that determined me; and as we three went back again up the flagged path to the house, and the servants round again to the yard, I spoke.

"Cousin Tom," I said. "Do you wish to know who our guests were?"

He looked at me in astonishment, and my Cousin Dolly too.

"Mr. Morton is the Duke of Monmouth," I said, "and Mr. Atkins, my Lord Essex."

CHAPTER V

It was a long time before my Cousin Tom recovered from his astonishment and his pleasure at having entertained such personages in his house. He told me, of course, presently, when he had had time to think of it, that he had guessed it all along, but had understood that His Grace wished to be *incognito*; and I suppose at last he came to believe it. He would fall suddenly musing in the evenings; and I would know what he was thinking of; and it was piteously amusing to see, how one night again, not long after, he rose and ran to the door when a drunken man knocked upon it, and what ill words he gave him when he saw who it was. His was a slow-moving mind; and I think he could not have formed the project, which he afterwards carried out, while I was with him, or he must have let it out to me.

*　　*　　*

It was a little piteous, too, to see with what avidity he seized upon any news of the Duke, and how his natural inclinations and those consonant with his religion strove with his new-found loyalty to a bastard. A week or two later we had news of the attempt made by my Lord Shaftesbury to injure the Duke of York's cause by presenting his name as that of a recusant, to the Middlesex grand jury. It was a mighty bold thing to do, and though the attempt failed so far as that the judges dismissed the jury while they were still deliberating, it shewed how little my Lord feared the Duke or His Majesty and how much resolved he was to establish, if he could, the Protestant succession and the Duke of Monmouth's pretended claim to it. A deal of nonsense, too, was talked at this time of how the Duke was truly legitimate, and how Mistress Lucy Walters had been secretly married to the King, before ever poor Queen Catherine had been heard of; and the proofs of all this, it was reported, were in a certain Black Box that no one had ever set eyes on; and the matter became so much a thing of ridicule that once at the play, I think, when one of the actors carried on a black box, there was a roar of laughter and jeering from the pit.

It was wonderful to hear my Cousin Tom hold forth upon the situation.

One evening in September, two months after our adventure of the Duke's coming, after a long silence, he made a little discourse upon it all.

"I should not be surprised," said he, "if there was more in the tale than most men think. It is not likely that the proofs of the marriage would be easy to come by, in such a case; for Mistress Walters, whom I think I once saw at Tunbridge Wells, was not at all of the King's position even by blood; and it is less likely that His Majesty, who was but a very young man at that time, would have stood out against her when she wished marriage. Besides there is no doubt that he knew her long before there was any prospect of his coming to the throne. Then too there has always appeared, to my mind at least, something in the Duke's bearing and carriage that it would be very hard for a bastard to have. He has a very princely air."

To such talk as this I would make no answer; but I would watch my Cousin Dorothy's face; and think that I read there something that I did not like — an interest that she should not feel: and, after a pause my Cousin Tom would proceed in his conjectures.

It was on the day following this particular discourse, which I remember very well, for my jealousy had so much worked up that I was very near breaking my resolution and telling my Cousin Dolly all that was in my heart, that a letter came for me from Mr. Chiffinch, so significant that I will write down some sentences of it.

"His Majesty bids me to write to you to come up to town again for a few days. He thinks that you may perhaps be of some use with His Royal Highness to urge him to go back to Scotland again, which at present he vows that he will not do. His Majesty is aware that the Duke scarcely knows you at all; yet he tells me to say this, and that I will explain to you when you come how you can be of service. There will be a deal of trouble this autumn; the Parliament is to meet in October, and will be in a very ill-humour, it is thought."

There was a little more of this sort; and then came a sentence or two that roused my anger.

"I have heard much here of your entertainment of the Duke of Monmouth, and of what a pretty girl your cousin is. His Majesty laughed very much when he heard of it; and swears that he suspects you of going over to the Protestant side after all. The Duke knows nothing of what you are, or of anything you have done; but he has talked freely of his entertainment at Hare Street, thinking it, I suppose, to be a Protestant house. In public the King has had nothing to say to him; but he loves him as much as ever, and would not, I think be very sorry, in his heart, though he never says so, if he were to be declared legitimate."

This made me angry then, for what the letter said as to the Duke of Monmouth's talk; and it disconcerted me too, for, if the King himself were to join the popular party, there would be little hope of the Catholic succession. The Duchess of Portsmouth, also, I had heard, had lately become of that side; and I dared say it was she who had talked His Majesty round.

Now my Cousin Tom knew that I had had this letter, for he had seen the courier bring it; but he did not know from whom it came; and, as already he was a little suspicious, I thought, of what I did in town, I thought it best to tell him that it was from a friend at Court; and what it said as to the Duke of Monmouth's talk, hoping that this perhaps might offend him against the Duke. But it had the very opposite effect, much to my discomfiture.

"His Grace says that, does he?" he said, smiling. "I am sure it is very courteous of him to remember his poor entertainment"; and (Dolly coming in at this instant) he told her too what the Duke had said.

"Hear what the Duke of Monmouth hath been saying, my dear! He says you are a mighty pretty girl."

And Dolly, greatly to my astonishment, did not seem displeased, as soon as she had heard the tale; for she laughed and said nothing.

*   *   *

As I rode up to London next day in answer to my summons, I was wondering how in the world I could be of service to the Duke of York. As Mr. Chiffinch had said, I knew next to nothing of him, nor he of me; but when I was gone round to the page's rooms the morning after I came, he told me something of the reasons for which I had been summoned.

"Such Jesuits as are left," he said, "and the Duke's confessor among them, seem all of opinion that the Duke had best remain in London and fight it out. We hear, without a doubt, that my Lord Shaftesbury, who seems most desperate, will bring in the Exclusion Bill again this Session; and the priests say that it is best for His Royal Highness to be here; and to plead again for himself as he did so well two years ago. His Majesty on the other hand is honestly of opinion — and I would sooner trust to his foresight than to all the Jesuits in the world — that he himself can fight better for his brother if that brother be in Scotland; for out of sight, out of mind. And he desires you, as a Catholic, yet not a priest, to go and talk to the Duke on that side. He hath sent half a dozen to him already; and, since he knows that the Duke is aware of what you have done in France, he thinks that your word may tip the balance. For the Duke, I think, is in two minds, beneath all his protestations."

For myself, I was of His Majesty's opinion; for the sight of the Duke irritated folk who had not yet forgotten the Oates Plot; and I consented very willingly to go and see him.

*   *   *

I was astonished to find that by now I had really become something of a personage myself, amongst those few who had heard what I had done in France; and I was received by His Royal Highness in his lodgings after supper that evening with a very different air from that which he had when I had last spoken with him.

The Duke was pacing up and down his closet when I came in, and turned to me with a very friendly manner.

"Mr. Mallock," he said, when I had saluted him and was sat down, "I am very glad to see you. His Majesty has told me all that you have done, and has urged me to see you, as you are devoted as I know, to the Catholic cause, and know the world too; and men's minds. Do you think I should go or stay?"

"Sir," I said, "my opinion is that you should go. There is a quantity of disaffection in town. I have met with a good deal of it myself. If Your Royal Highness is to be seen continually going about, that disaffection will be kept alive. Men are astonishingly stupid. They act, largely, upon that which they see, not on that which they know: and by going to Scotland you will meet them both ways. They will not see Your Highness at all; and all that they will know of you is that you are doing the King's work and helping the whole kingdom in Edinburgh."

"But they say I torture folks there!" said the Duke.

"They say so, Sir. They will say anything. But not a reasonable man believes it."

(It was true, indeed, that such gossip went about; but the substance of it was ridiculous. Good fighters do not torture; and no one denied to the Duke the highest pitch of personal courage. He had fought with the greatest gallantry against the Dutch.)

He said nothing to that; but sat brooding.

His closet was a very magnificent chamber; but not so magnificent as he who sat in it. He was but just come from supper, and wore his orders on his coat; but all his dress could not distract those who looked at him from that kingly Stuart face that he had. He was, perhaps, the heaviest looking of them all, with not a tithe of Monmouth's brilliant charm, or the King's melancholy power; yet he too had the air of command and more than a touch of that strange romance which they all had. Until that blood is diluted down to nothing, I think that a Stuart will always find men to love and to die for him. But it was Stuart against Stuart this time; so who could tell with whom the victory would lie?

So I was thinking to myself, when suddenly the Duke looked up.

"Mr. Mallock," he said, "I hear that you have a very persuasive manner with both men and women. There is an exceedingly difficult commission which I wish you would execute for me. You have spoken with the Duchess of Portsmouth?"

"Never, Sir," I said. "I have seen Her Grace in the park only."

"Well; she has thrown her weight against me with the King. God knows why! But I wonder you have not met her?"

"Sir, I never go to Court, by His Majesty's wish."

"Yes," he said. "But Her Grace is the King's chief agent in his French affairs; and you are in them too, I hear. But that is His Majesty's way; he uses each singly, and never two together if he can help it." (This was perfectly true, and explained a good deal to me. I had heard much of the Duchess in France, but nothing at all of her from the King.)

"Well," continued the Duke, "I wish you would see her for me, Mr. Mallock; and try to get from her why she is so hot against me. She is a Catholic, as you are, and she should not be so. But she is all on fire for Monmouth and the Protestant succession; and she is all powerful with the King."

"I shall be happy to do what I can, Sir," said I, "but I do not suppose Her Grace will confide in me."

"I know that," he said, "but you may pick up something. You are the fourth I have sent on that errand, and nothing come of it."

We talked a while longer on these affairs, myself more and more astonished at the confidence given me (but I think now that it was because the Duke had so few that he could trust); and when I took my leave it was with a letter written and signed and sealed by the Duke, which I was to present at Her Grace's lodgings immediately.

The Duchess, at this time, was, I think, the most powerful figure in England; since her influence over the King was unbounded. She had come to England ten years ago as Charles' mistress, a good and simple maid in the beginning, as I believe, and of good Breton parents, who would not let her go to the French Court, yet were persuaded to let her go to the English — where, God help her! she soon ceased to be either good or simple. In the year seventy-two she was created Duchess of Portsmouth who up to that time had been the Breton woman Madame Kéroual (or, as she was called in England Madam Carwell). Three years later her son had been made Duke of Richmond. At the time of the Popish Plot she had been terrified of her life, and it was only at the King's persuasion that she remained in England. I cannot say that she was popular with the people, for her coach was cried after pretty often unless she had her guards with her; and this always threw her into paroxysms of terror. Yet she remained in England, and was treated as of royal blood both by Charles who loved her, and James who feared her.

A couple of days later I received a message to say that Her Grace would receive me after supper on that same evening: so I put on my finest suit, and set out in a hired coach.

The Duchess lived at this time in lodgings at the end of the Great Gallery in Whitehall; and I think that of all the apartments I had ever set eyes on — even the royal lodgings themselves — this was the finest; and no wonder, for they had been pulled down two or three times before she was satisfied, thus fulfilling the old proverb of Setting a Beggar on Horseback. I was made to wait awhile in an outer chamber, all as if she were royal; and I examined the pieces of furniture there, and there was nothing in the Queen's own lodging to approach to them — so massy was the plate and so great and exquisitely carved the tables and chairs. When I was taken through at last by a fellow dressed in a livery like the King's own, the next room, where I was bidden to sit down, was full as fine. There was a quantity of tapestry upon the walls, of new French fabric, so resembling paintings that I had to touch before I was sure of them — of Versailles, and St. Germain, with hunting pieces and landscapes and exotic fowls. There were Japan cabinets, screens and pendule clocks, and a great quantity of plate, all of silver, as well as were the sconces that held the candles; and the ceilings were painted all over, as were His Majesty's own, I suppose by Verrio.

As I sat there, considering what I should say to her, I heard music continually through one of the doors; and when at last it was flung open and my Lady came through, she brought, as it were, a gust of music with her.

I bowed very low, as I had been instructed, in spite of the character of the woman, and then I kneeled to kiss her hand. Then she sat down, and left me standing, like a servant.

She appeared at that time to be about thirty years old, though I think she was far beyond this; but she had a wonderfully childish face, very artfully painted and darkened by the eyes. I cannot deny, however, that she was very handsome indeed, and well set-off by her jewels and her silver-lace gown, cut very low so as to shew her dazzling skin. Her fingers too, when I kissed them, were but one mass of gems. Her first simplicity was gone, indeed.

I loathed this work that I was sent on; since it forced me to be civil to this spoiled creature, instead of, as I should have wished, naming her for what she was, to her face. However, that had been done pretty often by the mob; so I doubt if I could have told her anything she did not know already. Her voice was set very low and was a little rough; yet it was not ugly at all. She spoke in French; and so did I.

"Well, Mr. Mallock," she said, "I have company; but I did not wish to refuse another of His Royal Highness's ambassadors. What is the matter now, if you please?"

Now I knew that this kind of personage loved flattery — for it was nothing but this that had ruined her — and that it could scarcely be too thick: so I framed my first sentences in that key: for, after all, my first business was to please her.

"His Royal Highness is desolated, madam," I said, "because he thinks he has displeased you."

"Displeased me!" she cried. "Why, what talk is this of a Prince to a poor Frenchwoman?"

She smiled very unpleasantly as she said this; and nearly all the time I was with her, her eyes were running up and down my figure. I was wearing a good ring or two also, and my sword-hilt was very prettily set with diamonds; and she always had an eye for such things.

"There can be no talk of Prince and subject, madam," I said, "when Her Grace of Portsmouth is in question."

She smiled once more; and I saw that she liked this kind of talk. So I gave her plenty of it.

"La! la!" she said. "This is very pretty talk. What is your business, sir, if you please?"

"It is what I have said, madam; and nothing else upon my honour! His Royal Highness is seriously discomposed."

"Then why does he not come to see me, and ask me himself?" snapped my Lady. "He hath not been these three months back.

Why does he send a — a messenger?"

(She was on the very point of saying *servant*; and it pleased me that she had not done so. I noted also in my mind that wounded vanity was one of the reasons for her behaviour, as it usually is with a woman.)

"Madam," I said, "His Royal Highness does not come, I am sure, because he does not know how he would be received. It seems that Your Grace's favour is given to another, altogether, now."

"God bless us!" said the Duchess. "Why not say Monmouth and be done with it?"

"It is Your Grace who has named him," I said: "but the Duke of Monmouth is the very man."

She gave a great flirt to her fan; and I saw by her face what I had suspected before, that it was not only with music that she was intoxicated. Then she jerked her pretty head.

"Sit down, sir," she said; and when I had done so, pleased at the progress I was making, she told me everything I wanted to know, though she did not think so herself.

"See here, Mr. Mallock: You appear an intelligent kind of man. Now ask yourself a question or two, and you will know all that I know myself. What kind of a chance, think you, has a Catholic as King of England, as against a Protestant; and what kind of a chance, think you, has the Duke of York beside the Duke of Monmouth? I speak freely, because from your having come on this errand, I suppose you are a man that can be trusted. I wonder you have not seen it for yourself. His Royal Highness has no tact — no *aplomb*: he sets all against him by his lordly ways. He could not make a friend of any man, to save his life: he can never forget his royalty. He sulks there in his lodgings, and will not even come to see a poor Frenchwoman. And now, sir, you know all that I know myself."

The woman's ill-breeding came out very plainly when she spoke; and I remember even then wondering that His Majesty could make so much of her. But it is often the way that men of good breeding can never see its lack in others, especially in women: or will not. However I concealed all this from Her Grace, and let go more of my courtesy.

"But, madam," I said, "with all the goodwill in the world it is Versailles to a china orange that His Royal Highness will succeed in the event. I do not say that he will make as good a King as the Duke of Monmouth, nor that his being a Catholic will be anything but a disadvantage to him; but disadvantages or no, if he is King, it is surely better to be upon his side, and help, not hinder him."

I would not have dared to say such a thing to a respectable woman; for it advised her, almost without disguise, to look to her own advantage only.

She gave me a sharp look.

"That is where we are not agreed," said she.

I made a little despairing gesture with my hands.

"Well, madam — if you do not accept facts —"

"Why do you think the Duke of York is so sure to succeed?" she asked sharply; and I saw that I had touched her.

"Madam," I said, "we English are a very curious people. It is true that we cut off His late Majesty's head; but it is also true that we welcomed back his son with acclamation. We are not quick and logical as is your own glorious nation; we have very much more sentimentality; and, among those matters that we are senti- mental about, is that of Royalty. I dare wager a good deal that if government by Monarchy goes in either of our countries, it will go in Your Grace's fatherland first. We abuse those in high places, and we disobey them, and we talk against them; yet we cling to them.

"And there is a second reason —" I went on rapidly; for she was at the point of speaking — "We are a highly respectable nation, with all the prejudices of respectability; and one of these prejudices concerns His Grace of Monmouth's parentage" — (I saw her flare scarlet at that; but I knew what I was doing) — "It is a foolish Pharisaic sort of prejudice, no doubt, madam; but it is there; and I do not believe —"

She could bear no more; for her own son had precisely that bar sinister also; and in her anger she said what I wished to hear.

"This is intolerable, sir," she flared at me, gripping the arms of her chair. "I do not wish to hear any more about your stupid English nation. It is because they are stupid that I do what I do. They can be led by the nose, like your stupid king: I can do what I will —"

"Madam," I entreated, and truly my accents were piteous, "I beg of you not to speak like that. I am a servant of His Majesty's — I cannot hear such talk —"

I rose from my chair.

Now in that Court there was more tittle-tattle, I think, than in any place on God's earth; and she knew that well enough; and understood that she had said something which unless she pre- vented it, would go straight to Charles' ears. It is true that she ruled him absolutely; but he kicked under her yoke a little now and then; and if there were one thing that he would not brook it was to be called stupid. She let go of the arms of her chair, and went a little white. I think she had no idea till then that I was in the King's service.

"I said nothing —" she murmured.

I stood regarding her; and I think my manner must have been good.

"I said nothing that should be repeated," she added, a little louder.

I still kept silence.

"You will not repeat it, Mr. Mallock?"

"Madam," I said, "I have only one desire: and that is to serve His Majesty and His Majesty's lawful heir. My mouth can be sealed absolutely, if that end is served."

I said that very slowly and deliberately.

I saw her breathe a little more freely. It was a piteous sight to see a woman so depending upon such things as a complexion, and whiffs of scandal, and servants' gossip.

"Mr. Mallock," she said, "I cannot veer round all in a moment, even though I must confess that what you have said to me, has touched me very closely."

She looked at me miserably.

"Madam," I said, for I dared not grasp at more than this, for fear of losing all, "that has wiped out your words as if they had never been spoken."

I kissed her hand and went out.

*   *   *

I did not go to the Duke, for I hold that, when a man has to sift carefully between what he must say and what he must not, it is best to do it on paper; but I went back to my lodgings and wrote to him that it was merely for her own advantage that the Duchess had behaved so, and because she thought that the Protestant succession was certain — her own advantage, that is to say, mingled with a little woman's vanity. I begged His Royal Highness therefore to go and see the Duchess, if he thought well, and, if possible, publicly, when she held her reception, before he went to Scotland — (for I was diplomat enough to know that the assuming he would go to Scotland would be the best persuasion to make him) — ; and at the end I told him that I thought my arguments had prevailed a little with Her Grace, and that though she could not at once turn weathercock, he might take my word for it that she would not be so forward as she had been. But I did not tell him what argument I had chiefly used; for I hold that even to such a woman as that, a man should keep his word.

Everything I told the Duke in that letter fell true. The Duchess began to cool very much in the Protestant cause, though perhaps that was helped a little by Monmouth's having fallen under the King's displeasure: and the Duke of York went two or three times to the Duchess' receptions; and to Scotland on the day before Parliament met.

CHAPTER VI

It was on Mr. Chiffinch's advice that I remained in London for the present, determining however to spend Christmas at Hare Street; and indeed I had plenty to do in making my reports to Rome on the situation.

There was a storm brewing. From all over the country came in *addresses to the King*, as they were called, praying him to assemble Parliament, and that, not only for defence against Popery, but against despotism as well; and all these were nourished and inspired by my Lord Shaftesbury. His Majesty answered this by proclaiming through the magistrates that such addresses were contrary to the laws that left such things at the King's discretion; and the court-party against the country-party presently begun to send addresses beseeching His Majesty to defend that prerogative of his fearlessly. Names began to be flung about: the court-party called the other the party of Whigs, because of their whey faces that would turn all sour; and the country-party nicknamed the others Tories, which was the name of the banditti in the wilder parts of Ireland. So it appeared that whenever Parliament should meet, there would be, as the saying is, a pretty kettle of fish to fry.

Parliament met at last on the twenty-first of October, the Duke of York having set out to Scotland with a fine retinue on the day before; (which some thought too pointed); and the King himself opened it.

With all my love for His Majesty I am forced to confess that he presented a very poor spectacle on that occasion. Not only did he largely yield to the popular clamour, and profess himself willing, within reason, to befriend any measures for the repression of Popery; but he stood at the fire afterwards in the House of Lords, for a great while, warming his back and laughing with his friends. I was in the gallery and saw it myself. Laughter is a very good thing, but a seemly gravity is no less good. As might be expected of curs, they barked all the louder when there was no one to stand up to them; and within a week, after numerous insulting proposals made to honour that horde of lying informers that had done so much mischief already, and of preferring such men as Dr. Tonge to high positions in the Church, once more that Exclusion Bill of theirs came forward.

The Commons passed it, as might be expected, since my Lord Shaftesbury had packed that House with his own nominees.

I was in Whitehall on the night that it was debated in the Lords — four days later — and up to ten o'clock His Majesty had not returned from the House; for he was present at that debate — a very unusual thing with him. I went up and down for a little while outside His Majesty's lodgings; and about half-past ten I saw Mr. Chiffinch coming.

"His Majesty is not back yet," he said; and presently he proposed that we should go to the House ourselves.

*   *   *

From the little gallery whither he conducted me, I had a very good view of the House, and, yet more, of one of the strangest sights ever seen there.

Upon the carpet that was laid by the fire, for it was a cold night, stood His Majesty himself with a circle of friends about him. Now and again there came up to him one of the Peers for whom he had sent; he talked to him a few minutes; and then let him go; for he was doing nothing else than solicit each of them for his vote.

The cry was raised presently to clear the House; and we went away; for their Lordships were to record their votes; and we had not stood half an hour in the court outside, before there came a great cheering and shouting; followed hard by a great booing from the crowds that stood packed outside. My Lords had thrown out the Exclusion Bill by above two-thirds of their number — which was ninety-three. Presently His Majesty came out by his private way, laughing and jesting aloud with two or three others.

It was to be expected that the country-party would make some retort to this; and what that retort was I heard a few days later, from a couple of gentlemen who came into the parlour at the Covent Garden tavern where I was taking my supper. They came in very eagerly, talking together, and when they had sat down, one of them turned to me.

"You have heard the news, sir?"

"No, sir. What news?"

"My Lord Stafford is to be tried for his life."

I did not know what political complexion these two were of; so I looked wise and inquired how that was known.

"A clerk that is in the House of Lords told me, sir. I have always found his information to be correct."

This was all very well for the clerk's friend, thought I; but not enough for me; and so soon as I had finished my supper and bidden them good-night I was off to Mr. Chiffinch.

"Why yes," he said. "It is like to be true enough. I had heard talk of it, but no more. It is he whom they have chosen as the weakest of the Five in the Tower; and if they can prevail against him they will proceed against the rest, I suppose. I wonder who the informers will be."

I inquired how it was that the Peers did not resist.

"They fear for themselves and their places," said Mr. Chiffinch. "They will yield up anything but that, if a man or two will but push them hard enough. And, if they try my Lord, they will certainly condemn him. There is no question of that. To acquit him would cause a yet greater uproar than to refuse to hear the case at all."

"And His Majesty?"

Mr. Chiffinch eyed me gravely.

"His Majesty will never prefer his private feelings before the public utility."

"And this is to the public utility?"

"Why yes; or the country-party thinks it is. It is the best answer they can make to their rebuff on the matter of the Exclusion Bill."

The rumour proved to be perfectly true. The Five Lords who were still in the Tower, had been sent there, it may be remembered, above two years ago, on account of their religion, although the pretended plot professed by Oates was of course alleged against them. Since that time Parliament had been busy with other matters; but such an opportunity was now too good to be lost, of striking against the court-party, and, at the same time, of feeding the excitement and fanaticism of their own.

The trial came on pretty quickly, beginning on the last day of November; and as I had never seen a Peer tried by his fellows, I determined to be present, and obtained an order to admit me every day; and the first day, strangely enough, was the birthday of my Lord Stafford himself.

*   *   *

Westminster Hall, in which the trial was held, was a very noble sight when all the folks were in their places. (I sat myself in a high gallery, in which sat, too, ambassadors and public ministers — at the upper end, above the King's state.)

I could not see that which was immediately beneath me, neither of the box in which sat His Majesty during a good deal of the trial, nor, upon the left side where the great ladies sat. But I had a very good view of the long forms on which the Peers sat, before the state (under which was the throne), the wool-packs for the Judges, and the chair of the Lord Steward — all which was ranged exactly as in the House of Lords itself. Behind the Peers' forms rose the stands, scaffolded up to the roof, for the House of Commons to sit in; so that the Hall resembled the shape of a V in its section, with a long arena in the midst. The lower end held, in the middle, the bar for the prisoner to stand at, and a place for him to retire into: a box for his two daughters, of whom one was the Marchioness of Winchester; and the proper places for the Lieutenant of the Tower (whence my Lord was brought by water), the axe-bearer, who had the edge of his axe turned away from the prisoner, and the guards that kept him. Upon either hand of the entrance, nearer to the throne, stood, upon one side a box for the witnesses, and upon the other, those that were called the Managers — being lawyers and attorneys and the like; but these were in their cloaks and swords, as were others who were with them, of the Parliamentary party, since they were here as representing the Commons, and not as lawyers first of all.

*   *   *

The two first days were tedious enough; and I did not stay a great while; for the articles of impeachment were read, and formalities discharged. One matter of interest only appeared; and that was the names of the witnesses, when I learned for the first time that Oates and Dugdale and Turberville were to be the principal. I think more than I were astonished to hear that Dr. Oates was in this conspiracy too, as in so many others; and that he would swear, when the time came, that he had delivered to my Lord a commission from the Holy Father, to be paymaster in the famous Catholic army of which we had heard so much.

I was much occupied too on these days in observing the appearance and demeanour of the prisoner, whom I could see very well. He was now in his seventieth year, and looked full his age; but he bore himself with great dignity and restraint. He had somewhat of a cold look in his face; and indeed it was true that he was not greatly beloved by anybody, though respected by all.

The principal witnesses, even before Oates, were Dugdale and Turberville. First these gave their general testimony — and afterwards their particular. Mr. Dugdale related how that the plot, in general, had been on hand for above fifteen or sixteen years; and he repeated all the stuff that had so stirred up the people before, as to indulgences and pardons promised by the Pope to those who would kill the King. I must confess that I fell asleep once or twice during this testifying, for I knew it all by heart already. And, in particular, he said that my Lord had debated with others at my Lord Aston's, how to kill the King: and that himself was present at such debates.

A great hum broke out in the Hall, when Dugdale swore that he had heard with his own ears my Lord Stafford and others who had been present, give their assent one by one to the King's murder. His Majesty himself, I was told later by Mr. Chiffinch, retired to the back of his box to laugh, when he heard that said; for neither then nor ever did he believe a word of it.

Next came Mr. Oates; and he too reaffirmed what he had said before, with an hundred ingenious additions and particularities as to times and places — and this, I think, as much as anything was the reason why so many simple folk had believed him in the first event.

Then Turberville, who said falsely that he had once been a friar, and at Douay, related how my Lord, as he had said, had attempted to bribe him to kill the King, and suchlike nonsense. This, he said, had happened in France.

My Lord Stafford questioned the prisoners a little; and shewed up many holes in their story. For instance, he asked Turberville whether he had ever been in his chamber in Paris; and put this question through the High Steward.

"Yes, my Lord, I have," said Turberville.

"What kind of a room is it?" asked my Lord.

"I can't remember that," said Turberville, who before had sworn he had been in it many times.

"No," said my Lord, "I dare swear you can't."

"I cannot tell the particulars — what stools and chairs were in the room."

*   *   *

On the third day, which was Thursday, my Lord was bidden to call his witnesses and make his defence; and I must confess that he did not do this very well; for, first he made a great pother about this and that statute, of the 13 Charles II. and 25 Edward — nothing of which served him at all; and next his witnesses did him harm rather than good; and Dugdale, whom he examined was so clever and quiet and positive in his statements that it was mere oath against oath. Third, my Lord Stafford himself did appear a little confused as to whether he had known Dugdale or not, not being sure of him, as he said, in his periwig; for when Dugdale was bailiff to my Lord Aston at Tixall, he wore no such thing. All that he did, in regard to Dugdale, was to shew by one of his witnesses that Dugdale, when bailiff at Tixall, had been a mean dishonest fellow; but then, as the Lord High Sheriff observed, it would scarcely be an honest man whom one would bribe to kill the King.

When he dealt with Turberville too, he did not do much better; for he stood continually upon little points of no importance — such points as a witness may very well mistake — as to where the windows of his house in Paris looked out, and whether the Prince of Conde lodged to right or left — such little points as a lawyer would leave alone, if he could not prove them positively.

On the fourth and fifth day I was not present; for I had a great deal to do in writing my reports for Rome; and on the sixth day — which was Monday — I was not there above an hour, for I saw that the trial would not end that day. But on the Tuesday I was there before ten o'clock; and at eleven o'clock my Lords came back to give judgment. It was a dark morning, as it had been at the trial of the Jesuits; and the candles were lighted.

As soon as all were seated my Lord Stafford was brought in; and I observed him during all that followed. He stood very quiet at the bar, with his hands folded; and although, before the voting was over, he must have known which way it was gone, he flinched never a hair nor went white at all. (His bringing in while the voting was done was contrary to the law; but no one observed it; and I knew nothing of it till afterwards.)

The Lord High Steward first asked humble leave from my Lords to sit down as he spoke, as he was ailing a little, and then put the question to each Lord, beginning with my Lord Butler of Weston.

"My Lord Butler of Weston," said he, "is William Lord Viscount Stafford guilty of the treason whereof he stands impeached, or not guilty?"

And my Lord answered in a loud voice, laying his hand upon his breast:

"Not guilty, upon my honour."

There were in all eighty-six lords who voted; and each answered, Guilty, or Not Guilty, upon his honour, as had done the first, each standing up in his place. At the first I could not tell on which side lay the most; but as they went on, there could be no doubt that he was condemned. Prince Rupert, Duke of Cumberland, voted last, as he was of royal blood, and gave it against him.

The Lord High Sheriff, who had marked down each vote upon a paper on his desk, now added them all up: and there was a great silence while he did this. (I could see him doing it from where I sat.) Then he spoke in a loud voice, raising his head.

"My Lords," said he, "upon telling your votes I find that there are thirty-one of my Lords that think the prisoner not guilty, and fifty-five that have found him guilty — Serjeant," said he; and then I think that he was about to call for the prisoner, when he saw him already there. Then, before he spoke again, I saw the headsman turn the edge of the axe towards my Lord Stafford; and a rustle of whispering ran through the Hall.

"My Lord Stafford," said the High Steward, "I have but heavy tidings for you: your Lordship hath been impeached for high treason; you have pleaded not guilty: my Lords have heard your defence, and have considered of the evidence; and their Lordships do find you guilty of the treason whereof you are impeached."

Then my Lord Stafford, raising his head yet higher, and flinching not at all, cried out:

"God's holy name be praised, my Lords, for it!"

Then the Lord High Steward asked him why judgment of death should not be given on him; and after saying that he had not expected it, and that he prayed God to forgive those that had sworn falsely against him, he went on, as before, upon a legal point — that was wholly without relevance — that he had not been forced to hold up his hand at the beginning as he thought to be a legal form in all trials; and when he had said that, my Lords went out to consider their judgment.

It was above an hour before they came back. During that hour my Lord Stafford was permitted to sit down in the box provided for him; but no one was admitted to speak with him. He sat very still, leaning his head upon his hand.

When all were come back again, he was made to stand up at the bar once more; and his face was as resolute and quiet as ever.

Then, when the Lord High Steward had answered his point, saying that in no way did the holding up of the hand affect the legality of the trial; he began to give sentence.

"My part, therefore, which remains," said he, "is a very sad one. For I never yet gave sentence of death upon any man, and am extremely sorry that I must begin with your Lordship."

My Lord Nottingham was silent for an instant when he had said that, seeking, I think, to command his voice: and then he began his speech, which I think he had learned by heart; and it was one of the most moving discourses that I have ever heard, though he committed a great indecency in it, when he said that henceforth no man could ever doubt again that it was the Papists who had burned London; and professed himself — (though this I suppose he was bound to do) — satisfied with the evidence.

When he came to give sentence, I watched my Lord Stafford's face again very hard; and he flinched never a hair. It was the same sentence as that to which the Jesuits too had listened, and many other Catholics.

"You go to the place," said my Lord Nottingham, "from whence you came; from thence you must be drawn upon a hurdle to the place of execution: when you come there you must be hanged up by the neck there, but not till you are dead; for you must be cut down alive, your bowels ripped up before your face and thrown into the fire. Then your head must be severed from your body; and your body divided into four quarters, and these must be at the disposal of the King. And God Almighty be merciful to your soul!"

There was a moment of silence; and then my Lord Stafford answered.

"My Lords," he said quietly, yet so that every word was heard, "I humbly beseech you give me leave to speak a few words: I do give your Lordships hearty thanks for all your favours to me. I do here, in the presence of God Almighty, declare I have no malice in my heart to them that have condemned me. I know not who they are, nor desire to know: I forgive them all, and beseech your Lordships all to pray for me —" (His voice shook a little, and he was silent. Then he went on again. All else were as still as death.)

"My Lords, I have one humble request to make to your Lordships, and that is, my Lords, that the little short time I have to live a prisoner, I may not be a close prisoner as I have been of late; but that Mr. Lieutenant may have an order that my wife and children and friends may come at me. I do humbly beg this favour of your Lordships, which I hope you will be pleased to give me."

His voice grew very low as he ended; and I saw his lips shake a little.

The Lord High Steward answered him with great feeling.

"My Lord Stafford," he said — (and that was an unusual thing to say, for he had said before that since he was to be attainted he could not be called My Lord again) — "I believe I may, with my Lords' leave, tell you one thing further; that my Lords, as they proceed with rigour of justice, so they proceed with all the mercy and compassion that may be; and therefore my

Lords will be humble suitors to the King, that he will remit all the punishment but the taking off of your head."

And at that my Lord Stafford broke down altogether, and sobbed upon the rail; and it is a terrible thing to see an old man weep like that. When he could command his voice, he said:

"My Lords, your justice does not make me cry, but your goodness."

Then my Lord Nottingham stood up, and taking the staff of office that lay across his desk, he broke it in two halves. When I looked again, the prisoner was going out between his guards, and the axe before, with its edge turned towards him in token of death.

*   *   *

I was at Mr. Chiffinch's again that night to hear the news; but he was not there. When he came in at last, he appeared very excited. Then he told me the news.

"They are at His Majesty already," he said, "that he cannot remit the penalty of High Treason. But the King swears that he will, law or no law, judges or no judges. I have never seen him so determined. He does not believe one word of the evidence."

"Yet he will sign the warrant for the beheading?" I asked.

"Why," said Mr. Chiffinch, "His Majesty does not wish to go upon his travels again."

CHAPTER VII

The night before I went down to Hare Street, — for I went on Christmas Eve — I was present for the first time at the high supper in Whitehall, which His Majesty gave to the Spanish Ambassador. I had never been at such a ceremony before; and went out of curiosity only, being given admission to one of the stands by the door, whence I might see it all. It would have appeared very strange to me that the King could be so merry, as he was that night, when so much innocent blood had been shed upon his own warrant, and when such a man, as my Lord Stafford was, lay in the Tower, expecting his death six days later; — had I not known the nature of His Majesty pretty well by now. For, beneath all the merriment, I think he was not very happy, though he never shewed a sign of it.

I stood, as I said, upon a little scaffold to the right of the entrance; and I was glad of it; for there was a great pack of people crowded in, as the custom was, also to see the spectacle; and they were all about me and in front, as well as in the gallery where the music was.

The Banqueting Hall had its walls all hung over with very rich tapestry, representing all kinds of merry scenes of hunting and fighting and the like, and there were great presses along the walls, piled with plate of gold and silver. The music was all on the balusters above — wind-music, trumpets and kettledrums, that played as Their Majesties came in, after the heralds and Black Rod. I had not had before an opportunity of seeing the Queen so well as I saw her now; and I watched her closely, for I was sorry for the poor woman. She was very gloriously dressed in a pale brocade, with quantities of Flanders lace upon her shoulders and at her elbows, that set off her little figure very well. She was very handsome, I thought, though so little; and her complexion and her face were both very good, except that her teeth shewed too much as she smiled. She had, however, nothing of that witty or brilliant air about her that pleased the King so much in women; and she sat very quietly throughout supper, beside the King, not speaking a great deal. But I thought I saw in her at first a very piteous desire to please him; and he listened, smiling, as a man might listen to a dull child; and, indeed, I think that that was all that he thought of her. His Majesty himself appeared very noble and gallant, in His Order of the Garter, and with the Golden Fleece too, over his rich suit. Both Their Majesties wore a good number of jewels.

Their Majesties sat at a little high table, under a state, with their gentlemen and ladies standing behind them; and the Spaniards, with the King's other guests at a table that ran down the middle of the hall, yet close enough at the upper end for the Ambassador and the King to speak together. My Lord Shaftesbury was there; and it was strange to see him, I knowing how much he was privately under His Majesty's displeasure, and Prince Rupert, very fat and pale and stupid; and Sir Thomas Killigrew and a score of others. His Majesty was served by the Lords and pensioners; and the rest by pages and the like, and gentlemen. About the middle of the dinner toasts were drunk — and first of all His Majesty's, and the trumpets sounded and the music played, all standing, and when they were sat down again I heard the guns shot off at the Tower; and I thought of him who lay there, and how he heard them near at hand, and how he might have been here, supping with the Spaniards, had he not fallen under the popular displeasure on account of his religion. It was a wonderful thing to see the toast drunk, all that company standing upon its feet, and shouting.

When the banquet came in, and the French wines, a very curious scene of disorder presently began — these gentlemen flinging the dessert about and at one another, for they were beginning to be a little drunk: and I saw Killigrew fling a bunch of raisins at one of the Spaniards, in sport. His Majesty sat smiling throughout, not at all displeased; but not drunk at all himself; and indeed he seldom or never drank to excess nor gamed to excess, though he loved to see others do so.

At the end, when all was finished, a choir under the direction of the King's Master of Music sang a piece very sweetly from the gallery, with the wind music sounding softly; but no one paid the least attention; and then we all stood up again, such as had seats on the scaffolds, to see Their Majesties go out. But such a scene as it all was, when the fruit and sweetmeats were flung about would not have been tolerated in Rome, nor, I think in any Court in Europe.

The next morning, very early, James and I set out for Hare Street.

*   *   *

Now the determination had been forming in my mind for some weeks past, that I would delay no longer in that which lay nearer to my heart by now, I think, than all politics or missions or anything else; and that was to ask my Cousin Dolly if she would have me or no; and all the way down to Hare Street I was considering this and rehearsing what I should say. I still had some hesitation upon the point, for I remembered how strange and shy she had been when I had last been there, and had thought it to be because perhaps she believed that she was being flung at me by her father. But the memory of my jealousy had worked upon me very much — that jealousy, I mean, that I had had when His Grace of Monmouth had come and made his pretty speeches; and I was all but resolved to put all to the test, one way or the other. I had thought of her continually: in all that I had seen — in even the sorrowful affair in Westminster Hall and the merry business a fortnight after at the supper — I had seen it, so to say, all through her eyes and wondered how she would judge of it all, and wished her there. The sting of my jealousy indeed was gone: I reproached myself for having thought ill of her even for a moment; yet the warmth was still there; and so it was in this mood that I came at last to the house, at supper-time.

It was extraordinary merry and pretty within. Neither was below stairs when I came; for my Cousin Tom was in the cellar, and my Cousin Dolly in the kitchen; and when I went into the Great Chamber it was all untenanted. But the walls were hung all over with wreaths and holly: and there were wax candles in the sconces all ready for lighting the next day. But the parlour, where were the hangings of the Knights of the Grail was even more pretty; for there were hung streamers across the ceiling, from corner to corner, and a great bunch of mistletoe united them at the centre.

As I was looking at this my Cousin Dolly ran in, her hands all over flour; and as I saw her — "Here," I said to myself, "is the place where it shall be done."

She could not touch me or kiss me, because of the flour; but she permitted me to kiss her, my cold lips against her warm cheek; and her eyes were as stars for merriment. There is something very strange and mystical about Christmas, to me — (which I think is why the Puritans were so savage against it) — for I suppose that the time in which our Lord was born as a little Child, makes children of us all, that we may understand Him better.

"Well, you are come then!" said Dolly to me — "and we not ready for you."

"I am ready enough for home," said I. And she smiled very friendly at me for that word.

"I am glad you call it that," said she.

*   *   *

There was but a little dried fish and rice for supper that night, as it was a fast day; but the supper of Christmas Eve is always a kind of sacramental for me, when midnight mass is to follow. There was no midnight mass for us that Christmas, nor any mass at all; though I suppose it was celebrated as usual in the Ambassadors' chapels, and the Queen's: yet the supper had yet that air of mystery and expectancy about it.

"We are all to dance tomorrow night," said Dolly.

"So that is why the floor is cleared in the Great Chamber," I said.

She nodded at me. She looked more of a child than I had ever seen her.

"Will you dance with me, Dolly?" I asked.

"Yes," she said, "but my first is with my father."

I told them presently, though it was but a melancholy tale for Christmas Eve, of my Lord Stafford's trial, and all that I had seen there; and of the supper last night in Whitehall.

"My Lord is to be beheaded in five days," I said. "We must pray for his soul. He will die as bravely as he has lived; I make no doubt."

"And you have no doubt of his innocence?" asked Cousin Tom.

I stared on him.

"Why no," I said, "nor any man, except those paid to believe his guilt."

He pressed me to tell him more of what I had seen in London; and whether I had seen the Duke of Monmouth again.

"He is in Holland," I said, "under His Majesty's displeasure. But I saw Her Grace of Portsmouth."

"Why, that is his friend, is it not?" asked Tom.

"Yes," I said, "and a poor friend to his father and the Duke of York."

*   *   *

The next night was a very merry one.

We had dined at noon as usual: and that was pretty merry too; for all the servants dined with us, and the men from the farm and their wives. It was sad to have had no mass at all; and all that we had instead of it was the sound of the bells from Hormead, from the church that had been our own a hundred and fifty years ago — which was worse than nothing. At dinner we observed the usual ceremonial, with the drinking of healths and the burning of candles; and Dolly and her father and her maid sang a grace at the beginning and end — with a carol or two afterwards that was a surprise to me. It was very homely and friendly and Christian; and I saw my man James with his arm around one of the dairy-maids — which is pretty Christian too, I think. We kept it up till it was near time to get supper ready, telling of stories all the while about the fire in the old way. Some of them were poor enough; but some were good. Dick, the cow-man, whom we had long suspected of poaching, exposed himself very sadly, when the ale was in him, by relating a number of poaching tricks I had never heard before. One was of how to catch stares, or shepsters, when they fly up and down, as they do before lodging in a thicket. Then you must turn out, said Dick, a quick stare with a limed thread of three yards long, when she will fly straight to the rest, and, flocking among them, will infallibly bring down at least one or two, and perhaps five or six, all entangled in her thread. And another was how to take wild ducks. Go into the water, said he, up to the neck, with a pumpkin put over your head, and whilst the ducks come up to eat the seeds, you may take them by the legs and pull them under quietly, one by one, till they be drowned. But I would not like to do that in cold weather; and indeed it seems to me altogether like that other method by which you take larks by a-putting of salt upon their tails. I asked Dick, very serious, whether he had tried that plan; and he said he had not, but that a friend had told him of it; and the company became very merry.

There were other tales too, more grave than these, of sacrilege, and suchlike. One, which my man James told, was of a man who took an altar stone from an old church, to press cheeses with; but the cheeses ran blood; so they took it from that and put it in the laundry to bat the linen on. But at night, such a sound of batting was heard continually from the laundry — and no one there — that the man took it back again to the church, and buried it in the churchyard. And another was of two men who had thrown down a village-cross upon a bowling-green; and when one of them next day tried to move it from there, for the playing — he being a very strong man, and lifting it on end — it fell upon him, backwards, and crushed his breast, so that he never spoke again. And there were many tales told of church-lands; and how my Lord Strafford, that was beheaded, before his death told his son to get rid of them all, for that they brought a curse always upon them that held them. And there was another story told at the end by a man from the farm who had been in London at the time, and had seen it for himself — how my Lords Castlehaven and Arran, in St.

James' Park, did, for a wager, kill a strong buck in His Majesty's presence, by running on foot, and each with a knife only. They took nearly three hours to do it in, but the wager was for six, so they won that. They killed him at last in Rosamund's Pond, having driven him in there with stones. I could well believe this latter tale, and that the thing had been done in the king's presence, having seen what I had at supper two nights before.

*   *   *

When we came into the Great Chamber after supper all was ready for the dancing; and Mr. Thompson, who was the Hormead schoolmaster, and a concealed Catholic — though he went to the church with the children and did teach them their religion, for his living — was at the spinet to which we were to dance. There was a fellow also to play the fiddle, and another for a horn.

The dancing was very pretty to see; and we did a great number, beginning as the custom is, with country dances; and it was in the first of these that my Cousin Dolly did dance with her father, and I with Dolly's maid. We were all dressed too, not indeed in our best, but in our second best — with silk stockings, and the farm men and the maids were in their Sunday clothes. But each one had put on something for the occasion; one had a pair of buckled shoes of a hundred years old, and another an old ring. My Cousin Tom and I wore our own hair, and no periwigs. My Cousin Dolly was very pretty in her grey sarcenet, with her little pearls, and her hair dressed in a new fashion.

It was all very sweet to me, for it was so natural and without affectation; and it all might have been a hundred years ago before the old customs went out and the new came in from France, in which men pay dancers to dance, instead of doing it for themselves. The room was very well decked, and the candles lighted all round the walls; and when some of the greenery fell down and was trodden underfoot, the smell of it was very pleasant. A little fire was on the hearth — not great, lest we should be too hot.

We danced country dances first, as I have said; and then my Cousin Dolly shewed us one or two town dances, and I danced a sarabande in her company; but then as the rest of the folk liked the country dances the best, we went back to these.

Presently I saw my Cousin Dolly go out, and went after her to ask if she needed anything.

"No," said she, "only to get cool again."

"Come into the parlour," said I; and made her come with me. This too had a couple of candles burning over the hearth, and a little fire, for any who wished to come in; but it was empty, for even my Cousin Tom was disporting himself next door in a round dance that had but just begun.

Then it was that all my resolution came to a point; for all circumstances looked that way — my determination to speak, the blessed time of Christmas, the extraordinary kindness of Dolly to me all day, and the very place empty, yet lighted and waiting, as if by design.

For a moment after she had sat down on one side of the hearth, and I on the other, I could not speak; for I seemed to myself all shaking, and again she looked such a child, with her pale cheeks flushed with the exercise, and her eyes alight with merriment. All went before me in that moment — my old thought that I was to be a monk, my leaving the novitiate, my mission from Rome, such as it was, and the work I had been able to do for the King. To all this I must say good-bye; and yet this price I should pay seemed to me scarcely to be considered as weighed against this little maid. So it went by me like a picture, and was gone, and I looked up.

There was that in my air, I suppose, and the way I looked at her, that told her what my meaning was; for before I had spoken even a syllable she was on her feet again, and the flush was stricken from her face.

"Oh! no! Cousin Roger," she cried. "No, no, Cousin Roger!"

"It is Yes, Yes, Cousin Dolly," said I. "Or at least I hope so." (I said this with more assurance than I shewed, for if I was sure of anything it was that she loved me in return. And I stood up and leaned on the chimney-breast.)

She stood there, staring on me; and the flush crept back.

"What have I said?" she whispered.

"You need say nothing more, my dear, except what I bid you. My dear love, you have guessed just what it was that I had to say. Sit down again, if you please, Cousin, while I tell you."

As I looked at her, a very curious change came across her face. I saw it at once, but I did not think upon it till afterwards. She had been a very child just now, in her terror that I should speak — just that terror, I should suppose, that every maid must have when a man first speaks to her of love. Yet, as I looked, that terror went from her face, and her wide eyes narrowed a little as she brought down her brows, and her parted lips closed. It was, I thought, just that she had conquered herself, and set herself to hear what I had to say, before answering me as I wished. She moved very slowly back to her chair, and sat down, crossing her hands on her lap. That was all that I thought it was, so little did I know women's hearts, and least of all hers.

I remained yet a moment longer, leaning my forehead on my hand, and my hand flat upon the tapestry, staring into the red logs, and considering how to say what I had to say with the least alarm to her. I felt — though I am ashamed to say it — as it were something of condescension towards her. I knew that it was a good match for her, for had not her father drilled that into me by a hundred looks and hints? I knew that I was something considerable, and like to be more so, and that I was sacrificing a good deal for her sake. And then a kind of tenderness came over me as I thought how courageous she was, and good and simple, and I put these other thoughts away, and turned to her where she sat with the firelight on her chin and brows and hair, very rigid and still.

"Dolly, my dear," I said, "I think you know what I have to say to you. It is that I love you very dearly, as you must have seen —"

She made a little quick movement as if to speak.

"Wait, cousin," I said, "till I have done. I tell you that I love you very dearly, and honor you, and can never forget what you did for me. And I am a man of a very considerable estate and a Catholic; so there is nothing to think of in that respect. And your father too will be pleased, I know; and we are —"

Again she made that little quick movement; and I stopped.

"Well, my dear?"

She looked up at me very quietly.

"Well, Cousin Roger; and what then?"

That confused me a little; for I had thought that she had understood. And then I thought that perhaps she too was confused.

"Why, my dear," I said very patiently as I thought, as one would speak to a child, "I am asking you if you will be my wife."

I turned away from the fire altogether, and faced her, thinking I should have her in my arms. But at first she said nothing at all, but sat immovable, scrutinizing me, I thought, as if to read all that was in my head and heart. But it was all new to me, for what did I know of love except that it was very strange and sweet? So I waited for her answer. That answer came.

"Cousin Roger," she said in a very low voice, "I am very sorry you have spoken as you have —"

I straightened myself suddenly and looked at her more closely. She had not moved at all, except her face. A kind of roaring murmur began to fill my ears.

"Because," said she — and every word of hers now was pain to me — "because there is but one answer that I can give, which is No."

"Why —" cried I.

"You have spoken very kindly and generously. But —" and at this her voice began to ring a little — "but I am not what you think me — a maid to be flung at the head of any man who will choose to take her."

"Cousin!" cried I; and then she was on her feet too, her face all ablaze.

"Yes, Cousin!" cried she; "and never any more than that. You have acted very well, Cousin Roger; and I thank you for that compliment — that you thought it worth while to play the part — and for your great kindness to a poor country maid. I had thought it to be all over long ago — before you went away; or I would not have behaved as I have. But since you have considered it again carefully, and chosen to — to insult me after all; I have no answer at all to give, except No, a thousand times over."

"Why, Cousin —" I began again.

She stamped her foot. I could not have imagined she could be so angry.

"Wait till I have done," she said — "I do not know what my father thinks of me; but I suppose that you and he have designed all this; and led me on to make a fool of myself — Oh! Let me go! let me go!"

Oh! the triple fool that I was! Yet who had ever taught me the ways of love, or what women mean, or what their hearts are like? If I had been one half the man that I thought myself, I would have seized her there, and forced back her foolishness with kisses, and vowed that, conspirator or not, she must have me; that we knew one another too well to play false coin like this. Or I should have blazed at her in return; and told her that she lied in thinking I was as base as that. Why, I should have just borne myself like a lover to whom love is all, and dignity and wounded pride nothing; for what else is there but love, sacred or profane, in the whole world that God has made? If I had done that! If only I had done that then! But I suppose that I was no lover then.

So I drew back, smarting and wounded; and let her go by; and a minute later I heard the door of her chamber slam behind her, and the key turn.

*　　*　　*

For myself I went out very slowly, five minutes after, and

upstairs to my own chamber, and began to consider what things I must take with me on the morrow; for I would not stay another day in the house where I had been so insulted and denied.

CHAPTER VIII

Pride is a very good salve, when one has no humility; and it was Pride that I applied to myself to heal the wounds I had.

I came down again to the Great Chamber, half an hour later, very cold and dignified, and danced again, like the solemn fool that I was, first with one and then with another; and all the while I told myself, like the prophet that "I did well to be angry"; and that I would shew her that no man, of my ability, could depend upon any mere woman for his content. Yet the pain at my heart was miserable.

It is very near incredible to me now how I, who truly knew something of the world, and of men and of affairs, could be so childish and ignorant in a matter of this sort. In truth this was what I was; I knew nothing of true love at all; how therefore should I be a proper lover? I saw my Cousin Tom, who mopped himself a great deal, eyeing me now and again; and he presently came up and asked me where Dolly was.

"In her chamber, I think," said I, with my nose in the air; and with such a manner that he said no more.

It was enough to break my heart to continue dancing; but it was the task I had set myself upstairs; and till near ten o'clock we continued to dance — but no Dolly to help us. I had even determined how I should bear myself if she came — and how superb should be my dignity; but she did not come to see it. We ended with singing "Here's a health unto His Majesty"; and I took care that my voice should be loud so that she should hear it. (I had even, poor fool that I was! walked heavily past her chamber-door just now, that she might hear me go.)

When all were gone away at last, I waited for my Cousin Tom, and then went with him into the parlour; where I told him very briefly all that had passed, with the same dignity that I had set myself to preserve. I even spoke in a high sort of voice, to shew my self-command and detachment. My Cousin Tom appeared as if thunderstruck.

"Good God!" said he. "The minx! to behave like that!"

"It is no longer any concern of mine," I said. "For myself I shall go back to town tomorrow."

"But —" began he.

"My dear Cousin," I said, "it is the only thing that I can do — to set to work again. Mistress Dorothy must recover herself alone.

I could not expect her to tolerate such a personage as I must appear in her eyes."

"But you will came back again," said Tom. "And I'll talk to the chit as she deserves."

I preserved my lofty attitude.

"That again," said I, "is no concern of mine. And as for coming back, when Mistress Dorothy has found her a husband whom she can respect — we may perhaps consider it."

He sat very silent for a while after that; and I know now, though I did not know then, what was the design he was considering — at least I suppose it was then that he saw it clear before him. At the time I thought he was giving his attention to myself; and I wondered a little that he did not press me again to stay, though I would not have done so.

It was a very desolate morning when I awakened next day, and knew what had happened, and that I must go away again from the house I had learned so much to love; but there was no help for it; and, as I put on my clothes, I put on my pride with them; and came down very cold and haughty to get my "morning" as we called it, in the dining-room before riding; and there in the dining-room was my Cousin Dolly, whom I had thought to be in her chamber, as the door was shut when I came past it.

We bade one another good morning very courteously indeed; but we gave no other salute to one another. She knew last night that I was going, as my Cousin Tom had told her maid to tell her; and I was surprised that she was there. Presently I had an explanation of it.

"Cousin Roger," said she, "I was very angry last night; and I wished to tell you I was sorry for that, and for the hard words I used, before you went away."

I bowed my head very dignifiedly.

"And I, too," I said, "must ask your pardon for so taking you by surprise. I thought —" and then I ceased.

She had looked a little white and tired, I thought; but she flushed again with anger when I said that.

"You thought it would be no surprise," she said.

"I did not say so, Cousin," said I. "You have no right to interpret —"

"But you thought it."

I drank my ale.

"Oh! what you must think of me!" she cried in a sudden passion; and ran out of the room.

*   *   *

I think that was the most disconsolate journey I have ever taken. It was a cold morning, with a fine rain falling: my man James was disconsolate too (and I remembered the dairy-maid, when I saw it), and I was leaving the one place I had begun to think of as my home, and her who had so much made it home to me. I had not even seen her again before I went; and our last words had been of anger; and of that chopping kind of argument that satisfies no one.

I tried to distract myself with other thoughts — of what I was going to; for I had determined to go straight to Whitehall and ask for some employment; yet back and back again came the memories, and little scenes of the house, and the appearance of the Great Chamber when it was all lit up, and of the figure of that little maid who had so angered me, and the way she carried her head, and the turns of her hand — and how happy we all were yesterday about this time. However, I need not enlarge upon that. Those that have ever so suffered will know what I thought, without more words; and those who have not suffered would not understand, though I used ten thousand. And every step of all the way to London, which we reached about six o'clock, spoke to me of her with whom I had once ridden along it. As we came up into Covent Garden I turned to my man James and gave him more confidence than I had ever given to him before — for I think that he knew what had happened.

"James," said I, "this is a very poor home-coming; but it is not my fault."

*   *   *

Though fortune so far had been against me, I must confess that it favoured me a little better afterwards, for when I went in to Mr. Chiffinch's on the next morning, he gave me the very news that I wished to hear.

"Mr. Mallock," he said, "you are the very man I most wished to see. There is a great pother in France again. I do not know all the ins and outs of the affair; but His Majesty is very anxious. He spoke of you only this morning, Mr. Mallock."

My heart quickened a little. In spite of my pain it was a pleasure to hear that His Majesty had spoken of me; for I think my love to him was very much more deep, in one way, though not in another, than even to Dolly herself.

"Mr. Chiffinch," said I, "I will be very plain with you. I have had a disappointment; and I came back to town —"

He whistled, with a witty look. "The pretty cousin?" he said.

I could not afford to quarrel with him, but I could keep my dignity.

"That is my affair, Mr. Chiffinch. However — there is the fact. I am come to town for this very purpose — to beg for something to do. Will His Majesty see me?"

He looked at me for an instant; then he thought better, I think, of any further rallying.

"Why I am sure he will. But it will not be for a few days, yet. There is a hundred businesses at Christmas. Can you employ yourself till then?"

"I can kick my heels, I suppose," said I, "as well as any man."

"That will do very well," said Mr. Chiffinch. "But I warn you, that I think it will be a long affair. His Majesty hath entangled himself terribly, and Monsieur Barillon is furious."

"The longer the better," said I.

On the twenty-ninth I went down to see my Lord Stafford die. I was in so distracted a mood that I must see something, or go mad; for I had heard that it would not be until the evening of that day that His Majesty would see me, and that I must be ready to ride for Dover on the next morning. Mr. Chiffinch had told me enough to shew that the business would be yet more subtle and delicate than the last; and that I might expect some very considerable recognition if I carried it through rightly. I longed to be at it. One half of my longing came from the desire to occupy my mind with something better than my poor bungled love-affairs; and the other half from a frantic kind of determination to shew my Mistress Dolly that I was better than she thought me; and that I was man enough to attend to my affairs and carry them out competently, even if I were not man enough to marry her. It must be understood that I shewed no signs of this to anyone, and scarcely allowed it even to myself; but speaking with that honesty which I have endeavoured to preserve throughout all these memoirs, I am bound to say that my mind was in very much that condition of childish anger and resentment. I had a name as a strong man: God only knew how weak I was; for I did not even know it myself.

*   *   *

There was a great crowd on Tower Hill to see my Lord Stafford's execution; for not only was he well known, although, as I have said, not greatly beloved; but the rumours were got about — and that they were true enough I knew from Mr. Chiffinch — that he had said very strange things about my Lord

Shaftesbury, and how he could save his own life if he willed, not by confessing anything of which he himself had been accused, but by relating certain matters in which my Lord Shaftesbury was concerned. However, he did not; yet the tale had gone about that perhaps he would; and that a reprieve might come even upon the scaffold itself.

When I came to Tower Hill on horseback, about nine o'clock, the crowd covered the most of it; but I drove my horse through a little, so that I could have a fair sight both of the scaffold, and of the way, kept clear by soldiers, along which the prisoner must come.

I had not been there above a few minutes, when a company went by, and in the midst the two sheriffs, on horseback, whose business it was to carry through the execution; and they drew up outside the gate, to preserve the liberties of the Tower. While they were waiting, I watched those that were upon the scaffold — two writers to take down all that was said; and the headsman with his axe in a cloth — but this he presently uncovered — and the block which he laid down upon the black baize put ready for it, and for the prisoner to lie down upon. Then the coffin was put up behind, with but the two letters W.S. as I heard afterwards: and the year 1680.

Then, as a murmur broke out in the crowd, I turned; and there was my Lord coming along, walking with a staff, between his guards, with the sheriffs — of whom Mr. Cornish was one and Mr. Bethell the other — and the rest following after.

When my Lord was come up on the scaffold, the headsman had gone again; but he asked for him and gave him some money at which the man seemed very discontented, whereupon he gave him some more. It is a very curious custom this — but I think it is that the headsman may strike straight, and not make a botch of it.

When my Lord turned again I could see his face very plainly. He wore a peruke, and his hat upon that. He was in a dark suit, plain but rich; and had rings upon his fingers, which I could see as he spoke. He was wonderfully upright for a man of his age; and his face shewed no perturbation at all, though it was more fallen than I had thought.

He read all his speech, very clearly, from a paper he took out of his pocket; but as he delivered copies of it to the Sheriffs and the writers — (and it was put in print, too, on the very same day by two o'clock) — I need not give it here. He declared his innocence most emphatically; calling God to witness; and he thanked God

that his death was come on him in such a way that he could prepare himself well for eternity; but he did not thank the King for
remitting the penalties of treason, as he might have done. He
made no great references, as was expected that he would, to dis-
closures that he might have made; but only in general terms. He
denied most strongly that it was any part of the Catholic Religion
to give or receive indulgences for murder or for any other sin; and
he ended by committing his soul into the hands of Jesus Christ, by
whose merits and passion he hoped to be saved. His voice was
thin, but very clear for so old a man; and the crowd listened to him
with respect and attention. I think all those Catholic deaths and
the speeches that the prisoners make will by and by begin to
affect public opinion, and lead men to reflect that those who stand
in the immediate presence of God, are not likely, one after
another, to go before Him with lies upon their lips.

When he was done he distributed the copies of his speech,
and then presently kneeled down, and read a prayer or two. They
were in Latin, but I could not hear the words distinctly.

When he rose up again, all observing him, he went to the rail
and spoke aloud.

"God bless you, gentlemen!" he said. "God preserve His Majesty; he is as good a prince as ever governed you; obey him as
faithfully as I have done, and God bless you all, gentlemen!"

It was very affecting to hear him speak so, for he did it very
emphatically; but even then one of their ministers that was on the
scaffold would not let him be.

"Sir," he asked, speaking loud all across the scaffold, "do you
disown the indulgences of the Romish Church?"

My Lord turned round suddenly in a great passion.

"Sir!" he cried. "What have you to do with my religion? However, I do say that the Church of Rome allows no indulgences for
murder, lying and the like; and whatever I have said is
true." "What!" cried the minister. "Have you received no absolution?"

"I have received none at all," said my Lord, more quietly;
meaning of the kind that the minister meant, for I have no doubt
at all that he made his confession in the Tower.

"You said that you never saw those witnesses?" asked the
minister, who, I think, must have been a little uneasy.

"I never saw any of them," said my Lord, "but Dugdale; and
that was at a time when I spoke to him about a foot-boy." (This
was at Tixall, when Dugdale was bailiff there to my Lord Aston.)

They let him alone after that; and he immediately began to prepare himself for death. First he took off his watch and his rings, and gave them to two or three of his friends who were on the scaffold with him. Then he took his staff which was against the rail, and gave that too; and last his crucifix, which he took, with its chain, from around his neck.

His man then came up to him, and very respectfully helped him off with his peruke first, and then his coat, laying them one on the other in a corner. My Lord's head looked very thin and shrunken when that was done, as it were a bird's head. Then his man came up again with a black silk cap to put his hair under, which was rather long and very grey and thin; and he did it. And then his man disposed his waistcoat and shirt, pulling them down and turning them back a little.

Then my Lord looked this way and that for an instant; and then went forward to the black baize, and kneeled on it, with his man's help, and then laid himself down flat, putting his chin over the block which was not above five or six inches high.

Yet no one moved — and the headsman stood waiting in a corner, with his axe. One of the sheriffs — Mr. Cornish, I think it was — said something to the headsman; but I could not hear what it was; and then I saw my Lord kneel upright again, and then stand up. I think he was a little deaf, and had not heard what was said.

"Why, what do you want?" he said.

"What sign will you give?" asked Mr. Cornish.

"No sign at all. Take your own time. God's will be done," said my Lord; and again applied himself to the block, his man helping him as before, and then standing back.

"I hope you forgive me," said the headsman, before he was down.

"I do," said my Lord; and that was the last word that he spoke; for the headsman immediately stepped up, so soon as he was down, and with one blow cut his head all off, except a bit of skin, which he cut through with his knife.

Then he lifted up the head, and carried it to the four sides of the scaffold by the hair, crying:

"Here is the head of a traitor," as the custom was. My Lord's face looked very peaceful.

*   *   *

I rode home again alone, thinking of what I had seen, and the innocent blood that was being shed, and wondering whether this might not be the last shed for that miserable falsehood. But even after that sight, the thought of my Cousin Dorothy was never very far away; and before I was home again I was once more thinking of her more than of that from which I was just come, or of that to which I was going, for I was to see His Majesty that evening and so to France next day.

PART III

CHAPTER I

It was on a very stormy evening, ten months later, that I rode again into London, on my way from Rome and Paris.

*   *   *

Now, here again, I must omit altogether, except on one or two very general points, all that had passed since I had gone away on the day after my Lord Stafford's execution on Tower Hill. It is enough to say that I had done my business in Paris very much to His Majesty's satisfaction, as well as to that of others; and that M. Barillon himself had urged me to stay there altogether, saying that I could make a career for myself there (as the Romans say), such as I could never make in England. But I would not, though I must confess that I was very much tempted to it; and I know now, though I did not know it altogether then, that there were just two things that prevented me — and these were that His Majesty and my Cousin Dorothy were in England and not France.

Of my Cousin Dorothy I had heard scarcely anything at all; for the last letter I had had from Hare Street was at Eastertide; and Tom said not very much about his daughter, except that she was pretty well; and that he thought of taking her to town in the summer for a little. The rest of his letter was, two-thirds of it all about Hare Street and the lambs and how the fruit promised; and one-third of the affairs of the kingdom.

These affairs, of which I learned from other sources besides my Cousin Tom, were, in brief, as follows.

His Majesty, for the first time, since he had come to the throne, had shewn an extraordinary open courage in dealing with the country-party. (I must confess that my success in France was not wholly without connection with this. He was so much strengthened in French affairs that he felt, I suppose, that he could act more strongly at home.)

First, in January, he had dissolved the Parliament that had threatened the exclusion of the Duke of York, and that would vote him no money till he would yield. First he prorogued it, though there was a great clamour in his very presence; and then he dissolved it, coming in so early in the morning that none suspected his design.

Then he summoned a new Parliament to meet at Oxford: for at Oxford he knew he would have the support of the city, whereas at London he had not. That Parliament at Oxford will never be forgotten, I think; for it was more like an armed camp than a Parliament. Both parties went armed. My Lord Shaftesbury, in order to rouse the feeling on his side, went there in a borrowed coach without his liveries, as if he feared arrest or even death. But His Majesty answered that by himself going with all his guards about him, as if for the same reason. There were continual brawls in the city, and duels too. The parties went about like companies of cats and dogs, snarling and spitting at one another continually; and so fierce was the feeling that nothing could be done. My Lord Shaftesbury's creatures were still strong enough to hold their own; and at last His Majesty did the bravest thing he had ever done. He caused a sedan-chair to be brought privately to his lodgings, and his crown and robes to be put in there. Then he went in himself, and away to where the House of Lords was sitting, and before anyone could utter a word, he dissolved the Parliament once more, and altogether, and never again summoned another.

But that was not all.

First, it appeared as if even His Majesty himself was frightened at what he had done, for he allowed my Lord Archbishop of Armagh, Dr. Oliver Plunket, to be convicted and executed in London, clean contrary to all evidence or right or justice — just because he was a Papist, and the popular cry had been raised against him that he was conspiring to bring the French over to Ireland, whereas he was a good and kindly old man, who lived in the greatest simplicity and neither did nor designed harm to any living creature. (I do not know whether it was the name *France* that frightened the King; but certainly at that time I was engaged on his behalf in some transactions with that country which would have ruined him had they ever been known.) But then he recovered himself, after the sacrifice of one more Catholic, and did what he should have done a great while ago, and caused my Lord Shaftesbury to be arrested and sent to the Tower on a charge of fomenting insurrection, which was precisely what my Lord had been doing for the last two years at least.

But His Majesty's scheme fell through; for the sheriffs, who were Whigs, and on my Lord's side, therefore, packed the grand jury of the City and acquitted him.

Then there was another affair of which I, in my business in France, saw something of the other side. My negotiations were coming to a successful end, when news came over to Paris that the Prince William of Orange was in England, and made much of by His Majesty. This last was a lie; but I wrote across to His Majesty of what a bad impression such a rumour made; and urged him to make amends — which he did very handsomely. The Duke of Monmouth too was back again in London, and so was the Duke of York; so the chess-pieces were all again for the present on the squares on which the game had begun. It was also a little satisfaction to me to hear that Her Grace of Portsmouth had urged the Duke of York's return; for I thought myself not a little responsible for her change of face. Once again, however, the Duke returned to finish affairs in Scotland, and then came back to Court; and it was on his journey there that the *Gloucester* was wrecked, and His Royal Highness so nearly drowned.

The Duke of Monmouth however saw that affairs were moving against him; so he determined on a very bold stroke; and, after returning to England once more without His Majesty's leave, went through all the country as if on a royal progress; and it was astonishing how well he was received. It was then that Mr. Chiffinch wrote to me at length, telling me of the spies he had sent to follow the Duke everywhere, and asking whether I would not come over myself to help in it. But I was just considering whether I would not go to Rome; and, indeed, before I could make up my mind, another letter came saying that the Duke was to be arrested, and then let out on bail, and that he could do no more harm for the present. So I went to Rome, and there I stayed a good while, reporting myself and all that I had done, and being received very graciously by those who had sent me.

Since then, not very much of public import had happened, until in the first week in November I received in Paris a very urgent letter from Mr. Chiffinch telling me to return at once; but no more in it than that.

*   *   *

It was a very stormy night, as I have said, when I rode in over London Bridge to where the lights of the City shone over the water.

I was very content at my coming; for in spite of all my resolutions, it was a terrible kind of happiness to me to be in the same country (and so near to her, too) as was my Cousin Dorothy. I had striven to put her out of my head, I had occupied myself with that which is the greatest of all sports — and that is the game that Kings play in secret — I had become something of a personage, and rode now with four servants, instead of one. Yet never could I forget her. But I was resolved to play no more with such nonsense; to live altogether in London, and to send my men in a day or two to get my things from Hare Street. It often appears to me very strange, when I see some great man go by whose name is in all men's mouths for some office he holds or for his great wealth or power, to reflect that he has his secret interests as much as any, and is moved by them far more deeply than by those public matters for which men think that he cares. I was not yet a great personage, though I meant to be so; and my name was in no men's mouths, for it was of the very essence of what I did that it should not be; yet I was held in high consideration by two kings. But for all that, as I turned westwards from London Bridge, I looked northwards up Gracechurch Street, and longed to be riding to Hare Street, rather than to Whitehall.

*　　*　　*

It was strange, and yet very familiar too, to go up those stairs again, all alone — (for I had sent my men on to Covent Garden, where I had taken two sets of lodgings now, instead of one) — to tell the servant that Mr. Chiffinch looked for me, and to be conducted by him straight through to the private closet where he awaited me over his papers. I was in my boots, all splashed, and very weary indeed. Yet I had learned, ever since the day when His Majesty had found fault with me so long ago, never to delay even by five minutes, when kings call.

"Well?" I said; as I came in.

"Well!" said he; and took me by the hands.

Now it may seem surprising that I could tolerate such a man as was Mr. Chiffinch, still more that I should have become on such terms with him. The truth is, that I regarded him as two men, and not one. On the one side he was the spy, the servant, the panderer to the King's more disgraceful secrets; on the other he was a man of an extraordinary shrewdness, utterly devoted to His Majesty, and very competent indeed in very considerable affairs. If ever the secret memoirs of Charles II. see the light of day, Mr. Chiffinch will be honoured and admired, as well as contemned.

"First sup;" he said. "I have all ready: and not one word till you are done."

He took me through into a little dining-room that was opposite the closet; and here was all that a hungry man might desire of cold meats and wine. He had had it set out, he told me ever since five o'clock (for I had sent to tell him I would be there that night).

While I ate he would say nothing at all of the business on hand; but talked only of France and what I had done there. He told me the King was very greatly pleased; and there were rewards if I wished them — or even a title, though he was not sure of what kind, for I was a very young man.

"He vows you have done a thousand times more than the Duchess of Portsmouth in all her time. But I would recommend you to take nothing. It will not be forgotten, you may be sure. If you took anything now, it would make you known, and ruin half your work. If you will take my advice, Mr. Mallock, you will tell the King, Bye and bye; and have a peerage when the time comes."

Now of course these thoughts had crossed my mind too: but it was more to hear them from a man like this. I nodded at him but said nothing, feigning that my mouth was full; for indeed I did not quite know what to say. I need not say that the thought of my Cousin Dorothy came to me again very forcibly. At least I should have shewn her what I could do.

When I was quite done, Mr. Chiffinch carried me back to the parlour; and there, having locked the door, he told me what was wanted of me.

When he had done, I looked at him in astonishment. "You are as sure as that?" I said.

"We are sure, beyond the very leastest doubt, that at last there is a plot to kill the King. There are rumours and rumours. Well, these are of the right kind. And we are convinced that my Lord Shaftesbury is behind it, and my Lord Essex, and Mr. Sidney; and who else we do not know. My men whom I sent to spy out how Monmouth was received in the country, tell me the same. But the trouble is that we have no proof at all; and cannot lay a finger on them. And there is only that way, that I told you of, to find it out."

"That I should mix with them — feign to be one of them!" said I.

The man threw out his hands.

"Mr. Mallock," he said, "I told the King you were too nice for it. He said on the contrary that he was sure you would do it; that it was not a matter of niceness, but of plot against counterplot."

"A pretty simile!" I said with some irony; for I confess I did not like the idea; though I was far from sure I would not do it in the end.

"'If one army is besieging a castle or town,' said he, 'and mines beneath the ground after nightfall secretly, is it underhand action to do the same, and to countermine them?' But I said I was not sure what you would think of it. You see, Mr. Mallock, I scarcely know a single person who unites the qualities that you do. We must have a gentleman, or he would never be accepted by them; and he must be a shrewd man too. Well, I will not say we have no shrewd gentlemen: but what shrewd gentlemen have we, think you, who are not perfectly known — and their politics?"

"The Duchess of Portsmouth knows me," said I, beginning to hesitate.

"But she does not know one word of this affair; nor will they tell her. She is far too loyal for that."

"But she will have told others what I am."

"It is not likely, Mr. Mallock. We must take our chance of it. Truly I see no one for it but yourself. I would not have sent for you, if I had, for you were very useful in France. But the difficulty is, you see, that we can take no observable precautions. We have doubled the guards inside the palace at night; but we dare not in the day; for if that were known, they would suspect that we knew all, and would be on their guard. As it is, they have no idea that we know anything."

"How do they mean to do it?"

"That again we do not know. If they can find a fanatic — and there are plenty of the old Covenanting blood left — they might shoot His Majesty as he sits at supper. Or they may drag him out of his coach one day, as they did with Archbishop Sharpe. Or they might poison him. I have the cook always to taste the dishes before they come into Hall; but who can guard against so many avenues?"

*　　*　　*

I sat considering; but I was so weary that I knew I could decide nothing rightly. On the one side the thing appealed to me; for there was danger in it, and what does a young man love like that? And there was a great compliment in it for me — that I should be the one man they had for the affair. Yet it did not sound to me very like work for a gentleman — to feign to be a conspirator — to win confidence and then to betray it, in however a good cause.

What astonished me most however was the thought that the country-party had waxed as desperate as this. Certainly their tide was going down — as I had heard in France; but I did not know it was gone so low as this. And that they who had lied and perjured themselves over the Oates falsehoods, and had used them, and had kept the people's suspicions alive, and had professed such loyalty, and had been the cause of so much bloodshedding — that these men should now, upon their side, enter upon the very design that they had accused the Catholics of — this was very nearly enough to decide me.

"Well," said I, "you must give me twenty-four hours to determine in. I am drawn two ways. I do not know what to do."

"I can assure you," said the page eagerly, "that His Majesty would give you almost anything you asked for — if you did this, and were successful."

I pursed my lips up.

"Perhaps he would," I said. "But I do not know that I want very much."

"Then he would give you all the more."

I stood up to take my leave.

"Well, sir," I said, "I must go home again and to bed. I am tired out. I will be with you again tomorrow at the same time."

He rose to take me to the outer door.

"You will not want to go to Hare Street this time," he said, smiling.

"To Hare Street!" I said. "Why should I go there?"

"Well — the pretty cousin!" said he.

I set my teeth. I did not like Mr. Chiffinch's familiarities.

"Well, then, why should I not go?" I asked.

"Why: she is here! Did you not know?"

"Here! — in London."

"Aye: in Whitehall. I saw her only yesterday."

"In Whitehall! What do you mean, Mr. Chiffinch?"

I suppose my face went white. I knew that my heart beat like a hammer.

"Why, what I say!" said he. "Why do you look like that, Mr. Mallock?"

"Tell me!" I cried. "Tell me this instant!"

"Why: she is Maid of Honour to Her Majesty. The Duchess of Portsmouth is protecting her."

"Where is she?"

"Why —"

"*Where is she?*"

"She is with the rest, I suppose.... Mr. Mallock! Mr. Mallock! Where are you going?"

But I was gone.

CHAPTER II

When I was out in the air I stopped short; and then remembering that Mr. Chiffinch would be after me perhaps, and would try to prevent me, I went on as quick as I could, turned a corner or two in that maze of passages, and stopped again. As yet I had no idea as to what to do; my brain burned with horror and fury; and I stood there in the dark, clenching my hands again and again, with my whip in one of them. It was enough for me that my Cousin Dolly was in that den of tigers and serpents that was called the Court, and under the protection of the woman once called Carwell. There was not one thought in my brain but this — all others were gone, or were but as phantoms — the King, the Duke, Monmouth, the Queen — they would be so many wicked ghosts, and no more — before me — and I would go through them as through smoke, to tear her out of it.

I suppose that some species of sanity returned to me after a while, for I found myself presently pacing up and down the terrace by the river, and considering that this was a strange hour — eight o'clock at night, to be searching out one of Her Majesty's ladies; and, after that, little by little, persons and matters began to take their right proportions on them again. I could not, I perceived, merely demand where Mistress Jermyn lodged, beat down her door and carry her away with me safe to Hare Street. Their Majesties of England still stood for something in Whitehall, and so did reason and commonsense, and Dolly's own good name. I began to perceive that matters were not so simple.

I do not think I reasoned at all as to her dangers there; but I was as one who sees a flower on a dunghill. One does not argue about the matter, or question whether it be smirched or not, nor how it got there. Neither did I consider at all how my cousin came to be at Court, nor whether any evil had yet come to her. I did not even consider that I did not know whether she were but just come, or had been there a great while. I considered only that she must be got out of it — and how to set about it.

I might have stood and paced there till midnight, had not one of the sentinels at the water-gate — placed there I suppose, as Mr. Chiffinch had told me just now, as an additional security, after nightfall — stepped out from his place and challenged me. I had had the word, of course, as I came in; and I gave it him, and he was contented. But I was not. Here, thought I, is my opportunity.

"Here," said I, "can you tell me where Mistress Dorothy Jermyn is lodged?"

He was a young fellow, plainly from the country, as I saw, by his look in the light of the lantern he had.

"No, sir," he said.

"Think again," I said. "She is under the protection of Her Grace of Portsmouth. She is one of the Queen's ladies."

"Is she a little lady, sir — from the country — that came last month?"

"Yes," I said, feigning that I knew all about it, and trying to control my voice. "That is she."

"Why, she is with the others, sir," he said.

"She is not with the Duchess then?"

"No, sir; I know she is not. There is no lady with the Duchess beside her own. I was on my duty there last week."

This was something of a relief. At least she was not with that woman.

Now I knew where the Queen's Maids lodged. It was not an hundred yards away, divided by a little passage-way from Her Majesty's apartment, and adjoining the King's, with a wall between. There were five of these; besides those who lodged with their families — but they changed so continually that I could not be sure whether I knew any of them or not. I had had a word or two once with Mademoiselle de la Garde; but she was the only one I had ever spoken with; and besides, she might no longer be there; and she was a great busybody too; and beyond her I knew only that there was an old lady, whose name I had forgot, that was called Governess to them all and played the part of duenna, except when she could be bribed by green oysters and Spanish wine, not to play it. Such fragments of gossip as that was all that I could remember; as well as certain other gossip too, as to the life of these ladies, which I strove to forget.

However, I could do nothing at that instant, but bid the man good-night, and go up into the palace again with a brisk assured air, as if I knew what I was about. A bell beat eight from the clock-tower, as I went. Then when I had turned the corner to the left, I stopped again to reckon up what I knew.

This did not come to very much. Her Majesty, I knew, was attended always by two Maids of Honour at the least; and at this hour would be, very likely, at cards with them, if there were no reception or entertainment. If there were, then all would be there, and Dolly with them; and even in that humour I did not think of forcing my way into Her Majesty's presence and demanding my cousin. These receptions or parties or some such thing, were at least twice or three times a week, if Her Majesty were well. The reasonable thing to do, I confess, was to go home to Covent Garden, quietly; and come again the next day and find out a little; but there was very little reason in me. I was set but upon one thing; and that was to see Dolly that night with my own eyes; and assure myself that matters were, so far, well with her.

At the last I set out bravely, my legs carrying me along — as it appears to me now — of their own accord: for I cannot say that I had formed any design at all of what I should do; and there I found myself after a minute or two of walking in the rain, at the door of the lodgings where all the ladies that had not their families at Court lived together. There were three steps up to the heavy oaken door that was studded over with nails; and in the little window by the door a light was burning. I had come by the sentinel that stood before the way up to the King's lodgings, and had given him the word; but I saw that he was watching me, and that I must shew no hesitation. I went therefore up the steps, as bold as a lion, and knocked upon the oaken door.

I waited a full minute; but there was no answer; so I knocked again, louder; and presently heard movements within, and the sound of the bolts being drawn. Then the door opened, but only a little; and I saw an old woman's face looking at me.

She said something; but I could not hear what it was.

"Is Mistress Jermyn within doors?" I asked.

The old face mumbled at me; but I could not hear a word. "Is Mistress Jermyn within?" I asked again.

Once again the face mumbled at me; and then the door began to close.

This would never do; so I set my foot against it, suddenly all overcome with impatience — (for I was in no mood to chop words) — and with the same kind of fury that had seized me in Mr. Chiffinch's rooms. I saw red, as the saying is; and it was not likely that a deaf old woman would stop me. She fluttered the door passionately; and then, as I pushed on it, she cried out. There was a great rattle of footsteps, and as I came into the little paved entrance, a heavy bald fellow ran out of the room where I had seen the light — (which was the porter's parlour) — in his shirt-sleeves, very angry and hot-looking.

He looked at me, like a bull, with lowered head; and I saw that he carried some weapon in his hand.

"Is Mistress Jermyn within doors?" I asked, putting on a high kind of air.

"Who the devil are you?" said he.

I was not going to argue that point, for it was the weakest spot in my assault. So I sat down on the stairs that rose straight up to the first floor. (It was a little oak-panelled entrance that I was in, with a single lamp burning in a socket on the wall.)

"You will first answer my question," I said. "Is Mistress Jermyn within doors?"

Then he came at me, thinking, I suppose that my sitting down gave him an advantage, and he lifted his weapon as he came. I had no time to draw my own sword — which was besides, somewhere between my legs; but I rose up, and, as I rose, struck out at his chin with all my force, with my whole weight behind.

He staggered back against the doorway he had come out by; and the same moment two things happened. The old woman screamed aloud; and Dolly sprang suddenly out on to the head of the stairs, from a door that opened there, full into the light of the lamp.

"Why-" cried she.

"Oh! there you are," I said bitterly. "Then Mistress Jermyn is within doors."

Then I turned and went straight upstairs after her; and, as I went heard the ring of running footsteps in the paved passage out of doors, and knew that the guard was coming up. The fellow still leaned, dazed, against the doorpost; and the old woman was pouring out scream after scream.

I went after Dolly straight into the room from which she had come. It was a little parlour, very richly furnished, with candles burning, and curtains across the windows. It looked out towards the river, I suppose. Dolly was standing, as pale as paper; but I could not tell — nor did I greatly care — whether it were anger or terror. I think I must have looked pretty frightening — (but then, she had spirit enough for anything!) — for I was still in my splashed boots and disordered dress, and as angry as I have ever been in my life. I could see she was not dressed for Her Majesty; so I supposed — (and I proved to be right) — that she was not in attendance this evening. It was better fortune than I deserved, to find her so.

"Now," said I, "what are you doing here?"

(I spoke sharply and fiercely, as to a bad child. I was far too angry to do otherwise. As I spoke, I heard the guard come in below; and a clamour of voices break out. I knew that they would be up directly.)

"Now," I said again, "you have your choice! Will you give me up to the guard; or will you hear what I have to say? You can send them away if you will. You can say I am your cousin?"

She looked at me; but said nothing.

"Oh! I am not drunk," I said. "Now, you can —"

Then came a thunder of footsteps on the stairs; and I stopped. I knew I had broken every law of the Court; I had behaved unpardonably. It would mean the end of everything for me. But I would not, even now, have asked pardon from God Almighty for what I had done.

Then Dolly, with a gesture, waved me aside; and confronted the serjeant on the threshold.

"You can go," she said. "This is my cousin. I will arrange with them below."

The man hesitated. Over his shoulder I could see a couple more faces, glaring in at me.

Dolly stamped her foot.

"I tell you to go. Do you not hear me?"

"Mistress —" began the man.

"How dare you disobey me!" cried Dolly, all aflame with some emotion. "This is my own parlour, is it not?"

He still looked doubtfully; and his eyes wandered from her to me, and back again. He was yet just without the room. Then Dolly slammed to the door, in a passion, in his very face.

Then she wheeled on me, like lightning. (I heard the men's footsteps begin to go downstairs.)

"Now you will explain, if you please —" she began, with a furious kind of bitterness.

"My maid," said I, "that kind of talk will not do with me" — (for at her tone my anger blazed up higher even than hers). "It is I who have to ask Why and How?"

"How dare you —" she began.

I went up without more ado, and took her by the shoulders. Never in all the time I had known her, had the thought ever come to me, that one day I might treat her so. She struggled violently, and seemed on the point of crying out. Then she bit her lip; but there was no yielding in me; and I compelled her backwards to a chair.

"You will sit there," I said. "And I shall stand. I will have no nonsense at all."

She looked at me, I thought, with more hate than I had ever seen in human eyes; glaring up at me with scorn and anger and resentment all mingled.

"Yes — you can bully maids finely —" she said. "You can come and cringe for their protection first —"

I laughed, very short and harsh.

"That manner is of no good at all —" I said. "You will answer my questions. How did you come here? How long have you been here?"

She said nothing; but continued to look at me. Then again my anger rose like a wave.

"Do you think to stare me down?" I said. "If you will not answer me, I'll begone to those who will."

"You dare not!"

"Dare not! Do you think to frighten me? — Dolly, my dear, I am not in the mood to argue. Will you tell me how you came here, and how long ago? I must have an answer before I go."

For an instant she was silent.

"Will you go straight home again if I tell you?"

"Yes — I will promise that," said I — for now that I had seen her with my own eyes most of what I desired was done. The rest could wait twelve hours.

"Well, then," she said, "I have been here a month; and my father put me here."

"Your father!"

"Yes, my father. Have you anything to say against him?"

"No: I will say it to him."

I wheeled about to go to the door.

"You have done enough mischief then, you think!" sneered Dolly.

I turned about again.

"Mischief!"

"Why, you have ruined my name," said Dolly, with the savage look in her eyes still there. "But you did not think of that! You thought only of yourself. The whole palace will know tomorrow that you beat down the porter to force your way in. And it will not lose in the telling."

I had nothing to say to that. It was true enough, and the very kind of talk with which the Court continually diverted itself. But I would not show my dismay. Indeed the very thought of any trouble to her had no more occurred to my mind than the conse-quences to a charging bull.

"We will see about that," I said, "when I speak with His Maj-esty."

Dolly laughed again, but without merriment.

"Oh! you will do this and that, no doubt," she said. "And when shall you see His Majesty?"

I took out my watch.

"It is nearly nine," I said. "I shall see His Majesty in thirteen hours. You had best be packing your valises. We shall ride at noon."

I waited no more to hear her laugh, as she did again; but went out and down the staircase. The porter's chamber had its door half open: I pushed the door and went in. The fellow started up.

"Here is a guinea," said I, throwing one upon the table; "and my apologies. But 'twas you that began it!"

Then I turned and went out.

As I came down the steps into the little lamplit way, a man was coming swiftly up it from the direction of the court, with one of the guards behind him. I stopped short, thinking I was to be arrested. But it was the page.

"Good God!" he said. "You have done finely indeed!"

I was still all shaking; and I simulated anger without any difficulty.

"And whose fault is that?" said I, as if in a fury. "Do you think —"

"And His Majesty may come by at any instant!" he said.

"Why; that is what I wish. In any case I must see him at ten o'clock tomorrow."

"You are mad!" he said. "You had best begone to the country before dawn: and even that will not save you." He looked over his shoulder at the young man who had fetched him, and who now stood waiting.

"Save me! What have I done? I have but been to visit my cousin." (I said this very loud, that the guard might hear.)

Again Mr. Chiffinch looked over his shoulder, and back again. I could see the shine of lanterns where others waited behind. We were just outside the King's lodging.

"Well, sir," he said. "But you will go now, will you not?"

"Why, yes," I said. "And I will be with you at half-past nine tomorrow."

He beckoned the young soldier up.

"See this gentleman to the gate," he said. "He will find his way home, after that."

CHAPTER III

I spent a very heavy evening before I went to bed; and when I was there I could not sleep; for it appeared to me that I had made a great fool of myself, having injured my own prospects and done no good to anyone. I understood perfectly that I had acted in an unpardonable manner; for Her Majesty's Maids of Honour were kept, or were supposed to be kept, in very great seclusion at home, as if they were Vestal virgins — which was indeed a very great supposition. Tale after tale came back to my mind of those Maids in the past — of Mademoiselle de la Garde herself, of Miss Stewart, Miss Hyde, Miss Hamilton, and others like them — some of whom were indeed good, but had the greatest difficulty in remaining so; for the Court of Charles was a terrible place for virtue. It was astonishing to me that the horror of the place had not before this affected me; but it is always so. We are very philosophical, always, over the wrongs that do not touch ourselves.

As to how my Cousin Dolly came to be in such a place, I began to think that I understood. It must all have dated from that unhappy visit of the Duke of Monmouth to Hare Street; my Cousin Tom must have followed up that strange introduction, and the affair must have been worked through Her Grace of Portsmouth. I think I could have taken my Cousin Tom by the throat, and choked him, as I thought of this.

Meantime I had no idea as to what I should do the next day — except, indeed, see His Majesty, and say, perhaps, one tenth of what I felt. I had told Dolly we should ride at noon next day; I was beginning to wonder whether this prediction would be fulfilled. Yet, though I had begun to consider myself more than in the first flush, I still felt my anger rise in me like a tide whenever I regarded the bare facts. But mere anger would never do; and I set myself to drive it down. Besides, it would be there, I knew, and ready, if I should need it on the next day.

*　　*　　*

When I arrived at Mr. Chiffinch's the next morning, I found him in a very grave mood. He did not rise as I came in, but nodded to me, only.

"Sit down, Mr. Mallock," said he. "This is a very serious affair."

"So I think," I said.

He waved that away.

"His Majesty hath heard every word of it, with embellishments. He is very angry indeed. Nothing but what you have done for him lately could have saved you; and even now I do not know —"

"Man," I said, "do not let us leave such talk as this. It is not I who am in question —"

"I think you will find that it is," he answered me, with a quick look.

I strove to be patient, and, even more, to appear so.

"Well," I said, "what have I done? I am come back from France: I hear my cousin is here; I go to see her; a fellow at the door is impertinent, and I chastise him for it. Then I go upstairs to my cousin's parlour —"

"That is the point," he interrupted. "It is not your cousin's. It is the lodging of the Maids of Honour."

Yes: he had me there. That was my weak point. But I would not let him see that.

"How was I to understand that distinction? I knocked at the door as peaceably as any man could."

"And after that," he said, smiling a little grimly, "after that, your cousinly affection blinded you."

"Well, that will do," I said.

He smiled again.

"Well; that is your case," he observed. "We will see how His Majesty regards it. For I must tell you, Mr. Mallock, that for five minutes last night it was touch and go whether you were not to be arrested. And I will tell you this too, that if you had not come this morning, you would have been brought."

"As bad as that?" I said, laughing. (But I must confess that his gravity dismayed me a little.)

"As bad as that," he said. "You must go to His Majesty at ten."

"As I arranged," I said.

"As His Majesty arranged," said Mr. Chiffinch, rising: "and it is close upon the time."

And then he added, with the utmost gravity.

"If there is one thing His Sacred Majesty is touchy upon, it is the reputation of the ladies of the Court. I would remember that, sir, if I were you."

I observed a while ago that Pride is a good weapon if one has not Humility. So is Anger a good weapon, if one has not Patience; and I do not mean simulated Anger, but the passion itself, held in a leash, like a dog, and loosed when the time comes. Now, so great was my feeling for His Majesty, and that not only of an honest loyalty, but of a real kind of respect that I had for his person and his parts — a real fear of the very great strength of will that lay beneath his weakness — that I understood that, unless my anger was fairly near the surface, I should be beaten down when I came into his presence. So, as we went together towards his lodgings, I looked to see that my anger was there, patted it on the head so to say, and called it Good Dog: and was relieved to hear it growl softly in answer.

Plainly we were expected; because the two guards at the door stood aside as soon as they saw us, and one of them called out something to a man above. There were two more at the door itself; and we went in.

As we came in at the door of the private closet, having had no answer to our knock, His Majesty came in at the other with two dogs at his heels. He paid no attention to me at all, and barely nodded at my companion. Then he sat down to his table, and began to write; leaving us standing there like a pair of schoolboys.

Again I stroked the head of my anger. I could see the King was very seriously displeased; and that unless I could keep myself determined, he would have the best of the interview; and that I was resolved he should not have.

Suddenly he spoke, still writing.

"You can go, Chiffinch," said he. "Come back in half an hour."

He looked up for a flash and nodded; and I thought, God knows why, that he had in mind the guards outside, and that they should be within call. I knew precisely what my legal offence would be — that of brawling within the precincts of the palace; and the penalties of this I did not care to think about; for I was not sure enough what they were.

When the door closed behind Mr. Chiffinch I felt more alone than ever. I regarded the King's dark face, turned down upon his paper; his dusky ringed hand with the lace turned back; the blue-gemmed quill that he used, his great plumed hat. I looked now and again, discreetly, round the room, at the gorgeous carvings, the tall presses, the innumerable clocks, the brightly polished windows with the river flowing beneath. I felt very little and lonely. Then, in a flash, the memory came back that not fifty yards away was Dolly's little parlour, and Dolly herself; and my determination surged up once more.

Suddenly His Majesty threw down his pen.

"Mr. Mallock," he said very sternly, "there is only one excuse for you — that you were drunk last night. Do you plead that?"

He was looking straight at me with savage melancholy eyes. I dropped my own.

"No, Sir."

"You dare to say you were not drunk?"

"Yes, Sir." His Majesty caught up an ivory knife and sat drawing it through his fingers, still looking at me, I perceived; though I kept my eyes down. I could see that he was violently impatient.

"Mr. Mallock," said he, "this is intolerable. You come back from France where you have done me good service — I will never deny that — and you win my gratitude; and then you fling it all away by a piece of unpardonable behaviour. Are you aware of the penalties for such behaviour as yours? — brawling in the Palace itself, knocking my men down, forcing your way into the lodgings of Her Majesty's Ladies? Have you anything to say as to why you should not go before the Green Cloth?"

A great surge of contradiction and defiance rose within me; but I choked it down again. It was there if I should need it. The effort held me steady and balanced.

"Do you hear me, sir?"

"Yes, Sir," said I.

"Well — what have you to say?"

He glanced past me towards the door; and I thought again that the guards were in his mind.

"Sir; I have a very great deal to say. But I fear I should offend Your Majesty."

The King jerked his head impatiently.

"It is of the nature of a defence?"

"Certainly, Sir."

"Say it then. You need one."

I raised my eyes and looked him in the face. He was frowning; and his lips were moving. Evidently he was very angry; and yet he was perplexed, too.

"Sir, this is precisely what took place. I returned from France last night, where, as Your Majesty was good enough to remark, I was able to be of some little service. Upon my return I heard from Mr. Chiffinch that my 'pretty cousin' as he was kind enough to call her, was in Whitehall, as one of Her Majesty's ladies. I went to see my cousin, perhaps a little precipitately, but I went peaceably, first inquiring of one of Your Majesty's guards where her lodgings were. I knocked, peaceably, upon the door. An old woman opened to me, and would give me no intelligible answer to my — peaceable — inquiry as to whether my cousin were there. I prevented her closing the door in my face, but peaceably; then a fellow ran out, and asked me who the devil I was. Again, peaceably, I inquired for my cousin. I even sat down upon the stairs. Then he made at me; and in self-defence I struck him once, with my hand. My cousin looked out of a door, and I went up into what I understood was her parlour. When the guard came, she sent them away, telling them I was her cousin. The serjeant was impertinent to her; and she shut the door in his face. I remained five minutes, or six, with my cousin, and then went peaceably away, and to my lodgings. That is the entire truth, Sir, from beginning to end."

The King laughed, very short and harsh.

"You put it admirably," he said. "You are a diplomat, indeed."

"That is my defence to Your Majesty; and it is perfectly true — neither less nor more than the truth. But I am not only a diplomat."

He did not fully understand me, I think, for he looked at me sharply.

"Well?" he said. "What else?"

"I have another defence for the public — Sir — not so courteous to Your Majesty."

He remained rigid an instant.

"Then for the public," he said, "you do not think the truth enough?"

"No, Sir; it is for Your Majesty that I think the truth too much."

"I will have it!" cried the King. "This moment!"

Interiorly I licked my lips, as a dog when he sees a bone. His Majesty should have the truth now, with a vengeance. All was falling out exactly as I had designed. He should not have kept me waiting so long; or I might not have thought of it.

"Well, Sir," said I, "you will remember I should not have dared to say it to Your Majesty, had I not been commanded."

He said nothing. Then, once more, I ruffled my growling dog's ears, so that he snarled.

"First, Sir; to the public I should say: If this is counted brawling, what of other scenes in Whitehall on which no charge was made? What of the sun-dial, smashed all to fragments one night, in the Privy Garden, by certain of the King's Gentlemen whom I could name? What of the broken door-knockers — not only in the City, but upon certain doors in Whitehall itself — broken, again by certain of the King's Gentlemen whom I could name? What of a scene I viewed myself in the Banqueting Hall last Christmastide in Your Majesty's presence, when a Spanish gentleman received full in his face a bunch of raisins, from —"

"Ah!" snarled the King. "And you would say that to the public?"

"Sir — that is only the exordium " — (my voice was raised a little, I think, for indeed I was raging again by now). "Next, I would observe that Mistress Jermyn is my own cousin, and that the hour was eight o'clock in the evening — not nine, if I may so far correct Your Majesty; whereas very different hours are kept by some members of the Court, and the ladies are not their cousins at all."

I had never seen the King so angry. He was unable to speak for fury. His face paled to parchment-colour under his sallow skin, and his eyes burned like coals. This time I lashed my anger, deliberately, instead of tickling it merely.

"Sir; that is not nearly all; but I will miss out a few points, and come to my peroration. My peroration would be after this fashion. Such, I would say, is the charge against one who has been of service to His Majesty; and such is the Court (as I have described) of that same King. There is not a Court in Europe that has a Prince so noble as our own can be, of better parts, or of higher ambitions, or of so pure a blood. And there is no Prince who is served so poorly; no Court that so stinks in the nostrils of God and man, as does his. He is capable," I cried (for by now I was lost to all consideration for myself; my loyalty and love for him had come to the aid of my anger; and I saw that never again should I have such an opportunity of speaking my mind), "He is capable of as great achievements, as any Prince that has gone before him; for he has already won back the throne which his fathers lost. Would it be of service, I would say, to such a Prince as this, to punish a man who would lay down his life for him to give him even a moment's pleasure; and to let go scot-free men and women who have never done anything but injure him?"

I ceased; breathless, yet triumphing; for I knew that I had held His Majesty with my words. How he would take it, when he recovered, I did not know: nor did I greatly care. I had spoken my mind to him at last; and what I had said was no more than my conviction. That blessed gift of anger had done the rest: and, having done its work, retired again to chaos; and left me clear-headed and master of myself.

When I looked at him he was motionless. He was still very pale, but the terrible brightness of his eyes was gone.

Then he roused himself to sneer; but I did not care for that;

for there was no other way for him just then, consonant with his own dignity.

"Very admirably preached!" said he; "even if a trifle treasonous."

"I am pleased Your Majesty is satisfied," I said, with a little bow.

Then he broke down altogether, in the only way that he could; he gave a great spirt of laughter; then he leaned back and laughed till the tears ran down. Presently he was quieter.

"Oddsfish!" he cried, "this is a turning of tables indeed! I sent for you, Mr. Mallock —"

The door opened softly behind me; and a man put his head in.

"Go away! go away!" cried the King. "Cannot you see I am being preached to?"

The door closed again.

"I sent for you, Mr. Mallock, to reprimand you very severely. And instead of that it is you who have held the whip. Little Ken is nothing to it: you should have been a Bishop, Mr. Mallock."

Again he spirted with laughter. Then he drew himself up in his chair a little; and became more grave.

"This is all very well," he said. "But I think I must get in my reprimand, for all that. You will not be sent to the guard-room, or the Green Cloth — (or whatever it is that would meet your case) — this time, Mr. Mallock; I will deal with you myself. But it is a very serious business, and your distinctions would not serve you in law. A sundial is not so important as a Christian lady; and a bunch of raisins is not, legally, a blow in the face. Still less are all the sundials and Spaniards in the world, equal to one of Her Majesty's Maids of Honour. You understand that?"

I bowed again; reminding myself that I was not done with him, even yet.

"Yes, Sir."

"Consider yourself reprimanded severely, Mr. Mallock."

I bowed; but I stood still.

"You have my leave — Oh! by the way, Mr. Mallock; there are just ten words I must have with you on the French affairs."

He motioned to a seat.

"I may kiss the hand that has beaten me?" said I.

He laughed again. He was a very merry prince when he was in the mood.

"It should be the other way about, I should think," he said. But he gave me his hand; and I sat down.

All the while we were talking, still, with one-half of my mind I was considering what was to be done next. It was a part, only, of my business that had been done; yet how to accomplish the rest without spoiling all? Presently His Majesty himself repeated that which Mr. Chiffinch had already said to me; and spoke of some kind of recognition that was due to me. That gave me my cue.

"Your Majesty is exceedingly kind," I said. "But I trust I am not to be dismissed from the King's service? Mr. Chiffinch appeared to think —"

"Why, no," said he; "not even after all your crimes. Besides we have something for you. Did he not tell you?"

"Any public recognition, Sir," I said, "would effectually do so. The very small value that my services may have would wholly be lost, if they were known in any way."

"Chiffinch said the same," observed the King meditatively. "But —"

"Sir," I said, "might I not have some private recognition instead? There is a very particular favour I have in mind, which would be private altogether; and which I would take as a complete discharge of that which Your Majesty has been good enough to call a debt of the King's."

"Not money, man! Surely!" exclaimed the King in alarm.

"Not in the least, Sir; it will not cost the exchequer a far-thing."

"Well, you shall have it then. You may be sure of that."

"Well, Sir," said I, "it is a serious matter. Your Majesty will dislike it exceedingly."

He pursed his lips and looked at me sharply.

"Wait!" he said. "It will not affect my honour or — or my religion in any way?"

I assumed an air of slight offence.

"Sir; I should not be likely to ask it, if it affected Your Majesty's honour. And as for religion —" I stopped: for one more opening presented itself which I dared not neglect. From both his manner and his words I saw that religion was not very far from his thoughts.

"Well — sir," he said. "And what of religion?"

"Sir, I pray every day for Your Majesty's conversion —"

"Conversion, eh?"

"Conversion to the Holy Catholic Church, Sir. I would give my life for that, ten times over."

"There! there! have done," said His Majesty, with a touch of uneasiness.

"But I would not ask a pledge, blindfold, Sir; even to save all those ten lives of mine."

"One more than a cat, eh? Do you know, Mr. Mallock, you remind me sometimes of a cat. You are so demure, and yet you can pounce and scratch when the occasion comes."

"I would sooner it had been a little dog, Sir," I said, glancing at the spaniels that were curled up together before the fire.

"Well — well; we are wandering," smiled the King. "Now what is this favour?"

I supposed I must have looked very grave and serious; for before I could speak he leaned forward.

"It is to count as a complete discharge, I understood you to say, Mr. Mallock, for all obligations on my part. And there is no money in it?"

"Yes, Sir," said I. "And there is no money in it."

He must have seen I was serious.

"Well; I take you at your word, sir. I will grant it. Tell me what it is."

He leaned back, looking at me curiously.

"Sir," I said, "it is now about half-past ten o'clock. What I ask is that my cousin, Mistress Dorothy Jermyn, receives an immediate dismissal from Her Majesty's service; and is ordered to leave London with me, for her father's house, at noon."

His Majesty looked at me amazed. I think he did not know whether to be angry, or to laugh.

"Well, sir," he said at last. "That is the maddest request I have ever had. You mean what you say?"

"Certainly, Sir."

"Well: you must have it then. It is the queerest kindness I have ever done. Why do you ask it? Eh?"

"Sir; you do not want my peroration over again!"

His face darkened.

"That is very like impudence, Mr. Mallock."

"I do not mean it for such, Sir. It is the naked truth."

"You think this is not a fitting place for her?"

"I am sure it is not, Sir," I said very earnestly, "nor for any country-maid. Would Your Majesty think —"

He jerked his head impatiently.

"What my Majesty thinks is one thing; what I, Charles Stuart, do, is another. Well: you must have it. There is no more to be said."

I think he expected me to stand up and take my leave. But I remained still in my chair.

"Well; what else, sir?" he asked.

"Sir; it is near a quarter to eleven. I have not the order, yet."

"Bah! well — am I to write it then?"

"If Your Majesty will condescend."

"And what shall I say to the Queen? It is not very courteous to dismiss a lady of hers so abruptly."

"Sir; tell Her Majesty it is a debt of honour."

He wheeled back to his table, took up a sheet and began to write. When he had done he scattered the sand on it, and held it out to me, his mouth twitching a little.

"Will that serve?" he said.

I have that paper still. It is written with five lines only, and a signature. It runs as follows:

> "This is to command Mistress Dorothy Jermyn, late Maid of Honour to Her Majesty, now dismissed by the King, though through no fault of her own, to leave the Court at Whitehall at noon today, in company with her cousin Mr. Roger Mallock, and never to return thither without his consent.
> "CHARLES R."

Then followed the date.

I had a criticism or two; but I dared not make them.

"That is more than I could have asked, Sir. I am under an eternal obligation to Your Majesty."

"I daresay: but all mine are discharged to you, until you earn some more. It might have meant a peerage, Mr. Mallock."

"I do not regret it, Sir," I said.

As I rose after kissing his hand, he said one more word to me.

"You are either a very wise man, or a fool, Mr. Mallock. And by God I do not know which. But I do know you are a very brave one."

"I was a very angry one, Sir," said I.

"But you are appeased?"

"A thousand times, Sir."

CHAPTER IV

I knew I could never carry the matter through alone; so, upon leaving the King's presence, I sought out Mr. Chiffinch immediately and told him what had passed.

He whistled, loud.

"You are pretty fortunate," he said. "Many a man —"

"I have no time for compliments," said I. "You must come with me to my cousin at once. We must ride at noon; and it is close upon eleven."

"You want me to plead for you, eh?"

"Not at all," said I. "There will be no pleading. It is to certify only that this is the King's writing, and that he means what he says."

"Well, well," said Mr. Chiffinch. "And what of the matter I spoke to you of last night? Have you decided? There is not much time to lose."

"You must give me a day or two," I said.

*　　*　　*

It was he who knocked this time; and it was not until the old woman had opened, and was curtseying to the King's page, that he called me up.

"Come, Mr. Mallock. Your cousin is within."

We went straight upstairs after the old lady; and upon her knock being answered, she threw the door open.

My Cousin Dolly was sitting over her needle, all alone. She looked, I thought, unusually pale; but she flushed scarlet, and sprang up, so soon as she saw me.

"Good-day, Mistress Jermyn," said the page very courteously. "We are come on a very sad errand — sad, that is, to those whom you will leave behind."

"What do you mean, sir?" asked Dolly, very fiercely. She did not give me one look, after the first.

He held out the paper to her. She took it, with fingers that shook a little, and read it through at least twice.

"Is this an insult, sir; or a very poor pleasantry?" (Her face was gone pale again.)

"It is neither, mistress. It is a very sober fact."

"This is the King's hand?" she snapped.

"It is," said Mr. Chiffinch.

"Dolly," said I, "I told you to be ready by noon; but you would not believe me. I suppose your packing is not done?"

She paid me no more attention than if I had been a chair.

"Mr. Chiffinch," said she, "you tell me, upon your honour, that this is the King's hand, and that he means what is written here?"

"I give you my honour, mistress," he said.

She tossed the paper upon the table; she went swiftly across to the further door, and opened it.

"Anne!" she said.

A voice answered her from within.

"Put out my riding-dress. Pack all that you can, that I shall need in the country. We have to ride at noon." She shut the door again, and turned on us — or rather, upon Mr. Chiffinch.

"Sir," she said, "you have done your errand. Perhaps you will now relieve me of your company. I shall be awaiting my cousin, Mr. Roger Mallock, as the King requires, at noon."

"Dolly —" said I.

She continued, looking through me, as through glass.

"At noon: and I trust he will not keep me waiting."

There was no more to be done. We turned and went out.

"Lord! what a termagant is your pretty cousin, Mr. Mallock!" said my companion when we were out of doors again. "You could have trusted her well enough, I think."

I was not in the mood to discuss her with him; I had other things to think of.

"Mr. Chiffinch," I said, "I am very much obliged to you; but I must be off for my own packing." And I bade him good-day.

*   *   *

When I rode into the court, five minutes before noon, a very piteous little group awaited me by the inner gate. Dolly, very white and angry, stood by the mounting-block, striving to preserve her dignity. Her maid was behind her, arguing how the bags should be disposed on the pack-horse, with the fellow who was to lead it. Dolly's own horse was not yet come; but as I rode up to salute her, he came out of an archway led by a groom.

I leapt off, and stood by the mounting-block to help her. Again it was as if I were not there. She jerked her head to the man.

"Help me," she said.

He was in a quandary, for he could not leave the horse's head.

"I am very sorry, Dolly," said I, "but you will have to put up for me for once. Come."

She gave a look of despair round about; but there was no help.

"It is on the stroke of noon," I said.

She submitted; but it was with the worst grace I have ever seen. She accepted my ministrations; but it was as if I were a machine: not one word did she speak, good or bad.

By the time that she was mounted, her maid was up too, and the bags disposed.

"Come," I said again; and mounted my own horse.

As we rode out through the great gate, the Clock Tower beat the hour of noon.

*　　*　　*

I am weary of saying that my journeys were strange; but, certainly, this was another of them.

*　　*　　*

Through the narrow streets I made no attempt to ride beside her. In the van went three of my men; then rode I; then, about ten yards behind, came Dolly and her maid. Then came two pack-horses, led by a fellow who controlled them both; and my fourth man closed the dismal cavalcade. So we went through the streets — all the way down the Strand and into the City, wheeled to the left, and so out by Bishopsgate. It was a clear kind of day, without rain: but the clouds hung low, and I thought it would rain before nightfall. I intended to do the whole journey in a day; so as to be at Hare Street before midnight at least. A night on the way, and Dolly's company at supper, all alone with me, or even with her maid, appeared to me too formidable to face.

When we were out in the country, I reined my horse in. I saw a change pass over Dolly's face; then it became like stone.

"We have a long ride, for one day," said I.

She made no answer. My anger rose a little.

"My Cousin," I said, "I had the honour to speak to you."

"I do not wish to have the dishonour of answering you," said Dolly.

It was a weakness on her part to answer at all; but I suppose she could not resist the repartee.

"A very neat hit," I said. "Must all our conversation run upon these lines?"

She made no answer at all.

"Anne," I said, "rein your horse back ten yards."

"Anne," said Dolly, "ride precisely where you are."

"Very good," said I. "I have no objection to your maid hearing what I have to say. I thought it would be you that would object."

"Anne," said Dolly, "did you pack the sarcenet?"

"Yes, mistress."

"Then tell me again the tale that you were —"

I broke in with such fury that even Dolly ceased.

"My Cousin," I said, "I have a louder voice than either of you; and I shall use it, if you do not listen, so that the whole country-side shall hear. I have to say this — that some time or another today I have to have a private conversation with you. It is for you to choose the time and place. If you give me no opportunity now, I shall make it myself, later. Will you hear what I have to say now?"

There was a very short silence.

"Anne," said Dolly, "now that we can hear ourselves speak, will you tell me again the tale that you began last night?"

She said it, not at all lightly, but with a coldness and a dis-tilled kind of anger that gave me no choice. I lifted my hat a little; shook my reins; and once more took up my position ten yards ahead. There was a low murmur of voices behind; and then silence. It appeared that the tale was not to be told after all.

*　　*　　*

We dined, very late, at a little inn, called the *Cross-Keys*, between Edmonton and Ware. I remember nothing at all, either of the inn or the host or the food — nothing but the name of the inn, for the name struck me, with a dreary kind of wit, as reflec-tive of the cross-purposes which we were at. We three dined together, in profound silence, except when Dolly addressed a word or two to her maid. As for me, she took the food which I carved, all as if I were a servant, without even such a thank-you as a man gives to a servant.

We took the road again, about three o'clock; and even then the day was beginning to draw in a little, very bleak and dismal; and that, too, I took as a symbol of my heart within, and of my cir-cumstances and prospects. Certainly I had gained my desire in one way; I had got Dolly away from Court; yet that was the single point I had to congratulate myself upon. All else, it appeared, was ruined. I had lost all the advantage, or very nearly all, that I had ever won from the King — (for I knew, that although he had been merry at the end of the time, he would not forget how I had wor-sted him) — and as for Dolly, I supposed she would never speak to me again. It had been bad enough when I had left Hare Street nearly a twelvemonth ago: my return to it now was a hundred times worse.

Although Dolly, however, would not speak to me, I was entirely determined to speak to Dolly. I proposed to rehearse to her what I had done, and why; and when that was over, I would leave it in her hands whether I remained at Hare Street a day or two, or left again next morning. More than a day or two, I did not even hope for. I had insulted her — it seemed — beyond forgiveness. Yet, besides my miserableness, there was something very like pleasure as well, though of a grim sort. I had spoken my mind to her, pretty well, and would do so more explicitly; and I was to speak my mind very well indeed to her father. There was a real satisfaction to me in that prospect. Then, once more, I would shut the door for ever on Hare Street, and go back again to town, and begin all over again at the beginning, and try to retrieve a little of what I had lost. Such then were my thoughts.

We supped, at Ware — at the *Saracen's Head*, and the same wretched performance was gone through as at the *Cross-Keys*. Night was fallen completely; and we had candles that guttered not a little. Dolly was silent, however, this time, even to her maid. She did not give me one look, all through supper.

When I came out afterwards to the horses, the yard was all in a mist: I could see no more than a spot of light where the lamp should be by the stable-door. The host came with me.

"It has fallen very foggy, sir," he said. "Would it not be best to stay the night?"

I was considering the point before answering; but my cousin answered for me, from behind.

"Nonsense," said she. "I know every step of the way. Where are the horses?"

(Even that, I observed, she said to the host and not to me.)

"The lady is impatient to get home," I said. "Is the fog likely to spread far?"

"It may be from here to Cambridge, sir," he said — "at this time of the year."

"Where are the horses?" said Dolly again.

There was no help for it. Once more we mounted; Dolly, again, assisted by the host, and not by me: but Anne was gracious enough to accept my ministrations.

For a few miles all went well: but the roads hereabouts were very soft and boggy; it was next to impossible sometimes to know whether we were right or not; and after a while one of my men waited for me — he that carried the lantern to guide the rest of us. The first I saw of him was his horse's ears, very black, like a pair of horns, against the lighted mist. "Sir," he said, "I do not know the road. I can see not five yards, light or no light."

I called out to James.

"James," said I, "do you know where we are?"

"No, sir," said he, "at least not very well."

"Cousin," I said — (for Dolly had reined up her horse close behind, not knowing, I suppose, that I was so near). "Cousin, I am sorry to trouble you; but unless you can lead us —"

"Give me the lantern," she said sharply to my man.

She took it from him, and pushed forwards. I wheeled my horse after her and followed. The rest fell in behind somewhere. I did not say one word, good or bad; for a certain thought had come to me of what might happen. She thought, I suppose, that Anne was behind her.

So impatient was my Cousin Dolly, that, certain of her road, as she supposed, she urged her horse presently into a kind of amble. I urged mine to the same; and so, for perhaps ten minutes, we rode in silence. I could hear the horses behind — or rather the sucking noise of their feet, — fall behind a little, and then a little more. The men were talking, too; and so was Anne, to them — for she liked men's company, and did not get very much of it in Dolly's service — and this I suppose was the reason why they did not notice how the distance grew between us. After about ten minutes I heard a man shout; but the fog deadened his voice, so that it sounded a great way off; and Dolly, I suppose, thought he was not of our party at all; for she never turned her head; and besides, she was intent on hating me, and that, I think, absorbed her more than she knew. I said nothing; I rode on in silence, seeing her like an outline only in the dark, now and again — and, more commonly nothing but a kind of lighted mist, now and then obscured. It appeared to me that we were very far away to the right; but then I never professed to know the way; and it was no business of mine. Truly the very courses of nature fought against my cousin and her passionate ways. Presently I turned at a sound; and there was James' mare at my heels. I knew her even in the dark, by the white blaze on her forehead. I had been listening for the voices; and had not noticed he was there. I reined up, instantly; and as he came level I plucked his sleeve.

"James," I whispered in Italian, lest Dolly should catch even a phrase of what I said — "not a word. Go back and find the others. Leave us. We will find our way."

James was an exceedingly discreet and sensible fellow — as I knew. He reined back upon the instant, and was gone in the black mist; and I could hear his horse's footsteps passing into the distance. What he thought, God and he alone knew; for he never told me.

The soft sound of the hoofs was scarcely died away, before I too had to pull in suddenly; for there were the haunches of Dolly's horse before the very nose of my poor grey. She had halted; and was listening. I held my breath.

"Anne," she said suddenly. "Anne, where are you?"

As in the Scripture — there was no voice nor any that answered. There was no sound at all but the creaking of the harness, and the soft breathing of the horses, for we had been coming over heavy ground. The world was as if buried in wool.

"Anne," she said again; and I caught a note of fear in her voice.

"Cousin," said I softly, "I fear Anne is lost, and so are the rest. You see you would not speak to me; and it was none of my business —"

"Who is that?" said she sharply. But she knew well enough.

I resolved to spare her nothing; for I was beginning to understand her a little better.

"It is Cousin Roger," I said. "You see you said you knew the road, and so —"

Then she lashed her horse suddenly; and I heard him plunge. But he could not go fast, from the heaviness of the ground; and he was very weary too, as were we all. Besides, she forgot that she carried the lantern, I think; and I was able to follow her easily enough; as the light moved up and down. Then the light halted once more; and I saw a great whiteness beyond it which I could not at first understand.

I came up quietly; and spoke again.

"Dolly, my dear; we had best have a little truce — an armed truce, if you will — but a truce. You can be angry with me again afterwards."

"You coward!" she said, with a sob in her voice, "to lead me away like this —"

"My dear, it was you who did the leading. Do me bare justice. I have followed very humbly."

She made no answer.

"Cousin; be reasonable," I said. "Let us find the way out of this; and when we are clear you can say what you will — or say nothing once more."

She took me at my word, and preserved her deadly silence.

I slipped off my horse; she was within an arm's length, and, not trusting her, I passed my arm with scarcely a noticeable movement through her bridle. It was well that I did so; for an instant after she tore at the bridle, not knowing I had hold of it, and lashed her horse again, thinking to escape whilst I was on the ground. I was very near knocked down by the horse's shoulder, but I slipped up my hand and caught him close to the bit — holding my own with my other hand.

"You termagant!" I said, as soon as I had them both quiet; for I was very angry indeed to be treated so after all my gentleness. "No more trust for me. It would serve you right if I left you here."

"Leave me," she wailed, "leave me, you coward!"

I set my teeth.

"I shall not," I said. "I shall punish you by remaining. I know you hate my company. Well, you will submit to it, then, because I choose so. Now then, let us see —"

Then she burst out suddenly into a passion of weeping. I set my teeth harder than ever. There was only one way, after all, to get the better of Dolly; and I had pitched on it.

"Yes: it is very well to cry," I said. "You nearly had me killed just now. Well: you will have to listen to me presently, whether you like it or not. Give me the lantern."

She made no movement. She had fought down the tears a little; but I could hear her breath still sobbing. I reached up and took the lantern from her right hand.

"Now; where in God's name are we?" said I.

We had ridden into some kind of blind alley, I presently saw; and that was why Dolly's horse had halted. Even that I had not owed to her goodwill. For we had ridden, I saw presently, lifting the lantern up and down, into a great chalk pit; and must have turned off along the track that led to it, from one of those sunken ways that drovers use to bring their flocks up to the high road. That we were to the right of the high road I was certain, of my own observation. *Ergo*; if we could get back into the sunken way and turn to the right, we might find ourselves on familiar ground again. However, I said nothing of this to Dolly. I was resolved that she should suffer a little more first. I took the bridles of the two horses more securely, slipping my hand with the lantern through the bridle of my own, turned their heads round and walked between them, looking very closely on this side and that, and turning my lantern every way. After twenty yards I saw that I was right. The bank on my left proved to be no bank, but the cliff-edge of the chalk pit only, by which the sunken way passed very near. I led the horses round to the right; and there were we, in the very situation I had surmised. Still holding Dolly's bridle, I mounted my own horse; and when I had done so, to secure myself and her the better, I pulled the reins suddenly over her horse's head, and brought them into my left hand.

"That is safer," I observed. "Now we can pretend to be friends again; and hold that conversation of which I spoke after we left London."

There was no answer, as we set out along the way. It was a little clearer by now; and I could see the bank on my right. I glanced at her; and in the light of the lantern I could see that she was sitting very upright and motionless like a shadow. I lowered the lantern to the right side, so that she was altogether in the dark and the bank illuminated. I felt a little compassion for her indeed; but I dared not shew it.

"Now, Cousin," I said, "I preached to His Majesty yesterday; and he told me I should be a Bishop at least. Now it is you that must hear a sermon."

Again she said nothing.

I had rehearsed pretty well by now all that I meant to say to her; and it was good for me that I had, else I might have fallen weak again when I saw her so unhappy. As it was I kept back some of the biting sentences I had prepared. My address was somewhat as follows. We jogged forward very gingerly as I spoke.

"Cousin," I began, "you have treated me very ill. The first of your offences to me was that, though I had earned, I think, the right to call myself your friend, neither you nor your father gave me any hint whatever of your going to Court. I know very well why you did not; and I shall have a little discourse to make to your father upon the matter, at the proper time. But for all that I had a right to be told. If you were to go, I might at least have got you better protection in the beginning than that of the — the — well — of Her Grace of Portsmouth.

"Now all that was the cause of the very small offence that I committed against you myself — that of forcing my way into your lodgings. For that I offer my apologies — not for the fact, but for the manner of it. And even that apology is not very deep: I shall presently tell you why.

"The next of your offences to me was that open defiance which you shewed, and some of the words you addressed to me, both then and afterwards. You have told me I was a coward, several times, under various phrases, and twice, I think, *sans* phrase. Cousin; I am a great many things I should not be; but I do not think I am a coward; at least I have never been a coward in your presence. Again, you have told me that I was very good at bullying. For that I thank God, and gladly plead guilty. If a maid is bent on her own destruction, if nothing else will serve she must be bullied out of it. Again, I thank God that I was there to do it."

I looked at her out of the tail of my eye. Her head seemed to me to be a little hung down; but she said nothing at all.

"The third offence of yours is the intolerable discourtesy you have shewn to me all today — and before servants, too. I put myself to great pains to get you out of that stinking hole called Whitehall; I risked His Majesty's displeasure for the same purpose: I have been at your disposal ever since noon; and you have treated me like a dog. You will continue to treat me so, no doubt, until we get to Hare Street; and you will do your best no doubt to provoke a quarrel between your father and myself. Well; I have no great objection to that; but I have not deserved that you should behave so. I have done nothing, ever since I have known you, but try to serve you —" (my voice rose a little; for I was truly moved, and far more than my words shewed) — "You first treated me like a friend; then, when you would not have me as a lover, I went away, and I stayed away. Then, when you would not have me as a lover, and I would not have you as my friend, I became, I think I may fairly say, your defender; and all that you do in return —"

Then, without any mistake at all, I caught the sound of a sob; and all my pompous eloquence dropped from me like a cloak. My anger was long since gone, though I had feigned it had not. To be alone with her there, enclosed in the darkness as in a little room — her horse and mine nodding their heads together, and myself holding her bridle — all this, and the silence round us, and my own heart, very near bursting, broke me down.

"Oh! Dolly," I cried. "Why are you so bitter with me? You know that I have never thought ill of you for an instant. You know I have done nothing but try to serve you — I have bullied you? Yes: I have; and I would do the same a thousand times again in the same cause. You are wilful and obstinate; but I thank God I am more wilful and obstinate than you. I am sick of this fencing and diplomacy and irony. You know what I am — I am not at all the fine gentleman that leaned his head on the chimney-breast — that was make-believe and foolishness. I am a bully and a brute — you have told me so —"

"Oh!" wailed Dolly suddenly — no longer pretending; and I caught the note in her voice for which I had been waiting. I dropped the lantern; the horses plunged violently at the flare and the crash; but I cared nothing for that. I dragged furiously on the bridle; and as the horses swung together, I caught her round the shoulders, and kissed her fiercely on the cheek. She clung to me, weeping.

CHAPTER V

Well; I had beaten her at last; and in the only way in which she would yield. Weakness was of no use with her, nor gentleness, nor even that lofty patronage which, poor fool! I had shewn her in the parlour at Hare Street. She must be man's mate — which is certainly a rather savage relation at bottom — not merely his pretty and grateful wife. This I learned from her, as we rode onwards and up into the high road — (where, I may say in passing, there was no sign of our party) — though she did not know she was telling it me.

"Oh! Roger," she said. "And I thought you were a — a pussy-cat."

"That is the second time I have been told so in two days," I said.

"Who told you so?"

"His Majesty."

"I thought His Majesty was wiser," said she.

"He has been pretty wise, though," I said. "If it were not for him, we should not be riding here together."

"I suppose you made him do that too," she said.

*　　*　　*

But it was not only of Dolly that I had learned my lessons; it was of myself also. I was astonished how inevitable it appeared to me now that we should be riding together on such terms; and I understood that never, for one instant, all through this miserable year away from her, had I ever, interiorly, loosed my hold upon her. Beneath all my resolutions and wilful distractions the intention had persevered. All the while I was saying to myself in my own mind that I should never see Dolly again, something that was not my mind — (I suppose my heart) — was telling me the precise opposite. Well; the heart had been right, after all.

*　　*　　*

She asked me presently what I should say to her father.

"I shall forgive him a great deal now, that I thought I never should," I said with wonderful magnanimity. "A few sharp words only, and no more. You see, my dear, it was through his sending you to Court —"

"Yes: yes," she said.

"He has behaved abominably, however," I said, "and I shall

tell him so. Dolly, my love."

"Yes," said she.

"I must go back very soon to town. I have been offered a piece of work; and even if I do not accept it, I must speak of it to them."

"Them?"

"Yes, my dear. I must say no more than that. It is *secretum commissum* as we say in Rome."

"And to think that you were a Benedictine novice!" exclaimed Dolly.

We talked awhile of that then; she asked me a number of questions that may be imagined under such circumstances: and my answers also can be imagined; and we spoke of a great number of things, she and I riding side by side in the dark, our very horses friendly one with another — she telling me all of how she went to Court, and why she went, and I telling her my side of the affair — until at last in Puckeridge a man ran out from the inn yard to say that our party was within and waiting for us. They had met, it appeared, a rustic fellow who had set them right, soon after they had lost us.

I do not know what they thought at first; but I know what they thought in the end; for I rated them very soundly for not keeping nearer to us; and bade James ride ahead with the lantern with all the rest between, and Dolly and I in the rear to keep them from straying again. In this manner then did she and I contrive to have a great deal more conversation before we came a little before midnight to Hare Street.

The village was all dark as we came through it; and all dark was the House when we pushed open the yard gates and rode in. We went through and beat upon the door, and presently heard a window thrown up.

"Who is there?" cried my Cousin Tom's voice.

I bade Dolly's maid answer. (She was all perplexed, poor wench, at the change of relations between her mistress and me.)

"It is Mistress Jermyn, sir," she said.

"Yes, father; I have come back," cried Dolly.

There was an exclamation from poor Tom; and in two or three minutes we saw a light beneath the door, and heard him drawing the bolts. I pushed Dolly and her maid forward as the door opened, and then myself strode suddenly forward into the light.

"Why — God bless —" cried Tom; who was in his coat and shoes. I could see how his face fell when he saw me. I looked at him very grimly: but I said nothing to him at once (for I was sorely tempted to laugh at his apparition), but turned to James and bade him see to the rest and find beds somewhere. Then I went after Dolly and her father into the Great Chamber, still with my hat on my head and looking very stern. He was talking very swiftly in a low voice to Dolly; but he stopped when I came in.

"Yes, Cousin Tom," I said, "I am come back again — all unlooked for, as I see."

"But, good God!" he cried. "What is the matter; and why is Dolly here? I was but just asking —"

I pulled out the King's paper which I had all ready, and thrust it down before the lantern that he had put on the table: and I waited till he had read it through.

"There, Cousin!" I said when he was staring on me again, "that is enough warrant for both you and me, I think. Have you anything to say?"

He began to bluster.

"Cousin," I said, "if I have any patience it is because Dolly has given it back to me. You had best not say too much. You have done all the harm you could; and it is only by God's mercy that it has not been greater."

He said that he was Dolly's father and could do as he pleased. Besides, she herself had consented.

"I know that," I said, "because she has told me so; and that it was in despair that she went, because we two fools bungled our business. Well, you may be her father; but the Scripture tells us that a woman must leave her father and cleave to her husband; and that is what I am to be to her."

Well; when I said that, there was the Devil to pay — we three standing there in the cold chamber, with the draughts playing upon poor Tom's legs. He looked a very piteous object, very much fallen from that fine figure that he had presented when I had first set eyes on him; but he strove to compensate by emphasis what he lacked in dignity. He said that he had changed his mind; that even third cousins once removed should not marry; that he had now other designs for his daughter; that I had no right to dictate to him in his own house. He waxed wonderfully warm; but even then, in the first flush of his resistance I thought I saw a kind of wavering. I sat with one leg across the corner of the great table until he was done; while Dolly sat in a chair, turning her merry eyes from the one to the other of us. For myself, I felt no lack of confidence. I had beaten the daughter; now I was to beat the father.

When he had finished, and drew breath, I stood up.

"Very bravely said, Cousin, bare legs and all," I said. "We will speak of it all again tomorrow. But now for a bite; we have been riding since noon."

It was very strange to go upstairs again after a mouthful or two, and a glass of warm ale, and see my chamber again from which I had departed in such unhappiness near a twelvemonth ago. James had made a little fire for me, before which I drew off my boots and undressed myself. For it was from this very chamber that I had gone forth in such despair, when Dolly had said that she would not have me: and now, here I was in it again, all glowing with my ride and my drink and my great content, having kissed Dolly just now in her father's presence as a symbol of our troth. And so I went to bed and dreamed and woke and dreamed again.

We had our talk out next morning, Tom pacing up and down the Great Chamber, until I entreated him for God's sake to sit down and save my stiff neck. He was very high at first; but I was astonished how quickly he came down.

"That is very well," I said, "to speak now of better prospects for Dolly. But you will do me the honour of remembering, my dear Cousin, that in this very room once you spoke to me very differently. If you have changed your mind, you might at least have told me so; for I have not changed mine at all; and Dolly, it seems, is come round to my way of thinking at last."

"But how did you do it?" asked he, stopping in his walk.

"I lost my temper altogether," said I; "and that is a very good way if you have tried all the rest."

"But the King, man, the King! How did you get that paper out of him? Why His Majesty himself, I am told, took particular notice —"

"Eh?" said I.

"That is no matter now," he said. "What were you going to say?"

"I must have that first," said I.

Tom began to pace the floor again.

"It is nothing at all, Cousin. It is that His Majesty spoke very kindly to my daughter upon her first coming to Court."

"I am glad I did not know that," I said, "or I might have said more to him."

"Well; but what did you say?"

Now I was in half a dozen minds as to what I should tell him. He knew for certain nothing at all of my comings and goings and of what I did for the King; yet I thought that he must have guessed a good deal. I judged it safer, therefore, to tell him a little, to stop his month; but not too much.

"Why," I said very carefully, "I have been of a little service to the King; and His Majesty was good enough to ask me if there were any little favour he could do me. So that is what I asked him."

Tom stopped in his pacing again: and it was then that I entreated him to sit down and talk like a Christian. He did so, without a word.

"In France, I suppose?" he said immediately after.

"Why, yes."

Tom looked at me again.

"And you travel with four men now, instead of one."

"I find it more convenient," I said.

"And more expensive too," he observed.

"Why, yes: a little more expensive, too," I answered. But I was a shade uneasy; because this increase of servants was at His Majesty's desire and cost. I made haste to turn the conversation back once more. I did not wish Tom to think that I was of any importance at all.

"Well; but what of Dolly?" I said.

It was then that my Cousin suddenly came down from his loftiness. He seemed to awake out of a little reverie.

"You come into the enjoyment of your property," he said, "in four years from now?"

"In less than that," I said. "It is three years and a half. My birthday is in June."

He asked me one or two more questions then as to its amount, and what arrangements I would make in the event of my marriage. When I had satisfied him upon these matters, he fell again into a reverie.

"Well?" said I, a little sharply.

"Cousin," he said, "I do not wish to stand in your way. But there must be no talk of marriage till '85. Will that content you?"

It did not in the least; but it was what I had expected. I was scarcely rich enough yet to support a wife, and knew that, well enough; for if I married and left the King's service there would be no more travelling expenses for me. Dolly and I last night had agreed upon that as the least that we could consent to.

"Four years is a long time," said I.

"You said three and a half just now," he observed a little bitterly.

"Well: three and a half. I suppose I must take that, if I can get nothing better."

*   *   *

Now I was secretly a little astonished that my Cousin Tom had consented so quickly, after his recent ambitions. Plainly he had aimed higher than at my poor standard during those months; for when a maid went to Court as one of the Queen's ladies the least that was expected of her was that she would marry a pretty rich man. But the reason of it all was unpleasantly evident to me. He must have gathered from what I had said and done that my favour was increasing with the King; and therefore he must have argued too that I must be serving His Majesty in some very particular way — which was the very last thing I desired him to know, as he was such a gossip. But I dared say no more then. We grasped one another's hands very heartily: and then I went to find Dolly.

*   *   *

The days that followed were very happy ones — though, as I shall presently relate, they were to be interrupted once more. I had in my mind, during them all, that I must soon go up to London again to tell Mr. Chiffinch my final decision that I could not undertake the work that he had proposed to me; for I had spoken of it at some length with Dolly, giving her a confidence that I dared not give to her father. But I did not think that I should have to go so soon.

It was in the hour before supper one evening that I told her of it, as we sat in the tapestried parlour, looking into the fire from the settle where we sat together.

"My dear," said I, "I wish to ask your advice. But it is a very private matter indeed."

"Tell me," said Dolly contentedly. (Her hand was in mine, and she looked extraordinary pretty in the firelight.)

"I am asked whether I will undertake a little work. In itself it is excellent. It concerns the protection of His Majesty; but it is the means that I am doubtful about."

Then I told her that of the details — of the how and the when and the where — I knew no more than she: but that, if all went well, I might find myself trusted by a traitor: and that I was considering whether in such a cause as this it was a work to which I could put my hand, to betray that trust, if I got it. But before I was done speaking I knew that I could not — so wonderfully does speaking to another clear one's mind — and that though I could not condemn outright a man who thought fit to do so, any more than I would condemn a scavenger for cleaning the gutter, it was not work for a gentleman to seek out a confidence that he might betray it again.

"Now that I have put it into words," I said, "I see that it cannot be done. Certainly it would advance me very much with His Majesty; (and that is one reason why I spoke to you of it) — but such advance would be too dearly bought. Do you not think so too, my dear?"

She nodded slowly and very emphatically three or four times, without speaking, as her manner was. "Then that is decided," said I, "and in a day or two I will go to town and tell them so."

So we put the matter away then; and spoke of matters far more dear to both of us, until Tom came in and exclaimed at our sitting in the dark as he called it.

*   *   *

The interruption came that very night.

We were at supper, and speaking of Christmas, and of how we would have again the dancing as last year, when we heard a man ride past the house, pulling up his horse as he came. Such interruptions came pretty often; — it was so that I had been first sent for by Mr. Chiffinch: and it was so again that the Duke of Monmouth had come, and others — but we had plenty too of others who came, seeing the house at the end of the village, to ask their way, or what not; so we paid no attention to it. Presently, however, we heard a man's steps come along the paved walk, and then a knocking at the door. James went out to see who was there; and came back immediately saying that it was a courier with a letter for me. My conscience smote me a little, for I had delayed more than a week now from answering Mr. Chiffinch: and, sure enough, when I went out, the man was come from him. I took the letter he gave me into the Great Chamber to read it, and was astonished at its contents. There were but four lines in it.

"Mr. Mallock," it ran, "come immediately — that is tomorrow. The Lord hath delivered them into our hands. Ride by Amwell; and go through the place slowly between eleven and twelve with no servant near." And it was signed with his initials only.

I went back again into the dining-room immediately, and shut the door behind me.

"I must go to town, tomorrow," I said, all short.

Dolly looked up at me, gone a little white. I shook my head and smiled at her, but secretly; so that Tom did not see.

CHAPTER VI

I do not think that I have yet related how great was the work that Mr. Chiffinch had done in the matter of the spies that he had everywhere during those later years of His Majesty Charles the Second. That which he had done during Monmouth's progress in the north — his receiving of reports day by day, and even hour by hour — this was only one instance of his activity. The secret-looking men, or even the bold-looking gentlemen, whom I had met on his stairs so continually, or for whose sake I was kept waiting sometimes when I went to see him — these were his tools and messengers. This company of spies was of all grades; and it was to serve in that company that he had sent for me from France, and that I was determined to decline.

Though, however, I was so determined, I did not dare to dis-obey the directions that his letter gave me; for I could not be sure that it was for this work in particular that he had summoned me; though I guessed that it was. I would go, thought I, and do in everything as he had said; I would ride through Amwell, with my servants behind at a good distance: I would see what befell me there — for that something would, was certain from the letter; then I would proceed on to London, and if the affair were against my honour, as I was sure it would be, I would refuse any further part in it. My one hardship was that I could do no more than tell Dolly in private that I would hold to my resolution. I dared not tell her anything of the contents of the letter which I had immediately destroyed. I promised her that I would be back for Christmas at the latest. She came out to the yard-gate to wish me good-bye: my servants were gone in front; and my Cousin Tom had the sense to be out of the way; so our good-byes were all that such miserable things ever can be. I waved to her at the corner, and she waved back.

When we came about two miles to the north of Amwell — which we did about eleven o'clock, as I had been bid, I bade my servants stay behind, and not come after me till half an hour later; further I bade them, if, when they came, they found me in any man's company, neither to salute me nor to make any sign of recognition; but to pass straight on to Hoddesdon and wait for me there, not at the inn where I was known, but at another little one — the *King's Arms* — at the further end of the village, and there they were to dine. Even then, when I came, if I did, they were not to salute me until I had spoken with them. All this I did, interpreting as well as I could, what Mr. Chiffinch had said; and they, since they were well-trained in that kind of service, understood me perfectly.

It was near half-past eleven when I came, riding very slowly, into the village street, looking this way and that so as to shew my face, but as if I were just looking about me. I noticed a couple of servants, in a very plain livery which I thought I had seen before, in the yard of the *Mitre*, but they paid no attention to me. So I passed up the street to the end, and no one spoke with me or shewed any sign. Now I knew that there was something forward, and that unless I fell in with it the arrangement would have failed; so I turned again and rode back, as if I were looking for an inn. Again no one spoke with me; so I rode, as if discontented, into the yard of the Mitre, and demanded of an ostler whether there was any food fit to eat there.

He looked at me in a kind of hesitation.

"Yes, sir," he said; "but — but the parlour is full. A party is there, from London."

Then I knew that I had been right to come; because at the same moment I remembered where I had seen those liveries before. They were those worn by the men who had come with Monmouth to Hare Street.

I said nothing to the ostler; but slipped off my horse, as he took the bridle, and went indoors. The fellow called out after me; but I made as if I did not hear. (I have found, more than once, that a little deafness is a very good thing.) There were voices I heard talking beyond a door at the end of the passage; I went up to this, and without knocking, lifted the latch and went in.

The room, that looked out, with one window only, into a small enclosed garden, was full of men. There were eight of them, as I counted presently; all round a table on which stood a couple of tall jugs and tankards. I raised my hand to my hat.

"I beg pardon, gentlemen. Is there room —"

"Why — it is Mr. —" I heard a voice say, suddenly stifled.

Beyond that, for a moment, there was silence. Then a man stood up suddenly, with a kind of eagerness.

"Mr. Mallock," he said, "Mr. Mallock! Do you not remember me?"

"Your back is to the light, sir —" I began; and then: "Why it is Mr. Rumbald."

"The same, sir; the same. There is a friend of yours, here, sir — Come in and sit down, sir. There is plenty of room for another friend."

There was a very curious kind of eagerness in the maltster's voice, which puzzled me not a little; and there was a change of manner too in him, that puzzled me no less. He spoke as if he had almost expected me, or was peculiarly astonished to see me there; and there was none of that hail-fellow air about him any more. He spoke to me as to a gentleman — as indeed I shewed I was by my dress — but yet manifested no surprise at seeing me so. However, I had neither time nor thought to consider this at the moment, for the friend of mine of whom he spoke, and who was now standing up to greet me, was no other than my Lord Essex — he who had been riding with Monmouth from Newmarket; and he whose name Mr. Chiffinch had expressly spoken of to me. Yet how did Mr. Rumbald know that we knew one another?

I made haste to salute him; for he too, I thought, had an air of eagerness.

"Come in and sit down, Mr. Mallock," he said. "We have dined early; and are presently off to town again. Are you riding our way?"

"Why, yes," I said, "I am going up to my lodgings for a little."

(As I spoke a thousand questions beseiged me. Why was there this air of expectation in them at all? How did Mr. Chiffinch know that they would be here at this time? Why had he arranged that I should meet them? Why had he not spoken of their names to me; since he had told me so freely of them before? Well; I must wait, thought I, and meantime go very gingerly. I was not going to put my hand to this kind of work; but I did not wish to spoil Mr. Chiffinch's design if I could help it.)

"Why," said my Lord, "if you are going to town, may I not ride with you? Some of these gentlemen are in a hurry; but I am sure I am not. Have you no servants, Mr. Mallock?"

"I have sent mine on before," I said, marvelling more than ever at the man's friendliness, "but I shall be very happy to ride with your Lordship, if you can wait till I have dined."

My Lord said a word to a man who sat near the door, who slipped out: and I heard his voice ordering dinner for me. Meantime I observed the company.

There were eight, as I have said; but I knew for certain two only — the maltster and my Lord Essex. The rest puzzled me not a little. They seemed well-bred fellows enough; but they were dressed very plainly, and appeared no more than country squires or lawyers or suchlike. They were talking of the most indifferent things in the world, with silences, as if they wondered what next to speak of; they hardly looked at me at all after a minute or two; and presently one by one began to stand up and take their leave, saluting my Lord by name, and bowing only to me. By the time that my dinner came there were left only my Lord, who was very attentive to me, and Mr. Rumbald; and before I was well set-to, even Mr. Rumbald stood up to say good-bye.

Again I was puzzled by the man; for again he appeared very friendly with me, and again shewed no sign of astonishment at my acquaintance with my Lord and at my appearance as a gentleman.

"I am very glad, sir," he said, shaking my hand with great warmth, "that you will have so pleasant a ride to town with your friend. And you will remember my house too, will you not, over the river, if ever you are by that way."

I told him that I would: and thanked him for his courtesy; and he went out, after shaking hands too with my Lord, taking care to exchange no glances with him, though it would be evident, even to a child, that there was some secret between them.

When he was gone, my Lord turned to me.

"A very good fellow, Rumbald — a very good fellow indeed."

I assented, heartily.

"Honest as the day," said my Lord.

"There is no doubt of it," said I, with my mouth full.

"And a good patriot too. It is what we want, Mr. Mallock."

Again I assented; and my Lord presently changed the conversation.

*   *   *

During the rest of dinner he said nothing that was significant of any of the things I suspected. I knew now, beyond a doubt, both from what Mr. Chiffinch had said and from the strangely mixed company, and the circumstances under which I found them, that something was forward; but as to what it was all about I knew no more than the dead. Neither did I as yet see a single glimmer of light on the questions that had puzzled me just now. So I determined that when we were safe out on the lonely road I would throw a bait or two; though my resolution still held that I would do no dirty work, even for His Majesty himself.

I dined very tolerably, and lit a pipe afterwards: (my Lord told me that he used no tobacco); and presently in a kind of impatience — for indeed the position I found myself in was a little disconcerting — I observed that it was past noon.

"You are quite right," said my Lord, "quite right. I will tell them to have the horses ready. Your servants are gone on before, I think you said, Mr. Mallock?"

I told him Yes; but I wondered why he did not shout for the maid, instead of going out himself; but I understood the reason when I found presently, when we took the road, that his own men kept a full hundred yards in the rear. Evidently he had gone out to tell them to do so.

*　　*　　*

So soon as we were clear of Amwell, I began. There was a little wind, and the weather was moist and thick, so there was no danger of our being overheard.

"My Lord," I said, "I am very much puzzled by what I have seen."

"Eh?" said he.

"It was a very mixed company just now, in Amwell."

He frowned a little.

"Very excellent gentlemen, all of them —" I hastened to add. "But I was wondering what it was that drew them all together. I can only think of two things."

"What are they, Mr. Mallock?" asked my Lord a little eagerly.

"Religion or politics, my Lord," I said. "And I am sure that it is not the first."

He appeared to reflect; but he was not a very good actor; and I could see that it was feigned.

"Why you are very sharp, sir," he said. "You have put your finger on the very place — the very place." (And he continued with far too short a pause): "On which side are you, Mr. Mallock? For the country or for the Court?"

"That is a dangerous question to answer, my Lord," I said, very short.

"It is only dangerous for one side," said he.

I nodded, in a grave and philosophical manner. Then I sighed.

"You are quite right, my Lord."

I could see that he was glancing at me continually. Yet no explanation of his behaviour yet crossed my mind.

"Mr. Mallock," said he after a silence, "it is no good fencing about the question. I can see that you are disaffected."

"That is a very safe way to put it," I said. "Who is not — on one side or the other?"

"Yes," said he, "but you are sharp enough to know what I mean."

Again I nodded; but my mind was working like a mill; for a new thought had come to me that seemed to illumine all the rest; and yet I could not understand. The thought was this. Plainly my Lord Essex knew a good deal about me: he knew enough, that is, to begin a conversation of this kind with one whom he had only met once before — a mad proceeding altogether, if that were all he knew. *Ergo*, thought I, he must know more than that; and if he knew more he must know that I was in the service of His Majesty and presumably devoted to that service; probably, too, from the understanding between himself and Rumbald, he knew that I had chosen on previous occasions to masquerade as if I were not a gentleman. Was he quite mad then? For to talk like this to one in the confidence of His Majesty was surely a crazed proceeding! Yet my Lord Essex was not a fool.

Looking back upon the matter as I write, it is hard for me to understand why I did not see through his design, since I saw so much of it. Yet it was not until London was in sight, or rather its lights against the sky, that all fell into its place; and I wondered at the simplicity of it. I think that it was the way he talked to me — the manner in which he skirted continually on the fringe of treason, yet said nothing that I could lay hold upon, and, above all, mentioned no names — that gave me the clue. I fear I fell a little silent as I perceived how point after point ratified the conclusion to which I had come; but I do not think he noticed it; and, even if he did, it would only encourage him the more. And when I saw the whole, as plain as a map, my scruples left me altogether. I would not have betrayed the true confidence of this man, or of any other; that resolution still held firm; but this was another matter altogether.

By the time that we reached Covent Garden — for he rode with me as far as that — I think he was satisfied that he had caught me in the way that he wished; for he had given me the names of one or two places where I could communicate with him if I desired; and was nearer actual treason in his talk than ever before — though he did not go much beyond deploring the Popish succession, and feigning that he did not know that I was a Catholic; and, on my side, I had feigned to be greatly interested in all that he had said, and had let him see, though not too evidently, that it was feigning on my side too. We parted, outwardly, the best of friends; inwardly we were at one another's throats.

So soon as I had dismounted — he having left me in the Strand — and gone indoors, I came out again, not fearing, indeed rather hoping, that he would be watching for me, and, in my boots just as I was, set out for Whitehall.

*　　　*　　　*

Mr. Chiffinch was within, expecting me. Even he looked a little excited; and no wonder. But first I made him answer my questions before I would say a word beyond telling him that his design had prospered.

"Mr. Chiffinch," said I over my supper which he had brought for me to his parlour. "Before I say one more word, you must tell me three or four things. The first is this. How did you know that it was in me that my Lord Essex would confide?"

"That is easily answered," said he. "My men told me that my Lord was after you everywhere — both in your lodgings and here."

"Ah!" I said, "and was there a fellow called Rumbald, with him?"

"You are right," he said. "How did you know that?"

"Wait," I said. "The next is, If you could tell me so much in your letter, why did you not tell me the names of the persons?"

He smiled.

"Mr. Mallock," he said, "from your hesitation I knew that you would refuse to do such work as this. So I intended to catch you unawares, and to entangle you in it. I knew that you would not refuse to go to Amwell, and behave there as I directed, if I said no more than I did."

"Well; you would have failed," I said.

"What!" said he. "You are still going to refuse?"

"No," said I, "I accept the work: but it is not what you think it is."

"Why — what is it then?"

"Wait," I said. "The next is, How did you know that they would be at Amwell at that time?" "Oh! that is easy enough; one of my fellows got that out of one of Rumbald's maids — that a party of six would lie at the Ryehouse last night; and that they would meet two more at dinner in Amwell at eleven o'clock today. Rumbald has been known to us a long while. But it is the others we are waiting for."

I was silent. There were no more questions I wished to ask at present; though there might be others later.

"Well," said the page, a little eagerly; and his narrow face looked very like a fox's, as he spoke. "Well; and what is your news?"

I finished my stew, and laid down the spoon.

"Mr. Chiffinch," said I, "let me first ask one more question. Why do you think that my Lord Essex was after me at all? How did he know of me?"

"Plainly from Rumbald," said he.

"And why did he want me?"

He smiled.

"Why, Rumbald thinks you disaffected towards the King; and yet knows you are in his service. You would be a very great helper to them, if you cared."

It was my turn to smile.

"My Lord Essex is not a fool," I said. "If they know so much of me, would they not know more?"

"Plainly they do not," he said. "Or they would not have tried to get you on their side."

I laughed softly.

"Sir," I said, "you are very sharp: but you are not sharp enough."

Then I related to him the behaviour of them all in the inn; and how Rumbald had shewn no surprise in seeing that I was a gentleman after all; and how my Lord Essex had talked in what would have been the maddest manner, if his intention had been as Chiffinch had thought it to be; and with every word that I said the page's face grew longer.

"Well," he cried, "it is beyond me altogether. What then is the explanation?"

"My friend," I said, "you were right. Neither before nor after what has passed today would I have done the work you designed for me which was to get these men's confidence, and then betray it again. But it is not their idea to give me their confidence at all. So I will work with you very gladly."

"But then what can you do —" he began in amazement.

"Listen," I said. "It will fall out just as I say. They will give me very few names; they will admit me to none of their real secrets; but yet they will feign to do so."

"But, what a' God's name —"

"Oh! man!" I cried, "you are surely slow-witted today. They will do all this —" (I leaned forward as I spoke for further emphasis) — "*in order that I may hand it on to His Majesty;* but they will give me no real secret till the climax is come, and their designs perfected. And then they will give me a false one altogether. They think that they will make me a tool to further their true plans by betraying false ones. We may know this for certain then — that whatever they tell me, knowing that I will tell you, is not what they intend, but something else altogether. And it will not be hard to know the truth, if we are certified of what is false."

*   *   *

There was complete silence in the room when I had finished, except for the wash of the tide outside the windows. The man's mouth was open, and his eyes set in thought. Then sense came back to his face; and he smiled suddenly and widely.

"God!" he said, and slapped me suddenly on the thigh. "Good God! you have hit it, I believe."

CHAPTER VII

From now onwards there began for me such a series of complications that I all but despair of making clear even the course that they ran. My diaries are filled with notes and initials and dates which I dared not at the time set down more explicitly; and my memory is often confused between them. For, indeed, my work in France was but child's play to this, neither was there any danger in France such as was here.

For consider what, not a double part merely, but a triple, I had to play. The gentlemen, who were beginning at this time to conspire in real earnest against the King and the Constitution, some of whom afterwards, such as my Lord Russell, suffered death for it, and others of whom like my Lord Howard of Escrick escaped by turning King's evidence — although their guilt was very various — these gentlemen, through my Lord Essex, had got at me, as they thought, to betray not truth but falsehood to His Majesty, and told me matters, under promise of secrecy, which they intended me to tell to the King and his advisers. To them, therefore, I had to feign feigning: I had to feign, that is, that I was feigning to keep their confidence, but that in reality that I was betraying it; while to Mr. Chiffinch I had to disclose these precious secrets not as true but as false, and conjecture with him what was the truth. (My evidence, later, was never called upon, nor did my name appear in any way, for that the jury would never have understood it.) I had, therefore, a double danger to guard against; first that which came from the conspirators — the fear that they should discover I was tricking them, or rather that I had discovered their trickery; and, on the other side, that I should become involved with them in the fall that was so certain from the beginning, and be myself accused of conspiracy — or of misprision of treason at the least. Against the latter I guarded as well as I could, by revealing to Mr. Chiffinch every least incident so soon as it happened; and on three occasions in the following year having a long discourse with His Majesty. But against the former danger I had only my wits to protect me.

The best thing, therefore, that I can do is to relate a few of the events that happened to me. (I have never, I think, experienced such a strain on my wits; for it went on for a good deal more than a year, since I could for a long time arrive at no certain proofs of the guilt of the conspirators, and His Majesty did not wish to strike until their conviction was assured.)

The first meeting of the conspirators to which I was admitted was in January. (I had not been able, of course, to go to Hare Street for Christmas; but the letters I had now and again from Dolly, greatly encouraged and comforted me. I had told her that I "was keeping to my resolution," but that "I should be in some peril for a good while to come," and begged her to remember me often in her pure prayers.)

A fellow came to my lodgings about the middle of January, with a letter from my Lord Essex. It ran as follows:

> "SIR, — With regard to some matters of which we spoke together on the occasion of our very pleasant ride to town last month, I am very anxious to see you again. Pray do not write any answer to this; but if you can meet me on Thursday night at the house of my friend Mr. West, in Creed Lane, at nine o'clock, we may have a little conversation with some other friends of ours. I am, sir, your obliged servant,
> "Essex."

I told the fellow that the answer was Yes. My Lord had been to see me in Covent Garden twice, but had said very little that was at all explicit; but Mr. Chiffinch had bid me hold myself in readiness, and put aside all else for the further invitations that would surely come. And so it had.

I found the house without difficulty; and was shewn into a little parlour near the door; where presently my Lord came to me alone, all smiles.

"I am very glad you are come, Mr. Mallock," he said. "I was sure that you would. I have a few friends here who meet to talk politics; and they would greatly like to hear your views on the points. I think I may now venture to say that we know who you are, Mr. Mallock, and that you have done a good deal for His Majesty in France. Your opinion then would be of the greatest interest to us all."

(I understood why he put so much emphasis on France; it was to quiet me as to any suspicions they thought I might have as to my being the King's servant in England too.)

I answered him very civilly, smiling as if I was at my ease; and after a word or two more he took me in. It was a long low room, with a beamed ceiling and shuttered windows, in which the men were sitting. There were six of them there; and I knew two of them, immediately. He that sat at the head of the table, a very grim-looking man, with pointed features, in an iron-grey peruke, was no other than my Lord Shaftesbury himself; and the one on his left, with a highish colour in his cheeks, was my Lord Grey. Of the rest I knew nothing; but those two were enough to shew me that I must make no mistakes. There were candles on the table.

My Lord Essex smiled as he turned to me.

"Mr. Mallock," he said, "I see you know some of these gentlemen by sight."

"I know my Lord Shaftesbury, and my Lord Grey by sight," I said, bowing to each. They each inclined a little in return.

"And this is Mr. West," said my Lord.

This was a very busy-looking active little fellow, with bright dark eyes. (He had the name of being an atheist, I learned afterwards.)

"Sit down, Mr. Mallock," said my Lord, pointing to a chair on my Lord Shaftesbury's right. I did so. There was no servant in the room. The two other men were presently made known to me as a Mr. Sheppard and a Mr. Goodenough. I knew nothing of either of these two at this time.

Now it may seem that it was extraordinary bold of all these persons to admit me, believing as they did, that I was on His Majesty's side, and would reveal all to him; and it was, in one way, bold of them; yet it was the more clever. For, as will appear, they said nothing to me at present that could be taken hold of in any way; and yet they sent, or rather thought they sent, to the King, false news that would help their cause.

When he had discoursed for a little while on general matters, yet drawing nearer ever to the point, my Lord Essex opened the engagement.

"That Mr. Rumbald," he said. "Do you know who he is, Mr. Mallock?"

"Why, he is a maltster, is he not?" I said.

"Well: he married a maltster's widow, who is dead now. But he is an honest old Cromwellian — loyal enough to His Majesty —" (the gentlemen all solemnly put hands to their hats) — "yet very greatly distressed at the course things are taking."

"An old soldier?" I asked.

"Yes: he was a Colonel under Oliver."

Such was the opening; and after that we talked more freely, though not so freely as, I doubt not, they had talked for an hour before I came. My Lord Shaftesbury did not say a great deal; he had a quick discontented look; but I think I satisfied him. He was in a very low condition at this time — all but desperate — so strongly had the tide set against him since my Lord Stafford's death and the reaction that followed it; and I think he would have grasped at anything to further his fortunes: for that was what he chiefly cared about. My Lord Essex did most of the talking, and Mr. West; and I could see that they were shewing me off, as a new capture, and one on whose treachery to them their hopes might turn.

Now there were three or four matters on which they were very emphatic. First, that no injury was intended to the King or the Duke of York; but this they did not disclaim for themselves so much as for the disaffected persons generally; as regards themselves they said little or nothing: and from this I deduced that the King's life would certainly be aimed at; and the more so, as they said what a pity it was that His Majesty's guards were still doubled.

"It shews a lack of confidence in the people," said my Lord Essex.

(From that, then, I argued that an attempt was contemplated upon Whitehall.)

The second thing that Mr. West was very emphatic upon was the need of proceeding, if any reform were to be brought about, in a legal and Parliamentary manner.

"Why does not His Majesty call another Parliament?" he added, "that at least we may air our grievances? It is true enough that my Lord Shaftesbury —" (here he bowed to my Lord who blinked in return) — "that my Lord Shaftesbury found Parliament against him in the event; but he does not complain of that. He hath at least been heard."

(From that I argued either that they thought they would be stronger in a new Parliament, or that they contemplated acting in quite another manner. I could not tell for certain which; but I supposed the latter.)

The third thing that Mr. Goodenough said, relating how he had heard it from a Mr. Ferguson of Bristol, was that the West of England was in a very discontented condition, and that His Majesty would do well to send troops there.

Now I knew that his statement was tolerably true; and that therefore the false part must be the second. The only conclusion I could draw was that they wished troops to be withdrawn from London.

To all these things, however, I assented civilly, arguing a little, for form's sake; but not too much.

When at last we broke up, my Lord Essex again came with me to the door, and carried me first, for an instant into the little parlour.

"Mr. Mallock," he said, "we have had a pleasant evening, have we not? But I need not tell you that our talk had best not be repeated. We have said not a word that is disloyal to His Majesty: but even a little fault-finding is apt to be misrepresented in these days." I said that I understood him perfectly (which indeed I did); and nodded very sagely.

"Let us meet again, then, Mr. Mallock — on that understanding. I have some more friends I would wish you to meet; and whom I am sure you could do good to. There is a quantity of discontent about."

I went to see Mr. Chiffinch the next day, and reported all that had passed, as they had intended me to do. We drew up a little report which was carried into effect: first, that no troops should be sent out of London; but that they should be dispersed as much as possible within the confines of the City; next that the guards at the gates of Whitehall should be diminished by one half — (this, to give colour to the malcontents' hope; and provoke them to action) — but the guards within increased by the same amount, yet kept out of sight so much as was possible; thirdly, that a rumour should be set about that the King would call a Parliament within the year at latest; and this Mr. Chiffinch promised to undertake (for a very great effect indeed can be produced on popular opinion by those who know the value of false rumours); but that His Majesty should be dissuaded from doing anything of the kind. Such then was the result of that first meeting to which I was admitted; and such more or less was our course of procedure all through the spring and summer. This I have related in full, to serve as an example of our method, because, since it was the first, I remember it very distinctly. In this manner I used the information I gained for the King's benefit; and, at the same time the conspirators were led to believe that I was their tool, and no more.

*　　　*　　　*

The next important incident fell in the beginning of the summer.

Now, in the meantime I had learned, from Mr. Chiffinch for the most part, though there were some matters I was able rather to inform him about, that there were two separate and distinct parties amongst the conspirators. There were those who intended nothing but some kind of a rising — scarcely more than an armed demonstration — and to this party would belong such a man as my Lord Russell — if he were of them at all; and there were those who meant a great deal more than this — who were hoping, in fact so to excite their followers as to bring about the King's death. But of these I found it very hard to get any names — and quite impossible, so far, to obtain any positive proof at all. The Duke of Monmouth, I knew, was of the moderate party; so, I thought then, was my Lord Grey — but Mr. Algernon Sidney whom I met once or twice was of the extreme side. But as to my Lord Shaftesbury, I knew nothing: he was pretty silent always; and it was with regard to him most of all that we desired evidence. It was this division of parties, no doubt, that hindered any action; the moderates were for ever trying to drag back the fanatics; and the fanatics to urge on the moderates; so that nothing was done.

From my diaries I find that I spoke with my Lord Essex no less than eight times between Christmas and July; I saw my Lord Russell only once as I shall relate presently, but did not speak with him: the rest I met now and again, but never all of them together. It was necessary, no doubt, that they should be well drilled before they could be trusted with me. Mr. Rumbald I met about four times, and my Lord Howard but once. I think all this time they were wholly satisfied that I passed on to Mr. Chiffinch what they told me, and nothing else; for he and I usually contrived to carry out part at least of their recommendations.

I first began to learn something of my Lord Russell's position in the matter in a meeting in July, in the house of the Mr. Sheppard (whom I had met at Mr. West's), that was situated in Wapping; and I learned something else too at the same time. My Lord Essex; came for me in his coach that day, and himself carried me down. (I need not say that on these occasions I carried always some pistol or other weapon with me beside my sword, for I never knew when they might not find me out.)

Mr. Sheppard's house was in a little street, that was a *cul-de-sac*, between the Garden Grounds, which was a great open space, and the Old Stairs on the river. It was about eight o'clock, and was beginning to be twilight when we came.

As we descended from the coach I noticed at a little distance away a number of fellows, very rough looking, standing together watching us; and I perceived that they saluted my Lord who returned the salute very heartily. I did not much like that. Who were these folks, I wondered, who knew my Lord?

The house was very ordinary within; it was flagged with stones that had some kind of matting upon them: the entrance was all panelled; and, what surprised me was that no servant was to be seen. Mr. Sheppard himself opened the door to us when we knocked.

We did not speak at all as we came in; and my Lord led me straight through into the parlour on the left that was full of tobacco-smoke. This was a very good room, hung all round with tapestry, though of a poorish quality, and, though it was not yet dark, the windows were shuttered and barred. At the table sat half a dozen persons, of whom I knew my Lord Shaftesbury at the head of the table as usual, and Mr. Goodenough that sat with his back to the hearth. Between these two sat a gentleman whom I knew to be my Lord Howard of Escrick, though I had never spoken with him. He carried himself with a very high air, and was the only man there dressed as if he were still in Westminster; the rest were subdued, somewhat, in their appearance. My Lord Howard looked at me with an intolerant kind of disdain, which my Lord Essex made haste to cover by directing me to my place.

I thought that my Lord Shaftesbury seemed very heavy this evening. He treated me with a silent kind of civility; and so, too, did he treat the rest. His eyes wandered away sometimes as we talked, as if he were thinking of something else. We spoke of nothing of any importance for a time, for Mr. Sheppard was bringing in wine with his own hands, though I saw a number of used glasses on the press which shewed me that the company had been here some time already.

It would be not until after ten or twelve minutes that Mr. Sheppard was deputed to open the affair on account of which I had been sent for.

"Now then, Sheppard," said my Lord Essex who sat on my right, "tell us the news."

Mr. Sheppard pushed his glass forward and leaned his elbows on the table. I could see that all that he said was directed principally at me.

"Well, my lords," he said, "I have very good news. You remember how I told you that I was beginning to fear for the people down here — that they would be provoked soon into some kind of a rising. They are still not wholly pacified —" (here he shot a look at me, which he should not have done) — "but I am doing my best to tell them that we have very good hopes indeed that His Majesty will be persuaded to call a Parliament; and I think they are beginning to believe me. I think we may say that the danger is past."

"Why; what danger is that, Mr. Sheppard?" said I, very innocently.

"Why — a rising!" he said. "Has not my Lord Essex told you?"

"Ah! yes!" said I, "I had forgot." (This was wholly false. He had told me once or twice at least that there was danger of this. This had been a month ago; and his object had been to persuade me that they had been telling the truth.)

"I saw some fellows as we came in," I said.

"Those are the malcontents," he said. "There are not more than a very few now, who go about and brag."

I assented.

"By the way," said my Lord Essex to Shaftesbury who looked at him heavily, "I spoke with my Lord Russell a week ago. You know my Lord Russell, Mr. Mallock?"

I said that I did not.

"Well; I had hoped he would have been here tonight. But he is gone down to the country — to Stratton — where he has his seat."

He talked a while longer of my Lord Russell; and I saw that he wished me to believe that my Lord was of their party: whence I argued to myself that was just what he was not; but that they wished to win him over for the sake of his name, perhaps, and his known probity. (And, as the event shewed, I was right in that conjecture.)

Two or three of them were still talking together in this strain, and while I listened enough to tell me that it was nothing very important that they said, I was observing my Lord Shaftesbury: and, upon my heart! I was sorry for the man. Three years ago he was in the front of the rising tide, in the full blast of popularity and power; he had so worked upon the old Popish Plot and the mob, that he had all the movement with him: His Majesty himself was afraid of him, and was forced to follow his leading. Now he was fallen from all this; the Court-party had triumphed because he had so overshot his mark, and here was he, in this poor quarter, in the house of a man that would have been nothing to him five years ago, forced to this very poor kind of conspiring for his last hopes. He sat as if he knew all this himself: his eyes strayed about him as we talked, and there were heavy pouches beneath them, and deep lines at the corner of his nose and mouth. It was this man, thought I, who was so largely responsible for the death of so many innocents — and all for his own ambition!

Presently I heard His Grace of Monmouth spoken of. It was Mr. Sheppard who spoke the name; and in an instant I was on the alert again. What he said fell very pat with what I was thinking of my Lord Shaftesbury.

"I declare," cried Mr. Sheppard, once more talking at me very evidently, "that His Grace of Monmouth breaks my heart. I was with his Grace a fortnight ago. His loyalty and love for the King are overpowering. I had heard" — (this was a very bold stroke of poor Mr. Sheppard) — "I had heard that some villainous fellows had proposed to His Grace — oh! a great while ago, in April, I think — that an assault should be made upon the King; and that His Grace near killed one of them for it. Yet His Majesty will scarce speak to him, so much he distrusts him."

This was all very pretty: and from it I argued that the Duke was deeper in the affair than we had thought, and perhaps belonged even to the extremest party, led, we supposed, chiefly by Mr. Sidney. But I murmured that it was a shame that His Majesty treated him so; and while I was listening to further eulogies on His Grace, a new thought came to me which I determined to put into execution that very night; for I felt we were not making any progress.

There was not much more conversation of any significance, and I was soon able to carry out what I determined; for my Lord Essex when we broke about half-past nine o'clock, again offered to take me home.

I said good-night very respectfully to the company; and followed him into the coach.

For a while I said nothing, but appeared preoccupied; so that at last my Lord clapped me on the knee and asked me if I ailed — which was what I wished him to do.

"My Lord," said I, with an appearance of great openness, "I have a confession to make."

"Well?" said he. "What is it?"

"I am disappointed," I said. "There is a deal of talk; and most interesting talk; and all very loyal and respectful. But I had fancied there was more behind."

"What do you mean?" asked he.

"Well:" I said. "If His Grace of Monmouth will do nothing, will none of his friends do it for him?"

"Of what nature?" asked my Lord.

"My Lord," said I, "need I say more?"

He was silent for a while; and I could see how his mind was a trifle bewildered. But he did presently exactly what I hoped he would do.

"Mr. Mallock," he said, "you are right: there is more behind.

And I promise you you shall hear of it when the time comes. Is that enough?"

"That is enough, my Lord," said I. "I am content."

*   *   *

I was with Mr. Chiffinch before the gates were shut for the night; and this was the report I gave him.

"I have learned three things at least," I said, when he had bolted the door, and drawn the hanging across it. "First that they are contemplating a rising as soon as they can get their men together; and that it will be from Wapping and thereabouts that the insurrectionists will come. Next that His Grace of Monmouth is more deeply involved than we had thought. And the third thing is, that I have persuaded my Lord Essex that I can be trusted to be a good traitor, and to report everything; but that if they do not commit more important falsehoods to me, I shall lose heart with them. We may expect then that after a little while I shall have more vital and significant lies told me, whence we can arrive at the truth."

"Is that everything?" said he.

"Ah! there is one thing more. They are trying to entangle my Lord Russell; and they think that they will succeed, and so do I; but at present he will not be caught."

CHAPTER VIII

We are drawing nearer now to the heart of the conspiracy that was forming little by little, as an abscess forms in the body of a sick man. For two months more no great move was made. I was summoned now and again to such meetings as those which I have described: and sometimes one man was there and sometimes another. They were becoming less cautious with me in this — since I had by now the names of nearly all the Londoners involved: and Mr. Chiffinch had the names of the principal men in Scotland and the provinces, especially in the West, with whom they were concerting. They still fed me with lies from time to time, in small points; and I gained a little knowledge from these as to what they wished me to believe, and hence as to what was indeed the truth.

It was in October that the next meeting of importance took place — the next, that is to say, to which I myself was admitted: and it was again in Mr. Sheppard's house in Wapping. There were gathered there, for the first time mostly all the principal gentlemen in the affair; and this was one more sign of how reckless they were becoming that I was admitted there at all. But I think it was because Mr. Chiffinch and I had been very discreet and careful that they thought that they had me in hand, and that I was somewhat of an innocent fool, and revealed no more than what they wished.

Before I went there — for I went by water this time, in a private wherry, to Wapping Old Stairs, I went first to Mr. Chiffinch to see if there were any news for me.

"Why, yes," he said, when he had me alone, "there is a little matter I would like you to find out about. The Duke of Monmouth was here with my Lord Grey, a day or two ago: they all dined with Sir Thomas Armstrong: and all three of them went round the posts and the guardroom, and saw everything. Now what was that for?"

"Sir Thomas Armstrong?" said I in astonishment. "Why he is —"

I was about to say he was one of His Majesty's closest friends and evil geniuses; but I stopped. There was no need.

The page smiled.

"Yes," he said. "Well; Mr. Mallock? If you can find out anything —"

"And the Duke too!" I said. "Well; I was right, was I not?" (For what I had found out was true enough — that His Grace was far more deeply involved than we had at first suspected. We had known that he was their *protégé*, but not that he was so much in their counsel, and of one mind with them.)

"His Grace will come to some disaster, I think," said Mr. Chiffinch very tranquilly.

*   *   *

When I came to Wapping Old Stairs it appeared that the watermen there knew well enough what was forward; for while one ran down to help me from the wherry, a number of others stood watching as if they knew what I had come for; and all saluted me as I went up. At the head of the stairs, I looked back, and two more wherries with a gentleman in each were just coming in.

Mr. Sheppard himself opened the door to me, and appeared a little confused, looking over his shoulder into the entrance-hall where two or three gentlemen were just going into the great parlour on the left. I could have sworn that one of them was the Duke, from the way he carried himself. With him was another whom I thought I knew, but he was not familiar to me. I appeared to notice nothing, but beat off the mud from my boots.

"Mr. Mallock," said Mr. Sheppard, "they are not yet all come; and two or three who are here have a little private business on another matter first. Will you wait a little in another room?"

I assented immediately; and he took me through the hall into another little parlour behind that in which the company was assembled.

"It will not be more than ten minutes," he said. "I will come for you myself when they are done."

When he was gone again I observed the room. It had but one window, which was shuttered; but it had two doors — the one by which I was come in, and another, beyond the hearth, leading to the great parlour. This door was closed.

Now it was of the greatest importance that I should hear what was passing in the next room. I should learn more in five words spoken there then, than in five hours when they were playing a part to me; and I had no scruple whatever, considering what they were at, and how they were using me, in learning by any means that were in my power what I wished to know. Even from where I stood I could hear the murmur of talk; and it was probable, it seemed to me, that if I laid my ear on the panel of the door I should hear every word of it. But first I pulled out a chair and set it by the table, with my hat and cane beside it. Then I went to the door into the hall, which opened, fortunately, with its hinge nearer to the hearth — (so that a man entering would not see immediately into that part of the room in which I should be) — and beneath the door I slipped a little sliver of wood from the wood-basket by the hearth, so that the door would stick a little. Having done that I went on tip-toe to the other door and put my ear to the panel. But I feared they would not say anything very significant, with me so close.

Now it was a little while before I could distinguish which voice belonged to what man. I got the Duke's at once; there was a lordly kind of ring in it that could never be forgotten; and I got presently my Lord Grey's voice; and then one with a drawl in it which I had never heard before; and then one that had no special characteristic, but was a little slow. These were the four whom I heard speak, besides Mr. Sheppard once. The conversation I heard was somewhat as follows. I set it all down on my way home.

The Duke said: "I am very pleased indeed that you are come after all, my Lord. We understand by that you have put aside all suspicions; and that is an encouragement."

The slow voice said; "I would do anything in my power, your Grace, which was not against my conscience, to help on that cause of which you have spoken; but I must confess —"

My Lord Grey said, sharply: "There, there! we understand, and are very glad of it. The thing can be arranged without any treason at all, or any injury to a soul. It is merely a demonstration — no more, upon my honour."

The drawling voice said: "No more will be needed. His Grace and we two went round everywhere. They are not like soldiers at all; they are remiss in everything."

The Duke said: "You see, my Lord, it is exactly as I said. God knows we would not injure a soul. I well know your Lordship's high principles."

The slow voice said: "Well, your Grace, so long as that is understood — I shall be very happy to hear what the design may be."

Mr. Sheppard said: "One instant, my Lord —" Then he dropped his voice; and I saw what he was at. I slipped back as quick as I could; drew out the sliver of wood from beneath the other door, and sat down. Then I heard his footstep outside.

When he came in, I was in the chair; but I rose.

"I beg pardon for keeping you, sir," he said: "there is just that trifle of business, and no more. I am come to keep you company."

Well; I resigned myself to it with a good air; and we sat and talked there of indifferent matters, or very nearly, for at least half an hour longer. It was highly provoking to me, but it could not be helped — that I should sit there with an affair of real importance proceeding in the next room, and I placed so favourably for the hearing of it. However I had gained something, though at present I did not know how much.

Suddenly Mr. Sheppard stood up; and I heard a door open and voices in the entrance hall.

"You will excuse me, sir, an instant," he said. "I must see these gentlemen out."

I bowed to him as I stood up and put myself in such a position that I could get a good look into the hall as he went out; and fortune favoured me, for there in the light of the pair of candles outside I caught a plain sight of the plump and rather solemn face of my Lord Russell. It was only for an instant; but that was enough; and at the same time I heard the drawling voice of someone out of sight, bidding good-night to others within the parlour. Then Mr. Sheppard shut the door behind him, and I sat down again.

Well; I had gained something; and I was beginning to repeat to myself what I had heard, for that is the best way of all to imprint it on the memory; when Mr. Sheppard came in again and invited me to follow him.

"Who was that that spoke?" I said carelessly, "as you went out just now? I can swear I know the voice."

He glanced sharply at me.

"That?" he said. "Oh! that must have been Sir Thomas Armstrong who is just gone out."

*   *   *

The parlour had no more than five men in it when we entered; and one seemed about to take his leave. That one was His Grace of Monmouth. I was a little astonished that they let me see him there, though I understood presently why it was so. He turned to me very friendly, while I was observing the two others I did not know — one of whom, Mr. Ferguson, was dressed as a minister.

"Why, Mr. Mallock," he said, "you come as I go!"

He recognized me a shade too swiftly. That shewed me that they had been speaking of me to him.

I said something civil; and then I saw that he was to say the piece they had just taught him; for that he was not sharp enough to be trusted long in the room with me.

"I hear you are all consulting," said he, "how to keep the peace. Well; I have given my counsel; and my Lord Essex here knows what I wish. I would I could stay, gentlemen; but that cannot be done."

There was a loyal and grateful murmur from the others. Indeed he looked a prince, every inch of him. He took his leave with a superb courtesy, giving his hand to each; and each bowed over it very low. I was not sure but that Mr. Sheppard did not kiss it. For myself, I kissed it outright. While I did so, I could have sworn that Mr. Sheppard said something very swiftly in the ear of my Lord Essex.

Now I was wondering why they had kept me from my Lord Russell. His probity was known well enough; and if they had wished to reassure me they could have done no better than tell me he was one of them; and then, of a sudden I recollected that to reassure me was the very last thing they wished; on the contrary, they wished to hold me tight, betraying only what they wished me to betray, until they were ready for their final stroke. And, just as I had arrived at that, when we were all sat down, my Lord Essex again dumfoundered me.

"Mr. Mallock," he said, "I wish to tell you, now we are in private, that my Lord Russell has been here, as well as His Grace and Sir Thomas Armstrong. You can tell from the presence of those three what our chief difficulty will be; for not one of them will hear of even the danger of any injury to His Majesty or the Duke of York. His Grace of Monmouth, of course, had to be consulted on one or two points; and he brought those other two with him to hear what we had to say. Well; I think we have satisfied them; though I fear, later, that they will not approve of our methods. But we did not wish my Lord Russell to see you until we had done talking to him; for fear that he might know something of your disaffection. We have satisfied him — and, what is more important — His Grace too, for the present; and they will not interfere with us."

Now this speech was an exceedingly ingenious one. Before he had done speaking I understood that Mr. Sheppard had suspected that I had seen my Lord Russell, and that that was why they were so open with me. But the rest of the speech was very shrewd indeed; and I think it might have deceived me, if I had not learned by the conversation that it was His Grace who was trying to reassure my Lord, and no one that was trying to reassure His Grace. But the web was so well woven that for the moment I could not see through it all; though I understood it all presently, when I had had a little time to think. For the instant, however, I saw one safe answer that I could make.

"I am obliged to your Lordship for telling me," I said, "and I trust from what you have said that it is but a preliminary to a little more information. Your Lordship told me in July that there would be more news for me presently."

He could not resist a glance at my Lord Grey — as if in triumph at his success.

"That is what we are met for," he said; and then — "Why, Mr. Mallock, I have not made these other gentlemen known to you."

They turned out to be — on the right of my Lord, the minister, Mr. Ferguson — he who had been spoken of before as an informant from Bristol; and a Colonel Rumsey — an old Cromwellian like the maltster of Hoddesdon — who sat next to Mr. Ferguson. We saluted one another; and then the affair began.

"Mr. Mallock," said my Lord, "the first piece of news is a little disappointing. It is that my Lord Shaftesbury is ill. It is not at all grave; but he is confined to his bed; and that throws back some of our designs."

(I made a proper answer of regret; and considered what was likely to be the truth. At the moment I could not see what this would be.)

"The next piece of news I have, gentlemen," went on my Lord — (for I think he thought he appeared to be speaking too much at me) — "is that owing to my Lord Shaftesbury's illness we must relinquish all thoughts of any demonstration in London. That, Mr. Mallock, was what we had hoped to be able to do in a week or two from now. Well; that is impossible. For the rest, Mr. Ferguson had better tell us."

This gentleman I took to be somewhat of an ass by his appearance and manner; but I am not sure he was not the cleverest liar of them all. He spoke with a strong Scotch accent, and an appearance of shy sheepiness, and therefore with an air too of extraordinary truth. He spoke, too, at great length, as if he were in his pulpit; and my Lord Essex yawned behind his hand once or twice.

Briefly put — Mr. Ferguson's report was as follows:

The discontent in the West was rising to a climax; and if a much longer delay were made, real danger might follow. It was sadly disconcerting, therefore, to him to hear that there was any hitch in the London designs: for the promise that he had given to some of the leaders in the West (whose names, he said, with an appearance of a stupid boorish kind of cunning, "had best not be said even here") was that a demonstration should be made simultaneously both here, in the West, and in Scot —

Here he interrupted himself sharply; and I saw that he had made a blunder. But he covered it so admirably, that if I had not previously known that discontent was seething among the Covenanters, I am sure I should have suspected nothing.

"In Scotland," said he, "we must look for nothing. They are forever promising and not performing — though I say it of my own countrymen. Any demonstration there would surely be a failure."

It was admirably done; and it was then that I perceived what an actor the man was.

Well; when he had done, we talked over it a while. I professed myself very well satisfied with what I had heard; and I put forward an opinion that it would be far better to delay no longer in the West. A demonstration there might lead to alarm here; troops might be withdrawn here, and relieve the pressure, and thus make possible a further demonstration in London. I spoke, I think, with some eloquence, remembering however that they all looked on me with the same confidence that I had in them — and no more: that is, that they believed me a liar. My observations were received with applause, very well delivered.

It was growing pretty late by the time we had done; yet before we went I had learned one more piece of news, partly through a little trap I laid, and partly through my Lord Essex's clumsiness.

"Well," said I, "I must be getting homewards, my Lords. I wish my Lord Shaftesbury had been here. Could I see his Lordship, do you think? — if I were to call at his town house? There is a very particular matter —"

My Lord Essex started a little. He was tired and overanxious, I think, with the continual part that he had to play before me; yet it was the first slip he made.

"My Lord is out of town —" he said. Then he paused. "You could not tell us, I suppose —"

I affected indifference. (Was my Lord out of town, I wondered?)

"Why; it is nothing," I said.

My Lord exchanged a look with Mr. Sheppard; and made his second mistake.

"I saw my Lord only — last week," he said suddenly. "He wishes his address to be private for the present; but —"

"Do not trouble yourself, my Lord," I said. "I assure you it has nothing to do with our business here."

I repeated this, I think, with a good enough manner to persuade them that what I said was true; and presently afterwards took my leave.

As I sat in the wherry that took me back to the Privy Stairs — (I had announced of course, "to the Temple") — I was preparing in my mind what I should say. I had learned a considerable amount for an evening; for the conversation I had overheard, added to what Mr. Chiffinch had told me, added to what they had all said in the parlour, interpreted and fitted together, was pretty significant.

These were the points I arranged.

First, that the visit of the Duke, my Lord Grey and Sir Thomas Armstrong to Whitehall was to see in what state the guards were in case of a surprise; and the conclusion they had arrived at was they "were not like soldiers at all" but "very remiss."

Second, that a "demonstration" in London was very imminent.

Third, that they had won over my Lord Russell enough at least to gain the help that his name would give.

Fourth, I was confirmed in what Mr. Chiffinch had told me as to the probability of a rising in Scotland.

Fifth, I was confirmed in my view that the Duke was very deeply involved.

Sixth, it appeared to me exceedingly probable that my Lord Shaftesbury was still in town, though not in his own house: and, all things considered, it was very nearly certain that he was hidden in Wapping. He was, probably also, a little ill, or he would have been at our meeting tonight.

One conclusion then, immediate and pressing, came out of all this; that an assault on Whitehall and an attack on the King's person was in urgent contemplation.

*   *   *

Then, as we went up under the stars, my waterman and I, one of those moods came upon me which come on all men in such stress as I was; and I appeared to myself, for the time, to be worlds away from all this sedition and passion and fever. The little affairs of men which they thought so great seemed to me in that hour very little and wicked — like the scheming of naughty children, or the quarrels and spites of efts in a muddy pond. In that hour my whole heart grew sick at this miserable murderous pother in the midst of which my duty seemed to lie; and yearned instead to those things that are great indeed — the love of the maid who had promised herself to me, and the Love of God that should make us one. My religion — though I am a little ashamed to confess it — had been very little to me lately: I had heard mass, indeed, usually, on Sundays, in one of the privileged chapels, and had confessed myself at Easter and once since, to one of the Capuchins, and received Communion; yet, for the rest it had largely been blotted out by these hot absorbing affairs in which I found myself. But, in that hour (for the tide was beginning to set against us) — it came back on me like a breeze in a stifling room. I thought of that cleanly passionless life I had led as a novice, and of that no less cleanly, though perhaps less supernatural life, that should one day be mine and Dolly's — and these politics and these plottings and this listening at doors, and this elaborate lying — all blew off from me like a cloud.

When we were yet twenty yards from the Privy Stairs a wherry shot past us, with no light burning. There was but one passenger in it, whom I knew well enough, though I feigned to see nothing; and once more my sickness came on me, that it was for a King like this, slipping out on some shameful pleasure, that I so toiled and endangered myself.

*　　*　　*

When I had reported all to Mr. Chiffinch, sitting back weary in my chair, yet knowing that I must go through with the work to which I had set my hand, he remained silent.

"Well?" I said. "Am I wrong in any point?"

"Why no," he said. "Your information tallies perfectly with all I know, and has increased the sum very much. For example, I had no idea where my Lord Shaftesbury was. I have no doubt whatever, from what you say, that he is in Wapping."

"Will you send and take him there?" I asked.

"No," he said shortly. "Leave him alone. We failed last time we took him. And he can do no great harm there. Plainly too, he is at the waterside that he may escape if there is need. I shall set spies there; and no more."

"What is to be done then? Double the guards again?"

"Why that of course," said he.

"And what else?" I asked; for I could see that he had not said all.

"A counterstroke," he said. "But of what kind? You say the

rising will be pretty soon."

"I do not suppose for a week or two at the most. They were decided, I am sure; but no more."

Suddenly the man slapped his leg; and his eyes grew little with his smile.

"I have it for sure," he said. "It will be for the seventeenth of November. That is the popular date. Queen Bess and Dangerfield and the rest."

"But what can you do?"

"Why," said he, "forbid by proclamation all processions or bonfires on that day. Then they cannot even begin to gather."

*   *   *

He proved right in every particular. The proclamation was issued, and met their intended assault to the very moment, as we learned afterwards, besides frightening the leaders lest their intention had been discovered: and the next night came one of the spies whom Mr. Chiffinch had sent down to Wapping, to say that my Lord Shaftesbury had slipped away and taken boat for Holland.

CHAPTER IX

Now indeed the fear grew imminent. I had thought that once my Lord Shaftesbury was gone abroad, one of two things would happen — either that the whole movement would collapse, or that the leaders would be arrested forthwith. But Mr. Chiffinch was sharper than I this time; and said No to both.

"No," said he, sitting like a Judge, with his fingers together, on the morning after my Lord Shaftesbury's evasion. "The feeling is far too strong to fall away all of a sudden. I dare predict just the contrary, that, now that the coolest of them all is gone — for he dare not come back again — the hot-heads will take the lead; and that means the sharpest peril we have yet encountered. This time they will not stop at a demonstration; indeed I doubt if they could raise one successfully; they will aim direct at the person of the King. It is their only hope left."

"Then why not take them before they can do any mischief?" I asked.

"First, Mr. Mallock," he said, "because we have not enough positive evidence — at any rate not enough to hang them all; and next we must catch the small fry — the desperate little ones who will themselves attempt the killing. It is now that I should be ready for a visit from your friend Rumbald, if I were you. They can have no suspicion that you have done anything but betray them in the way they intended: they have a great weapon, they think, in you, to continue carrying false news. Now, Mr. Mallock, is the very time come of which you once spoke to me — the climax, when they will feign to reveal everything to you, and then make their last stroke. You have seen my Lord Essex again?"

"Not a sight of him. I had only a very guarded note, two days ago, but very friendly: saying that the designs were fallen through for the present."

"Precisely what I have been saying," observed Mr. Chiffinch. "No, Mr. Mallock, you must not stir from town. I am sorry for your pretty cousin, and Christmas, and the rest: but you see for yourself that we must leave no loophole unguarded. His Majesty must not die out of his bed, if we can help it."

There, then, I was nailed until more should happen. I dared not ask my cousins to come to town; for God only knew what mischief my Cousin Tom might not play; and I had not eyes on both sides of my head at once. I wrote only to Dolly; and said that once more I was disappointed; but that I would most certainly see her soon, if I had to ride two nights running, from town and back.

I accomplished this, but not until Christmas was well over, and indeed Lent begun. During those weeks, certainly nothing of any importance happened to me, though my Lord Essex kept me in touch with him, and I even was present at one very dismal meeting with him and Mr. Ferguson, when it was deplored, in my presence, that the "demonstration" — as they still called it — of the seventeenth of November had been so adroitly prevented; and my Lord Shaftesbury's death — which had taken place (chiefly, I think, from disappointment) that very week — was spoken of with a certain relief. I think they were pleased to have matters entirely in their own hands now. However they proposed no immediate action, which more than ever persuaded me that this was what they intended. Yet the days went by: and no more news came, either from them or from Mr. Chiffinch — so I took affairs into my own hands, and one night, before the gates of the City were shut went down to Hare Street with a couple of men, leaving James at home, for I could trust him better than any other man.

Now I need not relate all that passed at Hare Street; for every lover knows how sweet was that day to me. I had seen her not at all for more than a year — (one year of those three that were to pass!) — and though we had written often to one another, when-ever we could get a letter taken, yet the letters had done no more than increase my thirst. I think she was dearer to me than ever; she was a shade paler and more grave, and I knew what it was that had made her so, for I had told her very plainly indeed that I was in peril and that she must pray much for me. My Cousin Tom was friendly enough, though I saw he was no more reconciled in his heart to our affair than he had been at the beginning; but I guessed nothing whatever of what he was contemplating. (How-ever perhaps he was not contemplating it then, for he did not attempt it till much later.) Yet he was pretty reasonable, and interrupted us no more than was necessary; so we had that day to ourselves, until night fell, and I must ride again. I was so weary that night, though refreshed in my spirit, that I think I drowsed a little on my horse, and thought that I stood again at the gate of the yard with Dolly, bareheaded in spite of the cold, holding the lan-tern to help us to mount.

*　　*　　*

I was still brooding all the way up Fleet Street, and even to my own door; until I saw James standing there; and at the sight of him I knew that something was fallen out.

I said nothing, but nodded at him only, as a master may, but he understood that he was to follow upstairs. There, in my chamber I faced him.

"Well?" said I. "What is it?"

"Sir," he said, "a fellow came last night and seemed much put out when I told him you were out of town."

"What sort of a fellow was he?" said I.

"He was a clean-shaven man, sir, rather red in the face, with reddish hair turning grey on his temples."

"Heavily built?"

"Yes, sir."

"Well; what did he say?"

"He said that you would know what affair he was come about — that it was very urgent; and that he could not stay in town beyond noon today. He said, sir, that he was to be found till then at the *Mitre* without Aldgate."

Well; that was enough for me. But I did not relish the prospect of no sleep again; for I cannot trust my wits when I have not slept my seven or eight hours. But there was no help for it.

"James," said I, "bring my morning up here at once, with some meat too. I may not be able to dine today, or not till late. When you have brought it I shall have a letter ready, for Mr. Chiffinch. That you must take yourself. Then return here, and pack a pair of valises, with a suit in them for yourself. Have two horses ready at eleven o'clock: you must come with me, and no one else. I do not know how long we may be away. You understand?"

"Yes, sir."

"Very well. I must get some sleep if I can before eleven."

Then a thought came to me. If Rumbald must be gone from town by noon, would he not likely want me to go with him?

"Wait," I said. "I do not know this man very well; but I will tell you that his name is Rumbald and that he lives at the Rye, near Hoddesdon. You had best not come with me. But do all else as I have said; but you must ride by yourself at eleven, to Hoddesdon; and put up at the inn there — I forget its name, but the largest there, if there be more than one. Remain there until you hear from me again: I may want a courier. Do not go a hundred yards from the inn on any account; and do not seem to know me, unless I speak to you first. You may see me, or you may not. I know nothing till I have seen Rumbald. If you do not hear of me before ten o'clock tonight, you can go to bed, and return here in the morning. I will communicate with you by tomorrow night at latest. If I do not, go to Mr. Chiffinch yourself and tell him."

My mind was working at that swift feverish speed which weariness sometimes will give. I was amazed afterwards at my own foresight, for there was very little evidence of what was intended; and yet there had come upon me, as in an illumination, that the time for which we had waited so long was arrived at last. I do not see how I could have guessed more than I did; neither do I now see how I guessed so much.

My letter to Mr. Chiffinch was not long. It ran as follows:

> "Rumbald hath been to see me; and bids me be with him, if I can, by noon today at the *Mitre*, without Aldgate. I know no more than that; but I am making ready to go down with him to the Rye at Hoddesdon, if he should want me there. I think that something is intended, if we are right in our conjectures. I shall have my man at the inn in Hoddesdon. You must send no one else for fear of alarming them, unless my man comes to you tomorrow to tell you that he does not know where I am. Is His Majesty still at Newmarket? If so, when does he purpose to return? Which road will he come by? Send an answer back by my man who bears this.
> "R.M."

Well; that was all that I could do. I gave the letter to James; telling him not to awaken me with the answer till he came at eleven o'clock; and after eating a good meal, I went to my bed and fell sound asleep; and it seemed scarcely five minutes, before James came knocking, with Mr. Chiffinch's answer. I sat up on my bed and read it — my mind still swimming with sleep.

"Prospere procede!" it ran. "I will observe all that you say. The King and His Royal Highness are together at Newmarket. They purpose to return on a Saturday, as the King usually does; but he hath not yet sent to say whether it will be tomorrow, the 18th or the 25th. I shall hear by night, no doubt. Neither do I know the road by which they may come."

I read it through twice; then I tore it into fragments and gave them to James.

"Burn all these," I said. "Are the horses ready?"

"Yes, sir," said James.

Undoubtedly my sleep had refreshed me; for by the time that I rode up to the *Mitre* without Aldgate, I was awake with a kind of clear-headedness that astonished me. It appeared to me that I

ROBERT HUGH BENSON ∽ 277

had thought out every contingency. I had with me a little valise, ready for the country, if need be; yet I could return to my lodgings without remark. James was already on his way to Hoddesdon, and would be there if I needed him. No harm was done if my conjectures were at fault; I had left no loophole that I could see, if they were not. It was with a tolerably contented heart, in spite of the dangers I foresaw — (for I think these gave spice to my adventure) — that I rode up to the *Mitre*, and saw Mr. Rumbald himself standing astraddle in the doorway.

I must confess however that the sight of him gave me a little check. He appeared to me more truculent than I had ever seen him. He had his hands behind him, with a great whip in them; he hardly smiled to me, but nodded only, fixing his fierce eyes on my face. He had, more than I had ever noticed it before, that hard fanatic look of the Puritan. After all, I reflected, this maltster had commanded a troop under Cromwell at Naseby. His manner was very different from when I had last seen him; he appeared to me as if desperate.

However, I think I shewed nothing of what I felt. I saluted him easily, and swung myself off my horse. He had gone into the house at my approach; and I followed him straight through into a little parlour to which, it seemed, he had particular access, for he turned a key in the door as he went in. When I was in, after him, and the door was shut, he turned to me, with a very stern look.

"Well, Mr. Mallock?" he said. "I see you are come ready for a ride." "Yes," I said. "I had your message."

He nodded. Then he came a little closer, looking at me with his fierce eyes.

"You understand what is forward?"

"I understand enough," said I.

"That is very good then. We will ride at once."

As we came out, a couple of men — one of them I noticed in particular, dressed as a workman — (I set him down for a carpenter or some such thing) — made as though they would speak to us; but Rumbald waved his hand at them sharply, as if to hold them off. I could see that he was displeased. I said nothing, but I marked the man closely: he was a little fellow, that looked ill. Mr. Rumbald's horse was already there; and mine was being held still by the ostler into whose hands I had given him. We mounted without another word; and rode away.

I think we did not speak one word at all till we were out from town. Such was his mood, and such therefore I imitated. He rode like a soldier, sitting easily and squarely in his saddle; and the more I observed him and thought of him, the less I liked my business. It was wonderful how some emotion had driven up the power that lay in him. All that genial hail-fellow manner was gone completely.

When we were clear of town he spoke at last.

"This is a very grave business, sir," he said. "We had best not speak of it till we are home. Have you no servants?"

He spoke so naturally of my servants that I saw he was astonished I had none. I had very little time to think what I should answer; it appeared to me that I had best be open.

"Yes," I said. "My man is gone on to Hoddesdon to await me there. I thought it was best he should not ride with us."

He looked at me with a peculiar expression that I could not understand; but only for an instant. Then he nodded, and turned his stern face again over his horse's ears.

My moods were very various as I rode on. Now I felt as a sheep being led to the slaughter; now as an adventurer on a quest; and, again, of a sudden there would sweep over me a great anxiety as to His Majesty's safety. The thought of Dolly, too, came upon me continually and affected me now in this way, now in that. Now I longed to be free and safe back at Hare Street; now I knew that I could never look her in the face again if I evaded my plain duty. One thing I can say, however, from my heart, and that is that never for an instant did I seriously consider any evasion. It was all in the course that I had chosen — to "serve the King." Well; I must do so now, wherever it led me. What, however, greatly added to the horror of my position was that I knew that this strong fellow at my side thought me to be a traitor to himself and was using that knowledge only for his own ends. He would surely be ruthless if he found I had served my turn; and here was I, riding to his house, and only two men in the world knew whither I was gone.

Rumbald had already dined; and thought not at all of me. We drew rein therefore, nowhere; but rode straight on, through village and country alike — now ambling for a little, once or twice cantering, and then walking again when the way had holes in it. So we passed through Totteridge and Barnet and Enfield Chase and Wood Green, and came at last to Broxbourne where the roads forked, and we turned down to the right. It was terrible that ride — all in silence; once or twice I had attempted a general observation; but he answered so shortly that I tried no more; and I am not ashamed to say that I committed myself again and again to the tuition of Our Lady of Good Counsel whose picture I had venerated in Rome. Indeed, it was counsel that I needed.

I did not know precisely where was the Rye, nor what it was like; for I had avoided the place, of design. I supposed it only a little place, perhaps in a village. I was a trifle disconcerted therefore when, as we crossed the Lea by a wooden bridge, he pointed with his whip, in silence, to a very solid-looking house that even had battlemented roofs — not two hundred yards away, to the left of the road. There was no other building that I could see, except the roofs of an outhouse or two, and suchlike. However, I nodded, and said nothing. No words were best: in silence we rode on over the bridge, and beyond; and in silence we turned in through a gateway, and up to the house, crossing a moat as we went.

Indeed, now I was astonished more than ever at the house. It was liker a castle. There was an arched entrance, very solid, all of brick, with the teeth even of a portcullis shewing. An old man came out of a door on our right, as our hoofs rang out; but he made no sign or salute; he took our horses' heads as we dismounted, and I heard him presently leading them away.

Still without speaking, the Colonel led me through the little guard-room on the right, hung round with old weapons of the Civil War, and up a staircase at the further end. At the head of the staircase a door was open on the right, and I saw a bed within; but we went up a couple more steps on the left, and came out into the principal living-room of the house.

It was a very good chamber, this, panelled about eight feet up the walls, with the bricks shewing above, but whitewashed. A hearth was on the right; a couple of windows in the wall opposite, and another door beyond the hearth. The furniture was very plain but very good: a great table stood under the windows with three or four chairs about it. The walls seemed immensely strong and well-built; and, though the place could not stand out for above an hour or two against guns, in the old days it could have faced a little siege of men-at-arms, very well.

Rumbald, when he had seen me shut the door behind me, went across to the table and put down his whip upon it.

"Sit down, sir," he said. "Here is my little stronghold."

He said it with a grim kind of geniality, at which I did not know whether to be encouraged or not: I did as he told me, and looked about me with as easy an air as I could muster.

"A little stronghold indeed," I said.

He paid no attention.

"Now, sir," he said, "we have not very much time. Supper will be up in half in hour; we had best have our talk first, and then you may send for your servant. Old Alick will find him out."

"With all my heart," I said, wondering that he made so much of my servant.

He sat down suddenly, and looked at me very heavily and penetratingly.

"Sir," he said, "you are going to hear the truth at last, I said we had not much time. Well; we have not."

"Then let me have the truth quickly," I said.

He took his eyes from my face. I was glad of that; as I did not greatly like his regard. What, thought I, if I be alone with a madman?

"Well, sir," he said, "we are driven desperate, as you may have guessed. I say, we; for you have identified yourself with our cause a hundred times over. My Lord Shaftesbury is gone; my Lord Essex is hanging back. Well; but those are not all. We have other men besides those that have been urged on and urged on, and now cannot be restrained. I have tried to restrain them myself" — (here he gulped in his throat: lying was not very easy to this man, I think) — "and I have failed. Well, sir, I must trust you more than I have ever trusted you before."

Again he stopped.

Then all came out with a rush.

"Not half a mile from here," said he, "along the Newmarket road there be twenty men, with blunderbusses and other arms, waiting for His Majesty and the Duke, who will come tomorrow."

"But how do you know?" cried I — all bewildered for the instant.

His head shook with passion.

"Listen," said he. "We have had certain information that they come this way — Why, do you think we have not —" (again he broke off; but I knew well enough what he would have said!) "I tell you we know it. The King is not lying at Royston, tonight. He comes by this road tomorrow. Now then, sir — what do you say to that?"

My mind was still all in a whirl. I had looked for sudden danger, but not so sudden as this. Half a dozen questions flashed before me. I put the first into words:

"Why have you told me?" I cried.

His face contracted suddenly. (It was growing very dark by now, and we had no candles. The muscles of his face stood out like cords.)

"Not so loud!" said he; and then: "Well, are you not one of us? You are pledged very deeply, sir; I tell you."

Then came the blessed relief. For the first moment, so genuine appeared his passion, I had believed him; and that the ambushment was there, as he had said. Then, like a train of gunpowder, light ran along my mind and I understood that it was the same game still that they were playing with me; that there was no ambushment ready; that they had indeed fixed upon this journey of the King's; but that they were unprepared and desired delay. His anxiety about my servant; his evident displeasure and impatience; his sending for me at all when he must have known over and over again that I was not of his party — each detail fitted in like a puzzle. And yet I must not shew a sign of it!

I hid my face in my hands for a moment, to think what I could answer. Then I looked up.

"Mr. Rumbald," said I, "you are right. I am too deeply pledged. Tell me what I am to do. It is sink or swim with me now."

He believed, of course, that I was lying; and so I was, but not as he thought. He believed that he had gained his point; and the relief of that thought melted him. He believed, that is, that I should presently make an excuse to get hold of my servant and send him off to delay the King's coming. Then, I suppose, he saw the one flaw in his design; and he strove, very pitifully, to put it right.

"One more thing, Mr. Mallock," said he, "this is not the only party that waits for him. There is another on the Royston road, among the downs near Barkway. They will catch him whichever way he comes."

I nodded.

"I had supposed so," I said; for I did not wish to confuse him further.

"Well," said he, "why I have sent for you is that you may help me here. There may be more guards with the King than we think for. It may come to a fight; and even a siege here — if they come this way. We must be ready to defend this place for a little."

It was, indeed, pitiful to see how poor he was as an actor. His sternness was all gone, or very nearly: he babbled freely and drunkenly — walking up and down the chamber, like a restless beast. He told me point after point that he need not — even their very code — how "swan-quills" and "goose-quills" and "crow-quills" stood for blunderbusses and muskets and pistols; and "sand and ink" for powder and balls. It was, as I say, pitiful to see him, now that his anxiety was over, and he had me, as he thought, in his toils. It was a very strange nature that he had altogether; — this old Cromwellian and Puritan — and I am not sure to this day whether he were not in good faith in his murderous designs. I thought of these things, even at this moment; and wondered what he would do if he knew the truth.

At supper he fell silent again, and even morose; and I think it possible he may have had some suspicions of me; for he suspected everyone, I think. But he brightened wonderfully when I said with a very innocent air that I would like my servant to be fetched, and that I would give him his instructions and send him back to London, for that I did not wish to embroil him in this matter.

"Why, certainly, Mr. Mallock," he said, "it is what I wish. I trust you utterly, as you see. You shall see him where you will."

He turned to his old man who came in at that instant, and bade him fetch Mr. Mallock's servant from Hoddesdon. I described him to Alick, and scribbled a note that would bring him. Then we fell to the same kind of talking again.

*   *   *

It was eight o'clock, pretty well, by the time that James came to the Rye. I had determined to see him out of doors where none could hear us; and before eight I was walking up and down in the dark between the gate and the house, talking to my host. When the two men came through the gate, Rumbald was very particular to leave me immediately, that I might, as he thought, send my man to Newmarket to put off the King's coming; and have no interruption.

"I will leave you," said he. "You shall see how much I trust you."

I waited till he was gone in and the door shut. Then I took James apart into a little walled garden that I had noticed as I came in, where we could not by any chance be overheard. Even then too I spoke in a very small whisper.

"James," said I, "go back to Hoddesdon; and get a fresh horse. Leave all luggage behind and ride as light as you can, for you must go straight to Newmarket; and be there before six o'clock, at any cost. Go straight to the King's lodgings, and ask for any of Mr. Chiffinch's men that are there, whom you know. Do you know of any who are there?"

"Yes, sir," whispered James; and he named one.

"Very good. With him you must go straight to His Majesty; and have him awakened if need be. Tell him that you come from me — Mr. Chiffinch's men will support you in that. Tell His Majesty that if he values his life he must return to town tomorrow — and not sleep anywhere on the way: and that the Duke of York must come with him. Tell him that there is no fear whatever if he comes at once; but that there is every fear if he delays. He had best come, too, by this road and not by Royston. You understand?"

"Yes, sir."

"I shall remain here until tomorrow night at the earliest. If I am not at home by Sunday night, go to Mr. Chiffinch, as I told you this morning. Is all clear?"

"Yes, sir."

"Then go at once. Spare no horses or expense. Good-night, James."

"Good-night, sir."

I watched him out of the gate. Then I turned and went back to the house.

CHAPTER X

It was a strange night and day that followed. On the one side my host found it hard, I think, to maintain the story he had told me, in action; for, in accordance with his tale, he had to bear himself as though he expected before nightfall the assassination of the King and His Royal Highness half a mile away, and the rush of the murderers to his house for shelter. On my side, it was scarcely less hard, for I knew nothing of how my man James had fared, or whether or no His Majesty would act upon my message. I guessed, however, that he would, if only my man got there; for Chiffinch's men (who now followed him everywhere) would be as eager as I that no danger should come to him.

My plans therefore were more secure than Rumbald's; since I knew, either that His Majesty would come, and no harm done, or that, merely, he would not come. In the latter case Rumbald would be certified that I had done as he thought I would; and would, no doubt, let me go peacefully, to use me again later in the same manner, if occasion rose. For myself, then, I intended after nightfall at the latest to ride back to London and report all that had passed; and, if the King had not come, to lay all in Mr. Chiffinch's hands for his further protection.

I was left a good deal to myself during the morning — Mr. Rumbald's powers of dissimulation being, I think, less than his desire for them; and I did not quarrel with that. I was very restless myself, and spent a good deal of time in examining the house and the old arms, used no doubt, forty years ago in the Civil War, that were hung up everywhere. Within, as well as without, it was liker an arsenal or a barracks, than a dwelling-house. Its lonely situation too, and its strength, made it a very suitable place for such a design as that which its owner had for it. The great chamber, at the head of the stairs, and over the archway, where we had our food, was no doubt the room where the conspirators had held their meetings.

A little before eleven o'clock, as I was walking in the open space between the house and the gate, I saw a fellow look in suddenly from the road, and then was away again. Every movement perturbed me, as may be imagined in such suspense; yet anything was better than ignorance, and I called out to let him see that I had observed him. So he came forward again; and I saw him to be the little carpenter, or what not, that had wished to speak to Rumbald yesterday at the inn.

He saluted me very properly.

"I beg your pardon, sir," said he, "but is Mr. Rumbald within?"

Now I had seen Mr. Rumbald, not ten minutes ago, slip back into the house from the outhouses where he had pretended to go upon some preparation or other for the reception of the assassins this evening; but he had not known that I saw him.

"He is very busy at present," said I. "Cannot I do your business for you?"

(I tried to look as if I knew more than I did.)

"Why, sir," he said, "I think not."

He seemed, I thought, in a very pitiable state. (I learned some months later that he was come down expressly to dissuade Rumbald from any attempt at that time; but I did not know that then.) Here, only, thought I, is one of the chicken-hearted ones. I determined to play upon his fears, if I could, and at the same time, perhaps, upon his hopes.

"I think I can, however," I said. "You would be out of the business, if you could, would you not?"

He turned so white that I thought he would have fallen. I saw that my shot had told; but it was not a hard one to make.

"Hold up, man," I said. "Why, what do you suppose I am here for?"

"What business, sir?" he said. "I do not know what you mean."

I smiled; so that he could see me do it.

"Very good, then," I said. "I will leave you to Mr. Rumbald;" and I made as if I would pass on.

"Sir," he said, "can you give me any assurance?... I am terrified." And indeed he looked it; so I supposed that he thought that the attempt was indeed to be made today. I determined on a bold stroke.

"My man!" I said. "If you will tell me your name, and then begone at once, back to town, I will tell you something that will be of service to you. If not —" and I broke off.

He looked at me piteously. I think my air frightened him. He drew back a little from the house, though we were in a place where we could not be seen from the windows.

"My name is Keeling, sir. You will not betray me? What is it, sir?"

"Well," said I, "I can give you an assurance that what you fear will not take place. There is not a man here beyond myself and

Mr. Rumbald and old Alick. Now begone at once. Stay; where do you live?"

He shook his head. A little colour had come back to his face again at the news.

"No, sir; that was not in the bargain. I will begone, sir, as you said; and thank you, sir."

He slipped back again very quickly, and was vanished. I suppose that he had ridden down in some cart all night, and that he went back in the same way, for I saw no more of him.

Well; I had gained two little points — I had kept him from Mr. Rumbald, which was one — (for I did not want my host to consult with any if I could help it) — and I had learned what perhaps was his name. This, however, I would test for myself presently.

At noon we dined; and having observed no difference in my host's manner, that might shew that he had any idea I had met with anyone, I made two remarks.

"I talked with a fellow at the gate this morning," I said; "he seemed to know nothing of the King's coming."

Rumbald jerked his head impatiently; and I perceived that we had not been seen. Presently I said:

"Who was that pale-looking fellow who wished to speak with you yesterday, Mr. Rumbald, at the *Mitre*?"

He looked sharply at me for an instant.

"His name is Thompson," said he. "He is one of my malting-men."

Then I knew that he had lied. A man does not invent the name of Keeling, but very easily the name of Thompson. So I saw that Rumbald had not yet lost all discretion; and indeed, for all his talk, he had hardly spoken a name that I could get hold of.

After a while I ventured on another sentence which suited my purpose, and at the same time confirmed him in his own view.

"If by any chance His Majesty should not come today — will it be done, do you think, tomorrow? Shall you wait till he does come?"

He shook his head and lied again very promptly.

"If it is not done today, it will never be done."

Looking back on the affair now, I truly do wonder at the adroitness with which we both talked. There was scarcely a slip on either side, though we were at cross-purposes if ever men were. But I suppose that in both of us there was a very great tension of mind — as of men walking on the edge of a precipice; and it was the knowledge of that which saved us both. After dinner I said I would walk again out of doors; and he thought it was mere affectation, since I must know by now that His Majesty was not coming.

"Well," I said, "if by any mischance His Majesty doth not come today, I will get back to town."

He looked at me; but he kept any kind of irony out of his face.

"You had best do that," he said.

*   *   *

Now it must have been forty miles from Newmarket to the Rye; and I had calculated that His Majesty would not start till nine o'clock at the earliest. He would have four horses and would change them at least three times; but they would not be able to go out of a trot for most of the way, so that I need not look for any news of him till three o'clock at the earliest. From then till five o'clock would be the time. If he were not come by five, or at the very latest half-past, I should know that my design had miscarried.

It is very difficult for me to describe at all the state I was in — all the more as I dared not shew it. It was not merely that my Sovereign was at stake, but a great deal more than that. My religion too was in some peril, for if, by any mischance things should not go as I expected; if, as certainly occurred to my mind as one possibility in ten, I had completely mistaken Rumbald, and he had spoken the truth for once — it was not the King only who would perish, but the Catholic heir also, and then good-bye to all our hopes. Yet, I declare that even this did not affect me so much as the thought that it was the man whom I had learned to love that was in peril — to love, in spite of his selfishness and his indolence and his sins. It was all but an intolerable thought to me that that melancholy fiery man who had so scolded me — whom, to tell the truth, I had scolded back — that this man might, even in imagination, be mixed up with the horror of the firing of guns and the plunging of the wounded horses — should himself be shot at and murdered, there in the lonely Hertfordshire lane.

At about three o'clock I could bear it no more. God knows how many prayers I had said; for I think I prayed all the time, as even careless men will do at such crises. There was the grim house behind me, the leafless trees overhead, the lane stretching up northwards beyond the gate. All was very silent, except for the barking of a dog now and again. It was a very solitary place — the very place for a murder; there were no meadows near us, where men might be working, but only the deep woods. It was a clearish kind of day, with clouds in the west.

At about three o'clock then I went to the stables to see my horse. These were behind the house. There was no one about, and no other horse in the stables but Rumbald's own black mare that had carried him yesterday.

It came to me as I looked at my horse that no harm would be done if I put the saddle on him. Rumbald would but think me a little foolish for so confessing in action that I knew the King would not come; and for myself it would be some relief to my feelings to know that if by any mischance I did hear the sound of shots, I could at least ride up and do my best, though I knew it would be too late.

I saddled my horse then, and put on the bridle, as quickly as I could. Then, again, I thought there would be no harm done if I led him out to the gate and fastened him there. I looked out of the stable door, but there was no one in sight. So I led my horse out, as quietly as I could, yet openly, and brought him round past the front of the house and so towards the gate. I thought nothing of my valise; for at that time I intended no more than what I had said. I was uneasy, and had no determined plans. I would tell Rumbald, if he came out, that I was but holding myself ready to ride out if I were needed.

Then, as I came past the front of the house, I heard, very distinctly in the still air, the tramp of horses far away on the hill to the north; and I knew enough of that sound to tell me that there were at least eight or nine coming, and coming fast.

Now it might have been the coach of anyone coming that way. The races were at Newmarket, and plenty went to and fro, though it is true that none had come this way all day. Yet at that sound my heart leapt up, both in excitement and terror. What if I had made any mistake, and enticed the King to his death? Well, it would be my death too — but I swear I did not think of that! All I know is that I broke into a run, and the horse into a trot after me; and as I reached the gate heard Rumbald run out of the house behind me.

I paid him no attention at all, though I heard his breathing at my shoulder. I was listening for the tramp and rattle of the hoofs again, for the sound had died away in a hollow of the road I suppose. Then again they rang out; and I thought they must be coming very near the place he had told me of; and I turned and looked at him; but I think he did not see me. He too was staring out, his face gone pale under its ruddiness, listening for what very well might be the end of all his hopes.

Then the distant hoofs grew muffled once more, though not altogether; and, at that, Rumbald ran out into the road as he was, bareheaded; and I saw that he carried a cleaver in his hand, caught up, I suppose, at random; for it was of no use to him.

Then, loud and clear not a hundred yards away I heard the rattle and roar of a coach coming down the hill and the tramp of the hoofs.

"Back, you fool," I screamed, "back!" for I dared not pull my horse out into the road. "Throw it away!"

He turned on me with the face of a devil. Though he must have seen the liveries and the guardsmen from where he stood, I think not even yet did he take in how he had been deceived; but that he began to suspect it, I have no doubt.

He came back at my cry, as if unwillingly, and stood by my side; but never a word did he say: and together we waited.

Then, past the gate on the left, over the hedge, I caught a flash of colour, and another, come and gone again; and then the gleam of a coach-roof; and, though I had no certainty from my senses, I was as sure it was the King, as if I had seen him.

So we waited still. I drew up in my hands my horse's bridle, not knowing what I did, and moved round to where I could mount, if there were any road; and, as I did it, past the gate, full in view there swept at a gallop, first three guards riding abreast, a brave blaze of colour in the dusky lane; then the four grey horses, with their postilions cracking their whips; then the coach; and, as this passed, as plain as a picture I saw the King lean forward and look — his great hat and periwig thrust forward — and behind him another man. Then the coach was gone; and two more guards flew by and were gone too.

I lost my head completely for the single time, I think, in all this affair; now that I knew that the King was safe. There, standing where I was, I lifted my hat, and shouted with my full voice:

"God save the King!"

*　　*　　*

I turned as I shouted; and, as the last word left my lips, I saw Rumbald, his face afire with anger, coming at me, round my horse from behind, with the cleaver upraised. If he had not been near mad with disappointment, he would have struck at my horse; but he was too intent on me for that.

I leapt forward, for I had no time to do anything else, dragging my horse's haunches forward again and round; and with the next movement I was across my saddle, all-asprawl, as my horse started and plunged. I was ten yards away before the man could do anything, and struggling to my seat; but, as I rose and gripped the reins, something flew over my head, scarce missing it by six inches; and I saw the blade of the cleaver flash into the ditch beyond.

At that, I turned and lifted my hat, reining in my horse; for I was as mad with success as the other man with failure.

"God save the King!" I cried again. "Ah! Mr. Rumbald, if only you had learned to speak the truth!"

Then I put in my spurs and was gone, hearing before me, the hollow tramp and rumble of the great coach in front, as the King's party went across the bridge.

CHAPTER XI

It was three months later that I sat once more, though not for the first time since my adventure at the Rye in Mr. Chiffinch's parlour.

*　　*　　*

Of those three months I need not say very much; especially of the beginning of them, since I received then, I think, more compliments than ever in my life before. My interviews had been very many; not with Mr. Chiffinch only, but with two other personages whose lives, they were pleased to say, I had saved.

His Majesty had laughed very heartily indeed at the tale of my adventures.

"Odds-fish!" said he. "We had all been done, but for you, Mr. Mallock. It was three or four days after, at the least, that I had intended returning; and by that time, no doubt, our friends would have had their ambushment complete. But when your man came, all a-sweat, into my very bed-chamber, telling me to fly for my life — well; there was no more to be said. There was a fire too at my lodgings that same morning; — and poor Sir Christopher's low ceilings all ruined with the smoke — but that would not have brought me, though I suppose we must give out that it did. No; Mr. Mallock, 'twas you, and no other. Odds-fish! I did not think I had such an accomplished liar in my service!"

His Royal Highness, too, was no less gracious; though he talked in a very different fashion.

To him there was no humour in the matter at all; 'twas all God's Providence; and I am not sure but that he was not more right than his brother; though indeed there are always two sides to a thing. His talk was less of myself, and more of the interests I had served; and there too he was right; for, as I have said, if there had been any mistake in the matter, good-bye to Catholic hopes.

My first interview with Mr. Chiffinch astonished me most. When he had finished paying compliments, I began on business.

"You will hardly catch Rumbald," said I, "unless you take him pretty soon. He too will be off to Holland, I think."

He shook his head, smiling.

"I am sorry not to be able to give you vengeance for that cleaver-throwing; but you must wait awhile."

"Wait?" cried I.

"What single name do you know besides that of Rumbald,

which was certainly involved in this affair? Why, Mr. Mallock, you yourself have told me that he observed discretion so far; and did not name a single man."

"Well; there is Keeling," I said.

"And what is Keeling?" he asked with some contempt. "A maltster, and a carpenter: a fine bag of assassins! And how can you prove anything but treasonable talk? Where were the 'swan-quills' and the 'sand and the ink'? Did you set eyes on any of them?"

I was silent.

"No, no, Mr. Mallock; we must wait awhile. I have even talked to Jeffreys, and he says the same. We must lime more birds before we pull our twig down. Now, if you could lay your hand on Keeling!"

He was right: I saw that well enough.

"And meantime," said I, smiling, "I must go in peril of my life. They surely know now what part I have played?"

"They must be fools if they do not. But there will be no more cleaver-throwing for the present, if you take but reasonable care. Meanwhile, you may go to Hare Street, if you will; though I cannot say I should advise it. And I will look for Keeling."

*　　*　　*

Well; I did not take his advice. That was too much to expect. I went to Hare Street in April and remained there a couple of months; but I do not propose to discourse on that beyond saying that I was very well satisfied, and even with Cousin Tom himself, who appeared to me more resigned to have me as a son-in-law. To neither of them could I say a word of what had passed, except to tell Dolly that my peril was over for the present, and to thank her for her prayers. During those two months I had no word of Rumbald at all; and I suspect that he lay very quiet, knowing, after all, how little I knew. If he went to Holland, he certainly came back again. Then, in June, once more a man came from Mr. Chiffinch, to call me to town. So here I sat once more, with the birds singing their vespers, in the Privy Garden, a hundred yards away, and the river flowing without the windows, as if no blood had ever flowed with it.

"Well," said Chiffinch, when I was down in a chair, "the first news is that we have found Keeling. You were right, or very nearly. He is a joiner, and lives in the City. He hath been to the Secretary of the Council, and will go to him again tomorrow."

"How was that done?" I asked.

"Why, I sent a couple of men to him," said the page, "when we had marked him down; who so worked on his fears that he went straight to my Lord Dartmouth; and my Lord Dartmouth carried him to Sir Leoline Jenkins. The Secretary very properly remarked that he was but one witness; and Keeling went away again, to see if he can find another. Well; the tale is that he hath found another — his own brother — and that both will go again to the Secretary tomorrow. So I thought it best that you should see him first here, tonight, to identify him for certain."

"That is very good," I said. "But, Mr. Chaffinch, if I appear too publicly in this matter, I shall be of very little service to the King hereafter."

"I know that very well," said the page. "And you shall not appear publicly at all, neither shall your name. Indeed, the King hath a little more business for you at last, in France; and you will wish perhaps to go to Rome. So the best thing that you can do, when we have seen that all is in order, is to wait no longer, but be off, and for a good while too. Your life may be in some peril for the very particular part that you played, for though we shall catch, I think, all the principal men in the affair, we shall not catch all the underlings; and even a joiner or a scavenger for that matter, if he be angry enough, is enough to let the life out of a man. And we cannot spare you yet, Mr. Mallock."

This seemed to me both reasonable and thoughtful; and it was not altogether a surprise to me. Indeed I had prepared Dolly for a long absence, thinking that I might go to Rome again, as I had not been there for a long while. Besides, waiting in England for the time laid down by Tom and agreed to by both of us, would make that time come no swifter; and, if there were work to be done, I had best do it, before I had a wife to engage my attention.

But I sighed a little.

"Well," said I; "and where is Keeling?"

"I have been expecting him this last ten minutes," said he.

Even as he spoke, a knock came upon the door. The page cried to come in; and there entered, first a servant holding the door, and then the little joiner himself, flushed in his face, I sup-posed with the excitement. He was dressed in his Sunday clothes, rather ill-fitting. He did not know me, I think, for he made no movement of surprise. I caught Mr. Chiffinch's look of inquiry, and nodded very slightly.

"Well, sir," began the page in a very severe tone, "so you have made up your mind to evade the charge of misprision of treason — that, at the least!"

"Yes, sir," said the man in a very timid way. (He must have heard that phrase pretty often lately.)

"Well; and you have found your other witness?"

"Yes, sir; my own brother, sir."

"Ah! Was he too in this detestable affair?"

"No, sir."

"Well, then; how do you bring him in?"

"Sir," said the man, seeming to recover himself a little, "I put my brother in a secret place; and then caused him to overhear a conversation between myself and another."

"Very pretty! very pretty!" cried the page. "And who was this other?"

"Sir; it was a Mr. Goodenough — under-sheriff once of —"

I could not restrain a start; for I had not thought Mr. Goodenough, the friend of my Lord Essex, to be so deep in the affair as this. Keeling saw me start, I suppose; for he looked at me, and himself showed sudden agitation.

"Good evening, Keeling," said I. "We have had a little conversation once before."

"Oh! for God's sake, gentlemen! for God's sake! I am already within an inch of my life."

"I know you are," said Mr. Chiffinch severely, "and you will be nearer even than that, if you do not speak the whole truth."

"Sir; it is not that I mean," cried the man, in a very panic of terror. "Rumbald hath been —"

"Eh? What is that?" said Mr. Chiffinch.

"Rumbald, sir, the old Colonel, of the Rye —"

"God, man! We know all about Rumbald," said the page contemptuously. "What hath he been at now?"

"Sir; he and some of the others caught me but yesterday. They had heard some tale of my having been to Mr. Secretary, and —"

"And you swore you had not, I suppose," snarled the other.

"Sir; what could I do? Rumbald was all for despatching me then and there. They caught me at Wapping. I prayed them for God's love not to believe such things: I entreated: I wept —"

"I'll be bound you did," said Mr. Chiffinch. "Well? And what then?"

"Sir! they let me go again."

"They did? The damned fools!" cried Chiffinch.

I was astonished at his vehemence. But, like his master, if there was one thing that the page could not bear, it was a fool. I made him a little sign.

"Keeling," said I, "you remember me well enough. Well; I need not say that we know pretty near everything that there is to know. But we must have it from you, too. Tell us both now, as near as you can recollect, every name to which you can speak with certainty. Remember, we want no lies. We had enough of them a while back in another plot." (I could not resist that; though Mr. Chiffinch snapped his lips together.) "Well, now, take your time. No, do not speak. Consider yourself carefully."

It was, indeed, a miserable sight to see this poor wretch so hemmed in. The sweet evening light fell full upon his terrified eyes and his working lips, as he sought to gather up the names. He was persuaded, I am sure, that we were as gods, knowing all things — above all, he feared myself, as I could see, having met me first at the very house of Rumbald, as if I were his friend, and now again in the chamber of his accuser. It was piteous to see how he sought to be very exact in his memories, and not go by a hair's breadth beyond the truth.

At last I let him speak.

"Now then," I said, "tell us the names." (I saw as I spoke that Mr. Chiffinch held a note-book below the table to take them down.)

"Sir, these for certain. Rumbald; West; Rumsey —"

"Slowly, man, slowly," I cried.

"Rumsey; Goodenough; Burton; Thompson; Barber — those last three all of Wapping, sir. Then, sir, there is Wade, Nelthrop, West, Walcot —" he hesitated.

"Well, sir," demanded Mr. Chiffinch very fiercely. "That is not all."

"No, sir, no no.... There is Hone, a joiner like myself."

"Man," cried the page, "we want better names than snivelling tradesmen like yourself."

The fellow turned even paler.

"Well, sir; but how can I tell that —"

"Sir," said the page to me sharply, "call the guard!"

"Sir," cried the poor wretch, "I will tell all; indeed I will tell."

"Well?"

"Sir, the Duke of Monmouth was in it — at least we heard so. He was certainly in the former plot!"

"And what was that?" asked the other very quietly.

"Why, sir; the plot to assault Whitehall; it is all one in reality; but —"

"We know all about that," snapped the page sharply. "Well; and what other names?"

"Sir; there was my Lord Russell."

I moved in my chair. Even to this day I cannot believe that that peer was guilty; though indeed he was found so to be. Mr. Chiffinch cast me a look.

"Proceed, sir," he said.

"And there was Mr. Ferguson, a minister; and Mr. Wildman; and my Lord Argyle in Scotland; and my Lord Howard of Escrick; and Mr. Sidney; and my Lord Essex. I do not say, sir, that all those —"

"There! there: go on. We shall test every word you say; you may depend upon it. What other names have you?"

"There was my Lord Grey, sir; and Sir Thomas Armstrong ... Sir; I can remember no more!"

"And a pretty load on any man's conscience!" cried the virtuous Mr. Chiffinch. "And so all this nest of assassins —"

"Sir; I did not say that. I said —"

"That is enough; we want no comments and glosses, but the bare truth. Well, Keeling, if this tale be true, you have saved your own life — that is, if your fellow murderers do not get at you again. You have been in trouble before, I hear, too."

"Sir; it was on the matter of the Lord Mayor —"

"I know that well enough. Well, sir; so this is the tale you will tell tomorrow to Mr. Secretary."

"Yes, sir, if I can remember it all."

"You will remember it, I'll warrant. Well, sir; I think I have no more questions for the present. Sir, have you any questions to ask this man?"

I shook my head. I was near sick at the torture the man was in.

"Well, sir; you may go," said the page. "And I would recommend you and your brother to lie very private tonight. There must be no more evasion."

*   *   *

When he was gone, Mr. Chiffinch turned to me.

"Well?" he said. "What do you think?"

"Oh! I think he speaks the truth, in the main," I said wearily. "Shall I be needed any more; or when may I leave town?"

"You must wait, Mr. Mallock, until we have laid hands on them."

*   *   *

It was not until the middle of July that I was able to leave. On the eighteenth of June a proclamation was issued, with the names of some of the conspirators; and numerous arrests were made. One matter pleased me a little, and that was that Keeling had been man enough after all, to warn some of the humbler folk, who had been led into the affair, of what he had done; and the most of these got clean away. Then Sheppard came forward and betrayed three or four who had met in his house, as I had seen for myself: and West added many details. A second proclamation containing the names, and offering rewards for the arrest of Monmouth, my Lord Grey, Sir Thomas Armstrong and the Reverend Robert Ferguson, was made after my Lord Russell's arrest; but all four of them escaped. My Lords Howard and Essex were taken on the tenth of July; and two days later Walcot, Hone and Rouse were convicted.

As soon as my Lord Russell's trial was begun, and the certainty that he would be convicted was made plain by my Lord Howard turning King's evidence, I left London with my man James. And before we were at Dover the news came to us that my Lord Essex, in despair, had cut his throat in the Tower. As for myself, I was glad enough to leave; for I was both sick and weary of intrigue. It would be of a very different sort in France; and of a kind that a gentleman may undertake without misgivings: so, though I was loth to leave the land where Dolly was, the balance altogether left me refreshed rather than saddened.

*   *   *

It was a clear day as the packet put out from Dover; and, as I stood on deck, watching the cliffs recede as we went, there came on me again that same mood that had fallen on me as I went up the river so long ago from Wapping. Once more it appeared to me as if I were in somewhat of a dream. Those men I had left behind, awaiting trial and death; Mr. Chiffinch; the King, the Court, even Dolly herself, appeared to have something phantom-like about them. Once more the realities seemed to close about me and envelop me — or rather that great Reality whom we name God; and all else seemed but very little and trifling.

PART IV

CHAPTER I

Once more it was high summer, a year afterwards, as I rode in, still with James, thank God! and three other men, over London Bridge.

*   *   *

My life abroad once more must remain undescribed. There is plenty of reason against the telling of it; and nothing at all for it. One thing only may I say, that I came last from Rome, having stayed over for the Feast of the Apostles, and carried with me, though verbally only, some very particular instructions for His Royal Highness the Duke of York from personages whom he should respect, if he did not. And what those counsels were will appear in the proper place. By those same personages I had been complimented very considerably, and urged to yet greater efforts. Briefly with regard to the two Royal Brothers, I was urged to press on the one, and to restrain the other; for I heard in Rome that it was said that they would listen to me, if I observed discretion.

As to what had passed in England, a very short account will suffice.

First, with regard to the conspirators, a number had been executed, among whom I suppose must be reckoned my Lord Russell — an upright man, I think; yet one who had at least played with very hot fire. Frankly, I do not believe that he aimed ever at the King's life, but that my Lord Howard witnessed that he did, in order to save himself. Of the others that were executed, I think all deserved it; and the principal, I suppose, was Mr. Sidney, that ancient Republican and Commonwealth man, who was undoubtedly guilty. Besides him, my Lord Essex had killed himself in prison — for I never believed the ugly story of the bloody razor having been thrown out of his window — and Sir Thomas Armstrong was executed — and richly he had earned it by a thousand crimes and debaucheries — and old Colonel Rumbald; whose fate, I must allow, caused me a little sorrow (even though he had flung a sharp cleaver at my head), for he was very much more of a man than that puling treacherous hound my Lord Howard, who was taken hiding in his shirt, up his own chimney, and turned traitor to his friends. Holloway too — a merchant of Bristol, and a friend of Mr. Ferguson — was executed, and several in Edinburgh, of the Scottish plotters under Argyle, among whom the principal was

Baillie of Jerviswood. The torture of the boot and the thumb-screws was used there, I am sorry to say; for they had plenty of evidence without it. Of the others some evaded altogether, of whom a good number went to Holland, which was their great refuge at this time, and others again saved their lives by turning King's evidence. The Reverend Mr. Ferguson proved himself a clever fellow, as indeed I had thought him, and a courageous one too, for after attending my Lord Shaftesbury upon his deathbed, he returned again to Edinburgh, and there, upon search being made for him, hid himself in the very prison to which they wished to consign him, and so escaped the death he had earned.

With regard to the Duke of Monmouth, affairs had taken a very strange course; and His Majesty, as I think, had behaved with less than his usual wisdom. Before even Mr. Sidney's death, the Duke had made his peace, both with the King and the Duke of York, and had, after expressing extraordinary contrition, and yet denying that he had been in any way privy to any attempt on the King's life, received a pardon. But he had not been content with that; and so soon as the *Gazette* announced that it was so, and had given men to understand that Monmouth had made his peace by turning King's evidence, what must His Grace do, but deny it again, and cause it to be denied too in all the coffee-houses in town? The King was thrown into a passion by this; and once again His Grace had to sign and read aloud a paper, in the presence of witnesses and of the King, in the private parlour of the Duchess of Portsmouth's lodgings — (where, it must be confessed, His Majesty did much of his business at this time). But the paper was not explicit enough, and must be re-written: and so the foolish shilly-shally went on — and he guilty all the time — and at last he evaded them all, and went back again to Holland.

There was another piece of news that had come to me lately that pleased me better; and that was of the trial of Oates, for treasonous speaking, and his condemnation in one hundred thousand pounds, which caused him to be shut up in prison without more ado, where he could do no more mischief. Indeed his credit was all gone now, thank God! and all that he had to do in prison was to prepare himself for his whippings which he got a year later. A few months earlier too, the four Popish lords that had been left in the Tower were released again, which I was very glad to hear of.

Other matters too had passed; but I think I have said enough to shew how affairs stood in the month of July when I came back to England — with the exception of what I shall relate presently as of my own experience.

The evening was as bright and fair as that on which I had come back to London near two years and a half ago, with so heavy a heart, to find Dolly at Court; but this time the heaviness was all gone. I had had letters from her continually, and all those I carried with me. She told me that her father seemed a little moody, now and again; but I did not care very greatly about that. He could be as moody as he liked, if he but let her and me alone. It was less than a year now from my twenty-eighth birthday, which was the period that had been fixed.

Now a piece of news had reached me at Dover that made me pretty content; and that was that His Majesty desired me to have lodgings now in Whitehall. These were very hard to come by, except a man had great influence; and I was happy to think that such as I had was from the King himself. So I did not return northwards this time from the Strand, but held on, and so to the gate of Whitehall. Here I was stopped and asked my name.

I gave it; and the officer saluted me very civilly.

"Your lodgings are ready, sir," said he. "Mr. Chiffinch was very urgent about them. And he bade me tell you you would find visitors there, if you came before eight o'clock."

It was now scarcely gone seven; but I thought very little of my visitors, supposing they might perhaps be Mr. Chiffinch himself and a friend: so I inquired very, leisurely where the lodgings were situate.

"They are my Lord Peterborough's old lodgings, sir," said the man. "He hath moved elsewhere. They look out upon the Privy Garden and the bowling-green; or, to be more close, on the trees between them."

This was a fine piece of news indeed; for these lodgings were among the best. I was indeed become a person of importance.

There were two entrances to these lodgings — one from the Stone Gallery, and the other from the garden; but that into the garden was only a little door, whose use was not greatly encouraged, because of the personages that walked there; so I went up the Stone Gallery, between all the books and the cabinets, and so to my own door; with my James behind me. My other men I bade follow when they had bestowed the horses and found their own quarters.

It was a fine entrance, with a new shield over the door; lately scraped white, for the reception of my own arms. I knocked upon it, and a fellow opened; and when I had told him my name, he let me through; and I went upstairs to the parlour that looked over the garden; and there, to my happiness were my visitors. For they were none other than my dear love herself and her maid.

I cannot tell what that was to me, to find her there.... The maid was sent into the little writing-room, next door, into which my visitors would usually be shewn; and we two sat down on the window-seat. Dolly looked not a day older: she was in a fine dress.

"See," she said, "you have caught me again at Court? Will you send me away again this time?"

She told me presently that she and her father were come up to town for a few days; but must be gone again directly. They had written to Mr. Chiffinch demanding news of me, and when should I be at liberty to come to Hare Street; and he had told them that at anyrate not yet for a while, and that they had best come and see me in my new lodgings. I was sorry that he had said I could not go to Hare Street for the present — though I had expected no less; but I soon forgot it again in her dear presence.

"You are a great man, now, I suppose," she said presently, "too great to see to the pigs any longer. We have no such rooms as this at Hare Street."

They were indeed fine; and we went through them together. They were all furnished from roof to floor; there were some good tapestries and pictures; and the windows, as the officer had said, looked out for the most part upon the trees beneath which so long ago I had watched ladies walking. But I told her that I loved my panelled chamber at Hare Street, and the little parlour, with the poor Knights of the Grail, who rode there for ever and never attained their quest, more than all Whitehall. Then I kissed her again, for perhaps the thirtieth time; and, as I was doing so Cousin Tom came in.

"Ah!" said he, "I have caught you then!" But he said it without much merriment.

If Dolly was no older, her father was. There were grey hairs in his eyebrows, for that was all that I could see of his hair, since he wore a periwig; and his face appeared a little blotchy.

I met him however with cordiality, and congratulated him on his looks. He sat down, and presently, to my astonishment, he too opened out upon my prospects, though in a very different manner from Dolly.

"You are a great man now," he said, "in these fine lodgings. I wonder His Majesty hath not made you at least a knight."

I was a little angry at his manner. He said it not pleasantly at all; but as if he found fault. I determined I would not meet his ambitions at all.

"My dear Cousin," said I, "indeed I am not a knight; and have no hope of being so. His Majesty hath a thousand men more competent than I."

"Then why hath he given you these lodgings?" said he, with a sharp look.

I shrugged my shoulders.

"I am of some convenience to His Majesty; and the more so if I am near him. I suppose that these lodgings fell vacant in the nick of time."

He looked at me very earnestly. He had, of course, no idea of in what matters I was engaged: I might have been a mere valet for all he knew.

"That is so?" he said.

"I have no reason to think otherwise," I answered him.

*　　*　　*

Well; it was growing late; and I had not supped, as Dolly presently remembered; it was near eight o'clock, and after that time there would be formalities at the gate as they went out. So they took their leave at last; and I kissed Dolly for the thirty-first time, and went downstairs with them, and watched them down the gallery; they having promised to come again next day.

*　　*　　*

I had scarcely done supper and looked about me a little, when Mr. Chiffinch's name was brought to me; and I went to see him in the little parlour and bring him through to what would be my private closet — so great was I become! He looked older; and I told him so.

"Well; so I am," said he. "And so are we all. You will be astonished when you see His Majesty."

"Is he so much older?" I asked.

"He has aged five years in one," said he.

We talked presently (after looking through my lodgings again, to see if all were as it should be, and after my thanking Mr. Chiffinch for the pains he had put himself to), first of France and then of Rome. He shewed himself very astute when we spoke of Rome.

"I do not wish to pry," he said, "but I hope to God's sake that the Holy Father hath given you a commission to His Royal Highness, to bid him hold himself more quiet. He will ruin all, if he be not careful."

"Why; how is that?" said I.

"Ah! you ecclesiastics," he cried — "for I count you half an one at least, in spite of your pretty cousin — you are more close than any of us! Well; I will tell you as if you did not know."

He put his fingers together, in his old manner.

"First," said he, "he is Lord High Admiral again. I count that very rash. We are Protestants, we English, you know; and we like not a Papist to be our guard-in-chief."

"You will have to put up with a Papist as a King, some day," said I.

"Why I suppose so — though I would not have been so sure two years ago. But a King is another matter from an High Admiral."

"Well; what else has he done?" I asked.

"He hath been readmitted to the Council, in the very face of the Test Act too. But it is how he bears himself and speaks that is the worst of all. He carries himself and his religion as openly as he can; and does all that is in His power to relieve the Papists of disabilities. That is very courageous, I know; but it is not very shrewd. God knows where he will stop if once he is on the throne. I think he will not be there long."

I said nothing; for indeed my instructions were on those very points; and I knew them all as well as Chiffinch, and, I think, better.

He spoke, presently, of myself.

"As for you, Mr. Mallock, I need not tell you how high you are in favour here. *Si monumentum requiris, circumspice*"; and he waved his hands at the rich rooms.

"His Majesty is very good," I said.

"His Majesty hath a peerage for you, if you want it. He said he had made too many grocers and lickspittles into knights, to make you one."

I cannot deny that to hear that news pleased me. Yet even then I hesitated.

"Mr. Chiffinch," said I at last, "if you mean what you say, I have something to answer to that."

"Well?" said he.

"Let me have one year more of obscurity. I may be able to do much more that way. In one year from now I shall be married, as I told you. Well, when I have a wife she must come to town, and make acquaintances; and so I shall be known in any case. Let me have it then, if I want it — as a wedding gift; so that she shall come as My Lady. And I will do what I can then, in His Majesty's service, more publicly."

"What if His Majesty is dead before that?" said he, regarding me closely.

"Then we will go without," said I.

He nodded; and said no more.

*　　*　　*

It was strange to lie down that night in a great room, with four posts and all their hangings about me, with my Lord Peterborough's arms emblazoned on the ceiling; and to know that it was indeed I, Roger Mallock, who lay there, with a man within call; and a coronet, if I would have it, within reach. It was not till then, I think, that I understood how swift had been my rise; for here was I, but just twenty-seven years old, and in England but the better part of six years. Yet, even then, more than half my thoughts were of Dolly, and of how she would look in a peeress' robes. I even determined what my title should be — taken from my French estates in the village of Malmaison, in Normandy, so foolish and trifling are a man's thoughts at such a time. One thing, however, I resolved; and that was to say nothing at all of all this either to Dolly or her father. It should be a wedding gift to the one, and a consolation to the other; for dearly would my Cousin Tom love to speak of his son-in-law the Viscount, or even the plain Lord Malmaison. As for His Majesty's death before another year, I thought nothing of that; for what young man of twenty-seven years of age thinks ever that anyone will die? Even should he die too — which I prayed God might not be yet! — there was His Royal Highness to follow; and I had served him, all things considered, pretty near as well as his brother.

So, then, I lay in thought, hearing a fountain play somewhere without my windows, and the rustle of the wind in the limes that stood along the Privy Garden. I heard midnight strike from the Clock-Tower at the further end of the palace, before I slept; and presently after the cry of the watchman that "all was well, and a fair night."

CHAPTER II

It was not until the third day after my coming to town that I had audience of the Duke — in the evening after supper, having bidden good-bye that morning, with a very heavy heart, to my cousins, at Aldgate, whither I had escorted them. I had promised Dolly I would come when I could; but God knew when that would be!

Even by then, I think, I had become accustomed to my new surroundings. I had made no friends indeed, for that was expressly contrary to my desires, since a man on secret service must be very slow to do so; but I had made a number of acquaintances even in that short time, and had renewed some others. I had had a word or two with Sir George Jeffreys, now a long time Lord Chief Justice, in Scroggs' old place; and found him a very brilliant kind of man, of an extraordinary handsomeness, and no less extraordinary power — not at all brutal in manner, as I had thought, but liker to a very bright sword, at once sharp and heavy: and sharp and heavy indeed men found him when they looked at him from the dock. It was in Mr. Chiffinch's closet that I was made known to him. I had spoken too with my Lord Halifax — another brilliant fellow, very satirical and witty, for which the King loved him, though all the world guessed, and the King, I think knew, that his opposition to our cause was so hot as even to keep him in correspondence with the Duke of Monmouth, safe away in Holland. At least that was the talk in the coffee-houses. He, like the Lord Keeper North, hated a Papist like the Devil, and all his ways and wishes. He said of my Lord Rochester, now made president of the Council — a post of immense dignity and no power at all — that "he was kicked upstairs," which was a very precise description of the matter.

*   *   *

I was taken straight through into the Duke's private closet, where he awaited me; and, by the rarest chance His Majesty was just about to take his leave, and they had me in before he was gone.

I was very deeply shocked by His Majesty's appearance. He was standing below a pair of candles when I came in, and his face was all in shadow; but when, after I had saluted the two, he moved out presently, I could see how fallen his face was, and how heavily lined. Since it was evening too, and he had not shaved since morning I could see a little frostiness, as it were, upon his chin. He dyed his eyebrows and moustaches, I suppose, for these were as black as ever. His melancholy eyes had a twinkle in them, as he looked at me.

"Well," said he, "so here is our hero back again — come to pay his respects to the rising sun, I suppose." (But he said it very pleasantly, without any irony.)

"Why, Sir," said I, "I have always understood that there is neither rising nor setting with England's sun; but that it is always in mid-heaven. The King never dies; and the King can do no wrong."

(Such was the manner in which we spoke at Court in those days — very foolish and bombastic, no doubt.)

"Hark to that, brother," said the King; "there is a pretty compliment to us both! It is to neither of us that Mr. Mallock is loyal; but to the Crown only."

"It is that which we all serve, Sir," said I; "even Your Majesty."

The King smiled. "Well," he said, "I must be off while you two plot, I suppose. Come and see me too, Mr. Mallock; when you have done all your duties."

I took him to the door of the closet where the servants were waiting for him; and even his gait seemed to me older.

Now James had very little — (though no Stuart could have none) — of his family's charm. He looked no older, no sharper and no lighter than a year ago; and he had learned nothing from adversity, as I presently understood. He very graciously made me sit down; but in even that the condescension was evident — not as his brother did it.

"You have been to Rome, again," he said pretty soon, when he had told me how he did, and how the King was not so well as he had been. "And what news do you bring with you?"

I told him first of the Holy Father's health, and delivered a few compliments from one or two of the Cardinals, and spoke of three or four general matters of the Court there. He nodded and asked some questions; but I could see that he was thinking of something else.

"But you have more to say to me, have you not?" said he. "I had a letter from the Cardinal Secretary —" he paused.

"Yes, Sir," said I. "The Holy Father was graciously pleased to put me at Your Royal Highness' disposal, if you should wish to know His Holiness' mind on one or two affairs."

I put it like this, as gently as I could; for indeed I had something very like a scolding, in my pocket, for him. He saw through it, however, for he lowered his eyelids a little sullenly as his way was, when he was displeased.

"Well; let us hear it," said he. "What have I done wrong now?"

This would never do. His Royal Highness resembled a mule in this, at least, that the harder he was pushed, the more he kicked and jibbed. He must be drawn forward by some kind of a carrot, if he were to be moved. I made haste to draw out my finest.

"His Holiness is inexpressibly consoled," I said, "by Your Royal Highness' zeal for religion, and courage too, in that course. He bade me tell you that he could say his *Nunc Dimittis*, if he could but see such zeal and obedience in the rest of Europe."

The Duke smiled a little; and I could see that he was pleased. (It was really necessary to speak to him in this manner; he would have resented any such freedom or informality as I used towards the King.)

"These are the sweets before the medicine," he said. "And now for the draught."

"Sir," I said, "there is no draught. There is but a word of warning His Holiness —"

"Well; call it what you will. What is it, Mr. Mallock?"

I told him then, as gently as I could (interlarding all with a great many compliments) that His Holiness was anxious that matters should not go too fast; that there was still a great deal of disaffection in England, and that, though the pendulum had swung it would surely swing back again, though, please God! never so far as it had been; and that meantime a great deal of caution should be used. For example, it was a wonderful thing that His Royal Highness should be Lord High Admiral of the Fleet again; but that great care should be observed lest the people should be frightened that a Papist should have the guarding of them; or again, that the Test Act should be set aside in His Royal Highness' case, yet the exception should not be pressed too far. All this my Lord Cardinal Howard had expressly told me; but there was one yet more difficult matter to speak of; and this I reserved for the moment.

"Well," said the Duke, when I had got so far, "I am obliged to His Holiness for his solicitude; and I shall give the advice my closest attention. Was there anything more, Mr. Mallock?"

He had received it, I thought, with unusual humility; so I made haste to bring out the last of what I had to say.

"There is no more, Sir," I said, "in substance. There was only that His Eminence thought perhaps that the extraordinary courage and fervour of Your Royal Highness' Jesuit advisers led them to neglect discretion a little."

"Ah! His Eminence thought that, did he?" said James meditatively.

His Eminence had said it a great deal more strongly than that; but I dared not put it as he had.

"Yes, Sir," I said. "They are largely under French influence; and French circumstances are not at all as in England. The Society is a little apt at present —"

Then the Duke lost his self-command; and his heavy face lightened with a kind of anger.

"Mr. Mallock," he said, "you have said enough. I do not blame you at all; but His Eminence (with all possible respect to him!) does not know what he is talking about. These good Fathers have imperilled their lives for England; if any have a right to speak, it is they; and I would sooner listen to their counsel than to all the Cardinals in Christendom. They know England, as Rome cannot; and, while I allow myself to be led by the nose by no man living, I would sooner do what they advise than what a Roman Cardinal advises. It is not by subtlety or plotting that the Faith will be commended in this country; but by courageous action; and since God has placed me here in the position that I hold, it is to Him alone that I must answer. You can send that message back to Rome, sir, as soon as you like."

Now there was James, true to himself; and I could see that further words would be wasted. I smoothed him down as well as I could; and I was happy to see that it was not with myself that he was angry — (for he made that very plain) — for that I still might hope he would listen to me later on. But anything further at that time was useless; so I prepared to take my leave; and he made no opposition.

"Well, sir," he said, "you have given your message very well; and I thank you for not wrapping it up. You have done very well in France, I hear."

"His Majesty hath been pleased to think so," I said. Then his face lightened again.

"Ah!" said he, "when the time comes, we shall shew Europe what England can do. We shall astonish even Rome itself, I think. We have long been without the light; but it is dawning once more, and when the sun is indeed risen, as His Majesty said, men will be amazed at us. We shall need no more help from France then. The whole land will be a garden of the Lord."

His face itself was alight with enthusiasm; and I wondered how, once more in this man, as in many others, the Church shewed itself able to inspire and warm, yet without that full moral conversion that she desires. He was not yet by any means free from the sins of the flesh and from pride — (which two things so commonly go together) — he could not be released from these until humiliation should come on him — as it did, and made him very like a Saint before the end. Meanwhile it was something to thank God for that he should be so whole-hearted and zealous, even though he lacked discretion.

As I was going down the stairs whom should I run into, coming up, but Father Huddleston, who stopped to speak with me. I did not know him very well; though I had talked with him once or twice. He was the one priest of English blood who was tolerated openly and legally in England, and who had leave to wear his habit, for his saving of the King's life after the battle of Worcester.

"So you are home again, Mr. Mallock," he said in his cheery voice.

I told him Yes; and that I was come for a good time.

"And His Majesty?" he said. "Have you seen him? He is terribly aged, is he not, this last year."

This priest was a very pleasant-looking fellow, going on for sixty years old, I would say; and, except for his dress, resembled some fine old country-squire. He wore a great brown periwig that set off his rosy face. He was not, I think, a very spiritual man, though good and conscientious, and he meddled not at all with politics or even with religion. He went his way, and let men alone, which, though not very apostolic, is at least very prudent and peaceful. He was fond of country sports, I had heard, and of the classics; and spent his time pretty equally in them both.

"Yes," said I; "the King is a year older since this time twelve-month."

He laughed loudly.

"There speaks the courtier," he said. "And you come from the Duke?"

I told him Yes.

"And I go to him. Well; good day to you, Mr. Mallock."

*   *   *

It was very pleasant to me, this new air in which I lived. Here was I, come from the Duke who had received me as never before, with a deference — (if the Duke's behaviour to any man could be called that) — such as he had never shewn me, being greeted too by this priest who up to this time had never manifested much interest in me, going back to my fine lodgings and my half-dozen servants. Indeed it was a great change. As I went past the sentry a minute or two later, he saluted me, and I returned it, feeling very happy that I was come to be of some consideration at last, with do much more, too, in the background of which others never dreamed.

*   *   *

I had my first audience of His Majesty a week later, and confirmed my impressions of his ageing very rapidly. He received me with extraordinary kindness; but, as to the first part of the interview, since this concerned private affairs in France, I shall give no description. It was the end only that was of general interest; and one part of it very particular, since I was able to speak my mind to him again.

He was standing looking out of the window when he said his last word on France, and kept silent a little. He stood as upright as ever, but there was an air in him as if he felt the weight of his years, though they were scarcely fifty-four in number. His hand nearest to me hung down listlessly, with the lace over it. When he spoke, he put into words the very thing that I was thinking.

"I am getting an old man, Mr. Mallock," he said, suddenly turning on me; "and I would that affairs were better settled than they are. They are better than they were — I do not dispute that — but these endless little matters distress me. Why cannot folk be at peace and charitable one with another?"

I said nothing; but I knew of what he was thinking. It was the old business of religion which so much entered into everything and distorted men's judgments: for he had just been speaking of His Grace of Monmouth.

"Why cannot men serve God according to their own conscience?" he said, "and leave others to do the same."

"Sir," I said, "there is but one Church of God where men are at unity with one another."

He paid no attention to that; and his face suddenly contracted strangely.

"Did you hear any gossip — I mean about myself — after the death of the Jesuit Fathers?"

I told him No; for I had heard nothing of it at that time.

He came and sat down, motioning me too to a seat; for I had stood up when he did.

"Well," he said, "it is certainly strange enough, and I should not have believed it, if it had not happened to myself."

Again he stopped with an odd look.

"Well," he said, "here is the tale; and I will swear to it. You know how unwilling I was to sign the death-warrants."

"Yes, Sir; all the world knows that."

"And all the world knows that I did it," he said with a vehement kind of bitterness. "Yes; I did it, for there was no way out of it that I could see. It was they or the Crown must go. But I never intended it; and I swore I would not."

"Yes, Sir," I said quietly, "you said so to me."

"Did I? Well, I said so to many. I even swore that my right hand might rot off if I did it."

His heavy face was all working. I had seldom seen him so much moved.

"Yes," he said, "that was what I swore. Well, Mr. Mallock, did you ever hear what followed?"

"No, Sir," I said again.

"It was within that week, that when I awakened one morning I felt my right hand to be all stiff. I thought nothing of it at the first; I believed I must have strained it at tennis. Well; that day I said nothing to anyone; but I rubbed some ointment on my hand that night."

He stopped again, lifted his right hand a little and looked at it, as if meditating on it. It was a square strong man's hand, but very well shaped and very brown; it had a couple of great rings on the fingers.

"Well," he said, "the next morning a sore had broken out on it; and I sent for a physician. He told me it was nothing but a little humour in the blood, and he bade me take care of my diet. I said nothing to anyone else, and bade him not speak of it; and that night I put on some more ointment; and the next morning another sore was broken out, between the finger and the thumb, so that I could not hold a pen without pain; and it was then, for the first time, that I remembered what I had sworn."

He had his features under command again, but I could see, as he looked at me, that his eyes were still full of emotion.

"Well, Mr. Mallock; I was in a great way at that; but yet I dared tell nobody. I wore my glove all day, so that no one should see my hand; and that evening when I went in to see Her Majesty, what should I see hanging up on the wall of the chamber but the pictures of the five men whose warrants I had signed!"

Once more he stopped.

Now I remembered that I had heard a little gossip as to the King's hand about that time; but it had been so little that I had thought nothing of it. It was very strange to hear it all now from himself.

"Well, sir," he said, "I am not ashamed to say what I did. I kissed their pictures one by one, and I begged them to intercede for me. The next morning, Mr. Mallock, the sores were healed up; and, the morning after, the stiffness was all gone."

I said nothing; for what could I say? It is true enough that many might say that it had all fallen out so, by chance, that it was no more than a strain at tennis, or a humour in the blood, as the physician had thought. But I did not think so, nor, I think, would many Catholics.

"You say nothing, Mr. Mallock," said the King.

"What is there to say, Sir?" asked I.

"What indeed?" he cried, again with the greatest emotion. "There is nothing at all to say. The facts are as I have said."

Then there came upon me once more that passionate desire to see this strange and restless soul at peace. Of those who have never received the gift of faith I say nothing: God will be their Judge, and, I doubt not, their Saviour if they have but been faithful to what they know; but for those who have received the knowledge of the truth and have drawn back from it I have always feared very greatly. Now that His Majesty had received this light long before this time, I had never had any doubt; indeed it had been reported, though I knew falsely, that he had submitted to the Church and been taken into her Communion while he was yet a young man in France. Yet here he was still, holding back from what he knew to be true — and growing old too, as he had said. All this went through my mind; but before I could speak he was up again.

"An instant, Mr. Mallock," he said, as I rose up with him; and he turned swiftly towards the door that was behind him, and was out through it, leaving it open behind him. From where I stood I could see what he did. There was a great press in the little chamber next door, and he flung the doors of this open so that I could see him pull forward his strong-box that lay within. This he opened with a key that he carried hung on a chain, and fumbled in it a minute or two, drawing out at last a paper; and so, bearing this, and leaving the strong-box open just as it was, he came back to me.

"Look at that, Mr. Mallock," said he.

It was a sheet of paper, written very closely in His Majesty's own hand, and was headed in capital letters.

Then there followed a set of reasons, all numbered, shewing that the Holy Roman Church was none other than the very Church of Christ outside of which there is no salvation. (It was made public later, as all the world knows, so I need not set it out here in full.)

"There, sir," he said when I had done reading it. "What do you think of that?"

I shall never forget how he looked, when I lifted my eyes and regarded him. He was standing by the window, with the light on his face, and there was an extraordinary earnestness and purpose in his features. It was near incredible that this could be the man whom I had seen so careless with his ladies — so light and indolent. But there are many sides to every man, as I have learned in a very long life.

"Sir," I cried, "what am I to say? There is nothing that I can add. This is Your Majesty's own conscience, written out in ink." (I tapped the paper with my finger, still holding it.)

"Eh?" said he.

"And by conscience God judges us all," I cried. Again I stared into his eyes, and he into mine.

"Your Majesty will have to answer to this," said I, "on Judgment Day."

I could say no more, so great was my emotion; and, as I hesitated a change went over his face. His brows came down as if he were angry, but his lips twitched a little as if in humour.

"There! there!" he said. "Give me the paper, Mr. Mallock."

I gave it back to him; and he stood running his eyes down it.

"Why, this is damned good!" he murmured. "I should have made a theologian."

And with that I knew that his mood was changed again, and that I could say no more.

CHAPTER III

I do not know which is the more strange that, when a great time of trial approaches a man, either he has some kind of a premonition that trouble is coming upon him, or that he has not. Certainly it is strange enough that some sense, of which we know nothing, should scent danger when there are no outward signs that any is near; but it appears even more strange to me that the storm should break all of a sudden without any cloud in the sky to shew its coming. It was the latter case with me; and the storm came upon me as I shall now relate.

*   *   *

It was now for the first time that I began to see something of the way the Court lived — I mean as one who was himself a part of it. I had looked on it before rather as a spectator at a show, observing the pageants pass before me, but myself, from the nature of my employment, taking no part in it from within.

A great deal that I saw was very dreadful and unchristian. Many of the persons resembled hogs and monkeys more than human beings; and a great deal of what passed for wit and merriment was nothing other than pure evil. Virtue was very little reckoned of; or, rather reckoned only as giving additional zest to its own corruption. I do not mean that there were no virtuous people at all — (there were virtuous people in Sodom and Gomorrah themselves) — but they were unusual, and were looked upon as a little freakish or mad. Yet, for all that, side by side with the evil, there went on a great deal of seemliness and religion: sermons were preached before the Court every Sunday; and His Majesty, who by his own life was greatly responsible for the wickedness around him, went to morning-prayers at least three or four times in the week; though I cannot say that his behaviour there accorded very well with the business he was engaged upon. Some blamed the Bishops and other ministers for their laxity and the flattery that they shewed to His Majesty: but I do not think that charge is a fair one; for they were very bold indeed upon occasion. Dr. Ken, who preached pretty often, was as outspoken as a preacher well could be, denouncing the sins of the Court in unmeasured language, even in His Majesty's presence: and a certain Bishop, whose name I forget, observing on one occasion during sermon-time that the King was fast asleep, turned and rebuked in a loud voice some other gentleman who was asleep too.

"You snore so loudly, sir," he cried, "that you will awake His Majesty, if you do not have a care."

I went sometimes to the chapel, with the crowd, to hear the anthem, as the custom was; for the music was extraordinary good, and no expense spared; and I heard there some very fine motets, the most of which were adapted from the old Catholic music and set to new words taken from the Protestant Scripture.

* * *

I went one night in August to the Duke's Theatre, as it was called, to see a play of Sir Charles Sedley, called *The Mulberry Garden*.

This extraordinary man, with whom I had already talked on more than one occasion, was, according to one account, the loosest man that ever lived; and indeed the tales related of him are such that I could not even hint at them in such a work as this. But he was now about forty-five years old; and a thought steadier. It chanced that he and my Lord Dorset — (who was of the same reputation, but had fought too both by land and sea) — were present with ladies, of whom the Duchess of Cleveland was one, in one of the boxes that looked upon the stage; and I was astonished at the behaviour of them all. Sedley himself, who appeared pretty drunk, was the noisiest person in the house; he laughed loudly at any of his own lines that took his fancy, and conversed equally loudly with his friends when they did not. As for the play it was of a very poor kind, and gave me no pleasure at all; for there was but one subject in it from beginning to end, and that was the passion which the author would call love. There were lines too in it of the greatest coarseness, and at these he laughed the loudest. He had a sharp bold face, of an extraordinary insolence; and he appeared to take the highest delight in the theme of his play — (which he had written for the King's Theatre a good while before) — and which concerned nothing else but the love-adventures of two maids that had an over-youthful fop for a father.

When the play was over, and I going out to my little coach that I used, I found that the Duchess of Cleveland's coach stopped the way, in spite of the others waiting behind, and Her Grace not come. However there was nothing to be done: and I waited. Presently out they came, Sedley leading the way with great solemnity, who knocked against me as I stood there, and asked what the devil I did in his road.

I saluted them as ironically as I could; and begged his pardon.

"I had no idea, Sir Charles," said I, "that the theatre and

street were yours as well as the play."

He looked at me as if he could not believe his ears; but my Lord Dorset who was just behind came up and took him by the arm.

"He is right," he said. "Mr. Mallock is quite right. Beg his pardon, I tell you."

"Why the devil —" began Sir Charles again, still not recognizing me.

My Lord clapped him sharply on his hat, driving it over his eyes.

"He is blind now, Mr. Mallock," he said, "in every sense. You would not be angry with a blind man!"

When Sir Charles had got his hat straight again he was now angry with my Lord Dorset, and very friendly and apologetic to myself, whom I suppose he had remembered by now; so the two drove away presently, after the ladies, still disputing loudly. But I think my Lord's behaviour shewed me more than ever that I was become a person of some consequence. Yet this kind of manners, in the midst of the crowd, though it commended gentlemen as well known as were those two — to the ruder elements among the spectators, who laughed and shouted — did a great deal of harm in those days to the Court and the King, among the more serious and sober persons of the country; and it is these who, in the long run, always have the ordering of things. God knows I would not live in a puritanical country if I could help it; yet decent breeding is surely due from gentlemen.

*   *   *

A week or two later I was at a *levée* in Her Majesty's apartments; and had a clearer sight than ever of the relations between the King and Queen.

Now His Majesty had behaved himself very ill to the Queen; he had flaunted his mistresses everywhere, and had even compelled her to receive them; he had neglected her very grossly; yet I must say in his defence that there was one line he would not pass: he would not on any account listen to those advisers of his who from time to time had urged him to put her away by divorce, and marry a Protestant who might bear him children. Even my Lord Bishop of Salisbury, Dr. Burnet, had, thirteen or fourteen years ago given as his opinion that a barren wife might be divorced, and even that polygamy was not contrary to the New Testament! This, however, Charles had flatly refused to countenance; and, when he thought of it, now and again, shewed her a sort of compassionate kindness, in spite of his distaste for her company. Yet his very compassionateness proved his distaste.

It was on occasion of a reception by Her Majesty of some Moorish deputation or embassage from Tangier, that I was present in her apartments; and it was immediately after this, too — (so that I have good cause to remember it) — that the first completely unexpected reverse came to my fortunes.

I arrived at Her Majesty's lodgings about nine o'clock in the evening; and was pleased to see that the Yeomen of the Guard lined the staircase up to the great gallery. This was an honour which the Queen did not very often enjoy; and very fine they looked in their scarlet and gold, with their halberds, all the way up from the bottom to the top.

The Great Gallery, when I came into it, was tolerably full of people, of whom I spoke to a good number, among whom again were Sir Charles Sedley and my Lord Dorset, as usual insepa-rable. But I was very much astonished at the manner in which the Moors were treated, for they were seated on couches, on one side of the state under which Her Majesty sat, as if they were some kind of raree-show, set there to be looked at. They were extraordi-nary rich and barbaric in their appearance; and when I had kissed Her Majesty's hand, I too went and looked with the rest of the crowd who jostled all together to stare at them. They were in very gorgeous silks, and wore turbans; and their jewels were beyond anything that I had ever seen — great uncut emeralds, and red stones of which I did not know the name, and ropes of pearls. The folks about me bore themselves with an amazing insolence, regarding them as if they had been monsters, and freely making comments on them which their interpreter, at least, must have understood. The Moors themselves behaved with great dignity; and it was impossible not to reflect that these shewed a far higher degree of dignity and civilization than did my own countrymen. They were very dark-skinned, and three or four of them of a won-derful handsomeness. They sat there almost in silence, looking gravely at the crowd, and observing, I thought, with surprise the bare shoulders and bosoms of the ladies who stared and screamed as much as any. It appeared to me that these poor Moors, too, thought that the civilization lay principally upon their own side. I presently felt ashamed of myself for looking at them; and turned away.

*   *   *

The gallery and the antechambers had some fine furniture in

them, pushed against the walls that the crowd might circulate; but all was not near so fine as the Duchess of Portsmouth's apartments, nor even as the King's. The cressets, I saw, most of them, were of brass, not silver; the brocades, which were Portuguese, were a little faded here and there; and there was not near the show of gold and silver plate that I had expected. But of all the sights there, I think Her Majesty was the most melancholy. She was dressed very splendid; and her skirt was so stiff with bullion that it scarce fell in folds at all. Her pearls were magnificent, but too many of them; for her *coiffure* was full of them. She resembled, to my mind, a sorrowful child dressed up for a play. Her complexion was very dark and faded, though her features were well-formed, all except her mouth. She was a little like a very pretty monkey, if such a thing can be conceived. She sat under her state, with an empty chair beside her — very upright, with the Countess of Suffolk and her other ladies round about her and behind her. She appeared altogether ill at ease, and eyed continually down the length of the gallery along which His Majesty would come, if indeed he came at all; for he had a way of sending a sudden message that he could not; and all the world knew where he would be instead.

Tonight, however, he kept his word and came.

I was in one of the antechambers at the time, talking to a couple of gentlemen and to one of the Queen's Portuguese chaplains who knew a little Italian, when I heard the music playing, and ran out in time to see him go past from the way that led from his own lodgings. He seemed in a very merry mood this evening, and was smiling as he walked, very fast, as usual. He was in a dark yellow and gold brocade that set off the darkness of his complexion wonderful well, and a dark brown periwig with his hat upon it; and he wore his Garter and Star. The crowd closed in behind his gentlemen so that I could not get near him; and when I came up he was on his chair by Her Majesty, and she smiling and tremulous with happiness, and the Moors coming up one by one to kiss his hand.

I could not hear very well what the interpreter was saying, when all this was done; but I heard him speak of a gift of thirty ostriches that this Moorish mission had brought as a gift to him.

His Majesty laughed loud when he heard that.

"I can send nothing more proper back again," said he, "than a flock of geese. I have enough and to spare of them."

Then, when all about were laughing, he turned very solemn. "You had best not tell them that," he said; "or they might take some of my friends away with them in mistake."

(This was pretty fooling; but it scarce struck me as suited to the dignity of the occasion.)

Presently the interpreter was saying how consumed with loyal envy were these Moors at all the splendour that they saw about them.

"It is better to be envied than pitied," observed His Majesty, with a very serious look.

*   *   *

At first be bore himself with extraordinary geniality this evening. He had been drinking a little, I think, yet not at all to excess, for this he never did, though he had no objection to others doing so in his company. There was related of him, I remember, how the Lord Mayor once, after a City Banquet, pressed His Majesty very unduly to remain a little longer after he had risen up to go. His Majesty was already at the door when the Mayor did this, even venturing — (for he was pretty far gone in wine) — to lay his fingers on the King's arm.

His Majesty looked at him for an instant, and then burst out laughing.

"Ah well!" he said, quoting the old song, "'He that is drunk is as great as a King.'"

And he went back and drank another bottle.

*   *   *

He was in that merry kind of mood, then, this evening: but such moods have their reactions; and half an hour later he was beginning first to yawn behind his hand and then to wear a heavy look on his face. Her Majesty observed it, too, as I could see: for she fell silent (which was the worst thing in the world to do), and began to eye him sidelong with a kind of dismay. (It was wonderful how little knowledge she had of how to manage him; and how she shewed to all present what she was feeling.)

Presently he was paying no more attention to her at all, but was leaning back in his chair, listening to my Lord Dorset who was talking in his ear; and nodding and smiling rather heavily sometimes. I felt very sorry for the Queen; but I had best have been feeling sorry for myself, for it was now, that, all unknown to me, a design was maturing against me, though not from my Lord Dorset.

As I was about to turn away, to go once more through the

rooms before taking my leave, I observed Mr. Chiffinch coming through very fast from the direction of the King's apartments, as if he had some message. He did not observe me, as I was within the crowd; but I saw him go up, threading his way as well as he could, and touching one or two to make them move out of his way, straight up to the King's side of the state. I thought he would pause then; but he did not. He put his hand on my Lord Dorset's shoulder from behind, and made him give way; and then he took his place and began to whisper to His Majesty. I saw His Majesty frown once or twice, as if he were displeased, and then glance quickly up at the faces before him, and down again, as if he looked to see if someone were there. But I did not know that it was for me that he looked. Then the King nodded thrice, sharply — Mr. Chiffinch whispering all the while — and then he leaned over and whispered to the Queen. Then both of them stood up, the King looking heavier than ever, and the Queen very near fit to cry, and both came down front the dais together, all the company saluting them and making way. And so they went down the gallery together.

I was still staring after him, wondering what was the matter, when I felt myself touched, and turned to find Mr. Chiffinch at my elbow. He looked very serious.

"Come this way, sir," said he. "I must speak with you instantly."

I went after him, down the gallery; and he led me into the little empty chamber where I had been talking with the priest half an hour ago. He closed the door carefully behind him; and turned to me again.

"Mr. Mallock," he said, "I have very serious news for you."

"Yes," said I, never dreaming what the matter was.

"It touches yourself very closely," he said, searching my face with his eyes.

"Well; what is it?" asked I — my heart beginning to beat a little.

"Mr. Mallock," he said, very gravely, "there is an order for your arrest. If you will come back with me quietly to my lodgings we can effect all that is necessary without scandal."

CHAPTER IV

I said never a word as we went back, first downstairs between the Yeomen, then to the right, and so round through the little familiar passage and up the stairs. I could hear the tramp of guards behind, and knew that they had followed us from the Queen's lodgings and would be at the doors after we were within. I was completely stunned, except, I think, for a little glimmer of sense still left which told me that the least said in any public place, the better. Mr. Chiffinch, too, I could see very well, was as bewildered as myself — for, so far as I was concerned, there was not yet the faintest suspicion in my mind as to what was the matter. At least, I told myself, my conscience was clear.

So soon as we were within the closet, the page, having again shut the door carefully behind me came forward to where I stood.

"Sit down, Mr. Mallock," said he, in a low voice, but very kindly.

I could see that his face was very pale and that he seemed greatly agitated. When I was seated, he sat himself down at his table a little way off.

"This is a terrible affair," he said, "and I do not know —"

"For God's sake," I whispered suddenly, "tell me what I am charged with."

He looked up at me sharply.

"You do not know, Mr. Mallock?"

"Before God," I said, "I have no more idea what the pother is about than —"

"Well, shortly," he said, "it is treason."

"Treason! Why —"

He leaned forward and took up a pen, to play with as be talked.

"I will tell you the whole thing from the beginning," he said. "You must have patience. An hour ago a clerk came to me here from the Board of the Green Cloth to tell me that the magistrates desired my presence there immediately on a matter of the highest importance. I went there directly and found three or four of them there, with Sir George Jeffreys whom they had sent for, it seemed, as they did not know what course to pursue, and had thought perhaps that I might throw some light upon it. They were very grave indeed, and presently mentioned your name, saying that a charge had been laid against you before one of the Westminster magistrates, of having been privy to the Ryehouse Plot."

"Why —" cried I, with sudden relief.

He held up his hand.

"Wait," he said, "I too laughed when I heard that; and gave them to understand on what side you had been throughout that matter, and how you had been in His Majesty's service and that I myself was privy to every detail of the affair. They looked more easy at that; and I thought that all was over. But they asked me to look at papers they had of yours —"

"Papers! Of mine!" I cried.

"Yes, Mr. Mallock. Papers of yours. I will tell you presently how they came by them. Well; there were about a dozen, I suppose, altogether; and some of them I knew all about, and said so. These were notes and reports that you had shewed to me: and there were three or four more which, though I had not seen them I could answer for. But there was one, Mr. Mallock, that I could not understand at all."

He paused and looked at me; and I could see that he was uneasy.

Now it may appear incredible; but even then I could not think of what paper he meant. To the best of my belief I had shewn him everything that I thought to be of the least importance — notes and reports, as he had said, such as was that which I had made in the wherry on my way up from Wapping one night.

I shook my head.

"I do not know what you mean," I said. "Where did they get the papers from?"

"Think again, Mr. Mallock. I said it was on a charge of treason just now. Well: I will say now that it may be no more than misprision of treason."

Still I had no suspicion. I was thinking still, I suppose, of my lodgings here in Whitehall and of a few papers I had there.

"You must tell me," I said.

"Mr. Mallock," he said, "this paper I speak of was in cypher. It contained —"

"Lord!" I cried. "Cousin Tom! —"

Then I bit my lip; but it was too late.

"Yes," said the other, very gravely. "I can see that you remember. It was your cousin who brought them up from Hare Street. He found them all in a little hiding-hole: and conceived it to be his duty —"

"His duty!" I cried. "Good God! why —"

Then again I checked myself.

"Mr. Chiffinch," said I, "I remember the paper perfectly: at least I remember that I had it, though I have never read it or thought anything of it."

"It is in very easy cypher, sir," said he, with some severity.

"Well; it was too hard for me," I said.

"Then why did you not shew it to me?" he asked.

"Lord! man," I said, "I tell you it was gone clean from my memory. I got it from Rumbald a great while ago — a year or two at the least before the Plot. It was on my mind to send it to you; but I did not. I had no idea that it was of the least importance."

"A letter, in cypher, and from Rumbald! And you thought it of no importance — even though the names of my Lord Shaftesbury and half a dozen others are written in full!"

"I tell you I forgot it," I said sullenly, for I had not looked for suspicion from this man.

He still looked at me, as if searching my face: and I suppose that I presented the very picture of an unmasked villain; for the whole affair was so surprising and unexpected that I was completely taken aback.

"Well," he said, "if you had but shewn me that paper, we could have forestalled the whole affair."

"What was in it?" I asked, striving to control myself.

"You tell me you do not know?" he asked.

Then indeed I lost control of myself. I stood up.

"Mr. Chiffinch," I said, "I see that you do not believe a word that I say. It will be best if you take me straight to those who have authority to question me."

He did not move.

"You had best sit down again, Mr. Mallock. I do not say that I do not believe you. But I will allow that I do not know what to think. You are a very shrewd man, sir; and it truly is beyond my understanding that you should have forgotten so completely this most vital matter. I wish to be your friend; but I confess I do not understand. Oh! sit down, man!" he cried suddenly. "Do not playact with me. Just answer my questions."

I sat down again. I saw that he was sincere and that indeed he was puzzled; and my anger went.

"Well," I said, "I suppose it may be difficult. Let me tell you the whole affair."

So I told him. I related the whole of my adventure in the inn, and how I got the paper, and tried to read it, and could not: then, how I took it to Hare Street and put it where he had described: then how I very nearly had asked a Jesuit priest if he had any skill in cypher; and then how, once more, it had all slipped my mind, and that, a long time having elapsed, even when Rumbald became prominent again, even then I had not remembered it.

"That is absolutely the whole tale," I said; "and I know no more than the dead what it is all about. What is it all about, Mr. Chiffinch?"

He drew a breath and then expelled it again, and, at the same time stood up, withdrawing his eyes from my face. I think it was then for the first time that he put away his doubts; for I had got my wits back again and could talk reasonably.

"Well," he said, "we had best be off at once, and see what they say."

"Where to?" asked I.

"Why to His Majesty's lodgings," he said. "I fetched him out to tell him. Did you not see me?"

"His Majesty!" I cried.

"Why yes; I thought it best. Else it would have meant your arrest, Mr. Mallock."

*   *   *

I must confess that my uneasiness came back — (which had left me just now) — as I went with the page to the King's lodgings, more especially when I saw again how the guards fell in behind us and followed us every step of the way. It was very well to say that I "should have been arrested" if such and such a thing had not happened: the truth was, I was already under arrest, as I should soon have found if I had attempted to run away. It seemed to me somewhat portentous too that His Majesty was so ready to see us, instead of mocking at the whole tale at once.

Mr. Chiffinch said nothing to me as we went. I think he himself was fully convinced of my innocence — at least of any deliberate treachery — but not so convinced that others would be; and that he was considering how he should put my case. It was a sad humiliation for me — this trudging along like a schoolboy going to be whipped, with a couple of guards following to see that I did not evade it.

We went straight upstairs, through the antechamber, and to the door of the private closet. I heard voices talking there — one of which cried to come in as the page knocked. Then we entered.

I had thought to find His Majesty alone, or very nearly so; and I was astonished and disconcerted at the number of persons that were there. The King himself was seated beyond his great table, with the rest standing about him, five in number. On his right was Sir George Jeffreys in his rich suit, just as he had come from some entertainment, his handsome face flushed with wine, yet none the less full of wit and attention. The officer of the Green Cloth was on the other side — (it was this gentleman's business to deal with all cases, within his jurisdiction, that took their rise in Whitehall itself); and a couple of magistrates beside him, with neither of whom I had any acquaintance. An officer, whose face again was new to me — named Colonel Hoskyns — a truculent-looking fellow, in the dress of His Majesty's Lifeguards, stood very upright beside Sir George Jeffreys, with his hat in his hand. A sheaf of papers lay before the King on the table.

I was even more disconcerted to see how His Majesty looked. An hour or two ago he had been smiling and gracious: now he wore a very stern look on his face; he made no sign of recognition as I came in after Mr. Chiffinch, but, so soon as the door was shut, spoke immediately to the page.

"Well?" he said. "What have you got from him?"

Chiffinch advanced a step nearer, glancing at the faces that all looked on him.

"Sir," he said, "I am convinced there has been nothing more than an indiscretion —"

Then the King shewed how angry he was. He threw himself back in his chair.

"Bah!" he cried — "an indiscretion indeed! With his guilt staring him in the face!"

There was a murmur from the others: and Colonel Hoskyns gave me a look of very high disdain, as if I had been a toad or a serpent. For myself I said nothing: I remained with my eyes down. Once or twice before I had seen His Majesty in this very mood. For the most part he was the least suspicious man I had ever encountered; but once his suspicion was awake there was none harder to persuade. So he had been with His Grace of Monmouth on two or three occasions; so, it appeared, he was to be with me now.

"Sir," said Mr. Chiffinch again, "I have examined Mr. Mallock very closely: but I have told him very little. Will Your Majesty allow him to hear what the case is against him?"

The King, who was frowning and pursing his lips, raised his eyes; and immediately I dropped my own. He was in a black mood indeed, and all the blacker for his past kindness to me.

"Tell him, Hoskyns," he said; and then, before the Colonel could speak he addressed me directly.

"Mr. Mallock," he said sharply, "I will tell you plainly why I have you here, and why you are not in ward. You have been of service to me; I do not deny that. And I have never known you yet to betray your trust. Well, then, I do not wish to disgrace you publicly without allowing you an opportunity of speaking and clearing yourself if that is possible. I tell you frankly, I do not think you will. I see no loophole anywhere. But — well there it is. Tell him, Hoskyns."

I will not deny that I was terrified. This was so wholly unlike all I had ever known of His Majesty. What in the world could be the case against me? (For I now saw that Mr. Chiffinch had not told me the whole, but only a part of the charge.) I fixed my eyes upon Mr. Hoskyns for whom I had conceived, so soon as I had set eyes on him, an extreme repulsion.

He made a kind of apologetic cringing movement towards the papers. The King made no movement, but rested heavily in his chair, with his hat forward, his elbows on the arms of his chair and his fingers knit beneath his chin. The Colonel took the papers up, shuffled them for a minute, and then began. There was an extraordinary malice in his manner which I could not understand.

"The charge against the — the gentleman — whose name, I understand, is Roger Mallock, consists of two distinct points:

"The first is that he has received and concealed a paper, containing an account of a debate held between certain of His Majesty's enemies, five years ago, in November of sixteen hundred and seventy-nine, with the list of the persons present and the votes that they gave as regards compassing the King's death. The first point to which Mr. Mallock has to answer is, How he came to be in possession of this paper at all?"

I made a movement to speak, as his voice ceased; but the King held up his hand. Then, as if by an afterthought he dropped it again.

"Well; speak if you like — point by point. But I would recommend you to hear it all first."

"Sir," I said, "I have no reserves, and nothing to conceal. I will answer point by point if Your Majesty will give me leave."

He said nothing. I turned back to the other.

"Well, sir," I said, "I had that paper from one Rumbald, in a private parlour in the *Mitre inn*, without Aldgate. He gave it me with some others, and forgot to ask for it again."

No one moved a finger or a feature, except the Colonel, who glanced at me, and then down again.

"The second point is, Why Mr. Mallock did not hand over the paper to the proper authorities." Again he paused.

"It was in cypher," said I, "and I could not read it."

"Then why did you preserve it so carefully, sir?" asked the Colonel angrily, speaking direct to me for the first time.

"I preserved it because it might be of interest, seeing from whom I received it."

"You preserved it then, because it might be of interest; and you did not hand it over because it might not," sneered the Colonel.

"Come! come!" said the King sharply. "We must have a better answer than that, Mr. Mallock."

Then my heart blazed at the injustice.

"Sir," I said, "I am telling the naked truth. If I were a liar and a knave I could make up a very plausible tale, no doubt. But I am not. The naked truth is that I preserved the paper for what it might contain; and then —"

I paused then; for I saw plainly what a very poor defence I had.

"And then —" sneered the Colonel softly.

"If you must have the truth," I said, "I forgot all about it."

Well; it was as I thought. Sir George Jeffreys threw back his head and laughed aloud — (he was a man of extraordinary freedom with the King) — a great grin appeared on the Colonel's face; and His Majesty, as I saw in the shadow beneath his hat, smiled bitterly, showing his white teeth. Even the magistrates chuckled together.

"Ah, sir," said Jeffreys, "for a clever man that is truly a little dull. You might have done better than that."

Then desperation seized me; and I flung all prudence to the winds.

"I thought you wanted the truth," said I. "I will lie if you drive me much further. Go on, sir," I cried to Hoskyns. "Let us have the rest."

The King stared at me, and his face was terrible.

"A word more like that in my presence, sir —"

"Sir," I cried, "I mean no disrespect. But I am hard put to it —"

"You are indeed," said Jeffreys. "Go on, Colonel Hoskyns."

The Colonel sniffled through his nose, lifting his papers once more.

"The next main charge against Mr. Mallock is even more grave. It is to the effect that when His Majesty and His Royal Highness were together at Newmarket, Mr. Mallock, knowing that there was a plot against their lives — of which the Rye was the centre — despatched a messenger to His Majesty bidding him come immediately, by the road that leads past the Rye, instead of directing him by Royston."

At that monstrous charge my spirit almost went from me. That it should be this thing, above all others that should be brought against me! I glanced this way and that; and saw how even Chiffinch, who had fallen back a little as I advanced, was looking askance at me!

"That is perfectly true," I said. "What of it?"

"Mr. Mallock does not seem to perceive," snarled the Colonel, "that the fact itself is enough. It is true that no harm came of it; but Mr. Mallock will scarcely deny that an armed man stood by him, waiting for the coach."

"Armed with a cleaver," said I, "which he presently flung at my head."

"So Mr. Mallock says," observed the Colonel.

"You say I am a liar?" I cried.

The King struck suddenly upon the table.

"Silence, sir!" he said. "Mr. Chiffinch, you told me before that you had something to say. You had best say it now."

I fell back, for I saw that my bolt was shot. If Chiffinch could not save me, no man could. It was gone clean beyond mere misprision of treason now: I saw that plain enough.

Then Mr. Chiffinch began; and I am bound to say that he shewed himself a better pleader than myself. I thanked God, as he spoke, that I had treated him with patience just now in his lodgings.

First, he remarked that I had been in His Majesty's service now for near six years, and that in all that time I had proved myself loyal and faithful. Then he proceeded to deal with the charges.

First, he said that the very weakness of my excuse with regard to the paper was my strength. If I were indeed the villain that I seemed, why in God's name had I not destroyed the paper? I had had near five years to do it in! Was not that an additional sign that I had, as I said, merely forgotten it? (As be said this I marvelled that I had not thought of that answer myself.) It was true that the paper was of the highest importance, but, as my story stood, I had not known that. Should not my word then be taken, considering all the other services I had done to His Majesty?

With regard to the second point, first let them divest their minds of any prejudice caused by the first; for the first was not proved. Having done that, it was necessary to remember how carefully I had reported every movement of the King's enemies to himself — Mr. Chiffinch. It was true that there had been found other papers in the hiding-hole which he himself had not seen, but he had at least known the substance of them — except of course of the cypher of which he had already treated. With regard to the affair at the Rye it was necessary to remember that my policy throughout had been to report all that I had learned and to interpret it as directly contrary to the truth; and that this policy had proved successful. (I saw the Colonel give a very odd look as this was said; and I saw that Mr. Chiffinch had seen it too.) At the worst it had been an error of judgment on my part that I had recommended the road by the Rye; but it was an error that had had no bad consequences; and to have recommended it was only in accordance with all my policy of taking as true the precise opposite to all that the conspirators had told me. So far as my policy was sound, all that I knew was that the Rye road would be safe on that one day; of the Royston road I knew little or nothing. As regards the incident of the cleaver, I had spoken of that to him immediately I returned to town; and, surely, it was true that a single man with a cleaver could do very little damage to a galloping coach. In short, though the evidence might be interpreted as against me — (here he shot a look at the Colonel) — it might also be interpreted for me, and, that this was the fairer interpretation, he pleaded my record of other services done to the King.

When he ended, there was a dead silence; and I think I knew even at that moment that the worst at any rate had been averted. But I was not sure: and I waited.

*　　*　　*

Sir George Jeffreys was the first to move. He had remained motionless, smiling a little, while the page had been speaking, watching him as a man may watch an actor who pleases him. At the end, after a little pause, he jerked his head a little, as if to throw off the situation. I think he had had no malice to me, but had watched the whole affair as a kind of sport, which was what he did upon the Bench too. He made a movement as if to move away, but remembered where he was, and stood still.

The two magistrates began to move also; and one nodded at the other.

Colonel Hoskyns shook his head sharply, and began to speak.

"Sir-" he began in his harsh voice.

The King held up his hand; and all was dead still again.

It was strange to me to watch the King, or rather to shoot a glance at him now and again; for I saw presently, in spite of the shadow of his hat and his dusky face, that he was looking from one to the other of us, as if appraising what had been said. I heard a fellow cough somewhere, not in the chamber, and knew by that that it was the guards, most likely, who were waiting for the verdict. Truly, during those moments all my confidence left me again; for this was a mood of the King that I never understood and had never seen so clearly as I saw it now. It was a sort of heaviness of mind, I think, that fell on him sometimes and obscured his clear wit, for to my mind nothing could be more plain than Mr. Chiffinch's argument. Yet I depended now, not only for my liberty, but for my very life, on the King's judgment. As a Catholic and a member of the secret service I could look for no hope at all if I were sent for trial. I looked at Mr. Ramsden, the Officer of the Green Cloth; for I had scarcely noticed him before, so quiet was he. It was through his hands first, I supposed, that the case would pass. He was still motionless, looking down upon the table.

Then the King spoke, not moving at all.

"Go into the antechamber, Mr. Mallock," he said dully, "and wait there till you be sent for."

*   *   *

I suppose that that waiting was the hardest I have ever done. Again my suspense came down on me, and I had no idea as to which way the matter would go. I sat very still there, hearing again one of the men hemming without the door on the one side: and very low voices talking in the chamber I had come from.

Then all of a sudden the door opened sharply, and Mr. Chiffinch came through. He smiled and nodded, though a little doubtfully, as he came through; and my heart gave a great leap, for I knew that the worst would not happen to me.

He said nothing, but beckoned me to follow, and we went straight through to where the guards wailed.

"You can go," he said; "this gentleman is no longer under arrest."

Still, all the way as we went, he said nothing; neither did I. He said nothing at all till we were back again in his closet, and the door shut. Then he faced me, smiling.

"Well, Mr. Mallock," he said, "His Majesty has determined to do nothing. You may even keep your lodgings for the present; but you will be watched, I need not tell you, very closely indeed: and you must expect no more employment for a while."

"But —"

"Wait," said he. "That black mood is on His Majesty; and you are very fortunate indeed to have come out of it so well. It was a very clever little design —"

"Design!" cried I.

"Why, of course," he said. "Did you not see that? I should have thought anyone —"

"Design," I said again. "Of whom? And why?"

He smiled.

"You are a very innocent young gentleman," he said, "in spite of your dexterity. Of course it was a design; and it nearly deceived even me —"

"My Cousin Tom —" I began.

"Your Cousin Tom is an ass," he said, "a malicious one, no doubt; but a mere tool. I have no doubt he intended to injure you; but he could have done nothing if he had not met with the right man. I have no doubt that he came up with the papers, and gossiped in the coffee-houses till he met other of your enemies: and they have done the rest. But it was Colonel Hoskyns no doubt who manipulated the affair."

"Colonel Hoskyns!" I said. "Why, I have never set eyes on the man before."

"I daresay not," said the page, still smiling. "But I have had his name in my books for a great while."

"Who is he?" I cried. "And what reason had he —"

Mr. Chiffinch shook his head at me lamentably.

"Why he is one of the party," he said, "though I can get no evidence that would hang a cat. I have no doubt whatever that he has been in the whole Shaftesbury affair from the beginning, and knows that they made shipwreck principally upon yourself. It is sheer revenge now, no doubt; for they cannot hope to make any further attempts upon His Majesty."

"But he is in the Guards!" I said, all in amazement.

The page shrugged his shoulders.

"What would you have?" he said. "I can get no evidence, even to warn His Majesty, though I have told him what I think. And, to tell the truth, I believe His Majesty to be safe enough. But that does not hinder them from wishing to have their revenge. Mr. Mallock —"

"Yes," I said, still all bewildered.

"I wonder what he will attempt next," said Mr. Chiffinch.

CHAPTER V

The dreariness of the time that followed is beyond my power of description. I besought Mr. Chiffinch to let me go abroad again, but he forbade me very emphatically; and I owed so much to him that I could not find it in my heart to disobey. For so desperate was I, at the ruin of all my hopes, that the thought even came to me that I would go back and try to be a monk again; for how, thought I, can I keep my word even to Dolly herself? Every prospect I had was ruined; my coronet was gone like the dream which it had always been; I had failed lamentably and hopelessly; and it was through her father's treachery and malice that all had come about. This I felt in my heaviest moods; but Mr. Chiffinch would hear none of it. He said that it was but a question of time, and His Majesty would come round once more; that he would never be content until I was reinstated; that he had not for an instant lost heart. Besides, he said, I was of use in another way, and that was to make Hoskyns disclose himself. Hoskyns would never rest, he said, till he had made at least one more attempt upon me; and next time, he hoped, he would catch him at it, and get rid of the fellow once and for all.

Neither could I even go to Hare Street; for how could I live again even for an hour in the house of my Cousin who had betrayed me? I could not even tell Dolly all that had fallen; for I was as sure as of anything in the world that her father would tell her nothing, and I did not have the heart to disgrace him in her eyes. I but wrote to her that I was a little out of favour with His Majesty at present, though I kept my lodgings, and that I must not stir from Court till I had regained my position. Meanwhile I reserved what I had to say to my Cousin Tom, until I should meet with him alone. I had no doubt whatever that he had done what he had, thinking to get rid of me as his daughter's lover.

The time dragged then very heavily; for I did not care to go much into the society of others, and had nowhere else to go, since I must not leave Whitehall; for it soon became known that I was out of favour, though I do not suppose that the reason was ever named. I spent my days principally in my own lodgings, and did a good deal of private work for Mr. Chiffinch, which occupied me. I went to the play sometimes, taking my man James with me; and I rode out with him usually, down Chelsea way, or to the north, coming back for dinner or supper. I never went alone, by Mr. Chiffinch's urgent desire.

*   *   *

It was after Christmas that matters were brought to a head, and that the last great adventures of my life came about that closed all that I thought to be life at that time. Even now, so many years after, I can scarce bear to write them down, though, as I look back upon them now, there were at least two matters for which I should have thanked God even then. I thank Him now.

*   *   *

It was on the last Thursday but one, in January, to be precise, that I was coming back from a ride, having been down the river-bank past Chelsea, where I had seen, I remember, Winchester House — that great place with all its courts — and my Lord Bishop returning in his coach: I do not remember anything else that I saw, for I was very heavy indeed and more than ever determined that, if matters did not mend very soon, I would be off to France (where, six months later, I should be obliged to go in any case when my estates would come to me), if not to Rome. It was near five months now that I had lived in disgrace, His Majesty not speaking to me above three or four times all that while, and then only to avoid incivility.

I could not understand why it was that he behaved so to me. He must know by now, surely, that I had never been anything but faithful to him; and I strove to put away the thought that it was mere caprice, and that he often behaved so to others. But I am afraid that such was the case. There were plenty of folks at Court, or who had left it, who had once been in high favour and had ceased to be, through no fault of their own. Neither would I seek consolation from any other source. The Duke was civil to me whenever we met, and I suppose he knew that I was in trouble, but he never spoke of it. Indeed it was a sad change from the time when I had returned so joyfully, and found my new lodgings waiting for me.

*   *   *

As we came up through Westminster I was riding alone, for I had bidden my man James to go aside to a little shop that was almost on our route, behind the abbey, to buy me something that I needed — I think it was a pair of cuffs; but I am not sure. It was very near dark, and the lamps were not yet lighted.

As I came towards the gate of Whitehall, I was riding very

carelessly and heavily, paying little attention to anything, for I was thinking, as it happened, of Dolly, with an extraordinary misery in my heart, and of how I should ever tell her (unless matters mended soon) of what her father had done; and whether in some manner he would not yet contrive to separate us. My horse swerved a little, and I pulled him up, for there were a couple of fellows immediately crossing before me. I saw that they looked hard at me; but I noticed no more, for at that instant I heard a horse coming up behind me, and turned to see that it was James. He looked a little strange, thought I, but he said nothing: only he came up, right beside me, and so rode with me through the gate.

He said nothing then, nor did I; and it was not until I was dismounted and a fellow had run out to take the horses that he asked if he might speak with me.

"Why, certainly," said I; and we turned together into the Court.

"Sir," he said, so soon as we were out of earshot of the guard, "did you see those two fellows without the gate?" I said that I had.

"Sir," he said, "they were following you all the way from Chelsea. I saw them at Winchester House; and I have seen them before today, too."

"Eh?" said I, a little startled.

Then he told me he had seen them for the last fortnight, three or four times at least, and that he was sure they were after some mischief. Once before today too, as we were riding in Southwark, and he had delayed for a stone in his horse's foot, he had seen them run out from behind a wall, but that they had made off when they saw him coming.

Now I knew very well what he meant. London was very far from being a safe place in those days for a man that had enemies. There was scarcely a week passed but there was some outrage, in broad daylight too, in less populated parts, and in the various Fields, and after dark men were not very safe in the City itself.

A year ago I should have thought nothing of it; but I was down in the world now, I knew very well, and I had enemies who would stick at nothing. It was true that they had let me alone for a while — no doubt lest any suspicion should attach to them — but the winter was on us now, and the mornings and evenings were dark; and, too, a good deal of time had elapsed. I remembered what Mr. Chiffinch had said to me at the beginning of the trouble.

"You did very well to tell me," I said. "Would you know them again if you saw them?"

"I think so, sir," he said.

"Well," I said, "I have no doubt that they are after me. You will tell my other men, will you not?"

"I told them a week ago," he said.

I said no more to him then; but instead of going immediately to my lodgings, I went first to see Mr. Chiffinch, and found him just come in. I told him very briefly what James had told me; but made no comment. He whistled, and bade me sit down.

"They are after you then," he said. "I thought they would be."

"But who are they?" said I, a little peevishly.

"If I knew their names," said the page, "I could put my hands on them on some excuse or other. But I do not know. It is the dregs of the old country-party no doubt." "And what good do they think to get out of me?"

"Why, it is revenge no doubt," he said. "They know that you are down with the king and have not many friends; and they suspect that you are still in with the secret service, no doubt."

"They are after my life, then?" I asked.

"I should suppose so."

He considered a minute or two in silence. At last he spoke again.

"I will have a word with His Majesty. He is treating you shamefully, Mr. Mallock; and I will tell him so. And I will take other measures also."

I asked what those might be.

"I will have my men to look out closely when you go about. You had best not go alone at all. Within Whitehall you are safe enough; but I would not go out except with a couple of men, if I were you."

I told him I always took one, at least.

"Well; I would take two," he observed. "There was that murder last week, in Lincoln's Inn Fields — put down to the Mohocks. Well; it was a gentleman of my own who was killed, though that is not known; and it was no more Mohocks than it was you or I."

*   *   *

As we were still talking my man James came up to seek me, with a letter that he had found in my lodgings, waiting for me. I knew the hand well enough; and I suppose that I shewed it; for when I looked up from reading it, Mr. Chiffinch was looking at me with a quizzical face.

"That is good news, Mr. Mallock, is it not?"

I could not refrain from smiling; for indeed it was as if the sun had risen on my dreariness.

"It is very good news," I said. "It is from my cousin — the 'pretty cousin,' Mr. Chiffinch. She is come to town with her maid; and asks me to sup with her."

"Well; take your two men when you go to see her," said he, laughing a little. "They can entertain the maid, and you the mistress."

*   *   *

I cannot say how wonderfully the whole aspect of the world was changed to me, as I set out in a little hired coach I used sometimes, with my two men, half an hour later, for my old lodgings in Covent Garden where, she said, she had come that evening. It was a very short letter; but it was very sweet to me. She said only that she could wait no more; that she knew how ill things must be going with me, and that she must see with her own eyes that I was not dead altogether. I had striven in my letters to her to make as light as I could of my troubles; but I suppose that her woman's wit and her love had pierced my poor disguises. At least here she was.

*   *   *

She was standing, all ready to greet me, in that old parlour of mine where I had first met her six years ago; and she was more beautiful now, a thousand times, in my eyes, than even then. The candles were lighted all round the walls, and the curtains across the windows; and her maid was not there. She had already changed her riding dress, and was in her evening gown with her string of little pearls. As I close my eyes now I can see her still, as if she stood before me. Her lips were a little parted, and her flushed cheeks and her bright eyes made all the room heaven for me. I had not seen her for six months.

"Well, Cousin Roger," she said — no more.

*   *   *

Presently, even before supper came in, she had begun her questioning.

"Cousin Roger," she said — (we two were by the fire, she on a couch and I in a great chair) — "Cousin Roger, you have treated me shamefully. You have told me nothing, except that you were in trouble; and that I could have guessed for myself. I am come to town for three days — no more: my father for a long time forbade me even to do that. If he were not gone to Stortford for the horse-fair I should not be here now."

"He does not know you are come to town!" I cried.

She shook her head, like a child, and her eyes twinkled with merriment.

"He thinks I am still minding the sheep," she said. "But that is not the point. Cousin Roger, I care nothing whatever for His Majesty's affairs, nor for secret service, nor for anything else of that kind. But I care very much that you should be in trouble and not tell me what it is."

Now I had not had much time to think what I should say, if she questioned me, as I knew she would; for it would not be an easy thing to tell her that her father was at the root of my troubles and had behaved like a treacherous hound. Yet sooner or later she must be told, unless I lost heart altogether. I might soften it and soften it — pretend that her father owed a greater duty to the King than to me, and must have thought it right to do as he had done. But she would see through it all: that I knew very well.

"Dolly," said I, very slowly, "I have not told you yet, because there was nothing in the world that you could do to help me. I have waited, thinking that matters might come straight again; but they have not. I will tell you, then, before you go home again. I promise you that. And on my side I ask you not to question me this evening. Let us have this one evening without any troubles at all."

She looked at me very earnestly for a moment without speaking; and I could see that her lightness of manner had been but put on to disguise how anxious she was. It is wonderful how a woman — in spite of her foolishness at other times — can read the heart of a man. I had said very little to her in my letters; and yet I could see now how she had suffered all the while. I had thought myself to have been alone in my unhappiness; now I understood that never for an instant had I been so; and my whole heart rose up in a kind of exultation and longing. Then she swallowed down her anxiety.

"I take you at your word, Cousin Roger," she said lightly. "I will ask no question at all."

Then Anne and my man James came in with the supper.

*　　*　　*

I think there is not one moment of that evening in my old lodgings that I have forgotten. As now I look back upon it it seems to me to have that kind of brightness which a garden has when a storm is coming up very quickly, and the clouds are very black, and yet the shadow has not yet reached it. I remember how the curtains hung across the windows; they were my own old curtains of blue stuff, a little faded but still rich and good; how the fire glowed in the wide chimney; how Dolly looked across the table, in her blue sac, with lace, and her wide sleeves, and her little pearls. She had dressed up, all for me, as indeed I had for her, for I was in my maroon suit, with my silver-handled sword and my black periwig. Ah! and above all I remember the very look in her eyes as she suddenly clapped her hands together. (The servants were out of the room at that instant.)

"Cousin Roger!" she said, "I shall never keep my promise unless I am distracted. We will go to the play: you and I and Anne, all together: and your man James shall wait upon us with oranges."

Well; she had said it; and I laughed at her merriment: she was so like a child on her holiday, and a stolen holiday too. The ways of God are very strange — that so much should hang upon so little! It was upon that sudden thought of hers that the whole of my life turned; and hers too! As it was, I said nothing but that it should be as she wished; and that my coach should set us down there and come again when the play was over. So the threads are caught up in those great unseen shuttles that are guided by God's Hand, and the whole pattern changed, it would appear, by a moment's whim. And yet I cannot doubt — for if I did, my whole faith would be shattered — that even those whims are part of the Divine design, and that all is done according to His Holy Will.

The rest of supper was hastened, lest we should be late for the play; and then, when James came up to tell us that the coach was waiting — though it was scarcely a hundred yards to the King's Theatre — and Dolly was gone for her hood and cloak, I stood, with a glass of wine in my hand, on the hearth, looking down at the fire.

Now I cannot tell how it was; but I suppose that the shadow that I spoke of just now, began to touch that little garden of love in which I stood; for a kind of melancholy came on me again. While she had been with cue, it had all seemed gone; we had been as merry at supper as if nothing at all were the matter; but now, even while she was in the next chamber with her maid, I fell a-brooding once more. I thought — God knows why! — of the little parlour at Hare Street which I had not seen for so long, and of the fire that burned there, upon that hearth too — the hearth on which I had stood in my foolish patronizing pride when I had first asked her to be my wife and she had treated me as I deserved. I did not think then of how we had sat there together afterwards so often; and of the happiness I had had there, but only of that miserable Christmas night when I thought I had lost her. The mood came on me suddenly; and I was still brooding when she came in again, alone. She was in her hood, and her face looked out of it like a flower.

"Cousin Roger," she said, "I have never told you why I came up today."

"My dear; you did," I said. "It was your father who —"

"No; no; but this day in particular. Cousin Roger, the woman came again last night."

"The woman! What woman?" I asked.

"Why — the tall old woman — to my chamber, up the stairs. You remember? She came the night before you were sent for — why — six years ago."

I stared on her; and a kind of horror came on me.

"Ah! do not look like that," she said. "It is nothing." She smiled full at me, putting her hand on my arm.

"You saw her!" I said.

"No; no. I heard her only. It was just as it was before. But I came up to town to — to see if all were well with you. And it is: or will be. Kiss me, Roger, before we go."

CHAPTER VI

I cannot think without horror, even now, of that play we saw on that night in the King's Theatre. It was Mrs. Aphra Behn's tragedy, called *Abdelazar,* or *The Moor's Revenge*, and Mrs. Lee acted the principal part of Isabella, the Spanish Queen. We sat in a little box next the stage, which we had to ourselves; and in the box opposite was my Lord the Earl of Bath with a couple of his ladies. He was a pompous-looking fellow, and a hot Protestant, and he looked very disdainfully at the company. In the box over him was Mistress Gwyn herself, and the people cried at her good-humouredly when she came in, at which she bowed very merrily as if she were royal, this way and that, so that the whole play-house was full of laughter. It was turned very cold, with a frost, and before the play was half done the whole house was in a steam under the glass cupola. Folks were eating oranges everywhere in the higher seats, and throwing the peel down upon the heads of the people below. The stage was lighted, as always, with wax candles burning on cressets; and the orange girls were standing in the front row of the pit with their backs to the stage.

Dolly, who was a little quiet at first, got very merry and excited presently at all the good-humour, as well as at the actors. She had thrown her hood back, so that her head came out of it very sweet and pretty; and a spot of colour burned on each cheek. I saw her watching Mistress Nell once or twice with a look of amazement — for she knew who she was — for Nell, though she was not on the stage, bore herself as though she were, and never ceased for an instant, though full of merriment and good humour, to turn herself this way and that, and bow to her friends, some of whom relished it very little; and to applaud very heartily, and then, immediately to throw a great piece of orange peel at Mr. Harris, who played the King. She had her boy with her — whom His Majesty had made Duke of St. Albans — and two or three gentlemen whom I did not know.

Dolly whispered to me once, to know who the boy was.

"That is her boy," I said.

Dolly said nothing; but I understood the kind of terror that she had to see them both there, so outrageous and bold; but she presently turned back again to the stage to observe the play.

*   *   *

I said just now that the play which we saw has very dreadful memories for me; but I do not know that more than once or twice at the time I had any such feeling. There were some pretty passages in the play that distracted me altogether, and a song or two, of which I remember very well one sung by a *Nymph, and answered* by her swain with his shepherds, of which the refrain was:

> *The Sun is up and will not stay;*
> *And oh! how very short's a lover's day!*

For the rest there was a quantity of bloodshed and intrigue and false accusation, but I was surprised, considering the subject, how little was against Popery; but Mrs. Behn was content at the end of it to make the *Cardinal* beg pardon of King Philip.

For the most part then I attended to the action — (and to Dolly, of course, all the while). Yet certainly there were other moments for me, when the shadow came down again, and I saw the actors and the whole house as if in a kind of bloody mist, though I had at that time no reason for it at all, and do not think that I shewed any sign of it. Two or three times before, as I have related, there came on me a strange mood — once when I came up from Wapping, and once as I put out from Dover in the packet. But it was not that kind of mood this time. Then it was as if all the world of sense were but a very thin veil, and all that was happening a kind of dream, or play. Now it was as if the play had a shocking kind of reality, as if the audience and the actors were monstrous devils in hell; and the paint on Mrs. Lee's cheeks her true colour, and her gestures great symbols, and the noise of the people the roar of hell. This came and went once or twice; and at the time I thought it to be my own humour only; but now I know that it was something other than this. When I looked at Dolly it went again in an instant, and she and I seemed to me the heart of everything, and all else but our circumstances and for our pleasure.

Well; it ended at last, and there was a great deal of applauding, and Mrs. Lee came on to the stage again to bow and smile. It was then, for the third time, I think, that my horror fell on me. As I stared at her, all else seemed to turn dim and vanish. She was in her costume with the blood on her arm and breast, and her great billowy skirts about her, and her stage-jewels, and she was smiling; and I, as I looked at her, seemed to see the folly and the shame of her like fire; and yet that folly and shame had a power that nothing else had. Her smile seemed to me like the grin of a devil; and her colour to be daubs upon her bare cheek-bones, and she herself like some rotten thing with a semblance of life that was not life at all. I cannot put it into words at all: I know only that I ceased applauding, and stared on her as if I were bewitched.

Then I saw my dear love's fingers on my arm, and her face looking at me as if she were frightened.

"What is the matter, Cousin Roger?" she whispered; and then: "Come, Cousin Roger; it is late."

Then my mood passed, or I shook myself clear of it.

"Yes; yes," I said. "It is nothing. Come, my dear."

*　　*　　*

The little passage by which we went out was crammed full of folk, talking and whistling and laughing; some imitating the cries of the actors, some, both men and women, looking about them freely with bold eyes. I saw presently that Dolly did not like it, and that we should be a great while getting out that way; and then I saw a little door beside me that might very well lead out to the air. I pushed upon this, and saw another little passage.

"James," said I, for he was close behind me, "go out and bring the coach round to this side if there is a way out." (And then to Dolly.) "Come, sweetheart, we will find a way out here."

I pushed my way behind a fellow who was just in front, and got through the door, and Dolly and her maid followed me.

It was a little passage with doors on the right which I think led to the actors' rooms and the stage, for I heard talking and laughing behind; but I made nothing of that, and we went on. As we went past one of the doors it opened all of a sudden and Mrs. Lee herself came out, still in her dress and her jewels, and her face all a-daub with paint, and the blood on her arm and dress, and ran through another door further along, leaving behind her a great whiff of coarse perfume. It was but for an instant that we saw her; yet, even in that instant, a sort of horror came on me again as if she were something monstrous and ominous, though — poor woman! — I have never heard anything against her more than was said at that time against all women that were actresses — all, that is, except Mrs. Betterton. She appeared more dreadful even than in the play, or than when she had spoken those terrible words as she sat in her chair, all bloody, as she died — stabbed by the mock Friar:

—but 'tis too late —
And Life and Love must yield to Death and Fate.

I looked at Dolly; but she was laughing, though with a kind of terror in her eyes too at that sudden apparition.

"Oh, Roger!" she said, "and now she will go and wash it all off, will she not?"

"Yes, yes," I said. "She will wash it all off." And I looked at her, and made myself laugh too. She said nothing, but took my arm a little closer.

*　　*　　*

I was right about the passage, that it led out to the air, yet not into Little Russell Street, but to a little yard by which, I suppose, the players came to their rooms. The frost had fallen very sharp while we had been in the theatre; overhead the stars tingled as if they shook, beyond the chimneys, and there were little pools of ice between the stones.

I stayed an instant when we came down the three steps that led into the yard, to pull Dolly's hood more closely about her head, for it was bitter cold, and to gather up my own cloak, and, as I did this, I saw that three men had followed us out, and were coming down the steps behind us. There was no one else in the yard. There was one little oil-lamp burning near one of the two entrances to shew the players the way, I suppose.

Then, when I had arranged my cloak, I gave Dolly my arm once more, and, as I did so, heard Anne, who was behind us, suddenly give a great scream; and, at the sound, whisked about to see what was the matter.

There was a man coming at me from behind with a dagger, and the two other fellows were behind him.

*　　*　　*

Now I had not an instant in which to think what to do, though I knew well enough what they were and whom they were after. What I did, I did, I suppose, by a kind of instinct. I tore my arm free from Dolly's hand, pushing her behind me with my left hand, and at the same time dashed my cloak away as well as I could, to draw out my sword. The fellow was a little on my right when I was so turned about, but appeared a little confounded by my quickness, for he hesitated.

"Back to the wall, Dolly!" I shouted. "Back to the wall"; and, at the same time I began to back myself, with her still behind me, to the wall that was opposite to the steps we had just come down.

My cloak was sadly in my way; but, as I reached the wall, still going backwards, I had my sword out just in time to keep off, by a flourish of it, the fellow who had recovered himself, and was coming at me again.

So for a moment, we stood; and in that moment I heard Anne screaming somewhere for help.

*   *   *

Then I saw how the two other men, at a swift sign from their leader, spread out on this side and that, so as to come at me from three directions together; and, at that saw that I must delay no longer. Before, I think, they saw what I intended, I leapt forward at the fellow in front, and lunged with all my force; and though he threw up his arms, with the dagger in one of his bands, and tried to evade a parry all at once, he was too late; my point went clean through his throat, and he fell backwards with a dreadful cry. And, at the same moment his two companions ran in on me from either side.

Now I do not even now see what else I could have done. I felt sure that one of them would have me, for I could not properly deal with them both; but I turned and stabbed quickly, with a short arm, at the face of the one on my right, missing him altogether, and, at the same time strove to strike with my left elbow the face of the other.

But, ah! Dolly was too quick for me. She must have run forward on my left to keep the fellow off, for I heard a swift dreadful sound as I shortened my right arm to stab at the other again; and I felt something fall about my feet.

I turned like a madman, screaming aloud with anger, careless of all else, or of whether or no anyone ran at me again, for I knew, in part at least what had happened; and, at the same moment the yard seemed all alive with folks running and crying out. The door at the head of the steps was open, and three or four players ran out and down; while from Little Russell Street on the right, where the coaches were, a great number ran in.

But I cared nothing for that at that instant. I had flung away my sword on to the stones and was stooping to pick up my dear love who had saved my life. There was already a great puddle of blood, and I felt it run hot over my left hand that was about her — hot, for it flowed straight from her heart that had been stabbed through by the knife that was aimed at me.

*   *   *

When I looked up again, I saw, standing against the light in the door opposite, at the head of the steps, the woman that had played the Queen with that mock-blood still on her arm and breast.

CHAPTER VII

"Mr. Mallock," said the page, "the King is heartily sorry, and wishes to tell you so himself."

I said nothing.

Of all that happened, after Dolly's death in the theatre-yard, I think now as of a kind of dream, though it changed my whole life and has made me what I am. I have, too, scarcely the heart to write of it; and what I say of it now is gathered partly from what I can remember and partly from what other folks told me.

It must have been a terrible sight that they all saw as they ran in from the lane, my man James first among them all. There lay, bloodying all the ice about him, the fellow whom I had run through the throat, as dead as the rat he was, but still jerking blood from beneath his ear; and there in my arms, as I kneeled on the stones, lay Dolly, her head fallen back and out of her hood, as white as a lily, dead too in an instant, for she was stabbed through her heart, with her life-blood in a great smear down her side, and all over my hands and clothes.

My man James proved again as faithful a friend as he had always been to me; for the affair had been no fault of his: I had sent him for the coach, and he was bringing it up to the yard-entrance from the lane, as Anne had run out screaming. Then he had run in, and my other man with him, and the crowd after him, in time to see the two living assassins make off into the dark entrance on the other side. A number had run after them, but to no purpose, for we never heard of them again; and my Dolly's murderer, I suppose, is still breathing God's air, unless he has been hanged long ago for some other crime.

The next matter was to get us home again; for James has told me that I would allow no one to touch either her or me, until a physician came out of the crowd and told me the truth. Then I had gathered her up in my arms like a child without a word to any; and went out, the crowd falling back as I came, to where the coach waited in Little Russell Street. Still carrying her I went into the coach, and would allow no one else within; and so we drove back to Covent Garden.

When we came there a part of the crowd had already run on before and was waiting. When the coach drew up, I came out of the coach, with my dear love still in my arms, and went upstairs with her to her own chamber and laid her on her bed; and it was a great while before I would let the women come at her to wash her and make all sweet and clean again. I lay all that night in the outer parlour that had been my own so long ago, or, rather, I went up and down it till daybreak; and no one dared to speak to me or to move away the supper-things from the table where she and I had supped the night before.

The inquest was held that day, but nothing came of it. I related my story in the barest words, saying that I knew nothing of the three men, and leaving it to Mr. Chiffinch to whisper in the officer's ear to prevent him asking what he should not. Of the man I had killed nothing was ever made public, except that he was a tanner's man and lived in Wapping, and that his name was Belton.

On the Saturday we went down to Hare Street, all together, with the body of the little maid in a coach by itself. I rode my horse behind, but would speak never a word to my Cousin Tom who went in a coach, neither then nor at any other time; neither would I lie in Hare Street House, nor even enter it; but I lay in the house of a farmer at Hormead; and waited outside the house for the funeral to come out next day, after the Morning Prayer had been said in the church. She lies now in the churchyard of Hormead Parva, where we laid her on that windy Sunday, in the shadow of the little Saxon church. I rode straight away again with my men from the churchyard gate, and came to London very late that night. I went straight to my lodgings, and refused myself to everyone for three days, writing letters here and there, and giving orders as to the packing of all my effects. On the Thursday, a week after my Cousin Dolly had come to town, I went to Mr. Chiffinch to take my leave.

Now of those days I dare say no more than that; and even if I would I could add very little. My mind throughout was in a kind of dark tumult, until, after my three days of solitude, I had determined what to do. There were hours, I will not deny, in which my very faith in God Himself seemed wholly gone; in which it was merely incredible to me that if He were in Heaven such things could happen on earth. But sorrow of such a dreadful kind as this is, in truth, if we will but yield to it, a sort of initiation or revelation, rather than an obscurer of truth; and, by the time that my three days were over I thought I saw where my duty lay, and to what all those events tended. I had come from a monk's life that I might taste what the world was like; I had tasted and found it very bitter; there was not one affair — (for so it appeared to me then) — that had not failure written all over it. Very well then; I would go back to the monk's life once more if they would have me. On the third day, then, I had written to my Lord Abbot at St. Paul's-without-the-Walls, telling him that I was coming back again, and had thrown up my affairs here.

"You were right, my Lord," I wrote at the end of it, "and I was wrong. My Vocation seems very plain to me now; and I would to God that I had seen it sooner, or at the least been more humble to Your Lordship's opinion."

At first I had thought that I would take no leave of the King; and had told Mr. Chiffinch so, after I had announced to him what my intentions were, and announced them too in such a manner that he scarcely even attempted to dissuade me from them. But he had begged me to take my leave in proper form; no harm would be done by that; and then he had told me that His Majesty knew all that had passed and was very sorry for it.

I sat silent when he said that.

"Yes, Mr. Mallock," he said again, "and I mean not only for your own sorrow, but for his own treatment of you. It hath been a whim with him: he treats often so those whom he loves. His Majesty hath something of a woman in him, in that matter. His suspicions were real enough, at least for a time."

"I had done better if I had been one of his enemies, then," said I.

"It is of no use to be bitter, sir," said the page. "Men are what they are. We would all be otherwise, no doubt, if we could. See the King, Mr. Mallock, I beg of you: and appear once at least at Court, publicly. You should allow him at least to make amends."

I gave a great sigh.

"Well: it shall be so," I said. "But I must leave town on Tuesday."

*   *   *

It was with a very strange sense of detachment that I went about my affairs all Friday and Saturday; for I had still plenty to do, and was not to see His Majesty till the Saturday night after supper. The weather was turned soft again, and we had sunshine for an hour or two. On one day I watched His Majesty go to dinner, with his guards about him, and his gentlemen; but I did not see it with the pleasure I had once had in such brave sights. It was with me, during those days, as it had been with me for those two or three moments during the play, though in a gentler manner; for I thought more of the humanity beneath than of the show above; and a rotten humanity most of it seemed to me. These were but men like myself, and some pretty evil too. Those gentlemen that were with the King — there was scarcely one of them about whom I did not know something considerably to his discredit: there was my Lord Ailesbury in strict attendance on him; and Killigrew — he that had the theatre — and the less said of him the better: and there were three or four more like him; the Earl of Craven was there, colonel of the foot-guards; and Lord Keeper Guildford; and the Earl of Bath; and there, in the midst, the King himself, with his blue silk cloak over his shoulders, and his princely walk, going fast as he always did, and smiling-well, what of those thirteen known mistresses of his that he had had, as well as of those other — God knows how many! — poor maids, who must look upon him as their ruin? It was a brave sight enough, there in the sunshine — I will not deny that — with the sun on the jewels and the silks, and on the buff and steel of the guards, with that swift kingly figure going in the midst; and it was a brave noise that the music made as they went within the Banqueting-Hall; but how, thought I, does God see it all? And for what do such things count before His Holy Presence?

I had not rehearsed what I should say to His Majesty when I saw him; for indeed it was of no further moment to me what either I or he should say. I should be gone for ever in three days to the secret service of another King than him — to that secret service where men need not lie and cheat and spy and get their hearts broken after all and no gratitude for it; but to that service which is called *Opus Dei* in the choir, and is prayer and study and contemplation in the cloister and the cell. There I should sing, week by week:

"Oh! put not your trust in princes nor in any child of man: for there is no help in them."

In such a mood then — not wholly Christian, I will admit! — I came into the King's closet, to take my leave of him, on that Saturday night, the last day of January, in the year of Salvation sixteen hundred and eighty-five.

He was standing up when I entered his private closet, with a very serious look on his face; and, to my astonishment, took a step towards me, holding out both his hands. I will not deny that I was moved; but I had determined to be very stiff. So I saluted him in the proper manner, very carefully and punctually, kneeling to kiss his hand, and then standing upright again. A little spaniel barked at me all the time.

"There! there! Mr. Mallock," he said. "Sit you down! sit you down! There are some amends due to you."

I seated myself as he bade me; and he leaned towards me a little from his own chair, with one leg across the other. I saw that he limped a little as he went to his chair; and learned afterwards that he had a sore on his heel from walking in the Park.

"There are some amends due to you," he said again: "but first I wish to tell you how very truly I grieve at the sorrow that has come on you, and in my service too, as I understand."

(Ah! thought I: then Mr. Chiffinch has made that plain enough.) He spoke with the greatest feeling and gravity; but the next moment he near ruined it all.

"Ah! these ladies!" he said. "How they can torment a man's heart to be sure! How they can torture us and yet send us into a kind of ecstasy all at once! We hate them one day, and vow never to see them again, and yet when they die or leave us we would give the world to get them back again!"

For the moment I felt myself all stiff with anger at such a manner of speaking, and then once more a great pity came on me. What, after all, does this man, thought I, know of love as God meant it to be?

"Well, well!" he said. "It is of no use speaking. I know that well enough. And it was that very cousin, I hear, that was Maid to Her Majesty!"

"Yes, Sir," said I, very short.

I wondered if he would say next that that circumstance made it all the sadder; but he was not gross enough for that.

"Well," he said, "I will say no more on that point. I am only grieved that it should have come upon you in my service; and I wish to make amends. I already owed you a heavy debt, Mr. Mallock; and this has made it the heavier; and before saying any more I wish to tell you that I am heartily sorry for my suspicions of you. They were real enough, I am ashamed to say: I should have known better. But at least I have got rid of Hoskyns; and he hath gone to the devil altogether, I hear. He had a cunning way with him, you know, Mr. Mallock."

He spoke almost as if he pleaded; and I was amazed at his condescension. It is not the way of Kings to ask pardon very often.

"Well, Mr. Mallock," he said next; "and I hear that you wish to leave my service?"

"If Your Majesty pleases," said I.

"My Majesty doth not please at all; but he will submit, I suppose. Tell me, sir, why it is that you wish to leave."

"Sir," I said, "the reasons are pretty plain. I have displeased Your Majesty for the past half-year; and I cannot forget that, even though, Sir, you are graciously pleased to compliment me now. Then I have quarrelled with my Cousin Jermyn, so that I have not a kinsman left in England; and — and I have lost her whom I was to make my wife this year. Finally, if more reasons are wanting, I am weary of a world in which I have failed so greatly; and I must go back again to the cloister, if they will have me there."

All came with a rush when I began to speak, for His Majesty's presence had always an extraordinary effect upon me, as upon so many others. I had determined to say very little; yet here I had said it all, and I felt the blood in my face. He listened very patiently to me, with his head a little on one side, and his underlip thrust out, and his great melancholy eyes searching my face.

"Well! well! well," he said again, "if you must be a monk there is no more to be said. But what of your apostleship in the world?"

"Sir," I cried — for I knew what he meant — "my apostleship as you name it has been a greater disaster than all the rest: and God knows that is great enough."

He was silent a full half minute, I should think, still looking on me earnestly.

"Are you so sure of that?" said he.

My heart gave a leap; but he held up his hand before I could speak.

"Wait, sir," he said. "I will tell you this. You have said very little to me; but I vow to you that what you have said I have remembered. It is not argument that a man needs — at least after the first — but example. That you have given me."

Then I flushed up scarlet; for I was sure he was mocking me.

"Sir," I cried, "you might have spared —"

He lifted his eyes a little.

"I assure you, Mr. Mallock," he said, "that I mean what I say. You have been very faithful; you have ventured your life again and again for me; you have refused rewards, except the very smallest; you have lost even your sweetheart in my service; and now, when all is within your reach again, you fling it back at me. It is not very gracious; but it is very Christian, as I understand Christianity."

I said nothing. What was there to say? I seemed a very poor Christian to myself.

"Come! come, Mr. Mallock," pursued the King very gently and kindly. "Think of it once again. You shall have what you please — your Viscounty or anything else of that sort; and you shall keep your lodgings and remain here as my friend. What do you say to that?"

For a moment again I hesitated; for it is not to everyone that a King offers his friendship. If it had been that alone I think I might have yielded, for I knew that I loved this man in spite of all his wickedness and his treatment of me — for that, and for my "apostleship" as he called it, I might have stayed. But at the word *Viscounty* all turned to bitterness: I remembered my childish dreams and the sweetness of them, and the sweetness of my dear love who was to have shared them; and all turned to bitterness and vanity.

"No, Sir," said I — and I felt my lips tremble. "No, Sir. I will be ungracious and — and Christian to the end. I am resolved to go; and nothing in this world shall keep me from it."

The King stood up abruptly; and I rose with him. I did not know whether he were angry or not; and I did not greatly care. He stepped away from me, and began to walk up and down. One of his bitch-spaniels whined at him from her basket, lifting her great liquid eyes that were not unlike his own; and he stooped and caressed her for a moment. Then the clocks began to chime, one after the other, for it was eight o'clock, and I heard them at it, too, in the bed-chamber beyond. There would be thirty or forty of them, I daresay, in the two chambers. So for a minute or two he went up and down; and I have but to close my eyes now, to see him again. He was limping a little from the sore on his heel; but he carried himself very kingly, his swarthy face looking straight before him, and his lips pursed. I think that indeed he was a little angry, but that he was resolved not to shew it.

Suddenly he wheeled on me, and held out his hand.

"Well, Mr. Mallock; there is no more to be said; and I must honour you for it whatever else I do. I would that all my servants were as disinterested."

I knelt to kiss his hand. I think I could not have spoken at that moment. As I stood up, he spoke again.

"When do you leave town?" he said.

"On Tuesday, Sir."

"Well, come and see me again before you go. No, not in private: you need not fear for that. Come tomorrow night, to the *levée* after supper."

"I will do so, Sir," said I.

*   *   *

On the following night then, which was Sunday, I presented myself for the last time, I thought, to His Majesty.

I need not say that half a dozen times since I had left him, my resolution had faltered; though, it had never broken down. I heard mass in Weld Street; and there again I wondered whether I had decided rightly, and again as I burned all my papers after dinner — (for when a man begins afresh he had best make a clean sweep of the past). I went to take the air a little, before sunset, in St. James' Park, and from a good distance saw His Majesty going to feed the ducks, with a dozen spaniels, I daresay going after him, and a couple of gentlemen with him, but no guards at all. The King walked much more slowly that day than was his wont — I suppose because of the sore on his heel. But I did not go near enough for him to see me; for I would trouble him now no further than I need. All this time — or at least now and again — I wondered a little as to whether I was right to go. I will not deny that the prospect of remaining had a little allurement in it; but it was truly not more than a little; and as evening fell and my heart went inwards again, as hearts do when the curtains are drawn, I wondered that it had been any allurement at all: for my life lay buried in the churchyard of Hormead Parva, and I had best bury the rest of me in the place where at least I had a few friends left. After supper, about ten o'clock, I put on my cloak and went across to the Duchess of Portsmouth's lodgings, where the *levée* was held usually on such evenings. My man James went with me to light me there.

I do not think I have seen a more splendid sight, very often, than that great gallery, when I came into it that night, passing on my way through the closet where I had once talked with Her Grace. It was all alight from end to end with candles in cressets, and on the great round table at the further end where the company was playing basset, stood tall candlesticks amidst all the gold. I had not seen this great gallery before; and it was beyond everything, and far beyond Her Majesty's own great chamber. If I had thought the closet fine, this was a thousand times more. There were great French tapestries on the walls, and between them paintings that had been once Her Majesty's, and those not the worst of them. The quantity of silver in the room astonished me: there were whole tables of it, and braziers and sconces and cressets beyond reckoning; and there were at least five or six chiming clocks that the King had given to Her Grace; and tall Japanese presses and cabinets of lacquer which she loved especially.

There was a fire of Scotch coal burning on the hearth, as in His Majesty's own bedchamber; and on a great silver couch, beside this, covered with silk tapestry, sat the King, smiling to himself, with two or three dogs beside him, and Her Grace of Portsmouth on the same couch. The Duchesses of Cleveland and Mazarin were on chairs very near the couch.

There was a great clamour of voices from the basset-table as I came in and the King looked up; and, as I went across to pay my respects to His Majesty, he said something to the Duchess, very merrily. She too glanced up at me; and indeed she was a splendid sight in her silks and in the jewels she had had from him.

"Why; here is my friend!" said the King, as he put out his hand to me; and once more the dogs yapped at me from his side. He put his left hand out over their heads and pressed them down.

"You must not bark at my friend Mr. Mallock," he said. "He is off to be a holy monk."

For a moment I thought the King was making a mock of me; but it was not so. He was smiling at me very friendly.

*   *   *

He was in wonderful good humour that evening; and I heard more of his public talk than ever before; for he made me draw up a stool presently upon the hearth. Now and again a gentleman came across to be presented to him; and others came and looked in for a while and away again. There were constant comings and goings; and once, as a French boy was singing songs to a spinet, near the door, I saw the serious face of Mr. Evelyn, with two of his friends, look in upon the scene.

I cannot remember one quarter of all the things that were said. Now the King was silent, playing with the ears of his dogs and smiling to himself; now he would say little things that stuck in the memory, God knows why! For example, he said that he had eaten two goose's eggs for supper, which shewed what a strong stomach he had; and he described to us a very fierce duck that had snapped his hand that afternoon in the park. History is not made of these things; and yet sometimes I think that it should be; for those be the matters that interest little folk; and most of us are no more than that. I do not suppose that in all the world there is one person except myself who knows that His Sacred Majesty ate two goose's eggs to his supper on that Sunday night.

He spoke presently of his new palace at Winchester that he was a-building, and that was near finished.

"I shall be very happy this week," said he, "for my building will be all covered in with lead." (He said the same thing again, later, to my Lord Ailesbury, who remembered it when it was fulfilled, though in another manner than the King had meant.)

He talked too of "little Ken," as he named him (who had been made Bishop last week), and of the story that so many told — (for the King told his stories several times over when he was in a good humour) — and the way he told it tonight was this.

"Ah! that little Ken!" said he. "Little black Ken! He is the man to tell me my sins! Your Grace should hear him" — (added he) — "upon the Seventh Commandment! And such lessons drawn from Scripture too-from the Old Testament!"

He looked up sharply and merrily at Her Grace of Portsmouth as he said this.

"Well; when poor Nell and I went down to Winchester a good while ago," he went on, "what must little Ken do but refuse her a lodging! This is a man to be a Bishop, thought I. And so poor Nell had to sleep where she could."

Her Grace of Portsmouth looked very glum while this tale was told; for she hated Mrs. Nelly with all her heart. She flounced a little in her seat; and one of the dogs barked at her for it.

"First a monk and then a Duchess!" said the King. "Did you ever hear of the good man of Salisbury who put his hand into my carriage to greet me, and was bitten for his pains? 'God bless Your Majesty,' said he, 'and God damn Your Majesty's dogs!' — Eh, Fubbs?" — (for so he called the Duchess).

So he discoursed this evening, very freely indeed, and there was a number of men presently behind his couch, listening to what he said. A great deal of what he said cannot be set down here, for it was extraordinary indecent as well as profane. Yet there was a wonderful charm about his manner, and there is no denying it; and in this, I suppose, lay a great deal of the injury he did to innocent souls, for it all seemed nothing but merriment and good-humour. His quickness of conception, his pleasantness of wit, his variety of knowledge, his tales, his judgment of men — all these were beyond anything that I have ever met in any other man.

There was silence made every now and then for the French boy to sing another song; and this singing affected me very deeply, so long as I did not look at the lad; for he was a silly-looking creature all dressed up like a doll; but he sang wonderfully clear and sweet, and one of the King's chapel-gentlemen played for him. His songs were all in French, and the substance of some of them was scarcely decent; but I had not the pain of hearing any that I had heard in Hare Street. During the singing of the last of these songs, near midnight, again that mood fell on me that all was but a painted show on a stage, and that reality was somewhere else.

The great chamber was pretty hot by now, with the roaring fire and all the folks, and a kind of steam was in the air, as it had been in the theatre ten days ago; and the faces were some of them flushed and some of them pale with the heat. The Duchess of Cleveland was walking up and down before the fire, with her hands clasped as if she were restless; for she spoke scarce a word all the evening.

When the song was done the King clapped his hands to applaud and stood up; and all stood with him.

"Odd's fish!" said he, "that is a pretty boy and a pretty song." Then he gave a great yawn. "It is time to go to bed," said he.

As he said that the door from the outer gallery opened; and I saw my Lord Ailesbury there — a young man, very languid and handsome who was Gentleman of the Bed chamber this week, though his turn ended tomorrow; and behind him Sir Thomas Killigrew who was Groom — (these two slept in the King's bed-chamber all night) — and two or three pages, one of them of the Backstairs. My Lord Ailesbury carried a tall silver candlestick in his hand with the candle burning in it. He bowed to His Majesty.

"Did I not say so?" said the king.

He did not give his hand to anyone when he said good-night, but turned and bowed a little to the company about him on the hearth, and they back to him, the three duchesses curtseying very low. But to me he gave his hand to kiss.

"Good-night, Mr. Mallock," said he, in a loud voice; then, raising it —

"Mr. Mallock goes abroad tomorrow; or is it Tuesday?"

"It is Tuesday, Sir," said I.

"Then God go with you," he said very kindly.

I watched him go out to the door with his hat on, all the other gentlemen uncovered and bowing to him, and him nodding and smiling in very good humour, though still limping a little. And my heart seemed to go with him. At the door however he stopped; for a strange thing had happened. As my Lord Ailesbury had given the candle to the page who was to go before them, it had suddenly gone out, though there was no draught to blow it. The page looked very startled and afraid, and shook his head a little. Then one of the gentlemen sprang forward and took a candle from one of the cressets to light the other with. His Majesty stood smiling while this was done; but he said nothing. When it was lighted, he turned again, and waved his hand to the company. Then he went out after his gentlemen.

CHAPTER VIII

It was a little after eight o'clock next morning that I heard first of His Majesty's seizure.

I had drunk my morning and was on the point of going out with my man — indeed I was descending the stairs — when I heard steps run past in the gallery outside; and then another man also running. I came out as he went past and saw that he was one of Mr. Chiffinch's men, very disordered-looking and excited. I cried out to know what was the matter, but he shook his head and flapped his hand at me as if he could not stay, and immediately turned off from the gallery and ran out to the right in the direction of the King's lodgings.

I turned to my man James who was just behind me.

"Go and see what the matter is," I said; for after seeing the King so well and cheerful last night, I never thought of any ill-ness.

While he was gone, I waited just within my door, observing one of my engravings, with my hat on. It was a very bitter morning. In less than five minutes James was back again, very white and breathing fast.

"His Majesty is ill," said he. "Mr. Chiffinch —"

I heard no more, for I ran out past him at a great pace, and so to the King's lodgings.

*   *   *

When I came to the door of them, all was in confusion. There was but one guard here — (for the other was within with the Earl of Craven) — and a little crowd was pestering him with questions. I made no bones with him, but slipped in, and ran upstairs as fast as I could. There was no one in the first antechamber at all, and the door was open into the private closet beyond. It was contrary to all etiquette to enter this unbidden, but I cared nothing for that, and ran through; and this again was empty; so I passed out at the further door and found myself at the head of a little stair leading down into a wide lobby, from which opened out two or three chambers, with the King's bedchamber at the further end. And here, in the lobby, I ran into the company.

There was above a dozen persons there, at least, all talking together in low voices; but I saw no one I cared to speak with, since I had no business in the place at all. But no one paid any attention to me. It was yet pretty dark here, for there were no candles; so I waited, leaning against the wall at the head of the stairs.

Then the voices grew louder; and the crowd opened out a little to let someone through; and there came, walking very quickly, and talking together, my Lord Craven leaning on the arm of my Lord Ailesbury. My Lord Craven — near ninety years old at this time — was in his full-dress as colonel of the foot-guards, for he had attended a few minutes before to receive from His Majesty the pass-word of the day: and my Lord Ailesbury was but half dressed with his points hanging loose; for he had been all undressed just now, when the King had been taken ill.

After they had passed by me I stood again to wait; but, almost immediately, across the further end of the lobby I saw Mr. Chiffinch pass swiftly from a door on the left to a door on the right. At that sight I determined to wait no longer: for there was but one thought in my mind, all this while.

I said nothing, but I came down the stairs and laid my hand on the shoulder of a physician (I think he was), who stood in front of me, and pushed him aside, as if I had a right to be there; and so I went through them very quickly, and into the room where I had seen Mr. Chiffinch go. The door was ajar: I pushed it open and went in.

It was a pretty small room, and there were no beds in it; it had presses round the walls: a coal fire burned in the hearth in a brazier, and a round table was in the midst, lit by a single candle, and near the candle stood a heap of surgical instruments and a roll of bandages. (This was the room, I learned later, next to the Royal Bedchamber, where the surgeons had attended half an hour ago to dress the King's heel.) There were three persons in the room beyond the table, talking very earnestly together. Two of them I did not know; but the third was Mr. Chiffinch. They all three turned when I came in, and stared at me.

"Why —" began the page — "Mr. Mallock, what do you —"

He came towards me with an air of impatience.

"Mr. Chiffinch," said I, in a low voice — "how is His Majesty. I —"

The further door which stood at the head of three or four steps leading up to it opened sharply, and the page whisked round to see what it was. A face looked out, very peaked-looking and white, and nodded briskly at the bandages and the instruments; the two other men darted at those, seized them, ran up the stairs and vanished, leaving the door but a crack open behind them.

Then Mr. Chiffinch turned and stared at me again. He appeared very pale and agitated.

"Mr. Chiffinch," said I, "I will take no refusal at all. How is His Majesty?"

His lips worked a little, and I could see that he was thinking more of what was passing in the chamber beyond than of my presence here.

"They are blooding him again," he said; and then — "What are you doing here?"

I took him by the lapel of his coat to make him attend to me; for his eyes were wandering back like a mule's, at every sound behind.

"See here," said I. "If His Majesty is ill, it is time to send for a priest. I tell you —"

"Priest!" snapped the page in a whisper. "What the devil —"

I shook him gently by his coat.

"Mr. Chiffinch; I will have the truth. Is the King dying?"

"No, he is not then!" he whispered angrily. "Hark —"

He tore himself free, darted back to the further door, and stood there, at the foot of the stairs, with his head lowered, listening. Even from where I was I could hear a gentle sort of sound as of moaning or very heavy breathing, and then a sharp whisper or two; and then the noise of something trickling into a basin. Presently all was quiet again; and the page lifted his head. I stood where I was; for I know how it is with men in a sudden anxiety: they will snap and snarl, and then all at once turn confidential. I was not disappointed.

After he had waited a moment or two he came towards me once more.

"Mr. Mallock," he whispered, "the King needs no priest. He is not so ill as that; and he is unconscious too at present."

"Tell me," I said.

Again he glanced behind him; but there was no further sound. He came a little nearer.

"His Majesty was taken with a fit soon after he awakened. Mr. King was here, by good fortune, and blooded him at once. Now they are blooding him again. Her Majesty hath been sent for."

"He is not dying? You will swear that to me?"

He nodded: and again he appeared to listen. I took him by his button again.

"Mr. Chiffinch," said I, "you must attend to me. This is the very thing I have waited for. If there is any imminent danger you must send for a priest. You promise me that?"

He shook his head violently: so I tried another attack.

"Well," I said, "then you will allow me to remain here? Is the

Duke come?"

"Not yet," said he. "Ailesbury is gone for him."

"Well — I may remain then?"

There came a knock on the inner side of the further door; and he tore himself free again. But I was after him, and seized him once more.

"I may remain?"

"Yes, yes," he snapped, "as you will! Let me go, sir." He whisked himself out of my hold, and went swiftly up the stairs and through the door, shutting it behind him, giving me but the smallest glimpse of a vast candle-lit room and men's heads all together and the curtains of a great bed near the door. But I was content: I had got my way.

*   *   *

As I walked up and down the antechamber, very softly, on tip-toe, it appeared to me that I was, as it were, two persons in one. On the one side there was the conviction and the determination that, come what would, I must get a priest to the King if he took a turn at all for the worse — since, for the present, I believed Mr. Chiffinch's word that His Majesty was not actually dying. (This was not at all what the physicians thought at that time; but I did not know that.) This conviction, I suppose, had always been with me that it was for this that in God's Providence I had been sent to England; at least, seven in the moment that I had left my house and run down the gallery, there it was, all full-formed and mature. As to how it was to be done I had no idea at all; yet that it would be done I had no doubt. On the other side, however, every faculty of observation that I had, was alert and tight-stretched. I remember the very pattern of the carpet I walked on; the pictures on the walls; and the carving on the presses. Above all I remember the little door in the corner of the chamber — the third; and how I opened it, and peeped down the winding staircase that led from it. (I did not know then what part that little door and winding staircase was to play in my great design!) Now and again I looked out of the single window at the river beneath in the early morning sunshine; now I paced the floor again. It seemed to me that I had found a very pretty post of observation, as this appeared a very private little room, and that I should not be troubled here. The great anterooms, I knew, where the company would be, must lie on the further side of the bedchamber.

I suppose it would be about five minutes after Mr. Chiffinch had left me that Her Majesty came. The first I knew of it was a great murmur of voices and footsteps without the door. I went to the door and pulled it a little open so that I could see without being seen, and looked up the lobby beyond the King's chamber; for in that direction, I knew, lay Her Majesty's apartments. A couple of pages came first, very hastily, with rods; and then immediately after them Her Majesty herself, hurrying as fast as she could, scarce decently dressed, with a cloak flung over all, with a hood. Behind her came two or three of her ladies. I saw the poor woman's face very plain for a moment, since there was no one between me and her; and even at that distance I could see her miserable agitation; her brown face was all sallow and her mouth hung open. Then she whisked after the pages through the door into the great antechamber that lay beyond the bedroom. I went back again, to shut the door and listen at the other; for I knew that the King's bed was close to it (though he was not in it at this time, but still in the barber's chair where he had been blooded); and presently I heard the poor soul begin to wail aloud. I heard voices too, as if soothing her, for all the physicians were there, and half a dozen others; but the wailing grew, as she saw, I suppose, in what condition His Majesty was — (for he still seemed all unconscious) — till she began to shriek. That was a terrible sound, for she laughed and sobbed too, all at once, in a kind of fit. I could hear the tone very plain through the door, though I could not hear what she said; and the voices of Mr. King and others who endeavoured to quiet her. Gradually the wailing and shrieking grew less as they forced her away and out again; till I heard it, as she went back again to her own apartments, die away in spasms. Poor soul indeed! she was nothing accounted of in that Court, yet she loved the King very dearly in spite of his neglect towards her. She could not even speak to him (I heard afterwards), though he had spoken her name and asked for her, after his first blooding.

*   *   *

Half an hour later — (in the meantime no one had come in to me, and I could only walk up and down and listen as well as I could) — I heard again the murmur of voices in the lobby, and steps coming swiftly down from the private closet. Again I was in time at the door to see who it was that went by; and it was the Duke of York, with my Lord Ailesbury who had gone to fetch him from St. James'. He went by me so near that I could hear his quick breathing from his run upstairs; and he had come in such a hurry that he had only one shoe on, and on the other foot a slipper. He went very near at a run up the lobby, and up a step or two, and into the great antechamber and so round to the Bedchamber; and I presently heard him enter it. Indeed I was very favourably placed for observing all that went on.

*   *   *

It was about eleven o'clock, as I suppose, when I first heard His Majesty's voice; and the relief of it to me was extraordinary.

I had ventured up the stair or two that led from this room into the Bedchamber, and had, very delicately, opened the door a crack so as to hear more plainly; but I dared not look through for fear that I should be seen.

For a long while I had heard nothing but whispers; and once the yapping of a little dog, very sharp and startling, but the noise was stifled almost immediately, and the dog, I suppose, taken out at the other door. Once or twice too had come the sudden chiming of all the clocks that were in the Bedchamber.

I heard first a great groan from the bed, to which by now they had moved him from the chair, and then Ailesbury's name spoken in a very broken voice. (My own heart beat so loud when I heard that, that I could scarce listen to what followed.)

"Yes, Sir," came Ailesbury's voice; and then a broken murmur again. (He was thanking him, I heard afterwards from Mr. Chiffinch, for his affection to him, and for having caused him to be bled so promptly by Mr. King, and for having sent Chiffinch to him to bring him back from his private closet.)

Presently he grew stronger; and I could hear what he said.

"I went there," he said, "for the King's Drops.... I felt very ailing when I rose.... I walked about there; but felt no better. I nearly fell from giddiness as I came down again."

He spoke very slowly, but strongly enough; and he gave a great sigh at the end.

Presently he spoke again.

"Why, brother," he said. "So there you are."

I heard the Duke's voice answer him, but so brokenly and confusedly that I could hear no words.

"No, no," said His Majesty, "I do very well now."

*   *   *

I came down the stairs again, shaking all over. I cannot say how affected I was to hear his voice again; and I think there could scarce be a man in the place any less affected. He was a man who compelled love in an extraordinary fashion. I felt that if he died I could bear no more at all.

I was walking up and down again very softly, when the door into the Bedchamber was noiselessly pulled open, and Mr. Chiffinch came down the stairs. That dreadful look of tightness and pain was gone from his face: he was almost smiling. He nodded at me, very cheerful.

"He is better. The King's Majesty is much better," he whispered. Then his face twitched with emotion; and I saw that he was very near crying. I was not far from it myself.

CHAPTER IX

How the hours of that day went by I scarcely know at all. I went back to dine in my lodgings, and to counter-order all preparations for my going on the morrow, so soon as I knew that His Majesty was out of any immediate danger; for I could not find it in my heart to leave town until he was altogether recovered. In the afternoon, before going back to inquire how he was, I walked a good while in the court and the Privy Garden, though the day was very raw and cold.

Whitehall had been put as in a state of siege from the first moment that the King's illness was known. The gates were closed to all but those who had lodgings in the Palace, and those who were allowed special entry by His Royal Highness. The sentries everywhere were greatly augmented; both horse and foot were placed at every entrance; and the greatest strictness was observed that no letter should pass out either to His Grace of Monmouth or to the Prince of Orange: even M. Barillon had but permission to send one letter to the French King as to His Majesty's state. All this was to hinder any rising or invasion that might be made either within or without the kingdom. I was in the court when the couriers rode out with despatches to the Lords Lieutenant of the Counties with advices as to what to do should His Majesty die; and I was there too when the deputies came from the Lord Mayor and Aldermen and Lieutenants of the City to inquire for the King and to assure His Royal Highness of their loyalty and support. This was of the greatest satisfaction to the Duke; for I suppose that he did not feel very secure.

A little before supper I went round to Mr. Chiffinch's; and, by the greatest good fortune found him on the point of returning to His Majesty's lodgings. He gave me an excellent account as we went together.

"The physicians declare," said he, "that His Majesty is out of danger: and bath permitted the Duke to tell the foreign ministers so. They have had another consultation on him; and have prescribed God knows what! Cowslip and Sal of Ammoniac, sneezing mixtures, plasters for his feet; and he is to have broth and ale to his supper. They are determined to catch hold of his disorder somehow, if not by one thing then by another. To tell the truth I think they know not at all what is the matter with him. They have taken near thirty ounces of blood from him too, today. If the King were not a giant for health he would have died of his remedies, I think!"

He talked so; but he was in very cheerful spirits; and before he left me at the door of the lodgings I had got an order from him to admit me everywhere within reason. It was something of a surprise to me to see how dearly this man — whose name was so evil spoken of, and, I fear with good cause enough — yet loved his master.

*　　*　　*

On Tuesday morning I was up again very early, and round at His Majesty's lodgings. I went up by the other way and into the great antechamber; and there I met with one of the physicians who was just come from the consultation that twelve of them had held together. He was a very communicative fellow and told me that six of them had been with His Majesty all night, and that His Majesty had slept pretty well; and that — to encourage him, I suppose! — ten more ounces of blood had been taken from his neck. He was proceeding to speak of some new remedies — and mentioned an anti-spasmodic julep of Black Cherry Water that had been prescribed, when another put out his head and called to him from the Bedchamber; and he went away back into it with an important air.

All that day too I never left Whitehall. There were great crowds in all the streets and outside the gates, I heard, but their demeanour was very quiet and sorrowful; and prayers were said all day long in the churches. When I went back to the antechamber in the evening I saw my Lord Bishop of Ely there, and heard from one of the pages that he was to spend that night in His Majesty's room. So I gathered from that that the physicians were not very confident even yet, though couriers had been sent out again today to bear the news of the King's happy recovery; and I was, besides, in two minds, when I saw the Bishop there, as to what I should do about a Catholic priest. If I had seen His Royal Highness then, I think I should have said something to him upon it; but the Duke was in the Bedchamber; and there I dared not yet penetrate.

*　　*　　*

On the Wednesday morning, when I went early to inquire, I heard that again His Majesty had slept well, and that the physicians were well satisfied; I saw no one but a man of Mr. Chiffinch's, who told me that; and that Dr. Ken, my Lord Bishop of Bath and Wells, was with the King; and I went away content:

but when I went back again, for the third time that day, just before supper-time, I saw from the faces in the antechamber that all was not so well. Yet I could get nothing out of anyone, and did not wish to press too hard lest I should be turned out altogether. I saw my friend of yesterday, whose name I have never yet learned, hurrying across the end of the chamber into another little room where the physicians had their consultations — (it was, I think, my Lord Ailesbury's dressing-room) — but I was not in time to catch him; so I went away again in some little dismay, yet not greatly alarmed even now. The Bishop, I thought, could at least do him no great harm.

On the Thursday morning, before I was dressed, my man brought me the *London Gazette* that had been printed about six o'clock the evening before. The announcement as to the King's health ran as follows. (I cut out the passage then and there and put it in my diary.)

> "At the Council Chamber, Whitehall, the 4th of February, 1684 [1685 N. S.], at five in the afternoon.
> "The Lords of His Majesty's most Honourable Privy Council have thought fit, for preventing false reports, I make known that His Majesty, upon Monday morning last, was seized with a violent fit that gave great cause to fear the issue of it; but after some hours an amendment appeared, which with the blessing of God being improved by the application of proper and seasonable remedies, is now so advanced, that the physicians have this day as well as yesterday given this account to the Council, viz. — That they conceive His Majesty to be in a condition of safety, and that he will in a few days be freed from his distemper.
> "JOHN NICHOLAS."

Yes, thought I, that is all very well; but what of yesterday after five o'clock, and what of this morning?

*　　*　　*

As I went to His Majesty's lodgings an hour afterwards I heard the bells from the churches beginning to peal, to call the folks to give thanks; yet the faces within the Palace were very different. When I went up into the great antechamber, the physicians were just dispersing; and, by good fortune I was at hand when my Lord Keeper North questioned Sir Charles Scarburgh as he went back to His Majesty's chamber.

"Well?" said he, very short. "What do you say today?"

"My Lord!" said Sir Charles, "we conclude that His Majesty hath an intermittent fever."

"And what the devil of that?" asked my Lord. "Could anything be worse?"

(There was a little group round them by now; and I could see one of the Bishops listening a little way off.)

"My Lord," said the other, "at least we know now what to do."

"And what is that?" snapped my Lord who seemed in a very ill humour.

"To give the Cortex, my Lord," said Sir Charles with great dignity; for indeed the manner of my Lord was most insolent.

My Lord grunted at that.

"Peruvian Bark, my Lord," said the physician, as if speaking to a child.

Well; there was no more to be got that morning. I was in and out for a little, again in two minds as to what to do. His Royal Highness went through the antechamber at one time (to meet M. Barillon, as I saw presently, and conduct him to the King's chamber), a little before dinner, but at such a quickness, and with such sorrow in his face that I dared not speak to him. I went back to dinner; and fell asleep afterwards in my chair, so greatly was I wearied out with anxiety; and did not wake till near four o'clock. Then, thank God! I did awake; and, with all speed went again to His Majesty's lodgings; and this time, guided, I suppose, by Divine Providence, for I had no clear intention in what I did, I went up the private way, through the King's closet where I found no one, down the steps, and so into the little chamber where I had talked with Mr. Chiffinch on the first morning of His Majesty's distemper.

The chamber was empty; but immediately after I had entered — first knocking, and getting no answer — who should come through, his face all distorted with sorrow, but Mr. Chiffinch himself! There was but one candle on the table, but by its light, I saw how it was with him.

I went up immediately, and took him by the arms; he stared at me like a terrified child.

"My friend," said I, "I must have no further delay. You must take me to His Majesty."

He shook his head violently; but he could not speak. As for me, all my resolution rose up as never before.

I gripped him tighter.

"I ask but five minutes," I said. "But that I must have!"

"I — I cannot," said he, very low.

I let go of him, and went straight towards the steps that led up into His Majesty's room. As I reached the foot of them, he had seized my arm from behind.

"Where are you going?" he whispered sharply. "That is the way to the King's room."

I turned and looked at him.

"Yes," I said very slowly, "I know that."

"Well — well, you cannot," he stammered.

"Then you must take me," I said.

He still stared at me as if either he or I were mad. Then, of a sudden his face changed; and he nodded. I could see how distraught he was, and unsettled.

"I will take you," he whispered, "I will take you, Mr. Mallock. For God's sake, Mr. Mallock —"

He went up the steps before me, in his soft shoes; and I went after, as quietly as I could. As he put his hand on the handle he turned again.

"For Christ's sake!" he whispered in a terrible soft voice. "For Christ's sake! It must be but five minutes. I am sent to fetch the Bishops, Mr. Mallock."

He opened the door a little, and peered in. I could see nothing, so dark was the chamber within — but the candles at the further end and a few faces far away. A great curtain, as a wall, shut off all view to my left.

"Quick, Mr. Mallock," he whispered, turning back to me. "This side of the bed is clear. Go in quick; he is turned on this side. I will fetch you out this way again."

He was his own man again, swift and prompt and steady. As for me, the beating of my heart made me near sick. Then I felt myself pushed within the chamber; and heard the door close softly behind me.

*   *   *

At first I could see nothing on this side, as I had been staring over the candle just now, except a group of persons at the further end of the great room, and among them the white of a Bishop's rochet; and the candlelight and firelight on the roof. The clocks were all chiming four as I came in, and drowned, I suppose, the sounds of my coming.

Then, almost immediately I saw that the curtains were drawn back on this side of the great bed that stood in this end of the room, and that they were partly drawn forward on the other side, so as to shroud from the candlelight him who lay within them, and beneath the Royal Arms of England emblazoned on the state.

And then I saw him.

He was lying over on this side of the bed, propped on high pillows, but leaning all over, and breathing loudly. His left, arm was flung over the coverlet; and his fingers contracted and opened and contracted again. I went forward swiftly and noiselessly, threw myself on my knees, laid my hand softly beneath his, and kissed it.

"Eh? eh?" murmured the heavy voice. "Who is it?"

I saw the curtain on the other side pulled a little, and the face of Sir Charles Scarburgh all in shadow peer in: it looked very lean and sharp and high-browed. The King flapped his hand in a gesture of dismissal, and the face vanished again.

"Sir," whispered I, very earnestly, yet so low that I think none but he could have heard me. "Sir: it is Roger Mallock —"

"Mallock," repeated the voice; yet so low that it could not have been understood by any but me. His face was very near to me; and it was shockingly lined and patched, and the eyes terribly hollow and languid: but there was intelligence in them.

"Sir," said I, "you spoke to me once of an apostleship."

"So I did," murmured the voice. "So I —"

"Sir: I am come to fulfill it. It is not too late. Sir; the Bishops are sent for. Have nothing to say to them! Sir, let me get you a true priest — For Christ's sake!"

The cold fingers that I yet held, twitched and pressed on mine. I was sure that he understood.

He drew a long breath.

"And what of poor little Ken?" he murmured. "Poor little Ken: he will break his heart — if he may not say his prayers."

"Let him say what he will, Sir. But no sacrament! Let me send for a priest!"

There was a long silence. He sighed once or twice. His fingers all the while twitched in mine, pressing on them, and opening again. Ah! how I prayed in my heart; to Mary conceived without sin to pray for this poor soul that had such a load on him. The minutes were passing. I thought, maybe, he was unconscious again. And the Bishops, if they were in the Palace, might be here at any instant, and all undone. I am not ashamed to say that I entreated even my own dear love to pray for us. She had laid down her life in his service and mine. Might it not be, thought I, even in this agony, that by God's permission, she were near to help me?

He stirred again at last.

"Going to be a monk," said he, "going to be a monk, Roger Mallock. Pray for me, Roger Mallock, when you be a monk."

"Sir —"

He went on as if he had not heard me.

"Yes," murmured he. "A very good idea. But you will never do it. Go to Fubbs, Roger Mallock. Fubbs will do it."

"For a priest, Sir?" whispered I, scarcely able to believe that he meant it.

"Yes," he murmured again, "for a priest. Yes: for God's sake. Fubbs will do it. Fubbs is always —"

His voice trailed off into silence once more; and his fingers relaxed. At the same instant I heard the door open softly behind, and, turning, I saw the page's face again, lean and anxious, peering in at me. Then his finger appeared in the line of light, beckoning.

I kissed the loose cold fingers once again; rose up and went out on tip-toe.

CHAPTER X

Then began for me the most amazing adventure of all. My adventures had indeed been very surprising — some of them; and my last I had thought to be the greatest of all, and the most heart-breaking, in the yard of the Theatre Royal. I had thought that that had drained the last energy from me and that I had no desires left except of the peace of the cloister and death itself. Yet after my words with the King and his to me, there awakened that in me which I had thought already dead — a fierce overmastering ambition to accomplish one more task that was the greatest of them all and to get salvation to the man who had again and again flouted and neglected me, whom yet I loved as I had never yet loved any man. As I went to and fro, as I shall now relate, until I saw him again, there went with me the vision of him and of his fallen death-stricken face there in the shadow of the great bed; and there went with me too, I think, the eager presence of my own love, near as warm as in life.

"What shall we do next? What shall we do next, Dolly?" I caught myself murmuring more than once as I ran here and there; and I had almost sworn that she whispered back to me, and that her breath was in my hair.

*   *   *

Within five minutes of my having left the King's bedchamber, I was running up the stairs to Her Grace of Portsmouth's lodgings. I had said scarce a word to Mr. Chiffinch when I came out into the little anteroom, except that I was sent on a message by His Majesty; and he stared on me as if I were mad. Then I was out again by the private way, through the closet and the rooms beyond, and down the staircase.

At the door of Her Grace's lodgings there stood a sentry who lowered his pike as I came up, to bar my way.

"Out of the way, man!" I cried at him. "I am on His Majesty's business."

He too stared on me, and faltered, lifting his pike a little. All were distraught by the news that was run like fire about the place that the King was dying, or he would never have let me through. But I was past him before he could change his mind again, and through a compile of antechambers in one of which a page started up to know my business, but I was past him as if he were no more than a shadow.

Then I was in the great gallery, where I had sat with the King and his company but four days ago.

*   *   *

It presented a very different appearance now. Then it had been all ablaze with lights and merry with laughter and music. Now it was lit by but a pair of candles over the hearth and, the glow of a dying fire. Overhead the high roof glimmered into darkness, and the gorgeous furniture was no more than dimness. I stopped short on the threshold, bewildered at the gloom, thinking that the chamber was empty; then I saw that a woman had raised herself from the great couch on which the King had lolled with his little dogs last Sunday night, and was staring at me like a ghost.

At that sight I ran forward and kneeled down on one knee.

"Madame," I said in French, "His Majesty hath sent me —"

At that she was up, and had me by the shoulders. Her face was ghastly, all slobbered over with crying, and her eyes sunken and her lips pale as wax. God knows what she was dressed in; for I do not.

"His Majesty," she cried, "His Majesty! He is not dead! For the love of God —"

I stood up; she still gripped me like a fury.

"No, Madame," said I, "His Majesty is not dead. He hath sent me. I spoke with him not five minutes ago. But he is very near death."

"He hath sent for me! He hath sent for me!" she screamed, as if in mingled joy and terror.

"No, Madame; but he hath sent to you. His Majesty desires you to get him a priest."

Her hands relaxed and fell to her side. I do not know what she thought. I do not judge her. But I thought that she hesitated. I fell on my knees again; and seized her hand. I would have kneeled to the Devil, if he could have helped me then.

"Madame — for the love of Christ do as the King asks! He desires a priest. For the love of Christ, Madame!"

She was still silent for an instant, staring down on me. Then she tore her hand free, and I thought she would refuse me. But she caught me again by the shoulders.

"Stand up, sir; stand up. I — I will do whatever the King desires. But what can I do? God! there is someone coming!"

There came very plainly, through the antechambers I had just run through, the tramp of feet. I stood, as in a paralysis, not knowing what to do next. Then she seized on me again as the steps came near.

"Stand back," she said, "stand back, sir. I must see —"

There came a knocking on the door as I sprang back away from the hearth, and stood out of the firelight. Then the door opened, as Her Grace made no answer, and the page whom I had seen just now stood bowing upon the threshold.

"Madame," said he. "M. Barillon, the French ambassador —"

She made a swift gesture, and he fell back. There was a pause; and then, through the door came M. Barillon, very upright and lean, walking quickly, all alone. He stopped short when he saw Her Grace, put his heels together and bowed very low.

She was at him in an instant.

"Monsieur!" she cried. "Yon are come in the very nick of time. How is His Majesty?"

He said nothing as he walked with her towards the hearth. She stood, waiting, with her hands clasped, and a face of extraordinary anguish.

"Madame," he said, "there is very bad news. I am come on behalf of His Majesty King Louis —"

"Sh!" she hissed at him, with a quick gesture to where I stood. He had not observed me. He straightened himself, as he saw me, and then bowed a little.

The Duchess went on with extraordinary rapidity, still talking in French.

"This is Mr. Mallock," said she, "Mr. Mallock — but just now come from His Majesty. He brings me very grave news. Monsieur Barillon, you will help us, will you not? You will help us, surely?"

All her anguish had passed into an extraordinary pleading: she was as a child begging for life.

"Madame —" began the ambassador.

"Ah! listen, Monsieur, the king desires a priest. He is a Catholic at heart, you know. He hath been a Catholic at heart a long time, ever since —" she broke off. "You will help us, will you not, Monsieur?"

He threw out his hands: but she paid no attention.

"Monsieur, I swear to you that it is so. Yet what can I do? I cannot go to him, with decency. The Queen is there continually, I hear. The Duke is taken up with a thousand affairs and does not think of it. Go to the Duke, I entreat you, Monsieur l'Ambassadeur; go to the Duke and tell him what I say. Mr. Mallock shall go with you. He is a friend of the Duke. He will bear me out. Monsieur, for the love of God lose no time. Come and see me again; but go now, or it may be too late. Monsieur, I entreat you."

She had seized him by the arm as she spoke. Even his rigid face twitched a little at the violence of her pleading. I knew well what was in his mind, and how he wondered whether he dared do as she asked him. God knew what complications might follow!

"Monsieur —"

He nodded suddenly and sharply.

"Madame," said he, "I will go. Mr. Mallock —"

He bowed to me.

"Ah! God bless you, sir —"

He stooped suddenly to her hand, lifted it and kissed it. I think in that moment something of the compassion of the Saviour Himself fell on him for this poor woman who yet might be forgiven much, for indeed, under all her foolishness and sin, she loved very ardently. Then he wheeled and went out of the room again; and I followed. No sound came from the Duchess as we left her there in the half lit twilight. She was standing with her hands clasped, staring after us as we went out.

*　　*　　*

He said nothing as we passed again through the anterooms and down the stairs. Then, as we went on through the next gallery he spoke to me. His men were a good way behind us, and another in front.

"Mr. Mallock," said he — (for he had known me well enough in France) — "His Majesty told you this himself?"

"Yes, sir," said I, "not a quarter of an hour ago."

"Then the Duke is our only chance," he said.

He said no more till we came to the great antechamber by the King's bedroom. It was half full of people; but the Duke was nowhere to be seen. I waited by the door as M. Barillon went forward and spoke to someone. Then he came back to me.

"The Duke is with the Queen," he said. "We must go to him there."

It was enough to send a man mad so to seek person after person in such a simple matter as this. Why in God's name, I wondered, might not even a King die in what religion he liked, without all this plotting and conspiring? Was I never to be free from these things?

At the door to the Queen's apartments M. Barillon turned to me.

"You had best wait here, sir," he said. "I will speak with the Duke privately first."

He was admitted instantly so soon as he knocked; and went through leaving me in a little gallery.

*   *   *

Of all that went through my mind as I walked up and down, with a page watching me from the door, I can give no account at all. Again one half of my attention was fixed, though with out any coherency, on the business I was at; the other half observed the carpet under my feet, the cabinets along the wall, and the pictures. It was not near as splendid as were the rooms I had left so short a while ago.

I had not to wait long. There was a sudden talking of voices beyond the door that the Ambassador had just passed through; and I heard the Duke's tones very plain. Then the page stiffened to attention, the door was flung open suddenly, and the Duke came out alone at a great pace, leaving the door open behind him. He never saw me at all. The page darted after him, and the two disappeared together round the corner in the direction of the King's rooms. As soon as they were gone, M. Barillon came out and beckoned to me; and together we went up and down the gallery.

"You are perfectly right, sir," he said. "His Royal Highness shewed great sorrow for not leaving thought of it. He is gone instantly to His Majesty."

"He will fetch a priest?"

"He will speak to His Majesty first. He will find out, at least, what he thinks."

"But, good God!" said I. "His Majesty hath told me himself what he wishes."

"You must let His Royal Highness do it in his own way," he said. "He must not be pushed. But I think you have done the trick, Mr. Mallock."

"How is Her Majesty?" I asked abruptly.

"The physicians have been at her too," he said dryly. "She had a fainting-fit just now in His Majesty's presence; and they have been blooding her."

"What priest can be got?" I asked next.

He made a gesture towards the chamber he had just come out of.

"There is a pack of them in there," he said, "next to Her Majesty's private closet. They have been praying all day in the oratory."

*   *   *

It was fallen dark by now; for it was long after five o'clock; and there were no candles lighted here. We went up and down a good while longer, for the most part in silence, speaking of this and that; and I will not deny that we talked a little of French affairs, though God knows I was in no heart for that, and answered very indifferently. It appeared to me extraordinary that a man could think of such little things as the affairs of kingdoms when an immortal soul was at stake.

A little before six o'clock, when at last the servants brought lights, the Ambassador left me again to go in to see the Queen, leaving me to watch for the Duke; and I had not very long to wait, for soon after I had heard a clock chime the hour, His Royal Highness came again, walking very quickly as before; and, when he saw me waiting there, beckoned me to follow him. We went through two or three rooms, all lighted up and empty — the Duke sending a page to fetch M. Barillon out of the Queen's private closet where he was talking with her — into a little chamber that looked out upon the court, where there was a fire lighted. We had hardly got there before the Ambassador came, all in haste, to hear what had been done.

"I have spoken with His Majesty," said the Duke, looking very white and drawn in the face. "He is in most excellent dispositions. He tells me that he hath put off the Bishops and has not received the sacrament from them and will not."

"And what of a priest, Sir?" asked the Ambassador sharply.

"I did not speak to him of that," answered the Duke so pompously that I raged to hear him. "He said that Dr. Ken hath read prayers over him, and told him that he need make no confession unless he willed; and that he willed not, and did not; but that Dr. Ken read an absolution over him which he values not at a straw."

"Sir," said I, very boldly, "this is very pretty talk; but it is not a priest. His Majesty wishes for a priest; he told me so himself."

The Duke turned on me very hotly.

"Eh, sir?"

I made haste to swallow down my wrath.

"Sir," I said, "I did not mean to be discourteous. But I assure Your Royal Highness that the King said so to me expressly. It is his immortal soul that is at stake."

Then I understood what was the matter. The Duke flung out his hands as if in despair.

"But what can I do?" he cried. "I am watched every instant. They will not leave me alone with him. Dr. Ken eyed me very sharply. They suspect something — I know they do — from my brother's having refused their ministrations. How can I get a priest to him?"

Then again, by God's inspiration as I truly believe, a thought came to me.

"Sir," I said, "I myself spoke with the King a while ago: and I do not think that a soul saw who I was. I came through the little door at the back of the bed. Why should not —"

The Ambassador struck his hands together.

"*Bon Dieu!*" he said. "I believe Mr. Mallock hath hit it again."

The Duke turned and eyed me very sternly.

"Well, sir, what is your plan?"

"Sir," I said, "let the chamber be cleared, or almost. Then let M. Barillon here go in as if he had a message from the French King. While he is there let a priest be brought by the back way, not through the antechamber at all —"

M. Barillon held up his hand.

"There would not be time," he said. "It does not take half an hour to deliver a message; and the priest's business would take full half an hour?"

"No! no!" cried James. "They would suspect something. Let Her Majesty come again to take her leave of the King; and then I will go in after for the same thing. While we are there, let the priest come, as Mr. Mallock has said —"

"Sir," said the Ambassador, "we must not have too many folks in this business —"

All this bargaining drove me near mad. Once more I broke in; and this time with more effect.

"Sir," I said to the Duke, "I entreat you to hear me. There is the little room at the back of His Majesty's bed, all ready, and empty too. We do not need all these devices. If you, Sir, will go to the King and prepare him for it, I will find a priest and bring him up the other way. I do not believe that even if there were folks in the bedchamber they would hear what passed."

"Which way would the priest come?" asked the Duke.

"There is a little stair in the corner of the room —"

"God! There is," cried the Duke. "I had forgotten it."

We stared on one another in silence. My mind raced like a mill. Then once more the Duke near ruined the whole design by his diplomacy.

"Gentlemen," he said, "we are too precipitate. His Majesty

hath not yet told me that he wishes for a priest —"

"Sir —" I began in desperation.

He looked at me so fiercely that I stopped.

"Listen to me," said he very imperiously. "I will have it my own way. M. Barillon, do you come with me now to His Majesty. I will bid the company withdraw into the antechamber — Bishops and all — on the pretext that I wish to consult with my brother privately. M. Barillon shall be in the doorway that none may come through. Mr. Mallock shall be with the company and hear what they say. Then, if the King wishes for a priest, we will consult again here, and see if Mr. Mallock's plan is a possible one."

He strode towards the door. There was no more to be said. It was a dreadful risk that we ran in so long delaying; but there was no gainsaying James when he had made up his mind.

*　　*　　*

The great antechamber was near full of folks of all kinds when we three came to it again. They fell back as they saw the Duke; and he passed straight through, as was arranged, with M. Barillon, leaving me behind, near the door. The King's bed-chamber was pretty dark, and I could see no more of the bed at the far distant end than its curtains.

Presently I heard the Duke in a low voice saying something to the company that was within: and immediately they began to come out, three or four Bishops, among them, my Lord Halifax, Lord Keeper North, and my Lord Craven; I noticed that M. Barillon was very careful to let all in the antechamber have a clear view of the bed, at which, by now the Duke was kneeling down, having drawn back the curtains a little, yet not so much as to shew us the King lying there.

Round about me they talked very little, though I saw the Bishops whispering together. The two brothers spoke together, very low, for ten minutes or a quarter of an hour; and I could hear the murmur of the Duke's voice. Of His Majesty's I heard nothing except that twice he said, very clear:

"Yes.... Yes, with all my heart."

And I thanked God when I heard that.

*　　*　　*

Yet, even so, all was not yet done.

So soon as I saw the Duke stand up again from his kneeling, and coming down the chamber, I slipped away to the door that leads out towards Her Majesty's apartments, that I might be ready for him. I saw him come through, all the people standing and bowing to him, and M. Barillon following him; and I noticed in particular a young gentleman whose name I did not know at that time — (it was the Comte de Castelmelhor, a very good Catholic) — standing out, a little by himself. I noticed this man because I saw that the Duke looked at him as he came and presently signed to him very slightly, with his head, to follow. So all four of us passed through the door into the long gallery that unites their Majesties' apartments and found ourselves alone in it. The Count was a little behind.

"He has consented," said the Duke in a low voice, "to my bringing him a priest. We must send for one. But I dare not bring one of the Duchess': they are too well-known."

"Sir," said Monsieur Barillon, "I will do so with pleasure. Why not one of Her Majesty's priests?"

The Duke nodded. We three were all standing together about the middle of the gallery. The Comte de Castelmelhor was halted, uncovered, a little behind us. The Duke turned to him.

"Count," said he, speaking in French, "we are on a very urgent business. His Majesty hath consented that a priest should come to him. Will you go for us to the Queen and ask for one of her chaplains?"

The young man flushed up with pleasure.

"With all my heart, Sir," he said. "Which priest shall I ask for? Is there one that can speak English?"

The Duke struck his forehead with his open hand.

"Lord!" he said. "I never thought of that. We must have an Englishman. Where shall we send?"

"Sir," said the Ambassador; "there is one at least at the Venetian Resident's."

Again I broke in. (My impatience drove me near mad. Time was passing quickly. I could have fetched a priest myself ten times over if the Duke had but allowed me to go in the beginning.)

"Sir," said I, "for God's sake let me go first to Her Majesty's apartments. I'll be bound there's one at least there that knows English. Let this gentleman come with me."

The Duke stared at me as if bewildered. I think he saw that he had done little but hinder the business, so far.

"Go," he said suddenly. "Go both of you together — Stay. Bring a priest with you, if you can find one, to the little room behind the King's bed; but bring him up the stairs the other way. Bid him stay till I send Chiffinch to him."

Then we were gone at full speed.

CHAPTER XI

It was eight o'clock at night; and the priest and I were still waiting in the little room; and no word was come through from the Bedchamber, beyond that Mr. Chiffinch had come through once to bid us be ready.

*   *   *

Once again God had favoured us in spite of all our blunders. The Count and I had run together through to Her Majesty's lodging and there we had found, as I knew we should, a priest that knew English. But I had not thought that God's Hand should be so visible in the matter as that we should find none other but Mr. Huddleston himself, the Scotsman, that had saved the King's life after the battle of Worcester. There was a very particular seemliness in this — though I had not much time to think of it then. But our difficulties were not all over.

First, Mr. Huddleston declared that he had never reconciled a convert in his life; and did not know how to set about it. Next he said that he was the worst man in the world to do it, as his face was very well known, and that he would surely be suspected if he were seen: and third that the Most Holy Sacrament was not in Whitehall at all, and that therefore he could not give *Viaticum*. He looked very agitated, in spite of his ruddy face.

I was amazed at the man; but I forced myself to treat him with patience, for he was the only priest we could get.

First I told him that nothing was needed but to hear the King's confession, give him absolution and anoint him: next, that we would disguise him in a great periwig and a gown, such as the Protestant Divines wore — (for, as I spoke, I actually spied such a gown hanging on the wall of the chamber in which I was speaking with him). Third, that another priest could go to St. James' and bring the Most Holy Sacrament to him from there.

At that point Father Bento de Lemoz, who was listening to our talk, came forward and interposed. He would get a little Ritual directly, he said (in very poor English) — that had in it all that was necessary: and he would go himself, not to St. James', for that was too far off, but to Somerset House, and get the Holy Sacrament from the royal chapel there. Mr. Huddleston had nothing to say to that; and in five minutes we had him in his periwig and gown, with the book in his pocket, with the holy oils, and away downstairs, and along the passage beneath, and up again by the little winding stair into the chamber beyond the King's bed. I gave him no time to think of any more objections.

*   *   *

That was a very strange vigil that we held for very near, I should think, twenty minutes or half an hour. We both sat there together without speaking. For the most of the time Mr. Huddleston was reading in his Ritual, and I could see his brow furrowed and his lips moving, as be conned over all that he would have to do and say to His Majesty. He was a man, as he had said, completely unaccustomed to such ministrations, though he was a very good man and a good priest too, in other matters. After a while he laid aside his book, and prayed, I think, for he covered his face with his hands.

*   *   *

A minute or two later I could bear the delay no longer. I rose and went up the three or four steps that led to the King's Bed-chamber, and listened. There was a low murmur of voices within; so that it seemed to me that the room was not yet cleared. I put my hand upon the door and pushed it a little; and to my satisfaction it was not latched, but opened an inch or two. But someone was standing immediately on the other side of it. I stepped back, and the door opened again just enough for me to see the face of Mr. Chiffinch. He looked past me quickly to see that the priest was there, I suppose, and then nodded at me two or three times. Then he pushed the door almost to, again. A moment after I heard the Duke's voice within, a little unsteady, but very clear and distinct. He was standing up, I think, on the far side of the bed.

"Gentlemen," he said, "the King wishes all to retire excepting the Earls of Bath and Feversham."

(Bath and Feversham! thought I. Why those two, in God's name, that were such a pair of Protestants? But, indeed, it was the one good stroke that the Duke made, for the names reassured, as I heard afterwards, all that had any suspicions, and even the Bishops themselves.)

There was a rustle of footsteps, very plain, that followed the Duke's words. I turned to the room behind me, again, and saw that Mr. Huddleston too had heard what had passed. He was standing up, very pale and agitated, with the book clasped in his hands. I moved down the steps again so as not to block the way; and again there followed a silence, in the midst of which I heard a door latched somewhere in the Bedchamber.

Then, suddenly, the door opened at the head of the stairs; and the Duke stood there, he too as pale as death. He nodded once, very emphatically, and disappeared again. Then the priest went by me without a word, up the steps and so through. The door, as before, remained a crack open. I went up to it, and put my eye to the crack.

On the left was the end of the bed, with the curtains drawn across it; and beyond the bed I could see the whole room down to the end, for the candles were burning everywhere, as well as the fire. I could see the great table before the hearth, the physician's instruments and bottles and cupping-glasses upon it, the chairs about it; the tall furniture against the walls, and at least half a dozen clocks, whose ticking was very plain in the silence. Three figures only were visible there. That nearest, standing very rigid by the table, was Mr. Chiffinch: of the two beyond I could recognize only my Lord Bath whose face looked this way: the other I supposed to be my Lord Feversham. The Duke was not within sight. He was kneeling, I suppose, out of my sight, beyond the bed.

Then I heard His Majesty's voice very plain, though very weak and slow.

"Ah!" said he, "you that saved my body is now come to save my soul."

There was the murmur of the priest's voice in answer. (The two of them were not more than three or four yards away from me, at the most.) Then again I heard the King, very clear and continuous, though still weak, and not so loud as he had first spoken.

"Yes," said he, "I desire to die in the Faith and Communion of the Holy Roman Catholic Church. I am sorry with all my heart that I have deferred it for so long; and for all my sins."

(He said it quite distinctly, as if he had rehearsed it beforehand.)

Then the priest and he spoke together — the King repeating the priest's words sometimes, and sometimes volunteering word or two of his own.

He said that through Christ's Passion he hoped to be saved; that he was in charity with all the world; that he pardoned his enemies most heartily, and desired pardon of all whom he had offended; that if God would yet spare him, he would amend his life in every particular.

All that I heard with my own ears, and with inexpressible comfort. His Majesty's voice was low, but very distinct, though sometimes he spoke scarce above a whisper; and I do not think that any man who heard him could doubt his sincerity — however

late it was to shew it. But he was not altogether too late, thank
God!

*   *   *

So soon as His Majesty began his confession, after Mr. Huddleston's moving him to it, I slipped away from the door and
began, as softly as I could to walk up and down the little chamber
again. I was satisfied beyond measure: yet it seemed to me sometimes near incredible that I should in very truth, be here at such a
time, and that I should have been, under God's merciful Providence, the instrument in such an affair. My life was ended, I knew
well enough now, in all matters that the world counts life to con-
sist of; yet was there ever such an ending? I had seen all else go
from me — my natural activities of every kind, my ambitions,
even the most sacred thing that the world can give, after the Love
of God, and that is the love of a woman! Yet the one purely supernatural end that I had set before me — that end to which, four
days ago, I had said, as I thought, good-bye for ever in the
Duchess of Portsmouth's gallery — this was the one single thing
that was mine after all. I could take that at least with me into the
cloister, and could praise God for it all my life long — I mean the
conversion of the man that was called King of England, the man
who, for all his sins and his treatment of me, I yet loved as I have
never loved any other man on earth. I think that in those minutes
of sorrow and joy as I paced up and down the little room, my
dearest Dolly was not very far away from me and that she knew
all that I felt.

Once — in a loud broken voice through the door — I heard
these words:

— "Sweet Jesus. Amen.... Mercy, Sweet Jesus, Mercy!"

That was the King's voice that I heard: and I kneeled down
when I heard them.

*   *   *

It would be about ten minutes later, as I still kneeled, that I
heard, upon the outside of the door that led down the winding
stairs, a very small tapping.

I ran to the door to open it, wondering who it could be; for I
had forgotten all about the Portuguese priest, though I had set
the candles ready burning, with a napkin on the table between
them, in readiness for his coming. And there he stood, with his
eyes cast down, and his hands clasped upon his breast.

I beckoned him forward, pointing to the table, and kneeled
down again.

He went past me without a word, kneeled himself before the table and then, unbuttoning his cloak he drew from round his neck the chain and the Pyx from his breast, and laid it all upon the table, continuing himself to kneel.

Presently he turned and looked at me, lifting his brows.

I knew what he wished; rose from my knees and went up the stairs, but very cautiously, lest I should hear anything that I should not. There was but a very faint murmur of the priest's voice, so I took courage and pushed the door a little open so that I could see the King.

It was very dark within the curtains, for they were drawn against the candlelight; but I could see what was passing. His Majesty was lying flat upon his back, with his hands clasped beneath his chin, and Mr. Huddleston was in the very act of arranging the coverlet over him again, after the last Anointing. As I looked the priest turned and caught my eyes, as he put the oil-stock and the wool away again in his cassock breast. I nodded three times very emphatically — (His Majesty did not see me at all, for his eyes were closed) — and went back again down the stairs and kneeled once more. A few moments later Mr. Huddleston came through.

I have never seen so swift a change in any man's face. He had been terrified as he had gone in — all pale and shaking. Now he was still pale, but his eyes shone, and there was a look of great assurance in his face. He came straight down the steps without speaking, kneeled, rose again, took up the Pyx and the corporal which Father de Lemoz had spread beneath it, and passed up and out again. His priesthood, I suppose, had risen in him like a great tide, and driven out all other emotions.

*   *   *

Again I followed him to the door, and kneeled there where I could see; and then there followed such a scene as I had never dreamed of.

The curtains on the other side of the bed had been drawn back just enough to admit the face of the Duke who now kneeled there, yet not so much that any of the three others at the further end of the chamber could see into the bed. The candlelight streamed in through the opening above the Duke's head; and in it, I saw His Majesty, all weak as he was, striving to rise, with his eyes fixed on That which the priest was holding in his right hand. I saw the priest's left hand go out to restrain him; but I heard the King's voice distinctly.

"Father," he said very brokenly, "let me receive my Heavenly Saviour in a better posture than lying on my bed."

"Sir," said Mr. Huddleston with great firmness, "lie down again, if you please. God Almighty who sees your heart will accept your good intention."

(But neither of them spoke loud enough to be heard at the further end of the great chamber.)

And so he was persuaded to lie down again.

Then the priest repeated again, still holding the Blessed Sacrament before the King's eyes, the Act of Contrition of which I had heard a word or two a while ago; and His Majesty repeated it after him, word for word, very devoutly.

Then, as the time was short Mr. Huddleston omitted several of the proper prayers, and proceeded at once to the Communion, saying but the *Agnus Dei* three times, and then communicating him immediately. With my own eyes I saw that holy act which sealed all and admitted the dying man to sacramental union with his God. His eyes were closed throughout; and when it was done he lay as still as a stone, his poor wasted face all dark against the white pillows. I caught a glimpse too of the Duke: his face was bowed in his hands, and he was weeping so that his shoulders shook with it.

Presently the priest was reading again as well as he could in a very low whisper the prayers for the Recommendation of a Departing Soul, down to the very end. His Majesty lay motionless throughout. At the end he opened his eyes.

"Father," he whispered, "the Act of Contrition once more, if you please. I have sinned, I have sinned very —" He could speak no more for weeping.

Then, once more, very slowly and tenderly, the priest repeated it; down to *Mercy, Sweet Jesus, Mercy!* My own eyes were all dim with tears, and as fast as I brushed them away, they came again. When at last I could see plainly once more, the priest was holding up a little crucifix before the King's eyes; and he made him a short address, very Christian and forcible. I remember near every word of it, as he said it.

"Lift up the eyes of your soul, Sir," he said, "and represent to yourself your sweet Saviour here crucified, bowing down His Head to kiss you; His Arms stretched out to embrace you; His Body and members all bloody and pale with death to redeem you. Beseech Him, Sir, with all humility that His most Precious Blood may not be shed in vain for you; and that it will please Him, by the merits of His bitter Death and Passion, to pardon and forgive you all your offences; and, finally, to receive your soul into His Blessed Hands; and, when it shall please Him to take it out of this transitory world, to grant you a joyful resurrection, and an eternal crown of glory in the next."

He bent lower, making a great sign of the cross with his right hand — (and the King too tried to bless himself in response).

"In the Name," said he, "of the Father and of the Son and of the Holy Ghost. Amen."

*   *   *

One more joy and sorrow all in one was yet to be mine before the end. As I opened the door for the priest to come back, His Majesty lifted his eyes and saw me there; and I perceived that he recognized me. The Duke had already risen up and gone down the room to bid them, I suppose, to open the door and let the folks in again. Then, as the King's eyes met my own he made a sign with his head that I should come near. I think that if the chamber had been filled with but one mob of priest-hunters and Protestants, I should have obeyed him then, even though I should have been torn to pieces the next instant.

I went forward without a word, leaving the door open behind me, and flung myself on my knees at the bedside.

His Majesty was too weary to speak, but, as I kneeled there, with my face in my hands on the bedclothes, and my tears raining down, he lifted his right hand and put it on my head, leaving it there for an instant. It was all he could do to thank me; and I value that blessing from him, a penitent sinner as he was, with the Body of our Saviour still in his breast, as much as any blessing I have ever had from any man, priest or bishop or Pope.

As he lifted his hand off again, I caught at it, and kissed it three or four times, careless whether or no my tears poured down upon it.

*   *   *

As I passed back again through the door to where Mr. Huddleston was waiting for me, I heard the doors at the further end of the chamber unlatched and the footsteps of the folks — physicians, courtiers, Bishops and the rest — that poured in to see the end.

EPILOGUE

I have said again and again how strange this or that moment or incident appeared to me as I experienced it; yet as I sit here now in my cell, thirty years later, looking out upon the cloister-garth with its twisted columns, and the cypresses and the grass, it is not so much this or that thing that appears to me strange, but the whole of my experiences and indeed human life altogether. For what can be more extraordinary than a life which began as mine did, when I first went to England in sixteen hundred and seventy-eight, should be ending as mine will end presently, if God will, as a monk of St. Paul's-Without-the-Walls, in Holy Rome? To what purpose, I ask myself, was that part of my life designed by Divine Providence? For what did I labour so long, when all was to come to nothing? For what was I to learn the passion of human love; if but to lose it again? For what was I to intrigue and spy and labour and adventure my life, for the cause of England and the Catholic Church, when all a year or two later was to fall back, and further than it had ever fallen before, into the darkness of heresy? There is but one effort in all those years of which I saw the fruition, and that was the conversion of my master upon his deathbed.

However, I have not yet related what passed after I had gone from the King again, and took Mr. Huddleston downstairs. I will relate that very shortly; and make an end. I had it all from Mr. Chiffinch before I left London.

*   *   *

His Majesty, after we were gone from him, rallied a little, in so far as to make some think that he would recover altogether; but the physicians said No; and they were right for near the first time in all their diagnosis of his state. But they continued to give him their remedies of Sal Ammoniac and Peruvian Bark, and later the Oriental Bezoar Stone, which is a pebble, I understand, taken from the stomach of a goat. Also they blooded him again, twelve ounces more, and all to no purpose.

His Majesty said a number of things that night that were very characteristic of him; for God gave him back his gift of merriment, now that he had the Gift of Faith as well: and he shewed a great tenderness too from time to time and a very Christian appreciation of his own condition.

For example, he said that he was suffering very much, but he thanked God for it and that he was able to bear it with patience, as indeed he did.

Two or three times however he seemed to sigh for death to come quickly; and once he looked round with his old laughter at the solemn faces round his bed, and begged their pardon that he was "such an unconscionable time in dying." "My work in this world seems over," he said — "such as it has been. I pray God I may be at a better occupation presently."

He thanked His Royal Highness the Duke of York (who was by his bed all that night, weeping and kissing his hand repeatedly) for all his attention and love for him, and asked his pardon for any hardship that had been done to his brother, through his fault. He gave him his clothes and his keys; telling him that all was now his; and that he prayed God to give him a prosperous reign.

To Her Majesty who came to see him again about midnight, he shewed the tenderest consideration and love: but the Queen, who swooned again and again at the sight of him, and had to be carried back to her apartments, sent him a message later begging his pardon for any offence that she had ever done to him.

"What!" whispered the King. "What! She beg my pardon, poor woman! Rather I beg hers with all my heart. Carry that message back to Her Majesty."

No less than twice did the King commend the Duchess of Portsmouth to the Duke's care — poor "Fubbs" as he had called her to me. Some blamed him for thinking of her at all at such a time; as also for bidding his brother "not to let poor Nell starve"; but for myself I cannot understand such blame at all. If ever there were two poor souls who needed care and forgiveness it was those two women, Mrs. Nell and Her Grace.

All his natural sons were there — all except the Duke of Monmouth whose name never passed his lips from the beginning of his sickness to the end — and these too he recommended to his brother — the three sons of the Duchess of Cleveland, and the rest. I do not wonder that he left out His Grace of Monmouth: it seems to me very near prophetical of what was to fall presently, when the Duke was to revolt against his new Sovereign and suffer the last penalty for it, at his hands. But His Majesty blessed all the rest of his children one by one, drawing them down to him upon the bed — they weeping aloud, as I heard.

A very strange scene followed this. One of the Bishops fell down upon his knees, and begged him, who was the "Lord's Anointed" — (and anointed too, lately, in a fashion the Bishop never dreamed of!) — to bless all that were there, since they were all his children, and all his subjects too. The Bedchamber was now full from end to end; and all the company fell together upon their knees. His Majesty, raising himself in bed, first begged the pardon of all in a loud voice for anything in which he had acted contrary to the interests of his country or the principles of good government; and then, still in a loud voice, pronounced a blessing on them all. Then he fell back again upon his pillows.

So that night went slowly by. The dogs were still in the room, whining from time to time, as Mr. Chiffinch told me afterwards — (for it was thought better that I myself, as one so deeply involved in what had lately passed should not be present) — and one of the little dogs sought repeatedly to leap upon the bed, but was prevented; and at last was carried away, crying. Again and again first one Bishop and then another begged him to receive the sacrament; but he would not: so they prayed by him instead, which was all they could do.

At about six o'clock, when dawn came, he begged that the curtains of his bed might be drawn back yet further, and the windows opened, that he might see daylight again and breathe the fresh air: and this was done. Then, at the chiming of the hour by the clocks in the room, he remembered that one of them, which was an eight-day one, should be wound up, for it was a Friday on which it was always wound. And this too was done.

At seven o'clock breathlessness came on him again, and he was compelled to sit up in bed, with his brother's arm about him on one side, and a physician's upon the other. They blooded him again, to twelve ounces more, which I suppose took his last remnant of strength from him; for in spite of their remedies, he sank very rapidly; and about half-past eight lost all power of speech. He kept his consciousness, however, moving his eyes and shewing that he understood what was said to him till ten o'clock; and then he became unconscious altogether.

At a little before noon, without a struggle or agony of any kind, His Sacred Majesty ceased to breathe.

Of all that followed, there is no need that I should write; for I remained in England only till after the funeral in Westminster Abbey — which was very poorly done — eight days later; and I left on the Sunday morning, for Dover, after being present first, for a remembrance, at the first mass celebrated publicly in England, with open doors, in the presence of the Sovereign, since over a hundred and thirty years. I had audience with King James on the night before, when I went to take my leave of him; and he renewed to me the offer of the Viscounty, of which I think Mr. Chiffinch had spoken to him. But I refused it as courteously as I could, telling him that I was for Rome and the cloister.

All the rest, however, is known by others better than by myself; and the events that followed. His Majesty shewed himself as he had always been — courageous, obstinate, well-intentioned and entirely without understanding. He was profuse in his promises of religious equality; but slow to observe them. He shewed ruthlessness where he should have shewn tenderness, and tenderness where he should have shewn ruthlessness. So, once more, all our labours went for nothing; and William came in; and the Catholic cause vanished clean out of England until it shall please God to bring it back again.

So here I sit near sixty years old, a monk of the Order of Saint Benet, in my cell at St. Paul's-Without-the-Walls. I have been Novice Master three times; but I shall never be more than that; for governmental affairs and I have said farewell to one another a long while ago. It was through my telling of my adventures to my Novices at recreation-time that the writing of them down came about; for my Lord Abbot heard of them, and put me under obedience to write them down. He did this when he heard one of my Novices name me to another as Father Viscount! I have written them, then, down all in full, leaving nothing out except the French affairs on which I was put under oath by His Majesty never to reveal anything: I have left out not even the tale of my Cousin Dolly; for I hold that in such a love as was ours there is nothing that a monk need be ashamed of. I will venture even further than that, and will say that I am a better monk than I should have been without it; and as one last piece of rashness I will say that amongst "those good things which God hath prepared for them that love Him" in that world which is beyond this (if I ever come at it by His Grace), will be, I think, the look on my Cousin Dolly's face when I see her again.

Of other personages whose acquaintance I made in England — excepting always His Majesty, and my master, Charles the Second — I neither speak nor think very much now. My Cousin Tom died of an apoplexy three years after I left England, and God knows who hath Hare Street House today! His Majesty James the Second, as all the world knows, made a most excellent end of it in France, dying as he had never lived till after his coming to France, a very humble and Christian soul. In regard to Mr. Chiffinch, I think of him sometimes and wonder what kind of an end he made. He was very reprobate while I knew him; yet he had the gift of fidelity, and that, I think, must count for something before God who gave it him. Of the ladies of the Court I know nothing at all, nor how they fared nor how they ended, nor even if they are all dead yet — I mean such ladies as was Her Grace of Portsmouth.

But all of them I commend to God every day in my mass living or dead; and trust that all may have found the mercy of God, or may yet find it. But most of all I remember at the altar the names of two persons, than between whom there could be no greater difference in this world — the names of Dorothy Mary Jermyn, the least of all sinners; and of Charles Stuart, King of England, the greatest of all sinners, yet a penitent one. For these are the two whom I have loved as I can never love any others.

The End